I0673032

DEALEY PLAZA

DEALEY PLAZA

JOHN A. RUSSO

Burning Bulb
PUBLISHING

Dealey Plaza
By **John A. Russo**

Burning Bulb Publishing
P.O. Box 4721
Bridgeport, WV 26330-4721
www.BurningBulbPublishing.com

PUBLISHER'S NOTE: This book is a work of fiction. Names, characters, places, and incidents are either the product of the author's imagination or are used fictitiously, and any resemblance to actual persons, living or dead, events, or locales is purely coincidental.

Copyright © 2012-2014 John A. Russo.

Cover designed by Gary Lee Vincent with licensed elements from fotolia.com (46217541, 48472016, 60901820, 55658243) and public domain archives. Back cover photograph of Mr. Russo taken by Tim Ferrante.

First printing.

Edition ISBN

    Paperback 978-0-61596-708-0

First edition.
Printed in the United States of America.

Library of Congress Control Number: 2014935356

This book is dedicated to Frank Imbrogno.

"We are sinking into the swamps of a plague and the massacre of strange people seems to relieve this plague. If one were to take patients in a hospital, give them guns and let them shoot on pedestrians down from hospital windows, you may be sure you would find a few miraculous cures."

-- Norman Mailer

PROLOGUE

Dealey Plaza is one of the most notorious places in America, and in the spring of 1964, I went there with some college pals, conspiracy buffs, who wanted me to help them film their own version of the Kennedy Assassination.

On the way home, four of them were murdered and their footage went up in flames.

It was the first link in a chain of violent death that spanned four decades and caused me to abandon all my youthful hopes and dreams.

As the years went by, some of us who had survived that trip became rich, some became famous or notorious, and some of us were entangled in tricky or dangerous situations that life had thrown our way.

Now we were gathered together for Homecoming Weekend 2000 at Belmont University.

But a killer was waiting for us.

And he was nursing a deadly grudge that had its roots in the trip to Dallas we had embarked on long ago when we were young, adventurous and innocent.

PART ONE
KENNEDY

"We were in a different country after those shots rang out in Dallas."
-- Tom Brokaw

"I didn't kill anybody."
-- Lee Oswald

"No American of that time will forget where, when, how he or she heard the news ... we sensed an era had ended ... we mourned our lost youth."
-- Theodore H. White

CHAPTER 1

I think of Dealey Plaza as a bellwether, a turning point, not just for me and my friends, but for America. It was as if we came, all unsuspecting, to a fork in the road, and got shoved by cataclysm onto a darker, more dangerous path. Things that might have happened did not happen and other, usually worse, things happened instead.

If President Kennedy had lived to be reelected, and if he had not been shot, he likely would have pulled our troops out of Vietnam. Lyndon Johnson would not have become president, the war would not have been escalated, and we would not have had the Tet Offensive, the My Lai Massacre, the shooting of four Kent State students, and all the other wartime blunders and atrocities that put the names of 58,000 Americans on a black granite wall.

Robert Kennedy might not have run for president and might not have been assassinated. Richard Nixon might never have gotten elected and we might never have heard of Woodward and Bernstein and the Watergate whistle blower named after a porno movie.

That movie, *Deep Throat,* helped launch a so-called Sex Revolution that liberated women to do what men wanted them to do and men to do it to them without the fear of responsibility for unwanted pregnancy.

Homicide became the leading cause of death of pregnant women.

Domestic violence reached epidemic proportions.

Weak, twisted men, scared of assertive women, turned their lusts onto children, and when they were released from prison as registered sex offenders, they hunted for more children to rape and kill.

Assassinations and assassination attempts proliferated. Diverse political and cultural figures such as Martin Luther King, Ronald Reagan, John Lennon, George Wallace and Larry Flynt were gunned down.

Angry, bitter people went ballistic and shot complete strangers or co-workers. A new phrase was coined for it: Going Postal.

Serial rapists and mass murderers stalked American streets with near impunity.

Charles Manson, Ted Bundy and John Wayne Gacy basked in their notoriety and sold souvenirs of their exploits on the Internet.

The Internet emerged as the blessing/curse of an Information Age that destroyed the slower, calmer patterns of past ages faster than we could comprehend or cope. We wallowed in affluence on the one hand and despair on the other, hooked on meth, heroin, household inhalants, airplane glue, intolerant religion and extremist politics. Our jaded, aimless youth rejected everything our civilization had to offer except computers, iPhones, video games and tattoo parlors. They pierced their noses, lips, tongues, navels and labia, as if forming a neo-primitive tribe of their own in lieu of accepting a trite, boring role in the confused, conflicted culture they were born into.

The teenage suicide rate sky-rocketed.

Since it was still possible to get richer here than practically anywhere else, and to do it faster and more gluttonously, we believed our boast that we were the Greatest Country on Earth. We kept on trying to make ourselves safe by bombing and killing people in less powerful, less affluent countries. When suicide bombers attacked us with our own fuel-laden airliners, we ran scared and waxed patriotic and sent our brave young soldiers to die in the wrong place.

Home-grown terrorists sprung up everywhere in our midst. Timothy McVeigh. The Unabomber. The Columbine Killers. They horrified us with their sudden and devastating body counts, so shockingly out of step with our slow, complacent habit of bumping each other off at a rate of 20,000 per year, with handguns.

Mere handguns weren't enough for us, though. We wanted bigger and better stuff. We wanted assault rifles, machine guns, tanks and bazookas. We claimed it was our Constitutional Right. Every crackpot cause had its militia, its militant fringe who wanted to be well armed. Some hated gays, some hated the government, some hated abortionists, some hated evolutionists, some hated anybody whose skin wasn't white. They said they'd give up their guns when the guns were pried from their cold dead hands.

And so the cold dead hands multiplied.

CHAPTER 2

Lori McCoy was scared and excited, afraid her voice would crack in front of all those people! She couldn't get over how *packed* the stadium was. Instead of staying away in droves, the way she thought they would, students and alumni had turned out in full force for the Belmont University Homecoming Game of October 27, 1962. Maybe they were hoping that if they acted *normal* God wouldn't let the world explode. Maybe the Russian ships down in Cuba would back off from the American blockade. Maybe there would be other years and other Homecomings.

" ... what so proudly we hailed, in the twilight's last gleaming ... "

Hitting the soul-stirring notes with pride in her own rich alto and pride in her heritage, Lori loved her country more than ever now that it was in special peril. Old-fashioned patriotism mixed with down-home religion, bred into her in the hills of West Virginia, coursed fervently through her veins. Thanks to a music scholarship, she was the first of her large backwoods family ever to go to college. Two years ago she had arrived on the Belmont campus terribly frightened and painfully shy, and had been taken under the wing of a smart, handsome, cocky young man who had married her and blessed her with a beautiful baby.

"And the rockets' red glare ... the bombs bursting in air ... "

Singing her heart out, Lori searched for her husband in the dense crowd high in the bleachers. There he was, with his long blonde hair and devil-may-care smile. She willed him to hold Missy up and make her wave her little hand, but it didn't happen. Lori could feel Keith's presence even at this distance, eyeing her intensely, passing judgment. She knew the crowd was with her, but his approval mattered most.

For the past year, except for a hiatus during the final trimester of her pregnancy, he had been booking Lori into campus bars, coffee houses and fraternity parties. He often used her as a guest on the campus radio station where he was a DJ and talk show host. Somehow he had talked the Homecoming Weekend Steering Committee into letting her sing the National Anthem today, and they were even going to let her sing one of the songs from her album at halftime. Miraculously, Keith had landed her a recording gig on a small record label, and she had let him select all the songs and supervise the arrangements. They were all public-domain folk ballads. Keith wouldn't let her sing her country songs anymore. She had written lots of them, ever since childhood, but he had kept them off the album. He said that Kingston Trio type stuff, Limelighters type stuff, was hot now, so that was the direction she had to go in, it would be stupid to buck the trend.

"Oh say, does tha-at star-spangled banner ye-et wa-ave ... "

Keith Santone cradled the baby against his chest, feeding her a bottle of formula, while he assessed Lori's performance. Her strong, folksy accent boomed over the loudspeakers, the stadium in such a strange hush that the anthem, sung a capella, was dramatically amplified. Vendors were quiet. The crowd was still. Pennants barely fluttered in the autumn sunshine.

"O'er the la-and of the freeee ... and the home of the-e braaaave ... "

Keith noted the cheers, whistles and applause that erupted with Lori's closing notes, and understood that the outpouring wasn't so much for her as for the Star-Spangled Banner that people feared would soon be under fire. But he didn't think it was going to happen. The world wasn't going to explode while he was in it. He had plans, big plans, and he believed he was destined to carry them out.

Looking down at Missy, he saw that she had finished the bottle of formula and was chewing contentedly on the nipple, and he could hand the baby over to Lori as soon as she got up here so she'd have to be the one to change the diaper. Just then, Keith saw his friend Charlie Guinard forcing his way between the jammed-up bleacher seats. Guinard was six five and weighed over three-hundred pounds, and was known as a campus wild man for instigating political protests and civil rights marches. Working his way closer, he was jostling people in the bleachers, but they didn't dare give him any lip; they didn't know what Keith knew, that the big, woolly-bearded law student wouldn't hurt a fly.

Keith had Missy's diaper bag next to him on the bench, saving a spot for Lori, so he tucked it under his legs, but still everybody in the row had to squeeze even tighter to make room for Charlie, who sat down with a worried, panicky look on his big, beefy face. "What the *hell* you doin' here?" he demanded of Keith.

"I was about to ask *you* that 'cause you don't give a damn about football."

"We got no time for this foolish shit!" Guinard shouted, waving his flannel-shirted arm, making the guy next to him spill some of the liquor he was pouring into a Coke. "We're only a stone's throw from the Big Apple! Any bombs that land there are gonna wipe *us* out, too! We gotta gather together a small group of *sane people!* We can set up a commune somewhere remote and safe -- like maybe Australia!"

Keith chuckled. "It's all gonna blow over. I'm not splitting to Australia when Lori's first album is about to be released."

"Like, who's gonna *buy* it, man, when everybody's *incinerated?*"

"Shhh," said Keith. "You'll make the baby cry."

Guinard lowered his voice to a hoarse whisper. "Man, babies are what it's all about! There won't *be* any future generations unless we find a safe haven! We don't wanna be here when the shit hits the fan, man! I hope it's not too late to apply for passports!"

"Here comes Lori," Keith said.

She was coming down the aisle on the thirty-yard line, beamingly accepting congratulations from fans, and working her way over to her husband and baby. When she got close enough, a young guy in a fraternity blazer gave her a nod and a smile and made room for her by squeezing down into the next row.

The opening kickoff sailed down the field and the crowd got on its feet cheering till the first tackle was made by the Belmont Bulldogs against the Darnell University Tigers, then things got quieter and everybody sat down.

"How'd I do?" Lori asked Keith. She took the baby from him and felt the rush of pleasure that always came over her when she looked into Missy's innocent little face.

Keith made no immediate comment. He liked keeping her in suspense.

"Sorry I didn't get here in time to hear you sing," said Guinard, momentarily stifling his anxiety about the dawning nuclear war.

Lori kissed and tickled Missy, both of them giggling and cooing.

"Not bad, not bad," Keith finally said. "But I want to see how you go over at halftime."

"Petty concerns," Guinard mumbled.

"What do you mean, petty? I've got an album coming out!" Lori said brightly.

"Kennedy and Khruschev are gonna vaporize us all," Guinard stated, as if he were an adult talking to a child.

Lori hugged her baby tighter than before.

Keith laughed and punched Charlie on the shoulder.

9

"Kennedy wants to get revenge for the Bay of Pigs fiasco," Guinard persisted. "That fuckup embarrassed the shit outta him and now he wants to save face. He's using the Russian missiles as an excuse for a full-scale invasion, and this time he's gonna use American troops instead of Cuban exiles! We're screwed, Keith -- we're gonna get drafted!"

"Not me. I got a wife and kid. They won't take me."

"Hah! Don't kid yourself," Guinard scoffed. "There's another world war, they're gonna need *everybody!*"

"Poor Frank Williams," Lori said sadly. "He's already *in* the army. Wonder how he's doin'."

"He shoulda declared himself a conscientious objector," said Guinard. "The poor sap's probably on his way to Cuba."

"Gay guys don't have to serve," said Keith. "Frank shoulda kissed the doctor when he was checkin' him for hernia."

"Huh?" said Lori.

"Doctor grabs your balls and tells you to cough," Guinard explained.

Lori burst out laughing. "Missy, don't you dare listen to this dirty talk!" she said, nuzzling the baby.

CHAPTER 3

I was lying on my bunk trying to read, but I couldn't concentrate. My thoughts kept buzzing and lighting like the flies in the barracks.

The Belmont University homecoming game was today, but I couldn't get it on my radio. Fort Bragg was too far away. I wondered how my ex-teammates were doing. I thought about how much better my life was when I was psyching myself up to dodge enemy linebackers instead of enemy bullets. I wished I had been big enough and fast enough to get drafted into the NFL instead of the army.

In the big, open bay of the barracks, where I lived communally with thirty other guys, there was no privacy, not even chicken wire between our bunks. We smelled each other's farts, heard each other's snores and moans, and felt each other's boredom, anxiety and fear. Some of the guys were sacked out, some were polishing their boots, some were playing solitaire or little games of gin rummy, sitting on their bunks and dealing the cards onto their footlockers.

When I tried to picture myself coming home in a coffin with a flag draped over it, it seemed like something that shouldn't happen to me but might anyway because pigheaded people were calling the shots. Khruschev had those missiles down there and Kennedy wanted them out. Maybe they were both crazy enough to leave the world in a pile of radiation and rubble. Even if the war didn't turn nuclear, I might never get to live the rest of my life as a civilian with dreams and ambitions.

The infantry company next door was already gone, on its way to Florida, the staging area for a Cuban invasion. On a dark, rainy night I had watched them scrambling out of their barracks, packs on their backs and M-14's clenched in their fingers, faces wet with rain and tears as they ran toward their convoy on the nearby baseball field. I wondered if they'd soon be blown to bits by a gang of Cubans forming up on a jai-alai court.

My company, the 50lst Chemical Company, was a dumping ground for over-the-hill noncoms, chicken-shit second lieutenants and cynical, disgruntled draftees like me. Fort Bragg's elite 82nd Airborne Division despised us and called us "the Five-Oh-Worst," yet in combat we'd often be up near the front lines and in danger of being ambushed. Our mission was to deliver truckloads of insecticides and germicides to keep bugs off of our own troops, and napalm to take everything off of enemy troops including their clothes, hair and skin.

The book I was holding in front of my face was a collection of combat memoirs by Ernest Hemingway who said that the book would not teach me how to die but would tell me how other men had fought and died so I would know that there were no worse things to be gone through than what other men had gone through before me. I never dreamed that Hemingway or anybody else was going to teach me how to die but I wanted some pointers on how to survive. In John Wayne movies you got pointers. Like propping your helmet on a rock so the enemy would think you were still there while you snuck behind him and shot him. In the movies you didn't shoot him in the back though. You had to give him a chance to see you and get his gun up so you could drill him honorably.

"Hey, Cheater!" somebody yelled. "Hey, you got any cotton balls?"

Rorthal Cheatwood, at the bunk next to mine, didn't miss a lick spit-shining his boots. "All my cotton balls is rotten," he said in his high, twangy drawl, aping a line from a hit folk song by the Highwaymen. I chuckled, but nobody else got it. The black guys only listened to R&B and the white guys didn't listen to anything but hillbilly music.

"Hey, Cheater, goddamn it, I ast you fer some cotton balls!"

"An' I tol' ya they's all rotten. You say borrow but you mean gimme. You ain't gonna pay me back an' you know it."

"Fuck you, hoss."

"You're too ugly to fuck," said Rorthal. "A face like yours, you oughta shave your ass and walk on your hands."

Sitting on his bunk, his broad forehead glistening with sweat, he kept dipping a cotton ball in water, then working it in tiny circles over every inch of black leather. His boots were already so shiny they'd be a danger in combat; he'd have to smear them with mud so they wouldn't draw sniper fire. My boots were combat ready. I never spit-shined my boots even though my platoon leader, Sergeant Barbarus Gibbon, was threatening to have me court-martialed for it.

Oh-oh, here he comes. I heard the door of his cadre room squeak open, so I hid my face behind my book. His shower shoes flapped toward me, and I hoped he would go to the water fountain at the other end of the bay. But the flap-flap-flap came to a stop right in front of my bunk. He liked to pick on people he outranked. Behind his back we called him Barbarian. His skin was blue-black like the skin of an eggplant, and he had a large grizzled head, a belly big as a basketball, and long skinny legs, so that in his white T-shirt and shorts he looked like an egg mounted on two black pipe stems.

Picking up my combat boots and holding them at arm's length as if they were a couple of dead rats, he said, "I wants these fuckin' boots spit-shined *right now.*"

"They're polished to a high gloss, that's what the regulations call for, Sarge."

"Don't sass me, perfessor, you nothin' but a smart-ass college boy."

"In college I was just a dumb jock."

"Well, in here you is a perfessor or anythin' else I wants to *call* you."

I understood his resentment. As an orderly room clerk, I had access to his file, so I knew he only had a fourth-grade education. New army regulations required all NCO's without a high-school diploma to start earning a GED, so he had to enroll in the fifth grade in an on-post school. He had fought in World War Two and Korea and had been decorated with a Bronze Star, a Silver Star and a Purple Heart, but now the army was modernizing and suddenly he was an anachronism. He had no family, no home other than the military, and he was afraid of flunking fifth grade and getting bounced out.

Dropping my boots onto the floor with a loud thud, he said, "I wants these boots spit-shined *today.* You gives me anymore crap, I calls the MP's and yer ass gets throwed in the *stockade.*"

He fastened his evil eye on me while I opened my wall locker and took out a can of polish, a brush and some rags. I didn't have any cotton balls, but I made a show of getting started with the polish and the brush. Finally he flap-flapped back into his cadre room and slammed the door.

Jimmy Green came down the aisle toward my bunk, waving around a paperback and shoving his hard-on aside so it wouldn't poke out of his boxer shorts. "Look!" he said. "It says motherfucker right there in black and white!"

The book was called *Love Lusty Amazons* and it did indeed say "motherfucker" right where he was pointing.

I said, "So what, Greenbean? Motherfucker, motherfucker, motherfucker. There, does that get your rocks off?"

"Aw, fuck you," said Greenbean. "This book is better'n the shit *you* read!"

He kept a foot-high stack of stroke books in the bottom of his footlocker and he liked to show everybody the ones that got him really hot. Of course he heard words like fuck and motherfucker and cunt and cocksucker all the time right in the barracks, but he never got a hard-on over them till he saw them in print.

He showed his book to Rorthal Cheatwood, who glanced at it and said, "Hey, hoss, if you're gonna cum in your shorts, don't sit on my bunk."

"Aw, fuck you too, Cheater," Greenbean said.

Barbarian flapped out of his room to make sure I was doing my boots, and Jimmy Bean showed him his stroke book. They stood in the aisle by my bunk, laughing and talking about pussy.

Barbarian had left his cadre room door open and I could make out that his radio was tuned to some football game where halftime scores from around the country were being announced. I tried to catch some mention of Belmont versus Darnell, but the station only covered the Top Twenty teams and Belmont and Darnell weren't even in the top hundred.

I wished I could offer Rorthal Cheatwood five bucks to spit-shine my boots for me. But Greenbean was keeping a hold on Barbarian by reading him another stroke passage out loud, and he'd climb all over me if he saw me trying to get out of polishing my own boots.

A wistful gleam in his eyes, Barbarian said, "When I come home from Korea, folks was slappin' my back and buyin' me drinks ever'where I went. I made sure I always had my uniform on, ribbons 'n' all. Got me all the pussy I c'd handle."

"You think that'll happen again, Sarge?" Bean asked hopefully.

"Once we beat the shit outta them Cubans, we gonna be heroes jus' like before. You won't hafta be readin' none of them kinda books, Greenbean. You be gettin' some pussy for real."

As soon as we were put on alert, some of our fat, lazy NCO's took to boasting about all the "gooks" they had killed or screwed in Korea and all the "spics" they were going to kill or screw in Cuba. They seemed to think that dying in combat wasn't for them, but just for us privates and PFC's, like KP and guard duty. For them, war and pussy seemed to go together somehow, just like football and pussy. To hear them talk, you would think that *they* weren't going to get shot at or killed, they were just gonna have one helluva ball blasting at Cubans with their guns and their dicks.

CHAPTER 4

When the missile crisis ended without any shots being fired, the lifers had to get off on the idea that "we" had made the Russians back down. They strutted around the mess hall bragging about what we coulda done and woulda done as they scarfed down tons of coffee and doughnuts and got fatter and fatter. The way they acted you would have thought they were a bunch of John Waynes who had saved nine wagon trains from Injun attacks and captured ten Iwo Jimas from the Japs.

Eventually, though, after the combat-ready alert was lifted, life on post settled back into normal military monotony. Barbarian had more time to pick on me now, but I started buttering him up by helping him with his arithmetic.

I also started to do a little writing, spurred on by a heightened awareness of my own mortality. I wanted to get something of myself down on paper before Kennedy and Khruschev got their undies in a twist again and sent me to get my head or my balls blown off. The purpose of the two dog tags is to hook one in between a dead soldier's teeth and let the other one dangle out of his mouth, for identification purposes. If my balls got blown off, they could stuff my dog tags in my mouth, and if my head got blown off they could stuff the dog tags up my arse, for all I cared.

I didn't feel up to writing a novel yet, so I was working on a series of sketches featuring characters based on Lori McCoy, Keith Santone and Charlie Guinard. Every day as soon as I got off duty, I'd take a quick shower, grab papers and notebooks, and go back up to the orderly room where I could use the typewriter in my clerk cubicle. Barbarian made a few suspicious remarks about "what kinda stuff the perfessor be writin' up there," as if I might be pounding out commie propaganda right under the army's nose. He was probably frustrated that he couldn't read well enough to check my stuff out and see if it merited a court-martial.

Most evenings I'd stay at the typewriter till lights-out time, ten o'clock, and walking down the hill from the orderly room on such nights, I'd see the barracks standing stark and white in the glow of the firelights, and no life in sight except an occasional duty soldier shoveling coal and blowing white breath into the cold, and sometimes I would feel alone and confident, and other times I would feel merely alone, dwarfed by the barracks and the giant pines and the stars like distant pinpricks in the black sky, and the pages of what I had written seemed as insignificant as the flyspecks on the mess hall walls.

Barbarian was so jubilant when he passed the fifth grade that he "rewarded" me for being his tutor by giving me the "honor" of representing the Five-Oh-Worst in the Battalion Soldier of the Month contest. I tried to squirm out of it, but he said, "I got nobody else, ever'body I put up flunked, so git yer swingin' dick over there."

It was no use to argue with him. I wanted to keep him in my camp. So I put on a clean uniform and paid Cheater five bucks to polish my boots and my brass.

On my way across the drill field, I passed a corporal kneeling in the dirt, laying out parade markers and listening to a portable radio lying on the ground beside him. He looked up at me and said, "I just heard a news bulletin claimin' President Kennedy got shot in Dallas."

I didn't know whether or not to believe the corporal, but when I got to Battalion Headquarters, the sergeant-major burst out of the interview room with tears rolling down his cheeks and said, "The president is dead."

A few minutes later I was called before a panel of commissioned officers and asked to recite the Chain of Command. I named my squad leader, my platoon leader, my company commander and so on, and a funny feeling came over me as I realized that I might be the first soldier in the army to name Lyndon B. Johnson as Commander in Chief. I went ahead and did it, and none of the officers corrected me. So it was true. JFK was actually dead.

I became intensely interested in the how and why of the assassination. The killing of Lee Harvey Oswald by Jack Ruby heightened my interest and increased my suspicions. I thought Oswald might not really be guilty. At first the authorities said that his rifle was a German Mauser, then they said it was a Mannlicher-Carcano. Why couldn't they get such a simple thing straight? And why were they claiming it was such a big deal that Oswald made Sharpshooter in the Marine Corps? *Expert* was the highest rating, not Sharpshooter, and it was achieved by shooting at stationary man-sized targets on an obstruction-free firing range, not by shooting down in the street at a man rolling past in a motorcade six stories below.

Around this time, I got my first-ever letter from my old college buddy, Keith Santone, who was holding down a low-paying job at a radio station in Belmont, New York, while his wife Lori finished her last year at the University. The envelope was plastered with Easter Seals and three-cent stamps, and when Barbarian handed it to me he said, "This guy like to lick glue?"

"Sniffs it too, Sarge," I said, more flippantly than I should have, as I ripped open the envelope and sat on my footlocker to read.

Hey, Frank, betcha you're sorry you didn't get to sun yourself in Cuba. Charlie Guinard said the Apple was gonna get hit with hydrogen bombs and Belmont was gonna get hit with nuclear fallout, so he pleaded with me and Lori to go to Australia with him to start a commune. We said we weren't about to screw up Lori's singing career, and he said if we didn't go we were going to be melted into a big radioactive clump. He's still caught up in civil rights marches and war protests. But he almost has his law degree and he offered to help us sue our piss-ant record company. The bastards only pressed a thousand copies of Lori's album, and they won't press more even though the whole batch sold out. I need your help, man. I'm going to Dallas to do my own investigation of the Kennedy Assassination. Oswald either didn't do it or didn't do it all by himself, and I want to be the first guy to prove it. I've got a couple of filmmakers, a black guy and his wife, who have promised to help me shoot a documentary down there during Easter break, so you have to come here as soon as you get out of the Army. Don't get a job right away, you can stay with me and Lori till we hit the road. This assassination investigation is gonna make me rich and famous. I even sent away to a mail-order house for a rifle just like Oswald's.

PART TWO
JOHNSON

"God knows many of them are fools, and most of them will be sellouts
but they're a better generation than we were."
-- Lillian Hellman

"The white man don't like nothing black but a Cadillac."
-- H. Rap Brown

"To the rest of the world the United States must look like a gigantic
insane asylum where the inmates have taken over."
-- Art Buchwald

"Let us, for God's sake, resolve to live under the law."
-- President Lyndon B. Johnson

CHAPTER 5

I walked past bananas and long Italian cheeses hanging in the window of Angelo's Groceria, a sight that made my mouth water, and pulled open the street-level door at the side of the building. Slamming it on a gust of cold wind, I climbed two flights of dirty uncarpeted stairs to a landing where a spill of light came through a high transom. I tapped on the door, and Keith bellered, "Come on in, Frank, it ain't locked!"

I stepped into the kitchen, but nobody was there.

Keith must've yelled from the master bedroom -- the door was ajar. Not wanting to interrupt anything, I stepped across the hall to the spare room, hung up my coat and sat on the studio couch I used for a bed. My open suitcase half full of clothes was in the middle of the floor. My record albums were stacked against a wall. I picked up a pile of dirty clothes, stuffed them in a plastic bag, stashed the bag behind the couch, then went into the living room, sat on a recliner and thumbed through an old copy of *Newsweek* with the assassinated President on the cover.

Living with a married couple when you're a single guy, there's no way not to sometimes feel like a third wheel. But I wasn't going to look for an apartment of my own till I got back from Dallas. I had no brothers or sisters, no close relatives. I was born and raised in Belmont, but my mother died of pancreatic cancer during my junior year at the University, and two years later my father hanged himself in a jail cell after he got arrested for a Drunk and Disorderly. I sold the modest home I inherited in order to pay off my student loans.

All our lives, my mother and I were terrorized by my father. I often had to get away from his drunken rages, so I was used to crashing in frat houses or dorms or young girls' apartments where a Big Man on the Gridiron was usually welcome. But eventually I got tired of hanging out with football groupies and was drawn toward the campus oddballs and nonconformists who were into something other than beer blasts. I got tight with Keith, Lori and Charlie. They made me feel that they liked me in spite of, not because of, the fact that I was a jock. They even said they saw writing talent in me, and encouraged me to put some stuff down on paper.

Keith came out of his and Lori's bedroom, pulling a pair of striped purple and gray bell bottoms over his naked loins, and said, "Gotta get laid while the baby naps. I'm on a fuckin' schedule."

The phone rang.

"Get that," Keith said. "A guy called earlier, someone calls himself Greenbean. I could barely understand him. He has a West Virginia twang like Lori's mom and dad."

I stepped into the kitchen and grabbed the wall phone and immediately recognized Jimmy Green's voice. He said, "Hey, hoss, how's your ding-dong hangin'?"

"I was out walking and thought about you when I passed a dirty book store."

"You shoulda bought me some good readin' material."

"I did. I got you some Edgar Allan Poe."

"Aw, hoss, you know I don't read that shit!"

Jimmy Green and Rorthal Cheatwood had both gotten out of the Army a month before I did, and we had stayed in touch. They had been my closest pals at Fort Bragg. They were rough-hewn guys, like some of the linemen who had blocked for me in college, and they would go to the wall for anybody they considered a friend. Both originally from West Virginia, these days they were sharing an apartment in Charleston, where they had taken low-level jobs in a chemical plant.

Bean suddenly said, "Me and Cheater heard Barbarian hung hisself in his cadre room."

Visions of my father's death hit me in the gut.

"Cheater tol' me Barbarian done it 'cause he flunked the sixth grade."

Greenbean let out a laugh that he couldn't hold in, and I realized he'd been joking.

"You fucker!" I said. "You got me!"

Greenbean horselaughed.

I was relieved. There were things that I honestly liked about Barbarian.

Still chortling, Bean said, "Well, he prob'ly *will* flunk sixth grade without you helpin' him with his 'rithmetic! I don't know if he'll hang hisself or not, but who gives a shit, hoss? Me and Cheater are up for visitin' cowboy country. We wanna join up with you in Dallas. Gotta find out 'xactly when you're gonna be headin' that way so we can report off."

"I already told you our trip is Easter week. I'll call you with the details soon as I know them."

"Lookin' forward to hookin' up with you, hoss."

I got off the phone and Keith came into the kitchen, flipped open a cigar box, took out a bag of grass and rolled a fat joint. Then Lori came out carrying two-year-old Missy. Blonde, like both her parents, the baby had Keith's dimples and Lori's green eyes and turned-up nose. Lori's hair was tied back in a ponytail and her body was hidden under a pleated housecoat. "C'mon now, honey," she cooed to Missy. "Say hello to Frank, he's company."

Missy buried her face against Lori's shoulder.

"Cat got your tongue?" Lori teased.

"Get her outta here!" Keith snapped. "I gotta talk to Frank about Dallas!"

"Well, I want to talk about the trip, too! Soon as I freshen up." Lori set Missy down, handed her a coloring book and some crayons, and marched huffily into the bathroom.

"I was better off when we just had a cat," Keith said. "She treats that kid like a cuddle toy."

I said, "We're going to hear Lori sing tonight, right?"

"I'm tired of hearing my old lady. There's a groovy jazz joint where Charlie Guinard hangs out with his moony-eyed groupies. That's where we're gonna go to talk about the trip, but if you really want to, we can catch Lori's last set."

I had noticed, ever since I got back, that Keith had lost enthusiasm for Lori's singing ever since her album failed to take off big.

Lori came out of the bathroom, freshened up and looking good in hot pants and halter. She joined us at the table and said, "How many days will it take to get down to Dallas?"

"Not days, hours," Keith told her. "We'll make it in about twenty-four driving straight through."

"We *can't* drive straight through!"

"Hell yes we can. It's less than fifteen-hundred miles."

"What about Missy! She's only a *baby*. She'll need to stop overnight and rest."

"She can get plenty of sleep in the car. We have to get there as fast as we can so we can spend all our time interviewing and filming. Longer the trip takes, the less time we'll have on the scene, right, Frank?"

He lit up another joint and passed it to me. I took a toke and passed it to Lori.

"It's true," I said tactfully, "that we probably need all the time we can get on location. But it's also true that we might wear ourselves out traveling and be less effective once we get there."

23

Keith said, "Maybe the wife and kid should stay home."

"No way!" Lori snapped.

He reached out to take her hand, but she yanked it away.

He leaned back, made eye contact with her and spoke in soft, soothing tones. "Listen, babe, we could cut down through West Virginia and drop you and Missy off at your mama's place. How would that be?"

"You're not gonna *dump* me, Keith! I'm looking forward to this trip. You promised me we could visit Nashville on our way back. I've been wantin' to see the Grand Ole Opry ever since I was a little girl. I told you how I used to hug my staticky portable radio and dream about bein' up on that stage for real someday! But *you* don't care one teeny bit about that, *do* you? Other people's dreams don't matter to you, long as you get to do what *you* want!"

"Aw, c'mon, babe, you know that's not --"

She got up in a huff, and Keith followed her into the bedroom. I could hear them arguing in there, then Keith came out carrying a rifle. Cradling it almost tenderly, he squinted through the telescopic sight. "Genuine Mannlicher-Carcano with a four-power scope, Frank. It has a weird, ugly kind of beauty, hey?"

This was my first look at what I thought of from then on as Lee Harvey Oswald's weapon, even though it wasn't the very one he had used.

Keith said, "You've gotta practice with this gun --"

"Army calls it a weapon, not a gun."

"I know, I saw *Battle Cry* -- Tab Hunter and Aido Ray. I want you to practice a *lot* next week before we leave for Dallas, till you can shoot this thing as fast and accurate as humanly possible. The Zapruder film shows that three shots were fired within very tight intervals, and so far nobody's been able to aim, shoot, eject spent cartridges and chamber fresh rounds as fast as Oswald would've had to. It's pretty strong proof that there had to've been another shooter."

I took the Mannlicher-Carcano in my hands and hefted it, picturing Oswald in the Book Depository window.

Keith handed me a box of big, evil-looking, brass-jacketed cartridges and I held three of them in my palm, realizing with a pot-enhanced jolt that this was the type of slug that had blasted President Kennedy's brain.

CHAPTER 6

The "Dallas Caravan" -- as Charlie Guinard dubbed it -- motored into Dallas in high spirits. Keith led the way, driving a big old station wagon with fake wooden panels, me in the front passenger seat and Lori and Missy in back. Guinard and his carload of peaceniks were directly behind us, Charlie in his typical bibbed coveralls and a plaid flannel shirt, driving with the seat pushed back and his big belly almost up against the steering wheel. Next came the van carrying filmmakers Carlisle and Brenda Dixon and a load of movie equipment. Then Jimmy Green and Rorthal Cheatwood in a beat-up 1955 Plymouth convertible with the top down because the canvas was rotted and half-shredded and even uglier than the rest of the car. Bean and Cheater had driven down from West Virginia to join the caravan at our rallying point, a truck stop just outside of Dallas. We were high on our prospects for success, but if we could've known what was in store for us, we never would've left the Belmont campus.

The ensuing days and nights went by in a blur of long hours, hard work and little sleep. Keith was fired up and manic. He popped uppers like candy to make himself stay on his feet twenty-four-seven. I was afraid he was going to keel over, but somehow he kept on going, organizing caravan members and bossing us around, conducting interviews with any residents who claimed to have a story to tell, obsessively scribbling down notes, trying to fit all the material he was gathering into some sort of perspective with what other people had said in books and articles about the assassination. If ever there was any down time, he kept me and Carlisle awake when we would rather have gone to bed, rapping about what we were doing and what we were going to do, and how great it was all going to turn out.

Keith was one of the most handsome, charismatic people I had ever known. He had utter confidence in his attributes and was convinced that he was destined for greatness. He felt he wouldn't be denied. Right now, as I said, he was working at a smalltime radio station in Belmont, where at least he got to be on the air spinning records and spouting off opinionated editorials, but as soon as Lori graduated they were moving to

Manhattan where Keith firmly believed that the big time was waiting for them. Shyly and to a lesser extent, Lori halfway believed it too, because he was always ranting about their golden destiny and trying to convince her of it.

He turned on all his charm and magnetism to make daring, almost impossible things happen on our Dallas trip because he saw it as his key to fabulous, instantaneous success. Somehow he wangled a permit to film inside the Texas Book Depository. But we weren't allowed to fire the rifle from there, not even using blanks, so we had to dry-fire it, with a guard watching us at all times. Keith set up a mock demonstration of Oswald's birds-eye view of the presidential limousine, by actually hiring a limo and driver and using Lori, Rorthal Cheatwood and Charlie Guinard as stand-ins for John and Jacqueline Kennedy and Governor Connally. I peered down at them from the same sixth-story window that Oswald had used, aimed the rifle and dry-fired it at them, and the creepiness of what I was doing made chills run up my spine.

Carlisle and Brenda said the film footage so far was "totally groovy," but we still needed to find someplace where we could actually fire the rifle, and this problem was solved when three of Charlie's groupies located a defunct office building just outside of town and got permission to use it as a substitute for the Book Depository. This was the most vital part of the filming. I took the part of Lee Harvey Oswald and fired down at the "actors" in the rented limo. Keith timed all the action scrupulously, and made us repeat it so many times that I got blisters on my fingers.

Finally he was not only satisfied, but elated. Try as I might, I had not managed to get off a group of three shots that beat the frame counts shown on the Zapruder film. If one shooter couldn't beat those shots or at least equal them, then it proved, according to Keith, that there had to have been more than one assassin.

On our last night in Dallas, Keith, Carlisle, Brenda and I got reckless, toking a dozen or so joints in the Dixons' room and joking that if we got caught the rednecks down here would probably lynch us. The Dixons were staying in a separate motel from the rest of us, a shabby fleabag for "coloreds." We brought in wine, cheese, cookies and crackers in order not to have to confront the fact that if we had tried to go into a local saloon or restaurant, Carlisle and Brenda would have been turned away or maybe even arrested.

This would be our last night down South together. I had made up my mind to cross into Mexico for a few days, to satisfy a yen that had built up in me from reading Jack Kerouac's novels and taking inspiration from them. Keith was making noises about wanting to go with me, but I didn't jump at that idea. He had promised Lori he'd take her to Nashville, and I thought he ought to keep his promise and didn't want to be blamed if he didn't.

Cheater and Bean didn't make it to the party in the Dixons' room, saying that they didn't want to be packed in there like sardines. The real reason was probably that they'd rather go out cruising on their own, maybe hit some of the road houses we had seen on the way down here, and hope for a chance to get laid even if they had to pay for it.

Charlie Guinard and his peacenik groupies had already hit the road for Oxford, Mississippi, where there was going to be a civil rights march that Charlie had helped organize. He had somehow talked the Dixons into filming it for him, and Keith and Lori were supposed to join up with him there and take part in the demonstration before continuing on to Nashville by themselves.

I liked the Dixons, and could tell by the way they worked together that they had a real passion for filmmaking. I wanted to get tighter with them, so I told them about the time that the Ku Klux Klan had driven my grandfather's family off of the little farm they had once owned in Pennsylvania. "My grandfather's last name was Guglielmi," I said, "but he had it changed to Williams when he came over from Italy. He imagined he'd be treated like a real American if he signed up and fought in the First World War, so he went over there and got mustard gas poisoning and found out that nobody respected him for it. My father was only eight years old when the Klan came in the middle of the night, men in white sheets on horses. They burned a cross in the yard and galloped around yelling and firing their guns. Around there, in the early nineteen-hundreds, immigrants were hated, no matter what color their skin was. Teddy Roosevelt even led a group called America for Americans that was fanatically against anybody who wasn't born here."

"Damn!" Carlisle said. "They wanted to drive out people who came to this country from someplace else, even if they were *white?*"

"When the First World War broke out, people blamed *all* foreigners, not just the Germans. There were quite a few lynchings. My grandfather moved the family to Belmont, New York, but he found out people were just as prejudiced up North. My dad never got over the way the Klan scared him to death when he was a little kid. He figured he was hated for who he was, so he decided to hate back. His whole life, he was prejudiced against every other race and nationality."

"I guess I understand it in a way," Carlisle allowed, shaking his head sadly.

"But that's no excuse!" Brenda said. "You can't let those kinds of people make you a hater just like them! Right, Frank?"

"Right. I could see how my father got that way, and I didn't want it to happen to me. He had a terrible mean streak, but he was still my father, and I always wanted to be close to him, but he never let me. He carried a grudge against everybody and everything till the day he died."

"How did he pass away?" Brenda asked.

"My mother died of cancer, and he went on a binge with the insurance money and got arrested for starting a bar fight with a black guy. The jailer checked his cell in the middle of the night and found him with his T-shirt knotted around his neck and his knees only a few inches from the floor. So the cops said he could've saved himself by standing up straight, so he must've really wanted to die. But I figured he must have hauled himself up and let himself drop and the jolt probably knocked him out."

"Oh man, I'm sorry," Carlisle said.

"I feel guilty about it," I said, "because he phoned me and wanted me to come and bail him out, but I said a night in jail would be good for him and hung up on him. I had hopes that maybe someday I'd get to have a better relationship with him, but now that will never happen. If he was trying to punish me, I guess he succeeded."

CHAPTER 7

On our last night in Dallas, Keith got up the nerve to tell Lori he wanted to go to Mexico with me. They were alone in their motel room when he broke it to her. "Frank's done a lot for me, babe. We can save him the expense of renting a car. I'd rather see Mexico, and you'd rather see Nashville, and this way we'll both have our druthers."

Lori had seen this coming, but she was still hurt by it, and her eyes smarted with held-back tears. She said, "What about Oxford? We promised Charlie."

"You promised Charlie, I didn't."

"Well, *you promised me!"*

"I've got to broaden my worldview, babe. It's good for my career."

"Bullcrap! Your *worldview* is gonna be the worms in the tequila bottles! If you don't get your damn throat slit in some back alley you'll get thrown in a Tijuana jail."

"C'mon, babe, you've gotta be back in class and I don't. It's not fair to deprive me of this opportunity."

"How in the world are me and Missy supposed to get to Oxford, then Nashville and then home? Am I supposed to hitchhike with a two-year-old in my arms?"

"Bean and Cheater said you can ride with them. They want to see Nashville, too. And they were drunk enough the other night to tell Charlie they'd meet up with him in Oxford."

"Hmph! You got your duckies all lined up in a row before you sprung this on me, didn't you!"

"C'mon, babe, be reasonable!"

Ignoring him, she got into the motel bed with her face to the wall so he couldn't see the tears running down her face. She didn't want to start sobbing and wake up Missy. The child loved her father unconditionally and was blind to his faults.

Lori was realizing more and more that her husband was like a selfish little boy who had never grown up. He got itchy pants as soon as Frank mentioned going to Mexico. He couldn't stand the thought of Frank coming back home with funny or outrageous stories to tell that the great Keith Santone did not have any part in.

Keith didn't even seem to appreciate how hard Lori had worked on his damned documentary. Desperate to prove her worth to him, she had done as much as she could to help out, and to be able to do so she had paid one of the girls with Charlie to watch Missy most of the time, using money she had earned on one of her singing gigs instead of wasting it to buy souvenirs and stuff. Seeing Lori working as a script girl, secretary and gofer all worked into one, Charlie had taken note of her efforts and had asked her to be a production assistant for the Dixons when they got to Oxford. But from Keith she got no compliments or caresses. He treated her like excess baggage. As her tears soaked silently into her pillow, she wondered just how big a fool she had allowed herself to become.

She had never been far from Cherry Hill, West Virginia, until she got accepted at Belmont University with a music scholarship, and she had stepped onto the campus like a chick that had just cracked out of its egg. Nobody else was as raw and naïve as she was. Just thinking about it made her blush. Everybody she laid eyes on seemed suave and sophisticated. Especially Keith. When he first started paying attention to her, she found it hard to believe. She was so grateful she became totally submissive to him.

But now she was beginning to find her wings. People not only liked her music, they liked her, and this had dawned on her gradually, as she began to get a sense of warmth, not just applause, from her audiences. She could tell that Frank Williams liked her, too, and he was smart and good-looking, even though he still had his too-short army haircut and he wasn't wearing the mod kind of clothes other guys were now wearing. He was able to attract women whether or not he was playing football.

Lori could tell by the look on Frank's face this morning that he knew his idea of going to Mexico had caused a rift between her and Keith, and he obviously felt sheepish about it. But she knew Frank wasn't to blame, even though she hadn't gotten a chance to tell him so.

More and more, she was aware that ever since her album had flopped, Keith had relegated her to second-class status in their marriage. When he was drunk or stoned he'd go into long rants about how, if he could hook onto a fad, a trend or a hot story, he'd become an overnight success. Lori suspected that he wasn't as interested in getting at the truth behind the Kennedy Assassination as he was in what it could do for *him*. His journalism was a vehicle for his own success, not something he was deeply passionate about. But maybe this was the way you had to think in the real world. Maybe it was foolish of her to feel that she would always want to write and sing even if she never got paid for it.

She couldn't help wondering if a major label would've picked up her album if there were some of her own original songs on it. She had tried singing a few of them in some of the campus hangouts, and people told her they liked them. But Keith said they were only saying that because it didn't cost them anything, and it'd be a different story if they had to plunk down cold hard cash.

Keith often made fun of her for being too trusting, too gullible, too stubborn about doing the right thing. But once she committed herself to someone or something, she was in for the long haul. Her Methodist religion did not prohibit divorce, but nobody where she grew up ever got one, even if the women had to put up with mean, drunken husbands who beat them, and the men had to put up with wives who became fat and bitchy. They all stuck it out somehow, and Lori figured that's what she ought to do too. She really did not want to make Missy grow up without a daddy.

CHAPTER 8

Brenda and Carlisle couldn't wait to get out of the Deep South. They'd been on edge for their whole four days down here, and what they were hearing on the radio right now was shaking them up worse. At first, Brenda thought she had hit on a preacher man as she spun the dial through the static, but it turned out he was the worst kind of fanatic, spouting hate-filled garbage on a low-wattage station with scary call letters: ARYN. His name was Conrad Pryzor, and he was the owner of the radio station and the leader of something called the Aryan Confederacy. Just like Keith Santone, he was taking advantage of people's widespread skepticism over the Warren Commission Report, but his slant was grotesque, totally deluded. He claimed that President Kennedy was killed by Cuban communists in retaliation for attempts by the CIA and the Mafia to kill Fidel Castro by sending him poisoned cigars.

"We Aryans must arm ourselves!" Pryzor ranted. "Our government is run by Zionists! America is the Promised Land God gave to white people, and we must win it back from the Jews and the nigras! Jesus Christ was an Aryan, not a Jew, and the final and greatest book of the Holy Bible is *Mein Kampf!* It was inspired by the Holy Ghost speaking through our prophet Adolf Hitler! Our savior *has* ordained our Armageddon! He *will* destroy all our enemies with great tongues of fire! And upon their smoldering ruins, we will build a glorious Fourth Reich that will last a thousand years!"

"Hell on earth!" Brenda said with disgust. "That's what the sick fool is preaching!"

"Right on," Carlisle agreed. "They call this the Bible Belt but it's more like a Bigotry Belt. Wild horses won't drag me down here ever again."

"Then why did you let Charlie talk you into going to Mississippi?"

"He's so damn *seductive.* And, look, babe, I don't want to be a hero, but I want to do my part. Charlie made sense when he pointed out that a whole lot of the guys getting killed in Vietnam are black, and down here they can't even vote, thanks to the Jim Crow laws."

"He played on your sense of pride and decency," Brenda said. "He knows how to push people's buttons. He's a travel agent for guilt trips, just like my mama."

They both laughed.

"Keith can be an insensitive clod, too," Carlisle said. "I felt like slapping him silly this morning when we were getting ready to leave."

They had been loading their van, and instead of helping, Keith had stood by cracking jokes in an exaggerated southern drawl. "If n I was y'all, I'd steer away from white sheets, even the ones hangin' on clotheslines -- might be eye-holes in 'em!"

"Very fucking funny, Keith!" Lori had snapped. She was burnt up at him because he wasn't taking her to Nashville. Instead he was going to Mexico with Frank Williams, forcing Lori and Missy to have to go to Oxford with Bean and Cheater, then catch a ride back to Belmont with Charlie. At least Bean and Cheater were up for stopping off at Nashville, so Lori would get to realize her dream. Luckily, they were goodhearted country boys who had grown up listening to the Wheeling West Virginia Jamboree, which was a sort of second cousin to the Grand Ol' Opry, and they, just like Lori, wanted to see the real thing. So now Lori and Missy were riding with Bean and Cheater in their beat-up old convertible, following closely behind the Dixons' van.

Conrad Pryzor was grating on Carlisle's nerves. He said, "Oxford is where the National Guard had to be called in a couple of years ago. I say we just film a little bit and then leave. It's gonna be like stepping into a snake pit."

"You're scaring me," Brenda said.

For the past several nights, hugging each other in cheap, sagging motel beds, they had spoken in whispers about the sad despair they had seen throughout the South. The rural roads were dotted with cotton pickers' shacks that had holes in their rusty tin roofs and ripped-off wall planks that had probably been used for fire wood. You could look right through some of the shacks and see babies being breast fed or naked little children that the whites called "pickaninnies" playing on the dirt floors. There were WHITE and COLORED drinking fountains in stores and public places, even in libraries and court houses. Often there were rest rooms FOR WHITES ONLY but no place for blacks to relieve themselves or wash their hands. They had to hold it till they got out of town and found some tall weeds way off the road, and even then they had to hope they wouldn't get caught and charged with indecent exposure or worse. Most of the white people they came across in the streets

33

ignored them as if they were dirt, but others, especially the cops, gave them menacing looks, conveying the clear message that they'd better watch their step at all times if they didn't want something really bad to happen to them.

"Turn that off, will you," Carlisle said. He was referring to Conrad Pryzor, who was fervently preaching that blacks needed to be either shipped back to Africa or returned to slavery.

Brenda said, "Sometimes it's good to listen to people like him, so we don't let ourselves get complacent."

"I lost my complacency a long time ago," Carlisle told her. "I keep on picturing all the slaves that suffered and died down here, and how unbelievable it is that it went on for three hundred years. Hatred is a way of life for a lot of folks down here, and it's hard for me not to hate back, like Frank said about his father."

"What about Keith? I don't trust him much. He sign a contract?"

"He says he'll take care of it when he gets back. Says he stuffed it in a desk drawer and forgot about it."

"You might have to get Lori to push him. She has a heart, and he doesn't. He's got a slew of people working for him for free. Working to make *him* famous. I don't think he even cares how Kennedy died, he just wants to exploit the situation."

With sudden alarm, Carlisle said, "There's a cop car coming up on us. Must've gotten between us and the Plymouth when I wasn't noticing."

"Does it have its rooflights on?"

"No."

"Don't panic, then. Act like nothing's wrong."

"Well, there *is* nothing wrong unless it's wrong with *them*," Carlisle said.

He watched in the rearview mirror as the shiny white patrol car swung out and then slowed, right alongside him. Two beefy red-faced cops glowered at him, then sped up and swung the patrol car in ahead of him, so close that he had to brake. He grimaced, thinking maybe they wanted him to ram them so he could be arrested for it. But then they hit the gas and took off.

Immediately a red pickup that must've been right behind the police car screeched up to within a few feet of the van's rear bumper. Carlisle goosed the gas pedal, but the pickup truck closed the gap, threatening to bump the van off the road. In the cab of the truck, two white men were laughing and chugging beer. Breaking into a sweat, Carlisle tried speeding up, but the pickup kept on tail-gating him so dangerously that he expected to be slammed. Abruptly the pickup swung out and got alongside him, the white men glowering at him, yelling obscenities and giving him the finger till an oncoming car forced them to cut over just in time to squeeze past the van without side-swiping it.

Then, just like the cop car, the pickup took off fast, giving Carlisle and Brenda a glimpse of a stars-and-bars rear bumper sticker and some other kind of sticker with a swastika on it.

"Asshole rednecks!" Carlisle spluttered.

"I sure hope they're gone for good," Brenda said breathlessly. "The cops too. Did you notice their car didn't have any markings on it?"

"It had a rack on it."

"Yeah, but there was no clue as to whether they were state troopers, county police or what."

"Could be from one of the dinky little towns we passed back aways – a couple of houses and a general store at a crossroads. Probably got one patrol car and can't afford to paint a logo on it."

"It looked like a brand new car though."

"Yeah," said Carlisle, "with two old-fashioned redneck assholes in it."

"Are Bean and Cheater still back of us?"

"I don't see them. Hope that jalopy of theirs didn't peter out somewhere. If they don't catch up soon, we'll double back and look for them. Maybe they broke down."

For a while they rode in silence. A sign said they were thirty miles away from Oxford, Mississippi, then they saw flashing lights up ahead. The police car and the pickup that had harassed them were stopped off to one side of the two-lane road. The blue light on the roof of the pickup was the detached kind with a wire leading over the roof and into the cab. The two beefy, red-faced cops were standing by their unmarked car, waving for the van to pull over. The other two guys were standing by their pickup with shotguns in their hands.

"Uh-oh," Carlisle said. He glanced at his wife and saw how scared she looked. "Don't panic, we'll get through this," he told her, squeezing her jean-clad knee. Even though he had done nothing wrong, he willed himself to put on an apologetic demeanor as he pulled the van onto the berm.

The cops watched him with poker faces, hands on hips. The shotgun-wielding rednecks dropped cigarette butts from between their lips and used their scuffed-up yellow clodhoppers to grind the butts into the asphalt. They were both wearing dirt-caked denims, rumpled flannel shirts and brown John Deere caps darkly stained with sweat and grease. They came up on either side of the van and pointed their shotguns at Carlisle and Brenda.

"Get out!" one of the cops barked.

Carlisle started reaching for his driver's license.

"Keep your filthy black paws visible!" the other cop commanded. "You reach fer somethin' we don't know what yer reachin' fer, our two deputies'll blow yer heads off!"

"Just my driver's license," Carlisle said mildly, stepping down onto the ground.

Brenda got out of the van, too. The shotgun barrels followed their every move. "My wife and I are both professors at Belmont University in—"

"Neeeewfuckin' Yawk!" one of the cops snarled. "We ain't *un literate,* we'uns can read license plates. You worse'n Yankees 'cause you *black* Yankees! Whatchoo doin' down here, boy? You aimin' to go fuckin' *peace* marchin'? Or makin' some of *our* fuckin' nigras addle-headed enough to think they can go vote same as their betters?"

About fifty feet up the road, two car doors slammed shut. Greenbean and Cheater got out of their clunker, and started toward the van from the gravel patch where they had parked, by a dinky little bridge. When they got close, the two cops drew out big, shiny revolvers and ordered Bean and Cheater to stop in their tracks.

"They're with *us,*" Brenda blurted, hoping to forestall any gunplay, even as she realized that a black woman couldn't vouch for two white men, it had to be the other way around.

Lori was watching apprehensively from the backseat of the ratty convertible, holding Missy protectively on her lap. She was too far away to hear much of what was being said, but she saw the guns. She glanced all around anxiously, hoping for help, or at least witnesses. But traffic was sparse here, and the couple of vehicles that came by were waved on by the cops.

"Whatchoo doin' travelin' behind two niggers?" one of the cops said to Jimmy Green and Rorthal Cheatwood. "You two some of them *white* deemonstrators?" That's the way he pronounced it, demon-strators, exaggerating the first syllable.

"White trash deemonstrators from up North," the other cop sneered.

"We're good ol' West Virginia boys!" Greenbean said heartily, trying to mollify the rednecks so the confrontation might end peacefully.

"West fuckin' Virginia!" snarled one of the shotgun toters. "Split off from the South and took sides with the North! You as much Yankees as these two niggers is. None of you got no fuckin' bizness down here!"

"Gimme yer keys," the other shotgun-toter demanded, and he snatched the keys out of Carlisle's hand. Leaning his shotgun against a guard rail, he went around and unlocked the back of the van. He immediately spotted the Oswald rifle and let out a loud whistle. "Lookee here!" he said, taking the weapon out of its box and holding it up for his buddies to see. Then he rummaged around, found a loaded ammunition clip, slid it into the slot under the breech and slammed it home with the heel of his hand.

Glowering at Carlisle, one of the cops said, "Who was you fixin' to *shoot,* black boy?"

"It's a souvenir," Brenda said shakily. "A war souvenir my father gave us."

"This *ain't* no American weapon!" the redneck who held it snapped.

"It's Italian," Brenda told him. "My father served in Italy as a medic. He saved a lot of white soldiers' lives."

She was lying, hoping to elicit a modicum of sympathy, if these assholes had any inside them. Her father had hoped to become a medic, but was denied. Instead he was put to work in a mess hall in Fort Benning, for the duration of the war.

"Yer daddy prob'ly sucked a lotta white soldiers' dicks," one of the cops said. "Lots of medics was faggots, sceered to fight."

The guy with the Mannlicher-Carcano worked the bolt, chambering a round, then pointed it at Carlisle's chest.

Brenda gasped.

Suddenly Cheater lunged for the rifle, and it went off -- an ear-splitting BLAM as he fought for it and was strong enough to yank it out of the redneck's hands. But the other redneck hit Cheater in the back of the neck with his shotgun, staggering him, and whacked him again as his knees sagged. It looked like he would crumple to the asphalt. But a loud shotgun blast hurtled him backwards, blowing a big gory hole in his chest. He reeled and fell dead in a pool of his own blood.

Brenda screamed.

"Shut the fuck up, bitch!" one of the cops yelled.

From down the road, Lori saw it all, and she grabbed Missy and ducked down between the car seats, hiding as best she could, hoping the bridge railing helped conceal her and the baby.

37

"You killed him!" Bean blurted, kneeling over Cheater's bloody body. He felt futilely for a pulse, and his hand came away smeary red. He rocked back on his heels, his mouth gaping.

"He was resistin' arrest," the redneck killer said.

"You had him knocked out, you didn't need to shoot him!" Bean cried out, getting to his feet.

"Well, if yer gonna be a hostile witness, I might just as well shoot *you.*"

He swung his shotgun onto Bean, who was using a handkerchief to wipe Cheater's blood off his hand. Bean seemed more sad than angry, muttering and shaking his head, as if he really didn't want to believe he was going to be shot.

BLAM! Bean was blown back and slammed down, his head a pulpy mass raggedly severed from the rest of his body. All that was left of his neck were some stringy, bloody ligaments and part of his spinal cord jutting out.

"You motherfuckers!" Carlisle shouted, his eyes wide with shock.

"Heh-heh," one of the cops jeered."I was wonderin' when you'd start talkin' like a reg'lar nigger 'steada a high-falutin' perfessor!"

The other cop said, "Pile what's left of the white trash into the back of that there van. Then we'll take their two nigger accomplices into custody." He said it with a sly leer that his partners picked up on.

"Like to take 'em someplace we won't be bothered fer a while, so's we can *interrogate* 'em afore we brings 'em in," the one with the Mannlicher-Carcano said, licking his lips. "Black wench is kinda cute fer a nigger. Betcha she'd like to have a taste of my *interrogatin' tool.*"

The man with the rifle snickered. "What about the white bitch over yonder?"

"Yer shittin' me. What white bitch? Where at?"

"In that there car them West Virginny boys was ridin' in, 'cross the bridge. I seen 'er duck down, tryin' to hide in the backseat." He snorted, "Stupid nigger-lovin' bitch!"

"Let's git 'er."

Lori peeped up and saw them coming for her. Scared out of her wits, she scrambled overtop of the front seat and turned the key in the ignition. Luckily, the engine started instead of stalling out as usual. She slammed the gearshift into Drive and peeled out, aiming to run the two killers over. But the one with the shotgun leaped out of the way and the one with the rifle fired, shattering her windshield. Glass exploded in her face but she kept on going, tramping the gas pedal to the floor. But flooring the old jalopy didn't produce the leap forward that she needed. She didn't know how in the world she was ever going to outrun the cops. In her rearview mirror she saw them running toward their patrol car, and she knew she couldn't hope to gain much of a lead.

Her only chance was to try trickery.

When she made it around a sharp bend in the road, she hoped she was temporarily out of the cops' sight, and she made a desperate decision to swerve the car into a farmer's field. The car humped over plowed ruts, Lori barely controlling it, and finally bounced onto a tractor trail and into a patch of woods and tall weeds.

She prayed that the cops would never figure she'd flee anywhere but straight down the highway as fast as she could go. The woods were hiding her pretty well. It helped that the top was down, creating a low profile. But she was afraid that a glimmer of red showing through the greenery or a glint of sunlight on chrome might give her away.

Leaning her face toward the rearview mirror, she saw trickles of blood where bullet-shattered glass had stung her. She hastily blotted her wounds with a tissue that she took from her pocket. Then she got out of the car, easing the door open and not bothering to shut it all the way so it wouldn't make any unnecessary noise.

Missy was crying and lifting her little arms, wanting to be patted and held. But Lori said, "Shhh ... shhh," and managed to make the child lie down with her again, between the car seats. Covering Missy's tiny body with her own, she kept on trying to soothe and quiet her, praying that if they were discovered and she was raped or shot, her baby would somehow be spared.

CHAPTER 9

Conrad Pryzor sat behind the gray steel desk in his office at his radio station, which was in a squat cinder-block building on a dirt road. Behind his desk was a framed portrait of Adolf Hitler. The grimy yellow paint of the opposite wall was all but hidden by a large red banner, much like a typical Nazi flag, except the swastika in the center was blue and was flanked by an A and a C that stood for the Aryan Confederacy.

Pryzor, a balding double-chinned man in his early thirties, was wearing a tan shirt with epaulettes, brown trousers and a black pistol belt, holster and German Luger. He also wore a red armband with the Aryan Confederacy emblem.

The two men who had shot Bean and Cheater faced him for a quizzing, hoping they had earned his approval. The one with the coarse black hair was Cletis Barrett and the other one, with patchy, thinning blonde hair was Albert Crane. They had shed their stained and bloody shirts, boots and jeans, had cleaned the boots as best they could, and left the rest to soak in a sink full of hot, soapy water. Then they had showered themselves off. They were now wearing brown trousers, black pistol belts and tan shirts with Aryan Confederacy armbands, like Pryzor's. In spite of their paramilitary-style dress, they didn't have the physically fit appearance of well-conditioned soldiers; they were big, jowly men with red, sunburnt faces, thick necks and thick, fat waists. The garage where their bloody clothes were soaking was where they repaired tractors and heavy equipment. Their fingernails and cuticles were caked with black grease.

"What did you do with the pickup?" Conrad Pryzor demanded of them.

"Got rid of the license plate," said Albert Crane with a suppressed grin. "Boosted it in a junkyard anyways, it wasn't even this year's. Hosed the bed out real good. Gonna repaint it, do it ourselves. Me and Cletis might hafta tussle it out. He says green, I say blue."

His attempt at a bit of humor didn't elicit so much as a token grin from Pryzor, who remained rigidly stiff and stern. "What about Herschel and Horace?" he asked. "What're they gonna do?"

"About what?" Cletis asked, scratching his head.

"About the goddamn *car!*"

Cletis smiled, confident that he could provide a good answer. "Took the rack off the roof already. Changed the license plate, too. You think we should repaint it? The upholst'ry already looks different. We took the seat covers off and burnt them up when we torched the van."

"With the two niggers and their white trash buddies inside it," Albert added, getting a charge out of replaying the exploit in his mind.

"There's no real need to repaint the car," Conrad Pryzor decided. "It looks like a million other white Chevrolets. How about Horace and Herschel? Could they be put in a line-up and picked out?"

"I don't see how," said Albert Crane. "Whoever comes nosin' around's gonna be lookin' fer two cops -- and Hershel and Horace gonna be out plowin' somewhere or feedin' their hogs. They got their uniform stuff hid real good in their barn. Never got no blood on their clothes neither."

"Okay, so far so good," said Pryzor. "Now tell me again how you let the *girl* get away."

His two underlings, who had started to relax, got fidgety again because they hated to relive the part of their escapade that had gone bad. Not only was it an embarrassment, it could cause their leader to see it as a threat to his own security. And they knew with certainty that if push came to shove, Pryzor wouldn't flinch at having them shot, chopped up, and fed to Herschel and Horace's hogs.

"Me and Albert had to stay watchin' the two niggers," Cletis said, pleading their case. "We couldn't just take off after the girl, once we found out she was hidin' there the whole time, by that bridge. *I* was the one spotted her! Herschel and Horace is the ones lost her, it's their fuckin' fault! No way she coulda outrun them in that ol' fucked-up Plymouth!"

"No *fuckin'* way!" Albert emphasized. "But she was cool-headed enough not to even try. Neither Herschel nor Horace spotted her tire tracks across that plowed field. Me and Cletis done it when we come back, after we took care of the two niggers."

"You came back to the scene of the crime," Prizor accused. "Don't you know how *dumb* that is?"

"Usually is, I admit," said Albert. "But there waren't no van there no more 'cause we had drove it away ourselves. No dead bodies neither, just a blotch of blood that coulda come from a road-kill deer that was layin' nearby. We figgered we'd mosey on back, maybe catch the girl walkin' or hitchin', then we could take care of 'er fer good."

"You said you took care of the niggers? Exactly how?"

"Kilt 'em both. Made 'er blow us while he watched. We didn't wanna put our lilly white dicks in 'er no place else."

"Put the rifle barrel in instead," Cletis said, smiling at his own cleverness. "You ought to've seen the look on her face. Pulled the trigger and shot one helluva load. It blasted her insides to shreds."

"Cut his pecker off and hung him," Albert added. "Then we cut 'im down, piled 'em both into the van with the white trash. Doused it real good with gas and burnt up everything that was in there. Them and all their stuff is charred to a crisp. Nothin' but a pile of twisted metal and roasted flesh."

"We couldn't get that ol' Plymouth started," Cletis complained, "or we woulda took it the hell outta there and hid it. We did take the license plate offa it, but we didn't wanna risk settin' it on fire right where it was. Didn't wanna be seen doin' that."

Conrad Pryzor stooped and picked up the Oswald rifle from behind his desk. He said, "I want this for a souvenir. It's a damn good rifle to own. It happens to be a Mannlicher-Carcano, the same kind Lee Harvey Oswald used -- or the liars said he used! It's worth the risk of keeping it because I don't see how anyone could trace it to me and match the ballistics to any slug they might find in the burnt-out van. The odds of that are slim to none. But still, a great deal of caution is warranted. I'm not going to openly display this rifle, I guarantee you that. I intend to keep it hidden somewhere for a long, long time."

CHAPTER 10

Lori and Missy were in the cab of a huge truck heading toward Chattanooga, Tennessee. The trucker was a fat, unshaven guy smelling of stale sweat and rancid cigar smoke and wearing a sweat-stained camouflage cap. Lori was scared of him even though he seemed to be nice. She didn't think she would ever trust anyone anymore. Even though she and Missy were a hundred miles from where the murders had taken place, she was terrified that somehow the two Mississippi cops, or other cops in cahoots with them, would appear out of nowhere and make the trucker pull over, then drag her and her baby out of the cab.

She had known that the bad guys would have found her sooner or later trying to hide in Bean and Cheater's car. Forcing herself to be brave, as soon as the white patrol car had sped by, she had run to the edge of the road, carrying Missy in her arms, along with a bag full of diapers, bottles and baby food. She had stuck her thumb out just as a big rig came up over the rise, and she had gotten very, very lucky -- somehow the driver had taken pity on her. Otherwise, she and Missy would probably be dead.

She couldn't get out of her mind what had happened to her friends. She had to keep choking back tears. She had known Carlisle and Brenda for a couple of years now, and they had been great fans of her music and always supportive in many other ways, even regarding her marriage; intuitively they had known it was on the rocks, and had offered to help her if she ever decided to leave.

She had just met Bean and Cheater a few days ago, and now they were gone. They were simple-hearted country boys, like most of the ones back home in Cherry Hill.

They even had the sense to act sheepish about how Keith had acted like an asshole by dumping her and Missy on their hands. At first she had wished she could be riding with Carlisle and Brenda, but the backseat of their van was piled with film equipment and footage, and to her relief Bean and Cheater didn't seem to mind putting up with her and the baby on the road. During pit stops, they told strangers that she was a recording star, and showed off her album jacket every chance they got, which made her have to smile and act sweet even though she was still pissed off at her selfish, high-handed husband.

Thinking about how kind Bean and Cheater were, by comparison, made her want to cry, and she had to work hard to hold back her feelings and not show them to the trucker.

Her story to the trucker was that her car had blown a tire and plowed into a patch of woods. He had offered to drop her off someplace close so she could get her car towed, but she said it was a junker anyway and was probably totaled, and she would just ride with him all the way to Chattanooga, after he told her he was on his way there to deliver a load of steel coils. She said she had a cousin who lived in Chattanooga, which was not true, and she didn't think the trucker totally believed her, but she was scared to give him any factual information about herself because she didn't know who might be coming after her to shut her up. And she couldn't take a chance on running to any police departments down here. She didn't trust any of them.

The trucker was kind enough to take her into downtown Chattanooga instead of staying on the interstate, which would have been an easier and faster route to his destination. She and Missy were dumped off in front of a hotel where there was a line of taxis. She got into a cab and almost asked to be taken to the police station, on the chance that maybe she had gotten far enough away from Mississippi and its murderous rednecks, but then she decided not to take that chance. Instead she asked the cabbie to take her to the Greyhound station.

Anxious to head North as fast as possible, she scanned the departure schedule and found that a bus would be leaving within the half hour for Cleveland and points beyond. To her great relief, there were some empty seats.

She bought seats for Missy and herself, and waited till ten minutes prior to departure time to use a pay phone. She placed an anonymous call to FBI headquarters in Washington, DC. Talking quickly, not saying who she was, she spouted off key details about the murders of Jimmy Green and Rorthal Cheatwood and the probable fate of Carlisle and Brenda Dixon.

When she hung up the phone, she only had five minutes left before her bus would pull out of the station. She had planned it that way, so that hopefully the FBI would not have enough time to trace her call and try to have her picked up and brought into custody.

She clung to a shred of hope that somehow the FBI would apprehend the killers and rescue Brenda and Carlisle.

44

CHAPTER 11

On our third day in Tijuana, Keith fed Mexican centavos into the phone hanging in the smelly hallway outside our fleabag of a hotel room and tried to get in touch with Lori at their apartment in Belmont. "Fuck!" he said. "Nobody's answering. Where the hell is she?"

I thought she might've decided not to come home ever again because of the way he treated her, but I didn't say so.

"Fuck this goddamn phone!" Keith said, pounding on it and slamming the receiver down when it wouldn't give back his centavos. "Fuck it, let's get drunk," he concluded finally.

So we spent that night in a cantina with a mariachi band, swilling down tequila and flirting with prostitutes.

Being in Mexico wasn't as romantic or even as much fun as Kerouac had made it seem. Next day our hangovers were so bad that Keith didn't make it to the phone till late in the afternoon. Again he plunked in centavos and again there was no answer. He gave the phone a solid hit with the heel of his palm, but again no centavos were disgorged. "I oughta rip the fucking thing off the wall!" he shouted angrily.

"I hope Lori wasn't in an accident," I said, thinking about Bean and Cheater's junker. "Maybe we should head home."

I felt I was more worried than he was about his wife and child. He didn't take another stab at reaching them till the following day, which was to be our final day in Mexico, and again the phone just rang and rang. But when he hung up this time a slew of centavos clattered into the coin-return slot and he said, "Fucking amazing," and scooped them up and put them in his pocket.

I said, "There has to be some way to reach her."

He thought for a moment, then phoned Angelo's Groceria, downstairs from the apartment in Belmont, and asked Angelo if he had seen Lori coming or going. He hadn't. And there was no point giving Angelo a number where we could be reached, because very shortly we were going to check out of our hotel, grab a quick lunch of tamales and refried beans, and head home.

"Maybe Lori stayed longer than expected in Nashville," Keith said. "I'll try calling her after we get across the border. If she still doesn't answer I'll phone her mother's place in West Virginia."

I said, "She has no way of getting in touch with us in case of an emergency."

"You think I don't fucking know that?" he snapped.

Sure, he knew it, but he hated to be reminded that his own selfish decisions may have put his wife and child in a bad spot. I had told him that Lori might put the blame on me if he bailed out of the trip to Nashville, but he had laughed and said don't worry, she wouldn't come down on me, she knew full well that nobody could stop him from doing whatever he wanted to do.

As soon as we passed through U.S. Customs, we headed for a pay phone. Again Keith got no answer. He then called Lori's folks in Cherry Hill, scaring them out of their wits because they hadn't heard from her and had no idea where she was. This was the Wednesday after Easter and Lori was supposed to have been back in her classes at the university two days ago.

We headed north in Keith's station wagon, seriously worried now and not bothering to heed the speed limit. Every hundred miles or so we tried the number in Belmont and the one in Cherry Hill. It wasn't until Thursday night, after a restless stay in a cheap motel in Kentucky, that we found out Lori had made it to her parents' place.

Her father, Tillman McCoy, yelled so loud at Keith that he had to hold the phone away from his ear. From outside the phone booth I could hear everything that was being said.

"She's here but she ain't about to talk to you! I'm hangin' up and don't you dare call back!"

Keith pleaded, "At least tell me if she's okay, her and the baby."

"Hell no they ain't okay, thanks to you! They been through hell, mister!"

I heard Mr. McCoy's receiver slam down.

Keith said, "Fuck you, Tillman." But he was talking to dial tone.

He stood there fuming for a while, then redialed, but all he got was a busy signal.

CHAPTER 12

In the cold, unheated bedroom they had shared while they were growing up, Lori and her sister Arlene hugged each other and cried. Arlene had a black eye and a cut lip, inflicted on her by Truman Shoaf, the big, crude, ugly-tempered 28-year-old coal miner she had married a year ago when she was just sixteen.

Lori had believed, up until the past couple of days, that she and Arlene were wed to two totally different kinds of men. But now she saw, to her dismay, that their husbands weren't so different after all. Truman Shoaf used his hands to work with and to batter his wife, and Keith Santone did those same things with his deviously manipulative mind.

At least Arlene didn't have any children yet, which ought to make it easier for her to leave her husband and start a new life. Lori felt like she was in more of a trap than her sister was. How was she going to finish college, get a job, pay bills, and pursue a musical career?

Missy was downstairs in the kitchen, hanging around her plump, kindly grandma and the warmth of the ancient coal-burning stove. Oatmeal cookies were baking, wafting delicious aromas throughout the house. But the familiar hominess didn't entirely quell Lori's uneasiness over not having her little girl close by. She didn't think she'd ever feel totally calm and safe anymore. Not after all she and Missy had been through.

The murders of Jimmy Green and Rorthal Cheatwood kept replaying through her mind. As grisly and horrible as those images were, thinking about Carlisle and Brenda was worse. She figured they must be dead. All she could hope for was that maybe their suffering hadn't been prolonged.

Thank God Missy hadn't seen much of what had happened, and was probably too young to understand very much of whatever she had seen. Lori tried to feel comforted by what she had learned in Psychology 101: that people almost never could remember anything that happened to them when they were younger than maybe two or three. Missy seemed almost like her normal self, so long as she wasn't allowed to see her mama cry, which was why Lori was doing it upstairs, with Arlene.

Lori knew that her mama was terribly worried about her and her sister, even though Mama McCoy's style was to keep her distance and let her grown children solve their own problems.

Lori's daddy, Tillman McCoy, wasn't so good at hiding his emotions.

He cast sad, helpless looks at Lori and Arlene anytime he was around them, so they were relieved when he went out with their brother Maylon this morning to start chopping dead roots out of the half-frozen ground in preparation for spring plowing.

The McCoy family owned eighty-four acres of rocky soil bordered on one side by a shallow creek and on the other side by a dirt road that wound through the valley. At the far end of the field was a large unpainted barn with a tarpaper roof, and near to it a pen that held about a dozen hogs. Inside the barn were several milking cows and a big, mean-spirited plow horse named Jed who wouldn't allow anybody but Tillman McCoy to put a harness on him.

The small farm didn't produce enough food for anyone to earn a living. Tillman and his son Maylon, who was nineteen, both had part-time jobs at a saw mill just outside the little town of Cherry Hill, about eighteen miles away. They grew beans, corn, tomatoes and such, mostly for canning, although they sold some of the produce in town, along with raw unpasteurized milk from the cows, and sides of pork once in a while when they butchered a hog.

From the time she was twelve until she was seventeen, Lori had kept a roadside stand every summer, where she sold jugs of homemade apple cider and candied apples, saving up her meager earnings to buy clothes for college. But she had gotten a rude awakening as soon as she set foot on the Belmont campus.

The apparel she had worked so hard for, which had looked so alluring in the show windows in Cherry Hill, was at least ten years out of style by New York standards. Thinking about it now still made her blush. She wasn't ashamed of her roots, but now that she had tasted a different kind of life, she realized that she could no longer be totally content here on the farm. She loved the old homestead as much as she loved her own flesh and blood, but sometimes she felt guilty that she might have allowed herself to become spoiled by the comforts and the larger view of the world that had opened up to her once she left home.

The farmhouse seemed too small for her now, as if it had shrunk while she was away. It was a two-story plank structure with a tin roof. The large front porch had no banisters. The same color paint, barnyard red, was used on the entire house, even the roof, even the window frames, which would have looked nice trimmed in white -- but cost, not beauty, had been Tillman's main concern. He had never had enough cash to pay for a septic tank and indoor plumbing, and so there wasn't a bathroom with a shower, sink and toilet. Instead there was an outhouse, dark and smelly inside, with husks of dead insects hanging in spider webs. Water for cooking, drinking and bathing had to be carried from the creek, and on days when the surface was frozen, ice had to be chipped away with a screwdriver or an axe.

The farmhouse had no basement and no furnace. No central heating. The only two heated rooms were the kitchen with its coal-burning cook stove, and the living room, with a fireplace that burned either logs or coal. The three upstairs bedrooms didn't even have space heaters.

There were seven or eight small farms in the valley, all as rudimentary as the one belonging to the McCoys. All of the families were dirt poor, still living in much the same way as other folks had lived here since the eighteenth century. At the mouth of the dirt road was a more elaborate dwelling, known as the Melford Mansion, currently inhabited by a retired lawyer and his wife, no relation to the original owner. Prior to the Civil War, Josiah Melford had owned slaves. Ten years ago when the place was auctioned off, an old ledger book had been found that showed the prices of the slaves and the fact that one of them had been sent to fight for the Union in place of one of Josiah Melford's sons. And the slave had been killed, and then written off as a property loss.

The entire valley had been owned by Melford. It was all worked by slaves, then by sharecroppers, and then by tenants or mortgagees like the McCoys. Lori often wondered whether the people of the valley nowadays were much better off than the slaves of old. There were no black people around here anymore. Gradually, after they were turned loose, they took off, probably wanting to shed the memories of their shackles. Ironically, lots of them ended up slaving on assembly lines in factories up North.

Shivering in spite of their woolen sweaters, Lori and Arlene wiped their tears before going downstairs. As they passed through the living room, they were startled by loud banging in the direction of the kitchen. Lori darted in there and snatched Missy up into her arms even as she realized that Truman Shoaf was yelling from out on the back porch, slurring his words, drunk as a skunk. "Let me in, goddamn it, or I swear I'll bust the goddamn door down!"

49

"Go away, Truman!" Mama McCoy shouted. "Don't you come around here causin' trouble! Go away and sober yourself up! Arlene ain't gonna deal with you in your disgustin' condition!"

"You send 'er out here, Mama! I got a right to take her home where she belongs!"

"No way! You ain't fit to be with nobody! Your drunken temper is what drove Arlene away from you! You're nothin' but a woman beater like half the so-called men in this valley!"

With Missy in her arms, Lori backed into the living room. Arlene was frozen there like a scared rabbit. "I better go with him," she said shakily. "I don't want none of you all to get hurt."

"Don't you dare go out there!" Lori said. "Stay right where you are!"

"But Mama is tryin' to stick up for me and he ain't about to let her stand in his way."

Lori was in awe of the pluck that it took for her mild little mama to confront big, mean Truman Shoaf. She was more scared of Truman than she'd ever been before. He reminded her of the rednecks she had narrowly escaped from, down in Mississippi -- hardheaded, pea brained and bent on destruction.

Suddenly Truman whooped and roared and delivered a vicious kick that splintered the jamb and banged the door against the plank wall so hard that one of the hinges was torn loose, leaving the door hanging sideways.

His scowling face black with coal dust, Truman barged in over the threshold. Mama McCoy stood in front of him, trying to bar his way, but he seized her shoulders and picked her up bodily and set her aside like a rag doll.

"Let me be, you big lunkhead!" she yelled, and as soon as her feet touched the linoleum she grabbed up a cast iron skillet from the coal stove, and swung it as hard as she could, banging Truman in the small of his back.

Truman didn't even flinch, and the skillet dropped to the floor with a heavy thud.

Lori and Missy backed away, but Arlene didn't move fast enough, and her husband grabbed her by her ponytail and yanked her into his bearlike arms.

She screamed and clawed at him, raking bloody streaks through his coal-blackened cheeks.

"I'll teach you, you bitch!" he bellowed, tightening his bear hug around her and walking her toward the battered doorway.

Mama McCoy ran out into the yard after them, pounding with both her little fists on Truman's broad, beefy back -- with no effect whatsoever. Overcome with futility, she stopped and started yelling toward the field and the barn. "Maylon! Tillman! *Help!* Hurry up! *Help us!*"

Keith and I pulled off the dirt road in time to see Truman Shoaf dragging Arlene toward his pickup truck.

Mrs. McCoy was out in the yard yelling for Tillman and Maylon. Lori was frozen a few feet behind her, and Missy was in Lori's arms.

Truman Shoaf, about six foot six and two-eighty, shoved Arlene into the cab of his truck and slammed the passenger side door on her.

With a running leap, Keith pounced on Truman and tried to bulldog him to the ground. No use. Truman flipped Keith over his back, then bent and picked him up by his throat and drove a big fist into his face, causing him to drop, unconscious.

I was about the same size as Keith, roughly six feet and one-ninety, in other words nearly a hundred pounds lighter than Truman Shoaf, but I boldly -- or foolishly -- moved in on him and a big sledgehammer left fist thudded into my chest, just below my right nipple. The blow had probably been aimed for my solar plexus, but luckily I had managed to bob and weave, making it land higher. It was like a mule kick against my rib cage, knocking me back several staggering steps, the explosion of pain so severe it felt like my heart might stop beating. At least the blow failed to deck me, as it surely would have had it crashed into my thorax. But my arms went limp and heavy -- I could barely get them up to defend myself. I backed away, trying to shake some sense into my groggy head, and Truman charged at me. I tried a straight jab, hoping to splatter his big nose, and only succeeded in hurting my fist as it was parried by a rock-hard forearm. At the same time, a countering right smashed into my face. My legs gave out and I crumpled, barely able to feel Truman's follow-up chop to the back of my neck.

I hit the ground hard, but somehow I didn't black out. I couldn't get up. My legs were rubbery, and I was in a daze. This was not a completely foreign experience. It had happened to me a couple other times when I was carrying a football and got crushed between two linemen. It's called "getting dinged." This time I didn't have to worry about fumbling -- I could use my hands to crawl away.

I barely got started crawling when one of Truman's clodhoppers stomped onto my upper back, pushing my face into the dirt. I managed to roll and grab his ankle, hoping I could throw him off balance, but he managed to stay upright by stepping on my chest. I hung onto the clodhopper, not wanting to get stomped again, and Tillman McCoy came running, red-raced and out of breath, and banged Truman Shoaf on his head with the blade end of a shovel.

He wobbled, trying not to go down, but his eyes glazed and he sagged and crumpled. Maybe I should've yelled, "Timber!" But I was too busy scrambling out of his way. I barely made it. He plowed into the ground with a one-seventh of a ton impact, then rolled onto his back and started to snore.

"C'mon, y'all get into the house!" Truman McCoy said. "I gotta call the sheriff. Maylon, you stay here. Take the shovel, and if he starts to get up, bang 'im with it ag'in."

While Tillman got on the phone in the living room, the rest of us spread out around the kitchen. Lori's mother tried futilely to pull the back door into its frame. "Guess Tillman's gonna have to fix it," she said with a sigh, leaving it still hanging off kilter.

Lori kept her distance from Keith, but Missy ran to him, gleefully yelling, "Daddy!" He picked her up onto his lap and gave her a kiss.

I got introduced to Arlene, blonde and green-eyed like a slightly younger version of Lori, and she brought me a basin of hot water and a washcloth so I could swab my face.

Mama McCoy put ice on Keith's shiner. Then she smelled something burning, gave a little shriek, and hustled to save the cookies still baking in the coal stove.

Lori watched all this, stoically peering at us from just beyond the archway that led to the living room. Tillman McCoy brushed past Lori and said, "Sheriffs a-comin'." Backing against a kitchen counter, he began telling me and Keith about all the bad things that had happened in Mississippi. He didn't try to soften the impact, and there was probably no way he could have done so. We had to face the hard truth that Jimmy Green and Rorthal Cheatwood were dead, and Carlisle and Brenda Dixon probably were, too. It was appalling to think of all that Lori had been through. I didn't know what I could say that might offer her the slightest bit of comfort.

Keith eyed her sheepishly with his right eye, the one that didn't have an ice pack on it, and mumbled, "I'm sorry, babe."

She stared at him, pursing her lips in a grimace of anger and contempt -- never before had I seen her look at him that way.

Maylon came through the gaping doorway and glowered at Keith, his fists clenched. "You asshole!" he barked. "You almost got your wife and baby killed!"

"I didn't—"

"Just shut the hell up before I black *both* your eyes!" Maylon said. He was a big, strapping fellow with hard, rangy muscles that didn't come from any fancy gym. I had no doubt that he could've trounced Keith, especially with Keith already hurting.

But Tillman stepped in front of Maylon, putting a hand on his chest. "Son, you get out there and check on Truman right now. I told you to keep an eye on him. "

Maylon said, "I tied him up with rope from the barn, drug him over to the maple tree and wrapped the rope around the trunk. He ain't goin' nowhere nohow. "

"Well, get on out there anyways," Tillman said.

Maylon cast a dirty look in Keith's direction before clomping down off the back porch.

"Any news from the FBI?" I asked.

"We ain't heard nothin'," Tillman McCoy said. "Anyhow, Lori didn't give 'em her name. I don't know if that was dumb or smart."

Turning toward me, Lori said, "I just wanted to get as far away from there as I could, Frank. Missy and I were lucky to be alive. I wasn't about to push our luck. "

"Yeah, babe, you did the right thing," Keith said, and her eyes went from me to him, which I think is what he wanted. "I'm glad you didn't stick around and try to save our film and tape. Your lives are more important." To illustrate how sincere and caring he was, he planted another kiss on Missy's forehead.

Lori said, "Hmph! I knew you were just dying to ask about your precious cans of film! Well, I don't know what happened to the damned stuff and I couldn't care less!"

"I wasn't asking about—"

"You brought it up in a sneaky roundabout way. It's probably all that's really on your mind."

"That's not true," Keith said. "I hope you realize we're gonna have to cooperate with the FBI. They'll probably track us down anyway, and then they'll treat us like suspects. Right now there's a lot we don't know. Who did it and why? Somebody might even be coming after you to shut you

53

up. We've gotta help the FBI get to the bottom of it all. Maybe it's tied in to the whole conspiracy thing. Lots of people knew what we were up to in Dallas. Maybe somebody didn't want our work to see the light of day."

"You and your pipe dreams!" Lori snapped. "Let me spell it out for you, Mr. Conspiracy Buff -- Carlisle and Brenda were stopped on the road for no other reason than because they were black! And when those rednecks found out we were with them, they called us nigger lovers. They never said a word about any film footage. They had no idea what was in the van. When they did open it up, the only thing that caught their attention was the rifle."

"Used it 'cause it couldn't be traced back to 'em," Tillman McCoy said.

"I have the serial number," I told him. "I wrote it down and kept it in my wallet."

"Smart fella."

"It's information the FBI needs," Keith said. "We have to help solve the murders any way we can. Maybe then we'll find out exactly what happened to Brenda and Carlisle."

"And maybe your cans of film will be with their dead bodies!" Lori scoffed. "Isn't that what you're hoping for?"

"Aw, give me a break, babe! I'm not that cynical. I stood up against Truman in defense of your sister, didn't I? And got a black eye for it."

A car door slammed shut, and we could hear Maylon talking with someone out in the backyard.

"Sheriff must be here," Tillman said.

Coming into the kitchen and doffing his "Smoky-the-Bear" hat, the sheriff said, "Howdy, Tilly, got a mite of trouble, do ya?" He was a portly, red-faced man about forty or so, wearing a tan and brown uniform and a bushy brown mustache.

Tillman introduced him, saying, "This here is Sheriff Gene Porter. Me and him go way back. Y'all answer whatever he asks and don't hold nothin' back."

Mama McCoy told how the confrontation with Truman Shoaf began, her voice growing more agitated with each recollection.

"Calm down, Mama," Tillman told her.

"I *can't* calm down!"

But she managed to tell her side of it. Then the rest of us filled in enough details to give Sheriff Porter a clear picture of what Truman had done and why he ended up getting himself banged over the head and tied to a maple tree.

"Well, now," the sheriff said, "if 'n y'all are prepared to swear out a complaint, I can hold him on assault and battery charges. That'll keep him in jail maybe three or four days. But he's gonna get out sooner or later. And then who can say what he might do. Probably gonna continue bein' a danger to you."

"I ought to've banged him hard enough to've kilt him," Tillman McCoy said. "That way we could've sent his sorry ass straight to the undertaker."

CHAPTER 13

Lori wouldn't let Keith sleep with her at the farmhouse, so he and I both took rooms at a little hundred-year-old hotel in the town of Cherry Hill. He knew his marriage was teetering on the brink of divorce, and he didn't want to return to Belmont without his wife. Instead he wanted to get her back under his spell. He kept rapping about it, using me as a sounding board.

"I wish Lori would wake up and act sensible. I don't really want to lose her. What would happen to Missy? She'd probably grow up poor. Why should I feel guilty for being concerned about my Dealey Plaza documentary? Am I supposed to smile while all our efforts go down the drain? What's wrong with wanting to retrieve something of value out of this disaster?"

"Nothing wrong with that," I conceded.

"Damn right there isn't. It doesn't mean I don't care about Carlisle and Brenda. I've got tons of respect for them."

It struck me that respect wasn't the same as caring. In the weeks since I had gotten out of the Army, I was starting to reevaluate Keith. He had charm. He had charisma. He was fun to be with. The zany escapades that he instigated were often exciting and seemingly worthwhile. Once I allowed myself to be sucked in, I usually had a lot of fun. But I was aware lately that some of the stuff he got me into was at best dangerous and at worst self-serving and even unprincipled.

On Saturday morning, Lori phoned Keith at the hotel. I could tell it wasn't a reconciliation call. He kept muttering, "Yeah, babe ... yeah, babe," and when he hung up, he said, "Lori wants us to meet her in the coffee shop down the street. She just got off the phone with the FBI. "

An hour later, the three of us were sitting in a booth, barely touching our coffee. Lori was wearing a cute red blouse and tight jeans and looked good in spite of the stress she was under. "I phoned the FBI in Washington this morning," she informed us. "I told who I was and where I'm at. I figured they would've traced the call anyhow. When I called them from Chattanooga, I was afraid they'd treat it like a crank call, but they must've taken me seriously, because they actually sent some of their people down to Oxford, Mississippi. They wouldn't tell me much, except they found the murder scene and they've been questioning people. They feel that their investigation down there ought to wrap up by sometime Sunday, then they intend to come here on Monday. "

"Any news on Carlisle and Brenda?" Keith asked.

Lori frowned, and appeared ready to unleash a snide comment, but she withheld it because two young girls in jeans, T-shirts and ponytails were coming toward our booth. They were wide-eyed and flustered and were carrying copies of Lori's record album with her picture on it.

"Oh my god, it's really her!" one of them blurted.

"Please, will you sign our albums?" the other one begged.

"Sure. What're your names?" Lori asked.

"We're cousins -- Roxanne and Mandy. I'm Roxanne."

Lori fished in her purse for a pen, and signed the album jackets. Keith teased the girls, saying, "You don't carry the albums around with you all the time, do you?"

They giggled. "No, we ran home and got them. We thought we died and went to heaven when we spotted Miss McCoy through the window."

It struck me, not for the first time, how imitative the album jacket was. Over a full facial shot of Lori was the title, *Lori is her Name*. Keith used to have a Julie London album featuring a glamor shot of Julie London and entitled, *Julie is her Name*. Not only did Lori's album contain nothing but "cover" songs, but even its jacket lacked originality, thanks to Keith's "guidance."

After some twittery chatter, the two young fans went hopping and skipping down the street outside, and Lori was able to shed her obligatory smile. Returning to the business at hand, she said, "Whatever the FBI knows about Brenda and Carlisle, they aren't telling. The agent I talked to on the phone was very tight-lipped. I think they want to eliminate us as suspects before they let us in on anything. We may have to take lie detector tests. "

"It's okay with me," Keith said. "I'm prepared to fully cooperate."

"Due to your vested interest," Lori said snidely.

"Hey, babe, why don't you give me a break? Really. How about sticking around for some lunch, just you and me, so we can talk things out between us and avoid making some rash decisions?"

"Right now I have nothing to say to you."

"Maybe I screwed up, but I still love you and I want to make things right."

"Your eye looks much better," she said. "I like the yellow and blue color scheme."

"Glad to see you still got your sense of humor, babe. That gives me hope."

Standing outside the coffee shop, Keith and I watched her get into her father's pickup and drive away. As we turned and headed back toward the hotel, he said, "Shit, Frank, I hope she believes me when I say I still love her. I'm not as much of a bastard as she's letting on. I might've acted a bit selfish, but who the hell could've imagined we'd run into *this* kind of bad luck?"

I said, "It wasn't exactly bad luck -- it was more like premeditated reckless endangerment, and you and I are both to blame. If we hadn't peeled off for Mexico, the whole gang of us would've stuck together in one caravan and maybe the rednecks would've backed off. A bigger group of us wouldn't have been easy prey."

"You wanna blame *us*?" Keith snapped, staring at me incredulously. "If you wanna wallow in some kind of guilt complex, leave me out of it. I'm not perfect, but I'm not totally evil either. I don't believe in self-flagellation. I've gotta move on with my life. *I* never shot *nobody*."

Come Sunday morning, he wanted to go to church, which made me think that maybe he felt at least a shred of guilt in spite of his denials. But it was hard to picture him being eager to pray or to humble himself.

I figured we would walk to one of the several churches right in the main part of town, but when we came out of the hotel Keith headed for his station wagon, and I followed him and got in. As he started the engine and pulled out, I asked where we were going.

He said, "You're in for an existential experience, Frank, old buddy. You ever been to a shit-stomping, bible-thumping, holy roller church?"

"No, I was raised Roman Catholic, but it didn't quite take. I guess you'd call me a fallen Catholic. But I sort of still believe in God. Or at least I'm still trying to."

"Come on, you're an agnostic, like me."

"Yeah, I guess. But I still want to think that maybe there's a heaven. and maybe praying does some kind of good."

"Sure, sure," he said. "How come I never saw you kneel in the end zone after you made a touchdown?"

"No, I never did that, but sometimes I did used to pray before the game that I wouldn't get hurt."

"Well, maybe this morning you can pray that Lori and I can get back together. We're gonna go to the little old country church in the valley that

Lori and her family go to. The preacher never even went to divinity school, he's just a farmer who got the calling. And the valley people love him because he whips 'em up and scares the shit out of 'em with visions of the devil, then makes 'em renounce their sinful ways so they can feel 'saved' and ready for paradise. "

"Doesn't sound like your kind of thing, Keith."

"Well, I'm thinking I can use it to make Lori stop pretending to hate me. If she thinks she can go on and build a career without me, she's fulla crap. Down deep, she doesn't really want to leave me. If I can open her up a little, I'll be able to work my charm on her. And then if I can manage to behave myself like a proper little husband for a while ... "

His voice trailed off as we turned onto the dirt road that led to the McCoys' farm. He said, "The church is a mile, mile and a half, past where we were the other day."

We had gone through some foggy patches out on the two-lane blacktop, but here in the valley the fog was so thick that the headlight beams bounced off of it and we could see better with the lights shut off. We saw ghostly images of cars and pickup trucks nestled in the enveloping whiteness, and that's how Keith knew we had arrived at the church's gravel parking lot. He nosed the station wagon into a space under the trees without colliding into anything, then killed the engine. As we got out he said, "Lori and Arlene gotta be worried about Truman Shoaf. He'll get outta jail tomorrow or the next day and he might come after Arlene and kill her. She's got to get away from him. I've been thinking, what if I told Lori that her sister is welcome to come and stay with us in Belmont?"

"That'd be a generous offer," I said. But inwardly I had doubts about how such an arrangement would work out. Keith had a congenital inability to control himself when he was around an attractive woman for any length of time, especially one as young and pretty as Arlene.

We could hear people singing *That Old Rugged Cross* as we approached the front door of the church. "Service already started," Keith said. "Good. We won't have to sit through the whole darn thing. This time of year, Tillman comes here real early, before anyone else, and fires up the potbellied stove. Gets so hot everybody sweats like mad, like they're already tasting some of the hellfire the preacher's warning them about. "

The raucous hymn ended about the same time as we found our way to a pew filled with valley folk. I spotted Lori and the rest of her family on the other side of the aisle, way up in front. All the pews near them were so packed that we could not have gotten any closer.

Keith was right about the potbellied stove. It was already making me sweat, although it was forty feet away, in a back corner of the church.

At first, the worship service wasn't drastically different from anything I was used to. The preacher told the story of Mary Magdalene washing the feet of Jesus Christ and begging to be forgiven. Then he elaborated upon the meaning of confession, forgiveness and atonement. It wasn't anything I hadn't heard before, and yet his delivery had me riveted.

Noticing how intently I was taking it in, Keith nudged me and with a knowing smile whispered, "His name is Preacher Barlow. He's somethin' else, ain't he?"

I nodded. Preacher Barlow indeed had an unusual gift. His voice was deep and melodious, rising and falling in spellbinding cadences. The man was so charismatic I could almost feel the Hand of God upon his shoulder. His face was craggy, weather-beaten and unshaven. His clothes were shabby: a worn and rumpled brown suit and a faded blue shirt with a tuft of coarse black chest hair curling from under the open collar.

Suddenly he stopped waving his bible around. His deep-set black eyes scanned each and every one of us, then he closed them, slumping his shoulders and bowing his head. After a long solemn pause he raised his head and great tears rolled down his face. "I'm a sinner!" he cried out. "An awful sinner! A terrible sinner!" He wiped his tears with the back of his hand. His voice got softer. "I'm a pitiful wretch who doesn't keep his promises. I call myself a preacher, a servant of the Lord, but I'm a miserable failure. Right here, one week ago, on Easter Sunday, Joe Johnson came up to me after worship services, took my hand in his and looked me in the eye, and said he had a problem that he sorely needed to talk to me about. I told him I'd come see him on Saturday, which would have been yesterday -- but I didn't go. And it wasn't like I forgot neither, I just didn't go. My daughter and my two grandchildren came by, and I got caught up in their visit, and before I knew it nightfall came and they were saying goodbye, and I didn't feel like going out of the house. But I was a fool because I let Satan use my own flesh and blood for temptation. Satan didn't want me to go see Joe Johnson so he used my daughter and grandchildren to distract me -- and I fell for it. Joe Johnson, only 47 years old, died in his sleep last night. His funeral is tomorrow. I know he'll be looking down on me from heaven with rebuke in his eyes, and I know I deserve it. So I'm here to ask for mercy and forgiveness.

Lord forgive me! Please, Lord, forgive me! Forgive this wretched sinner!"

He hung his head.

Suddenly, directly behind me in the next pew, a woman let loose with a bloodcurdling scream.

I whirled around, my heart pounding.

The scream had come from a big, fat lady in a dark green coat the size of a tent. I thought she must be having a seizure, so I got up to help her. But nobody else made a move; they all kept their seats. She kept on screaming, tears streaming down her chapped, ruddy cheeks. Then she dropped to the floor, moaning, babbling and twitching, crawling on all fours in the middle of the aisle. I seemed to be the only one shaken up by this, so I sat back down and tried not to stare at her.

Right after that, another woman stood up and told everybody that she had badly beaten her three-year old boy for snitching some oatmeal cookies before supper. The bruises and welts she had given him were so awful she was afraid he'd die in his sleep. She burst into tears, begging God to strike her dead because she didn't deserve to be forgiven.

My own feeling was that she deserved to do some jail time and also to have her little boy taken away from her.

When she sat down, another lady stood up. She said she was guilty and ashamed for being angry and impatient with her old and feeble grandmother and not taking proper care of her. She asked God to drive the devil out of her -- it was because of Satan's presence inside her that she was feeling so sad and worn out and sorry for herself.

The fat woman was still rolling on the floor, moaning, but softer now, as if she didn't want to miss out on any of the "dirt" that her fellow worshipers were dishing out about themselves. By now I had realized that this church believed in public confessions. Preacher Barlow had taken the lead and encouraged others by expressing his own sinfulness and guilt over not visiting the late Joe Johnson.

When I totally believed in Catholicism, I always hated to have to tell my sins to a priest, but it was definitely preferable to doing it in front of everybody. It didn't appear to be mandatory, however. Only about a dozen people stood up, and none of them were men, except for the preacher. I imagined that the men's sins might be the kind they wouldn't want their wives to hear.

Suddenly Keith stood up. I wondered what he was up to. His in-laws were gawking at him, turning around in their pew. Lori had a bemused look on her face. The fat woman who had been rolling in the aisle stopped moaning and got up slowly and squeezed back into her seat, eyeing Keith expectantly.

"I'm the worst sinner here," he said, as though he were claiming a prize. "My own selfishness, my own pigheadedness, got some of my good friends killed and almost led to the deaths of my lovely wife and child. By a miracle they were saved but I can't take any credit for that, I can only take the blame I richly deserve. My wife wants to leave me now and who am I to say she shouldn't? Who am I to say that she shouldn't take my little girl away from me? I can only ask for God's forgiveness hoping that his promise to forgive all sinners includes even me, the most miserable and wretched man in this church today."

His face was now wet with tears, and he would've probably had me crying if I hadn't been convinced he was merely making a well thought out grandstand play. Half the congregation was bawling, especially the women.

"I just hope that some of you know where I'm coming from," Keith said. "And I pray that you all can find some forgiveness and understanding deep in your hearts."

I would have liked to think that he had somehow experienced a genuine epiphany, but no matter how hard I tried to give him the benefit of the doubt, his words sounded hokey to me. I knew him too well. And Lori knew him even better. I didn't think this "heartrending" display could fool her.

When the services were over, on the steps outside the church Preacher Barlow shook Keith's hand as men, women and children pressed in, awaiting their turns.

Lori was standing at the bottom of the steps with the rest of her family, gazing up at the "repentant sinner." Keith spotted her and smiled, then worked his way down to her.

She took his hand.

Watching from where the station wagon was parked, I was struck by the fact that the fog must have lifted some time ago, and right now there was blue sky and bright sunshine, as if we were all characters in some movie with a happy, uplifting ending.

CHAPTER 14

Coleman Jamison was 37 years old, and had worked for 23 years at the general store in the tiny hamlet of Jonesville, eighteen miles south of Oxford, Mississippi. To call it a hamlet might be an exaggeration. It consisted mainly of the general store and a gasoline station at a dusty crossroads, with a few cottages and shacks dotting the countryside roundabout. In 1964 the population of Jonesville was 187, according to a tin sign nailed to a telephone pole by Pete Jones, the owner of the general store.

Pete called Coleman Jamison his "store nigger" and always guffawed when he said it because he thought it was a witty pun on the term "house nigger." Coleman's lot in life wasn't much different from that of an outright slave on one of the plantations of old. He got paid fifty cents an hour, got fed on leftovers from his boss's table, and wore clothing donated to the black church he belonged to. He slept on an army-surplus cot in a room at the back of the store, in a narrow aisle between rows of steel shelves full of dry goods and canned goods. The storeroom had one grimy window, but any sunlight that might have penetrated was mostly blocked out by the stuff on the shelves. And Bossman Pete didn't like it if Coleman wasted electricity by turning on the naked bulb that dangled from the ceiling.

There were three hooks by the storeroom door. Two of them held a few of Coleman's most-used garments, and one held Bossman Pete's pointy white hood and his white gown with the big red cross on it.

Coleman's chores consisted of mopping, sweeping and cleaning, chopping firewood, toting heavy boxes of merchandise and putting them wherever he was told to, and lugging customers' purchases to the counter or to their vehicles for them if they wanted him to do it. No tips required. Any and all other kinds of manual labor fell to Coleman also. For him to be given this job and to be paid "good money" for it was considered by Pete Jones and others in the white community to be a work of genuine Christian charity. This was not only because Coleman was black but because he was considered mentally retarded.

But in spite of the fact that folks called him "slow," he caught on that he had seen the old, faded red convertible before -- the one that got towed out of a half-plowed field a week ago, on orders of the two FBI men that all the white folks hated.

He had stood back from a little crowd on the side of the road, catching glimpses of men moving around among the trees a far piece away, where the trees were strung with yellow crime scene tape. He had left before getting to see what the car looked like, but he saw the tow truck drive in.

He had to leave sooner than he wanted to, because his boss, who was with the crowd of white folks, showed off to them, yelling, "Get back to work, nigger, or I'll take the strap to ya!"

Later that afternoon, the tow truck pulled into the store's gravel lot and two big-bellied white men got out to buy cans of cold soda pop and to jaw with Bossman Pete for a spell. Coming outside to fetch the sodas, Coleman recognized the car they were towing -- but he knew better than to pipe up about it. The tow truck men had perpetual sneers on their faces to show how mean and dangerous they were. One of them tripped Coleman after he handed them their sodas, and when he fell and skinned his hands and knees, they called him a clumsy nigger and laughed so hard the soda pop sprayed out of their mouths.

Bossman Pete and his cronies, plus many other white people, started treating Coleman worse after everybody found out about the murders and body burnings that happened nearby. Instead of being angry and scared over the horror of it all, they seemed to be secretly or even openly pleased, as if the victims had gotten what they deserved. Bossman Pete was one of the worst. He said, "Damn yankees come down here tryin' to get our niggers all riled up, and instead they got theyselves *fried* up!"

Coleman thought carefully about who he should tell about the red car. He finally decided he'd tell Reverend Staisy, pastor of the River Jordan Colored Baptist Church down the road. But he'd have to wait till Sunday when he went to services, or till the next time the reverend came to the general store, which could take a while.

As it happened, Reverend Staisy and his daughter showed up on the same day the car had been towed, but later on when the sun was low in the sky. Coleman was nervous and tongue-tied around seventeen-year-old Correlle Staisy because she was so pretty.

He knew he was considered ugly, especially by white people.

His skin was very dark. His lips were thick but the bottom one was thicker than the upper one and stuck out like a nubby shelf over his receding chin. He had bulging eyes, and the left one had an odd black spot on the white part of it that nobody knew the reason for. He was only about five-feet-four and a hundred and nineteen pounds, but he was wiry and much stronger than he looked, and when Bossman Pete made him help build a garage, the bossman said, "That little nigger can carry a hod of bricks up a ladder like nobody's bidness. Why, I believe he c'd outdo most white boys twice his size -- must be the gorilla in him."

There was a sink and toilet in the general store, but it was for white folks. Bossman Pete made Coleman use a plastic basin to wash himself, and he had to do it in the store room, setting the basin on his cot. When he needed to go Number One or Number Two, he must do it in the woods out back where nobody could see him.

On the day that Reverend Staisy and his daughter Correlle came by, Coleman waited till it looked like they were ready to leave with their packages, then he asked permission to "go out back for a minute," which was a euphemism for having to empty his bladder. "Don't you let this purty l'il gal see you or she might get all worked up!" Bossman Pete snickered, and a couple of white customers who had just come in snickered right along with him, lewdly ogling Correlle all the while, smirkingly confident that she and her father would meekly swallow whatever insults were hurled at them, without daring to give back any sass.

Shyly turning his eyes from Correlle to the reverend, Coleman stammered. "Uh ... uh ... I c'd he'p tote somethin' f-f-fer y'all since I's about to go out."

"Much obliged," Reverend Staisy murmured. He handed Coleman two bags of groceries, and Correlle went out ahead of them and held the door open.

As they crossed the gravel lot, Coleman glanced all around, then said under his breath, "Reverend, I done seed the red car those gov'ment men was lookin' at."

"Out in the field? When it was being towed?"

"No, suh, afore that."

The reverend blinked his eyes, a grim look on his face as he stopped by his battered old Chevy. Unlocking the door without looking directly at Coleman, he pretended he was just going about his normal business in case anyone was watching. At the same time, he said in a lowered voice, "Are you sure, Coleman?"

"Yessuh, I seed it by the bridge down the road a piece."

He handed Reverend Staisy the groceries, one bag at a time, and added, "There was a girl with a baby sittin' inside it, and the girl looked sceered. Some policemen was arrestin' two white men who musta been with 'er -- and a colored man and woman, too."

"Better not say nothin' about it," Correlle said, biting her lip, nervous and scared.

The reverend's eyes darted around sharply, then he asked, "When did you see this, Coleman?"

"I dunno, c'd be ten days ago, mebbe. Shook me up and stuck in my mind, but I dint know zackly what was happenin'. Men with guns waved us on by. I's sittin' in the bed of Mista Pete's pickup makin' sure some big cans of tar and tarpaper stayed put. Nothin' I c'd do 'bout what I seed."

"Listen to me, Coleman," Reverend Staisy said sternly. "Don't tell anyone what you saw till I think this all over. You hear me? This information could get somebody killed."

"Like us," Correlle whispered. "We better just forget about it, push it out of our minds."

Coleman was about to stammer an apology for letting them know stuff they didn't want to know, when Bossman Pete banged open the front door of the general store and yelled, "Get yer black ass in here, nigger! What y'all jawin' about out here? What's that sneaky look doin' on yer face? You swipe somethin' from me? I pick through them bags of groceries and find somethin' nobody paid for, y'all gonna have hell to pay!"

"We didn't steal nothin', Mister Pete," the reverend said.

"Well, you better get yer black asses outta here! You got what you came for -- now *get*!"

Coleman forgot all about his excuse for going outside, which was to go back in the woods to urinate. Instead, he hustled back across the gravel lot, wondering if he was going to get a few licks from Bossman Pete's leather strap. On his way, not daring to look over his shoulder, he heard Reverend Staisy's worn out engine grind a couple of times before it turned over, and the crunch of gravel as the car rumbled onto the blacktop.

Late that night, Bossman Pete, Cletis Barrett and Albert Crane burst in on Coleman as he was kneeling by his cot in the dark, saying his bedtime prayers. Pointing guns at him and yanking him to his feet, they immediately started beating him. Bossman Pete and Albert Crane held Coleman up while Cletis Barrett delivered punch after punch. When he crumpled to the floor, they tied his wrists and ankles with rope. Then they dragged him half-conscious out back into the woods.

"I'll whale into him with my belt till he fesses up," Bossman Pete said.

"Cigarette burns're better," Albert said. "Big fire later on'll cover up what we done."

The cold of the late April evening and the descending fog made Coleman come to. His attackers' breath was white, and they were wearing the kind of warm clothing and boots used by hunters. Meekly he muttered through his pain, "Why you doin' me this way, Mister Pete? Whatchou think I done wrong? I dint steal nothin' noway."

"I know you didn't, you wouldn't have the guts," Bossman Pete barked. "But you blabbed about somethin' to that blackass preacher and his daughter, and we wanna know what it was."

Albert Crane and Cletis Barrett both lit up cigarettes and got the ends glowing red hot.

"Uh ... I d-dint tell 'em n-nothin," Coleman said pleadingly. "Talked about the w-w-weather is all."

"Bullshit! How dumb you think I am? You made an excuse to go out and piss -- then you come back in without pissin'."

"I's s-s-sceered when you yelled at m-me, figgered I b-bbetter jest h-h-h-hold it in."

"I ain't buyin' it. You three was huddled together like thieves. Guilt was written all over your faces."

Albert Crane took a puff on his cigarette to make it stay real hot. A sinister look on his face, he said, "I don't like that li'l black speck on his eyeball. He'd look better with it burnt off."

"Please, n-no, d-d-don't do me that way, suh," Coleman said, cringing. "I d-doesn't know n-n-nothin' 'bout nothin' important ... neither d-does Reverend Staisy. We's jest jawin' 'bout the w-weather, the c-c-crops and such."

"I told you don't bullshit me," Bossman Pete said.

"You ain't nothin' but a lyin' nigger," snarled Cletis Barrett.

"Hold him down. I'll burn him," said Albert Crane.

The other two men sat on Coleman's chest and legs, and Albert Crane knelt beside him and touched the hot red tip of his cigarette against the side of Coleman's neck.

Coleman had the desperately nutty idea that maybe if he showed a lot of guts and did not scream, the men would have more respect for him and would start believing what he told them.

He tried hard not to scream but did not succeed.

"Maybe we oughta gag him," Cletis Barrett suggested.

"Then how's he gonna tell us what we wanna know?" Bossman Pete said. "Just keep going, nobody nearby to hear him anyways."

"Yeah, I still wanna burn that black speck," Albert Crane said. "Like a doctor burnin' off a wart."

"Better talk right now, Coleman," the general store owner said, "unless you itchin' to become a blind man."

Perspiration flooded out of Coleman, and he started to shake all over. His granddaddy, who had lived to be 93, had been 18 years old when slavery ended in 1863, and up till then he had been a slave working in the cotton fields. From his grandfather, Coleman had heard lots of stories about the cruel punishments that the plantation owners and their overseers inflicted upon hapless human beings. Black men were beaten to death and their women were raped. Runaways were branded when they were caught, or made to wear iron collars welded around their necks so they could never be taken off. Slaves who persisted in running away sometimes had their feet chopped off, and if that didn't pacify them, they were hanged, their corpses left to rot in the hot sun for days on end, as a warning to others who might be tempted to flee on their own, or somehow hook up with abolitionists from the North who were running something they called underground railroad. These kinds of Yankees were shot or hanged when the southern boys caught them, or else they were tortured to death.

Coleman realized deep down that Bossman Pete and his henchmen were living reincarnations of their exceedingly cruel ancestors. They were upholders of an insanely devilish tradition of hatred and white supremacy. And he knew he could expect no mercy from them.

They meant what they said.

For him there was no escape.

They were going to burn his eyes out. And probably worse.

Reverend Staisy had a sermon to write, but he had not been able to start on it. He sat at his kitchen table with a tablet and pencil but no words would come to him that he dared to put on paper. His conscience told him that he ought to be preaching against the utter meanness of men like Bossman Pete, but his reward for doing so was sure to be harassment or even death. He was not a brave man, but a godly one. He could picture himself as a martyr under certain circumstances, but he honestly did not feel that those circumstances had arrived. He did not believe that subjecting himself to punishment and persecution right now would serve any high or even marginally useful purpose.

He felt that his main job was to shepherd his flock. And to keep his own daughter safe from harm, by any lawful means necessary. He was burdened by the knowledge that he had not been able to protect his own wife. She had been raped and murdered while she was pregnant with what would have been their second child. Who could now blame him if he hovered over Correlle in an almost fanatical protectiveness? She resented it, too. She had wanted to go away to college, but he had prevented it. He insisted that she stay close to home, under his wing. So here she stayed, getting an inferior education at the underfunded and understaffed two-year college for Negroes who wanted to become teachers.

Like many who got accepted into that college, Correlle didn't really want to be a teacher. She wanted to be a scientist. But the closest she could get to it was to be a science *teacher*. She often ranted about the way that black people were denied the chance to realize their full potentiality. But Reverend Staisy made sure she didn't talk that way outside the house. And even indoors he told her to keep her voice down, for fear that somebody walking by or coming up onto the porch might hear her.

He heard her coming downstairs from her room, and he steeled himself to face her. He knew she was still wound up over the confrontation at Bossman Pete's general store, and she was likely to carry on her rant about it.

Sure enough, she stood over him by the kitchen table and said, "I hate living here. I want to go to school in the north."

"I'm not trying to hold you here," he said.

"That's a lie, Daddy. You were scared to lose me like you lost Mama. So you kept me here where there's more danger, not less."

He took off his wire-rimmed reading glasses and rubbed his sore eyes, and thought deeply about what she just said.

"Think about what happened today," she told him. "Those men would kill us just as soon as look at us."

He knew she was right.

"They don't treat you with any respect," she persisted. "They treat you with utter contempt. If you were a white pastor they'd damn near genuflect. But they won't even allow you in their church."

"Listen here, young lady," he told her sadly. "You don't have to rob me of my pride in order to make your points. You can start researching which school up north you can afford to go to. I won't try to stop you anymore. But you'll have to find some kind of job up there in order to support yourself. I'll help as much as I can ... but it won't be a whole lot, and you know it."

"I know, Daddy, and I realize you'll always do your best."

She bent over him, gave him a warm, loving hug, and kissed him on his forehead.

CHAPTER 15

Sometime after midnight, an arson fire erupted inside the River Jordan Colored Baptist church.

The flames had a three-hour head start on the Jonesville Volunteer Fire Department, but they couldn't have put out the fire and saved the tiny wooden church even if they'd have gotten there a lot sooner.

Three bodies were found in the smoking pile of charred rubble.

The bodies were too burnt up, shrunken and shriveled for a meaningful autopsy, but Preacher Staisy's house was far enough from the church that it was unscathed by fire, and this made identification of the two ghastly corpses and reconstruction of the crimes that had been committed here rather obvious.

The county sheriff photographed bloody smears and pools of blood left in the house, along with a bloody pocket knife that had been dropped on the porch. Blood spots and ripped panties and bra were found on Correlle Staisy's bed. And blood trails led downstairs, off the porch and across the stepping stones to what was left of the church.

The bloody pocket knife was identified by Bossman Pete as one he had given to Coleman Jamison for Christmas. "Goes to show what generosity can lead to," Pete told the local sheriff. "Who'd of thought he c'd manage to kill two people with a li'l ol' pocket knife."

"Musta caught 'em by surprise," the sheriff said sagely. His part-time job had been obtained largely through Bossman Pete's influence, and besides that they were drinking buddies, and anyhow who really could care if some niggers wanted to burn each other up?

"I knew he had eyes for that purty l'il black gal," Bossman Pete said. "Kept followin' her around and oglin' her every time she come into the store. Never thought he'd do nothin' to her though. This here is a great shock."

The scenario that went out for public consumption was that the little addlebrained nigger went nuts and raped Correlle, having first sneaked up on her father and killed him by stabbing him or cutting his throat. After he got his perverted sexual cravings satisfied, he stabbed Correlle

71

to death, too. Then he must have dragged both of the bloody bodies into the church.

He splashed gasoline all over, probably in a large circle, which was stupid, because he didn't stand outside the circle when he struck a match and tossed it. He found out with a sudden WHOOSH that he had trapped himself inside a wall of flames. Couldn't get out. Couldn't save himself.

Burnt himself up along with his victims.

Har! Har!

Shows you what you can expect from a dumb nigger.

PART THREE
NIXON AND FORD

"Only the triggerman in this monstrous crime has been convicted
... the nation, which permitted rampant opposition to the
aspirations of Dr. King and his people, is the real culprit."
-- Roy Wilkins

"If we ever let the communists win this war, we are in great
danger of fighting for the rest or our lives and losing a million kids."
-- Bob Hope

"That's what bothers me about this war. Sometimes I feel
like one of the bad guys."
-- a Marine in Vietnam

"I am not a crook."
--Richard M. Nixon

CHAPTER 16

Murder changes the lives connected to the lives that were lost. I often wonder what would have happened to me and to all of us if the murders had never taken place.

After fleeing from her husband, Arlene lived with Keith, Lori and Missy in Belmont. It was a dysfunctional, stressful arrangement. Keith was having a hard time getting over his lost chance at overnight success, Lori was having constant nightmares, and Missy was unnaturally sad and withdrawn for a child her age, probably sensing the lack of normalcy among the adults.

Keith was taking a few graduate courses so he could keep his job at the on-campus radio station while he waited for Lori to finish earning her degree. She was still singing at frat house parties, coffee houses and bars. Arlene was earning a little money waitressing part-time, and she'd babysit or clean while Lori was out performing.

Arlene was on edge all the time, expecting Truman Shoaf to come after her. He finally showed up drunk one Sunday when no one was home and tried to break into the Santones' apartment -- except he didn't realize that they lived upstairs, not in back, and ended up damaging the rear door to Angelo's Groceria and setting off the alarm. After getting arrested and paying a heavy fine, he slunk back home to his coal mining job, and not long thereafter he was crushed to death in a tunnel collapse-- bad news or maybe good news depending on one's point of view.

Arlene felt relief mixed with guilt. "Maybe I should've stayed," she said. "Maybe it wouldn't have turned out so bad. Maybe he would've started treating me better. "

"Yeah, dream on, Arlene," Keith told her. "Be happy you saved the cost of a divorce lawyer."

Lori and Arlene drove to West Virginia for the funeral, taking Missy along with them so the baby could spend time with her grandparents. Keith and I took advantage of the opportunity to go out on the town and get high, and he told me he was tired of keeping up the "born again" personna he had contrived in order to make his wife stick with him. "It was okay as a means to an end," he lamented, "but I'm not cut out to be a goody-two-shoes kinda husband. Maybe I can get a stray piece now and then without her catching on. I find myself eyeballing Arlene, and she eyeballs me back. I swear, if she wasn't my sister-in-law, I wouldn't mind banging her."

He laughed, but I didn't think he was entirely joking. I said, "Lori's been through a hell of a lot, Keith. She needs you to cling to right now, give her stability. "

"Not to worry," he said. "She's a lot stronger than you think. She's gonna be just fine."

I had my doubts. She wasn't the same Lori. It seemed to me that a sea change had occurred in all of our lives and it was hard to predict what direction any of us would take.

My goal of becoming a published novelist was slipping away from me. I couldn't stop thinking about the murder case, and I pestered the FBI agents so much that they got curt with me. I suspected that another case that came to light around that same time -- the murder/arson of a black minister and his daughter -- was too coincidental not to have a connection, but if there was one, the feds were unable to come up with it. They told me they weren't getting cooperation from local law enforcement. I got the sense that there was so much stonewalling going on down there that "local law enforcement" might be an oxymoron.

Meantime, I had to support myself, so I went to work in Belmont as a substitute teacher. I told people that a fulltime job wouldn't give me enough time to write, but I think I really wanted time to follow the murder case. I managed to complete the collection of vignettes about my college days that I had started while I was still in the Army, sent it around to agents and publishers, and landed a pile of rejection slips, including one handwritten note from a literary agent who said, "I'm afraid I must tell you, Mr. Williams, that I found your little stories to be utterly disjointed, unrelated and pointless." My confidence was knocked for a loop, and I got writer's block. Everything in my life seemed disjointed, unrelated and pointless, like the two unrelated murder cases in Mississippi. *If* they were unrelated. I kept hoping somebody would get caught and punished, but it never happened.

Out of blind frustration, I signed up to take a test and got accepted into the Belmont Police Department. I told myself that maybe I'd stick with it long enough to glean material for a crime novel or a mystery -- something with a clever hook and tight plot that couldn't be labeled "disjointed, unrelated and pointless" -- that phrase kept preying on my mind.

One day Keith called me and said that he had dropped some LSD two nights ago, and the real true key to my future came to him on an acid trip. All I had to do was go back into the Army and get myself sent to Vietnam so I could write the Great American Novel about that war, capitalizing on it like Ernest Hemingway and Norman Mailer had capitalized on World War One and World War Two. "You gotta write something good," he said, "like *A Farewell to Arms* or *The Naked and the Dead*."

"Right now I'm not writing anything," I said. "I've got writers' block."

"Well, shit, you better get on the stick before they fuck you up by pulling the troops out like Charlie Guinard and his flock of peaceniks are pushing for. Don't forget, if you get rich and famous, I want ten percent of your book and movie deals."

"Don't hold your breath. I'd operate on my own balls with a rusty can opener before I'd reenlist in the Army. Anyhow, I'm a cop now."

"Dumb," Keith said. "I don't even know where the hell that shit came from."

"I told you. I was a substitute MP at Fort Bragg when James Meredith tried to be the first Negro to go to Ole Miss and the regular MPs were sent there to do riot control."

"That was what, a couple of weeks at most as an MP?"

"Yep. Nineteen days."

"Probably about as long as you'll last as a flatfoot."

But Keith was wrong. The thing I liked about working as a street cop was the excitement that juiced up the routine. I must've been craving the adrenaline highs that had been largely missing from my life since my days on the football field.

I started going to law school at night and taking courses in criminology. I wanted to get a law degree, then apply for the FBI Academy. My ambition was to become one of the special agents who dealt with terrorism and hate crimes.

I thought a lot about Jimmy Green, Rorthal Cheatwood and the Dixons. Outwardly it might have looked like I didn't have much in common with Bean and Cheater, but I had played football with guys like them. They didn't have much formal education but they had their own brand of wit. They were personable and likable. They weren't the dummies other people thought they were. I still smiled remembering Bean's naive feistiness and his notion that stroke books were just as good as any other kind of literature. And I'd never forget some of Cheater's

sayings like, "That gal got an ass purtier'n the hips on a ten-dollar mule."
Or, "I knew a salesman so smooth-talkin' slick if he tol' you a turkey c'd
pull a plow you'd run out and buy a harness."

I hadn't known Carlisle and Brenda for very long before they were
killed, but I had taken an immediate liking to them and admired the way
they worked together as filmmakers. Their sensitivity and talent might
have enabled them to make some kind of mark on the world. But instead
they were cut down by ruthless bigots too stupid to appreciate their
artistry and too hateful to acknowledge their humanity.

Before I left for the FBI Academy I went to see the families of the
four victims. In Jimmy Bean's case, his family consisted of only his
maternal grandmother; he was basically an orphan; his father was still
alive but in prison. Rorthal's mother and father were hard-scrabble
Appalachian farmers, about as dirt-poor as Lori McCoy's parents.
Carlisle and Brenda came from black middle-class families in Syracuse,
New York.

None of them treated me impolitely but they didn't welcome me with
open arms either. I felt awkward around them and found myself trying to
cope with survivor's guilt. Gazing at me sadly as I got ready to leave,
Carlisle's father said, "I guess it's a good thing that you're becoming a
federal agent and that you want to do something to help find my son's
murderers. But the case has already gone cold and every day makes it go
even colder. I hope you'll forgive me if I can't really believe you'll ever
accomplish anything."

Still, I couldn't let go of a vague, wistful hope that maybe somehow,
someday, circumstances might put me in the right place at the right time
to bring the survivors a taste of justice if not closure.

CHAPTER 17

Lori broke into hard, wracking sobs and ran from the apartment, taking Missy with her, scarcely knowing where she was or where she was going, just walking and walking, down one city street after another, tugging Missy by the hand when she got too heavy to carry. They were like two wounded birds with no nest. Missy was crying because her mother was crying, and people on the sidewalks were staring at them. The tears would not stop, and neither would the ugly thoughts playing through Lori's head.

Keith had seduced Arlene, but Arlene had given in to him. To Lori, what her sister and her husband had done was worse than adultery -- it was incest, according to the Bible -- one of the worst sins imaginable. She almost wished she would have caught them in the act. Then she could've rained blows on both of them or even stabbed them to death, which would have gratified the part of her that ached to hurt them every bit as badly as they had hurt her.

But it didn't happen that way.

When Arlene broke down and confessed, crying and begging for forgiveness, she reached out to be hugged, but Lori flung her aside and ran from the apartment. She was already hurting so badly in the wake of the murders that this additional hurt inflicted upon her by people she loved was more than she could bear. Worse, there was no one she could tell. She was filled with pain and shame. She didn't want anyone to know. Didn't want to be pitied or talked about. Didn't want Missy to ever find out what her aunt and her father had done.

When she wore herself out with walking and crying, she realized that she had to get Missy off the streets and find some way to soothe her rather than making her feel the pain in her mother's heart. They went into a doughnut shop, used the ladies' room to wash and dry their faces, then got a coffee and a Coke. Lori had very little money in her purse. She couldn't pay for a hotel room. All of her belongings were back at the apartment. She had no choice but to return, stay there for at least one final night, and make plans and get out.

79

Keith would probably be there by now, back from his job at the campus radio station. Lori didn't want to even look at him. By now Arlene had probably told him that the game was up, their transgression had been revealed. Going back there would be like stepping into a hollow, hellish den of anguish and despair.

This time Lori knew it was finally all over between her and Keith. She couldn't ever forgive him. She must file for a divorce.

At this moment she hated Arlene just as much as she hated her husband. The sisterly bond had been so horribly shattered that it could never be put back together in any semblance of innocent affection and warmth. Yet she knew, even through her pain and grief, that she probably couldn't sustain an implacable revulsion toward her own sister. It was easier to focus the bulk of her anger on Keith. She wished she could be as mean and vindictive toward both of them as the situation demanded. She wished she knew how to hate and continue to hate till death wiped those who had wronged her from the face of the earth.

She forced herself to go back to the apartment and let herself in, her hand trembling when she used the key. It was dark inside except for a light in the kitchen, above the sink.

On the counter was a note handwritten in caps:

DEAR LORI,

GONE OUT TO DROWN MY SORROW. WISH I HAD HAD THE

GUTS TO BREAK IT TO YOU. DIDN'T MEAN TO HURT YOU.

GUESS I'M JUST NO GOOD. MAYBE I'LL TAKE A BRIDGE.

I'D CRAWL ON BROKEN GLASS IF YOU'D GIVE ME

ANOTHER CHANCE.

LOVE, KEITH.

She crumpled the note up and hurled it into the trash, despising its aura of whiny self-pity.

She gave Missy cereal, milk and cookies, then got her into her pajamas and then into her crib. The crib was in Lori and Keith's bedroom because of Arlene occupying the spare room. When Lori went down the hall she heard soft sobs coming from behind Arlene's door.

She locked Keith out of their bedroom. He came home late and slept on the living room couch. She heard him moving around and wondered what she'd have done if she had a gun. She decided that instead of yelling and screaming at him, she'd simply begin the process of freezing him out of her life.

Next morning he wanted to talk, even tried putting his arm around her, but she slapped it away. With all the iciness she could muster, she said, "It's over, Keith. Stay away from me."

But she couldn't stand losing two people at once. A double loss at this low point in her life would totally devastate her. And what would it do to her parents? If she had to tell them why she had abandoned her own sister, the shock and sudden pain might be too much for them. They'd be disgraced in their own church. They might not be able to take the blow.

Cursing herself for her weakness, she felt a twinge of pity, not for herself but for her miserable sister. She rapped lightly on Arlene's door, got no response, and went in and sat on the edge of the bed, her eyes puffy and red.

Arlene was lying there, not moving. In a meek, barely audible voice, she said, "I'm sorry for asking you to forgive me. I know that you can't, and I don't blame you."

Lori reached out and touched Arlene's cheek. She didn't mean to do it. It was done on impulse. She didn't say anything. Just touched Arlene's cheek and left, softly shutting the door, feeling the wetness of Arlene's tears on her fingertips.

When Arlene came out and started silently helping Lori to pack up her things, Lori didn't stop her. They didn't exchange many more words than the task needed, and their eyes didn't meet very often, and Lori found herself getting angry at the fact that Arlene was moving around in a daze, like a wounded doe.

"Hey, little sister!" Lori snapped. "Why're you looking so damned hurt? I'm the victim here! Is he going to marry you after I divorce him?"

Arlene shook her head no.

"I didn't think so. He'll stick it in anything warm and willing. You meant nothing to him but a spare piece of ass."

"I know. I'm a fool, a dumb hick. I wish I was dead."

"Hating yourself and feeling sorry for yourself is probably what made you do wrong. You need to work on your self-esteem. Ask Jesus for help."

"I'm not as strong as you. I never have been. "

"Well, you're gonna have to get stronger."

"Where are *you* gonna go?"

"Well, I was gonna go to Manhattan with Keith, and I'm still gonna go, only without him. I have a girlfriend there that I used to sing with before she graduated, and she's gonna let me and Missy stay with her till we find our own apartment."

"Can I come with you? I'll never hurt you again, I promise."

"You've got a lot of nerve, Arlene! I don't believe you asked me that!"

"I know ... I know ... I'm sorry."

"Look ... maybe I'll think about it ... find out if my friend even has room." Scarcely believing what she had just said, she backed off, saying, "Don't get your hopes up. I'm not promising anything."

To Lori's surprise, it turned out that her girlfriend was willing to temporarily squeeze everybody into her apartment. Lori wondered if she should tell Arlene that, or just wheedle out of her half-hearted promise. But she really didn't want Arlene to run back home and tell everyone all the gory details about what had happened. Heaven forbid she should stand up and confess it in front of Reverend Barlow and the whole darn congregation!

"You hurt me so bad I don't know if I can ever get over it," she told her sister. "But I guess I can try real hard to forgive you, like the Bible says."

Long after the move to Manhattan and the search for her own apartment was accomplished, Lori had many days when she walked unfeeling and uncaring through her daily chores. She could force herself to perk up when she had to, for her singing gigs, but afterwards she went totally flat and sank back into despondency.

One night she finally forced herself to tell Arlene that she forgave her, hoping that merely saying the unfelt words might help make them true. The old saying, easier to forgive than forget, kept playing through her mind, mocking her. She had spoken the words of forgiveness, but could she ever truly mean them? And could she ever truly forget?

She thought that God was putting her to a cruel test by asking her to turn the other cheek. As a Christian she was supposed to comply with

Jesus's teachings, but how could she ever again look at Arlene with the same guileless affection that they used to share?

Lori knew that if Arlene hadn't owned up to what she had done, she would have gone on in her sham of a marriage, letting Keith play her for a fool. Getting hit in the face with the truth had enabled her to wipe out the last vestiges of her love for Keith. But she still couldn't shake the image of her husband and her own sister doing it right under her nose, even in her own bed.

She had no doubt that Keith was the master manipulator and that Arlene was an easy mark, especially after Truman died and she was going around blaming herself. She was pretty much a basket case even before she moved to Belmont. She had no time to prepare herself for facing what to her was a frighteningly big city of 55,000 people, twenty times bigger than Cherry Hill. It was clear that she felt more overwhelmed than Lori had felt upon her own arrival here, partly because Arlene was forced into it, it wasn't a goal of hers, a step in a long-term plan. Lori had worried that Arlene might fall under the spell of some smooth-talking guy, and sure enough she had done so with a slickster close at hand. Keith had preyed on her vulnerability. He couldn't keep it in his pants, even where his own sister-in-law was concerned.

Lori didn't intend to do any forgiving and forgetting on his behalf, no matter what the Bible said. Hopefully Jesus would understand. Keith was her ex-husband and the father of her child, but he wasn't her flesh and blood. He was more expendable than Arlene.

As the weeks and months dragged by, though, the relationship between Lori and her sister continued to be one of human bondage rather than deep affection. Although they lived in the same apartment, and although Lori watched Arlene play with Missy and read to her and take care of her, and although they made everyday plans and did everyday things together, it was as if they talked at each other instead of to each other, moved around each other but didn't quite touch, and lived behind walls of unexpressed feelings that could never be totally breached.

One of Arlene's unfortunate responses to tension and depression was to eat too much, and to eat what wasn't good for her. Potato chips, candy, cookies and cake. Not cake and cookies made from scratch, not even sweet stuff "homemade" out of a box of premix, but mushy little store-bought goodies wrapped in cardboard and cellophane and filled with artificial ingredients.

Once every bit as pretty as Lori and so much of a lookalike that they used to often be taken as twins, the gathering pounds ballooned Arlene into a caricature of her former self. Out of guilt and shame, she lost her own identity in service to her sister and her sister's child. She didn't date and didn't pursue interests of her own. Living in the heart of one of the world's great cities, surrounded by dazzling opportunities and cosmopolitan diversions, she sampled almost none of it. She waitressed and came home, denying herself any "frills," stoically refusing to spend any household money on herself.

But as the months wore on her self-imposed exile became so unbearable that she broke down and began to show up at some of her sister's singing gigs. By this time Lori had made some breakthroughs and was starting to get hired at better places for better pay, so that they could more easily afford a babysitter, which eased Arlene's guilt over permitting herself to go out once in a while.

From the sidelines, she watched her sister's growing success with surprise mixed with satisfaction -- and a constant fear that the bubble might burst. She had always been proud, even a bit envious of Lori back when Lori was thought of as a genuine celebrity nowhere but in Cherry Hill. But now Lori was starting to make it in the toughest, most demanding city in the world and she was doing it by singing her own songs!

The secret was timing. And luck. Lori came on the scene just as avant garde entertainers like Bob Dylan, Joan Baez and Simon & Garfunkel were creating a music revolution by bringing a modern slant and an urban social consciousness to the folk idiom. The material that Keith had rejected some years earlier when Lori cut her first album now fit in perfectly with the current trend. Her lyrics were honest and meaningful and her style of delivery was poignant and unaffected. She became a favorite of the Manhattan sophisticates who delighted in discovering fresh young voices with something new to say and a new way of saying it. She achieved billing as a featured performer, a headliner, in some of the best venues.

As Lori McCoy's name grew in recognition and commercial value in the New York night scene, Arlene slowly morphed from waitress, babysitter and "chief cook and bottle washer" into something much more. She found herself becoming passionate about aiding Lori's blossoming career, and she gradually worked herself into a position of authority and responsibility as her sister's secretary, bookkeeper and personal manager.

Lori had a booking agent who lined up gigs and negotiated contracts, but for many other items of significance people had to go through Arlene, and she was often so zealously protective that she got called a "hatchet lady." The feisty side of her, which had been long buried, was now on display. Lori tended to shy away from confrontation, but Arlene overcompensated for that and became the "meany." Anyone she considered detrimental to her sister's career had better walk on eggs around her. If a publicist, a backup musician, a sound engineer or lighting man did not perform up to snuff, it was Arlene who did the scolding or the firing.

She envisioned greater success, even perhaps stardom, ahead for Lori. And yet, basking vicariously in the glow of her sister's limelight wasn't enough for her. She had never fully explored her own talents and wasn't really sure she had any. A nagging part of her knew that she couldn't ever be fulfilled as long as she remained her sister's handmaiden.

But for now she would continue doing it. It was her form of sackcloth and ashes.

CHAPTER 18

Keith kept an eye on his ex-wife's burgeoning career by reading notices in *Variety* and *Billboard* and scrutinizing ads and articles in the entertainment sections of the New York newspapers. He couldn't help being jealous. He dwelt upon all the key things he had done for her and how he had knocked himself out giving her the proper grooming while she was under his control. He congratulated himself that her success was belated evidence of his own good judgment. Hadn't he always known that she was a diamond in the rough? The last vestiges of guilt over the end of his marriage melted away as he told himself that his betrayal had turned out to be actually good for Lori -- it had pushed her out into the world where she was forced to either sink or swim, and she appeared to be rising, not sinking.

It was bitterly ironic that his own richly deserved rise to the top was plagued by bad luck. He had always believed in a grand destiny for himself. In high school he was voted King of Hearts and Most Likely to Succeed. In college he got the best roles in Drama Department productions, from tragedies to light musicals. He was always on the Dean's List (with just a little cheating). He hosted a popular on-campus radio show and had an on-air job waiting for him in the Big Apple. But just when the carousel's golden ring was within his grasp, his plastic horse melted and his dreams evaporated in the wake of the Dealey Plaza fiasco.

None of it was his own fault. Charlie Guinard was to blame for getting involved with that accursed peace march in Mississippi and persuading Carlisle and Brenda Dixon to go there and film it. If they would have gone straight home from Dallas, they'd never have been set upon by those asshole rednecks. The movie would've gotten finished and they'd still be basking in glory. An Academy Award in the documentary category wouldn't have been out of the question, and Keith as the producer would have been up on stage accepting it.

Other people were always letting him down out of stupidity or lack of imagination, or else they purposely took advantage of him and screwed him up. The pitfalls and near misses in his life weren't of his own doing. Everybody betrayed him, especially women.

Arlene broke up his marriage with her stupid blabbing. He wondered if she really had a guilty conscience or a subconscious desire to hurt her own sister. At bottom he hadn't really believed he'd be able to seduce her; she'd probably push him away because they were related by marriage. But he gave it a halfhearted try and bingo -- all the Bible training that had been pounded into her went out the window. She should have staved him off. What was he to do if women found him so irresistible?

As for Lori, she should have forgiven him. That's what her religion taught her to do. But no, she had to file for a divorce. Right up until the day the final papers were signed, Keith thought she'd break down and ask him to take her back. When it didn't happen, it was a blow to his pride. Now her career was on the upswing, thanks to how he had groomed and polished her while they were together, and instead of sharing in the limelight he was on the outside looking in.

Another woman who was abusing Keith was Margot Dane, the owner of the TV/radio station where he was employed. She wasn't keeping the promises she had made when he was just a college kid, several rungs below her socially, but with the kind of hard body she rarely got to touch at her age. He had gotten money out of her for Lori's first album, but so far for himself he had gotten doodly squat. She had promised him that this job at her station would be the key to his future, but so far it was the key to nowhere. Bitterly he remembered how Margot had gotten him hard by talking about making him a news anchor in the largest media market in the United States, where his handsome face would be seen daily by millions of people. But instead he was doing voice-overs for cheesy TV spots cranked out for low-end clients who could maybe afford to buy a bit of air time but had nothing to spend on production.

Since Keith was given the dirt cheap stuff to produce, his paycheck was dirt cheap too. To add insult to injury, when he had ventured to ask for a raise, Margot had snidely offered to make him a lowly time-slot salesman, which would have shoved him into a "slot" so deep he could never climb out of it. She knew damn well he deserved to be on camera. But that's exactly what she was afraid of. He'd be able to charm audiences and build sky-high ratings. Then he'd step up to a bigger and better station.

He was scrimping along paycheck to paycheck, unable to live with any semblance of flash and style in this extremely expensive city. His mother wouldn't give him any money either, even though she had copped a huge insurance settlement when his father died. Keith was living with her in the penthouse apartment he had grown up in, on Park Avenue, and she wasn't charging him any rent. But beyond that she wouldn't let loose of the purse strings. And she constantly nagged him about how he should've gone into his father's medical practice. "Listen, dear, would it have been so bad? You would've been immediately successful. Maybe it's not too late. I pray to God you'll wise up someday soon and get the stars out of your eyes." She always turned her eyes toward heaven when she said this.

His father hadn't even been a specialist, just a general practitioner. But Dad had a genius for wooing wealthy patients, and it enabled him to build his practice to the point where it became a respected clinic with an impressive staff of internists, nurses and medical technicians. He was as charming and reassuring as an undertaker, and he used his bedside manner to work on his patients' pocketbooks while his more medically gifted employees worked on the patients' bodies.

Keith wryly admired the subtlety and sophistication of his father's money-making enterprise but at bottom he wanted no part of it. It lacked pizzazz. It was mundane. He wanted to get rich but in a glitzy flamboyant style. He wanted everybody to know who Keith Santone was, the way everybody knew of Howard Hughes.

One day when he was especially disgusted with his mundane job at the TV station, he placed a call to the attorney who had handled his side of the divorce and asked if he had grounds to sue Lori for a portion of her income now that it must be amounting to some kind of substantial figure. "Better yet, could I claim that I'm due half of everything she earns in show business from now and for the rest of her life, because of the fact that I helped launch her when I was her husband and manager?"

"You signed all that away in the settlement papers," the attorney said.

"What about alimony and child support? If she's making more money now, I should have to pay less, right?"

"I could try for a reduction, but your payments are already so low I don't think a judge would act in your favor."

"Well, hell, could we overturn the settlement somehow? I read about contract renegotiations every day in the newspapers. Nothing's carved in stone anymore."

"Yeah, you're talking about big-time athletes and movie stars, not us peons," the attorney said. "But let me mull it over, maybe I can find an angle."

"Pete Best got a fat settlement from the Beatles," Keith said. "He was kicked out before they made it big, but he was with them when they first started out. That's like me and Lori. "

"Legally speaking, I don't think the Beatles had to give their old buddy Pete a damn thing. They did it out of the goodness of their hearts."

"Well, Lori has a good heart, too. It's her greatest weakness."

A week or so later, while Keith was stewing over the fact that his lawyer hadn't even bothered to get back to him, he was buzzed by the receptionist and asked if he wanted to take a call from Charlie Guinard. Annoyed, he considered telling her to tell Charlie that he was out sick. He hadn't spoken to the big blustery oaf for a long time and he was of a mind to keep it that way.

A couple of years ago when Keith was going through his messy divorce, Charlie kept calling up and pestering him to get a TV crew down to Mississippi to stir things up and put pressure on the State Police and the FBI so the local officials could be pushed out of the way and the Dixon murders could be solved. After the fifth or sixth phone call, Keith said, "Look, Charlie, don't you have sense enough to stop bugging me with this shit? I can't deal with it right now, my life's in a total fucking mess."

"Oh, come on, Keith," Charlie said, "don't expect me to shed crocodile tears over you. You and Margot Dane gotta be regular bed buddies now that you and Lori are splitting up. Whisper sweet nothings in Margot's ear and make this happen."

"You're pissing me off, Charlie. Number one, what you're talking about is a job for the networks, not an affiliate. And number two, there's no way in hell Margot would fork out a ton of bread to send a TV crew to Mississippi even if the entire Senate got blown away down there, much less two blacks and two obscure white guys."

"You could do it freelance, couldn't you?"

"Yeah, and kiss my job good-bye."

"Fuck your job, Keith; this is a story that needs to be told and you're the one who should be telling it because not only were you personally involved but you made it happen. Don't you give a shit that you contributed toward the deaths of four of our friends?"

"It was your fucking fault! You and your goddamn peace march!"

"But you brought us all together down there, and that's what set the whole chain of events in motion."

"Fuck off," Keith said, and slammed the receiver down.

He was glad when Charlie didn't call back. To hell with him, his schtick had lost its charm. He was still acting like a campus radical and refusing to wake up to the fact that he wasn't on a college campus anymore. He was working out of a shabby storefront office in Brooklyn, living in a room above the office, and playing legal beagle for a bunch of stumblebums and misfits who couldn't pay him a damn cent. Instead of putting on a suit and tie and going to work in a big corporate law firm where he could rake down a ton of money, he was still going around in wrinkled flannel shirts and baggy jeans, looking like an over-the-hill beatnik. His rabble-rousing civil rights and antiwar activities had earned him a degree of notoriety in the tabloids. His scowling, bearded face was plastered all over the eleven o'clock news several weeks ago when he got himself arrested during a sit-in, which should've been an embarrassment for him but instead he acted like it was a badge of honor.

Keith couldn't think of any reason why Charlie would be suddenly phoning him, except maybe to hit him up for a donation to some stupid cause he couldn't care less about. He reluctantly picked up the receiver and said with an obvious lack of enthusiasm, "Hey, Charlie, how's it going?"

"Believe it or not, I might have some business for you. I've got a fellow here in the office --"

"You've got an office?" Keith said with mock amazement. "With a real phone and a real desk and chair?"

"And a rusty brown file cabinet and an old manual Smith Corona, all paid for by Legal Aid."

"Some guys get all the breaks," Keith quipped.

"The reason for my call," Charlie said, "I've got a fellow here that you should meet, his name is Ed Baumgardner. He has a line of health and beauty products and he needs a TV commercial. He saw you on the air and he likes your style, wants you to be the on-camera spokesman."

"What about you?" Keith needled. "I saw you on the news, you're a celebrity now."

"My big hairy face won't sell health and beauty products to the sex-starved housewives. You're the razor-cut manicured cat, not me, Keith. That's why you get the big bucks."

"I'm raking it in," Keith said, hoping Charlie would think it was true.

"Well, we're not asking you to do anything for free, but if you could talk Margot into cutting us a little break on the time buys that'd be great. Can I send Ed over to see you?"

"I just had a shoot wrap up early," Keith lied, not wanting to admit he wasn't busy. "I've got to supervise some postproduction details, but I'll be loose by three. How does that sound?"

"Good, Ed will be there. Thanks, buddy."

"I appreciate the referral," Keith said, not really meaning it. He fully expected this gig to result in just another down-and-dirty TV spot, a big fat zero for his sample reel, but at least he might score some points with Margot for bringing in a billable job.

Ed Baumgarder was a little baldheaded guy with a quirky smile and a fringe of frizzy red hair, and even if he hadn't been wearing a green blazer with brass buttons he would have reminded Keith of a leprechaun. They shook hands by the elevator and went into the conference room to talk, and in short order it dawned on Keith that the "leprechaun" was holding a key to a pot of gold, and there might be a possibility of dipping his own fingers into the pot.

Baumgardner had a fledgling company called Natural Life Products, a one-man operation selling herbal remedies, shampoos, ointments and vitamins out of a string of concessions in a New Jersey supermarket chain. He didn't own any of the stores so he had no overhead costs for light, heat and air conditioning, and he didn't even have to pay for his own cashiers because shoppers took his items straight to the check-out lines. The deal was that he would set up a section of each store with shelves and displays for Natural Life, and the chain would do the tabulating and accounting and take a piece of the action.

Baumgardner didn't even have to bear manufacturing costs; he got the products on consignment from a wholesaler in California. So far, they were carried in just one chain of thirty-six stores, which last year had generated an average profit of about eight-hundred dollars per store for a combined net of just over twenty-eight thousand dollars. This was barely enough for one man to live on, and if Baumgardner would've had to split it with a partner it would've been starvation city. But Keith wanted in, and he wanted in badly. He had no doubt that buckets and buckets of money would start pouring in if Natural Life could expand into bigger and bigger chains with more and more stores. It didn't even matter much if a few of the concessions failed; they could be closed down with no muss no fuss and not even any laid-off employees collecting workman's comp.

"Ed, you've got a diamond in the rough here," Keith said. "You've done a good job of getting it off the ground and to the point where it can become very lucrative, if handled the right way. I'd really like to become your partner. I'd write your spots, produce them for you and act in them for free. "

"That's not really worth a lot," Baumgardner said. "I'm already able to pay for my own commercials, including the air time, and I'm the kind of guy who likes to call his own shots."

Baumgardner apparently wasn't as dumb as he looked. Flattery wasn't going to do the trick, it was going to take hard cold cash. And Keith didn't have any. He didn't even have any idea whom he might ask to back him, except his mother or Margot Dane, and they'd almost certainly turn him down. Nevertheless he had to start talking as if he had money, or this opportunity would fly right out the window. In his most sincere tone he said, "Look, Ed, I can tell your company is cash poor because of the limits you set on time buys. If you can't get major capital as expeditiously as possible, competitors will come out of the woodwork and you won't be able to beat them off. They'll co-opt your marketing concept, overpower you in the marketplace, and all your hard work will go down the drain. I'm willing to come up with money because I believe wholeheartedly in what you're doing. You've probably approached fat-cat bankers and brokers who've refused to listen to you. They're stodgy and shortsighted and I'm not that way, you and I are on the same wavelength. With the cash I can provide, you and I could work beautifully together as a team. "

Mulling it over, Baumgardner said, "I came to you because of Charlie Guinard. He gave you a good recommendation. He's a great guy and I trust him."

"We're old college buddies," Keith said brightly. "There isn't a better guy on the face of the earth. Totally honest and straight forward, that's why we respect each other. But I have cash and he doesn't. I'm going to level with you, Ed, I see Natural Life becoming a multimillion-dollar enterprise in less than five years, but it's going to take fifty-thousand in new capital."

"You have that kind of money?"

"I have access to it."

"What're you gonna do, rob a bank?"

Keith chuckled, wishing he could do just that.

"I'll lend you a ski mask, but you'll have to get your own gun," Baumgardner said.

Keith chuckled again.

Clapping Baumgardner on the shoulder, he said, "Let me put a business plan together and get back to you by early next week. I promise you I can make this work, and I don't make promises I can't keep."

They shook hands on it. Getting on the elevator, Baumgardner smiled his lopsided smile and Keith kept a facsimile of a smile pasted on his own face until the elevator doors closed. Then he walked away frowning, wondering where in the hell he was going to come up with fifty-thousand dollars.

Two weeks later, after introducing Ed Baumgardner to his mother and pitching her over tea and cookies, Keith found out that he didn't need to go to the bank with a gun and a ski mask. His mother was going to invest with him, and not because he was her son or because she was snowed by his business plan. Amazingly, she took quite a liking to little Ed Baumgardner, to the point where she was quite smitten with him. Of course it helped greatly that his Natural Life Company could show a good balance sheet. Betty Santone understood balance sheets very well from being the real brains behind her late husband's medical clinic; truth be known, she deserved most of the credit for turning it into a cash cow.

With the windfall of his mother's money, Keith worked like a demon, fueled by the manic enthusiasm he always applied to ventures that turned him on. He produced powerful TV spots with eye-catching production values, expanded the time buys, jazzed up the point-of-purchase displays, and hired a strong sales team to persuade bigger chains to devote supermarket space to the Natural Life concessions.

He devised a new advertising campaign that capitalized on the "back to nature" craze of the sixties and seventies. The brand name Natural Life was perfect for the increasing number of health-conscious people. The redesigned logo featured a rainbow shining on a pot of gold, which was Keith's tongue-in-cheek homage to the Leprechaun who had brought him his good fortune -- but it was an homage that he kept to himself.

He got a kick out of seeing his mother and Ed Baumgardner together as a couple. They didn't seem to want to get married but they were oddly compatible. Keith doubted that there was any sex in their relationship, but he didn't totally rule it out either. Picturing such a thing was amusing. Ed was about five-three and a hundred-and-ten pounds, and Betty

Santone was a big woman, five-ten and two-sixty. At social events she introduced him as her friend Ed, not her fiancé or "significant other." But they seemed as affable and at times as nippy and naggy with each other as an old married couple.

By 1975, Keith Santone was chief financial officer of a company with assets of over two hundred million dollars. Ed Baumgardner was chief executive officer and Betty Santone was a major shareholder.

Although Keith was shelling out a great deal of cash nowadays for increased alimony and child support, he did it with benevolent dispatch, like Daddy Warbucks. He wasn't living with his mother anymore; he now had his own penthouse apartment in Manhattan and the lavish accouterments to go with it. Magnanimously, he donated large chunks of money to several of Charlie Guinard's causes, as payback for the introduction to the Leprechaun, even though he couldn't care less about the causes. He was living the high life that he deserved, and he didn't have to give a damn whether his ex-wife's career prospered or flopped.

CHAPTER 19

In 1972, Lori wrote and recorded her first hit song. It was inspired by her worries over her brother Maylon, who was fighting in Vietnam.

One night just before going to bed she watched news footage of flag-draped coffins being unloaded from a cargo plane. Unable to sleep, she tossed and turned, tormented by the idea that one of those coffins could have been Maylon's. She wondered if the bodies of soldiers killed in action might sometimes reach the United States ahead of the much feared telegrams from the Defense Department. Telling herself this was unlikely didn't enable her to rest any easier. She thought about all the mothers and fathers and brothers and sisters praying fervently for their loved ones to come home safely, just as she was praying for Maylon, and it seemed terrible but true that some of those prayers would be answered and some wouldn't be. This inspired the lyrics for the chorus of her song, which was the first part that came to her. She got up and wrote down the words:

In the dark a soldier cries,
In the dark another dies.
The folks at home will hope and pray,
The one they love still lives today.

The other lyrics flowed from the chorus and in less than an hour she had it done. She called it *A Soldier's Song*. Prior to its ever being recorded, she sang it at a peace rally in Central Park that was organized by a committee headed by Charlie Guinard. He flipped out over the song, declaring that it wasn't just a personal statement, it could be the anthem for the entire peace movement. And, he said, there were supporters of the movement who had money and connections to make it go over big. "Write more songs like that," he added, "and I think you'll have a hit album."

Lori almost didn't dare to believe him, but over the next month and a half lyrics kept coming to her and she poured herself into her writing every time she got a chance, even during breaks at her nightclub gigs. She wrote eight new songs and revamped and polished some of the ones she had kept locked in a drawer for several years, scared to show them to anybody because they were so different from what she was hearing on the radio.

She sang the new songs for Charlie, Missy and Arlene, accompanying herself on her acoustic guitar. Again Charlie was blown away. Missy was only ten, but she was moved by many of the tunes and lyrics, humming along and tapping her feet. Arlene was hesitant, saying that she had no idea how people might respond to songs that were admittedly good but quite unusual in theme and concept. Her noncommittal comments shook Lori's confidence. But Charlie didn't flinch. He said, "Take it from me, this stuff is dynamite and the world is ready for it right now." He and Lori decided together which of the new songs would make it onto the tracks of her new album.

A month prior to the recording session, Charlie showed up at Lori's apartment, handed her two Simon & Garfunkel albums in worn and tattered jackets and said, "Put these on the stereo."

They listened together, sipping coffee. One of the albums had the duo's signature song *The Sounds of Silence* on it, but it was an earlier, lesser known version, done in a simple unadorned "folk" arrangement. The other album had the same song on it, but in a souped-up "folk rock" arrangement with more emphasis on drums and electric guitars -- and it was this later version that had become a monster hit.

"See what I mean?" Charlie said, a gleam in his eyes.

"Yeah," Lori agreed. "I don't think the earlier version ever would've made it onto the sound track of *The Graduate*. None of their other songs would've made it either, they don't have enough punch. "

"Some A&R man must've seen that and pushed them in the right direction," Charlie said. "And that's what made their careers. Think of the serendipity, their songs perfectly complimenting the movie. Without the Simon & Garfunkel music I don't think it would've become the top box-office picture of, when, 1968?"

"Uh-huh," Lori said. "I remember 'cause that was the year Missy started first grade."

She decided then and there to give all the songs on her new album the contemporary folk rock sound. True to his word, Charlie found a backer who was willing to pay for some of the best studio musicians in New York. The recording sessions were euphoric. Everyone got caught up in the feeling that they were taking part in something wonderfully unique and full of potential.

But the album didn't take off when it debuted. It took a long time for word of mouth to come into play because the record company didn't promote heavily. Lori was terribly disappointed in the early weeks of the release, but Charlie never wavered and in the end his expectations paid off. The album slowly gathered momentum, garnered more and more air play, and eventually made the *Billboard* Top Twenty. *A Soldier's Song*, the featured single, shot to number one on pop stations all over the country.

Suddenly Lori was a star, in demand for a major concert tour. She appeared on the *Ed Sullivan Show* and *The Tonight Show*. Mike Wallace interviewed her on *Sixty Minutes*. She was featured in articles and photo spreads in *Time, Newsweek,* and *Life* magazines. Tabloid reporters dug into her past and spread lies, truths and half-truths about her divorce and her relationships with her daughter, her sister and her ex-husband.

The story of her narrow escape from the rednecks in Mississippi was told and retold. Even Mike Wallace asked her about it. Because of the circumstances of her ordeal, and because her hit ballad and all of her other songs thematically revolved around social issues, she got thrust into the forefront of the antiwar and civil rights movements, a role that she didn't especially want. However the leaders of the movements, including Charlie Guinard, wanted *her*. They welcomed her, even coveted her, just as they coveted other highly visible spokespersons for their causes, and this exposed her to a nasty barrage from the more hateful elements of the mass media.

She got called a peacenik, a pinko, a traitor. Right-wing commentators labeled her "Lefty Lori McCoy" and loved linking her with actress Jane Fonda who had been given the derisive nickname "Hanoy Jane."

When Lori made the cover of *Newsweek*, two huge sacks of hate mail were forwarded to her by the magazine's editors. Out of more than three hundred letters, only fifteen were favorable, the rest were full of venom. Some folks wanted to see her shot, some wanted her to be tarred and feathered, others wanted her to be hanged. One lady wrote, "I'm going to come to New York one of these days and I hope I get to see you walking in one of those despicably misguided peace marches because I'll come right up to you and gouge your eyes out."

Tears rolled down Lori's cheeks as she dumped the sacks of letters into a garbage can so Missy wouldn't see them when she came home from school. Even though she told herself that *Newsweek* had about eight million readers and only a few hundred of them had responded so hatefully, they still succeeded in making her feel miserable. When she was an unknown struggling singer she had no idea how much it could hurt to be despised by masses of people that she had never even met.

Charlie told her to just laugh it off. "Millions of people like you," he said, "or you wouldn't have sold a couple million records. The ones who're in your camp enjoy reading about you, then they toss the magazine aside. They don't bother to write letters to the editor. The rabid nut cases are in the minority, they don't deserve a moment of your time. Pay no attention whatsoever to their mindless ranting and raving. Tell yourself sticks and stones et cetera."

One day Lori's mother phoned her, very upset. "Lorelei, you have to be careful these days. I worry about you and Missy. Some of the folks in Cherry Hill are saying bad things about you."

"What kind of bad things?" Lori asked, alarmed.

"They say you forgot where you came from. They don't like the way you're speaking out against the government. They say the New York Jews got ahold of you and turned you into a communist. They give me and your daddy dirty looks when they pass by us in town. I swear, sometimes I'm scared our home might get fire-bombed. "

"Oh, Mama, they'd never do a thing like that," Lori said. But she was afraid that maybe they *would* do it. It was bad enough to find out she was hated by strangers, but it hurt even worse to think that folks she had grown up with could be turning against her. She suggested that maybe her parents ought to move away, and she offered to buy them a newer, much nicer place, but her mother said, "Oh, Lorelei, we could never leave here now, you know that, honey. We're gonna live out our years right where we're at."

Lori started trying to develop a thicker skin to protect herself against the hate mongers. She remembered something her father used to say, "Be careful what you wish for because you might get it." She wasn't sorry that she was enjoying a large measure of success but she knew she had to learn to cope with the downside. And she couldn't afford to rest on her laurels. Her next album had to be at least as good as and hopefully better than the last one.

She finally had to admit to herself that she had become a so-called celebrity, a target for people's prejudices as well as a focus for their enchantment. It was vaguely embarrassing to be looked at as an icon instead of a real person. Andy Warhol, the pop artist who got famous painting mundane items such as Campbell's soup cans, had remarked recently that a celebrity was, "somebody famous for being famous." That implied a certain uselessness, a lack of real ambition or accomplishment, and Lori didn't want the quip to epitomize her even if it did justly pertain to certain other people in the news or on the society pages.

In her coffee house and saloon singing days, many of the patrons, especially men who might have been smitten with her, liked to hang around her or show off that they knew her. But now this effect was on a whole different level. Whenever she walked into a room full of people, the timbre of the room altered. There was a heightened awareness of her presence. She could affect many of the people around her more than they could affect her. It was clear that some of them felt inferior to her even though she disdained feeling superior to anybody. She wanted them to treat her as an equal, not as somebody put up on a pedestal.

Arlene was still acting as Lori's manager and publicist, and Charlie had done a surprisingly good job of negotiating her contract with Strayhorn Records. Royalties were pouring in and the money Lori was being paid for concerts was almost obscene. She and Missy were living in a lovely, spacious apartment now, actually almost a double apartment with a separate little wing for Aunt Arlene.

Missy spent every other weekend with her father. Keith always sent a limo to pick her up so he could keep his distance from Lori and Arlene. Apparently they all had decided this was best, without ever discussing it openly.

Now that Charlie was negotiating deals for Lori, there was a change in him. He went to business meetings with his beard and mustache neatly trimmed and wore sportcoats and slacks instead of baggy jeans. He seldom wore a necktie, preferring open-necked shirts, dressy but casual. He also lost a lot of weight and toned down his blustery mannerisms, shading them toward a hearty and robust kind of dignity.

Many of the heaviest backers of the civil rights and anti-war movements were famous actors, artists, musicians and sports figures. They observed the excellent job Charlie was doing as Lori McCoy's personal attorney and were impressed by the way he had remade himself, displaying a charismatic intensity tempered by restraint, and quite a few of them sought to be represented by him. By 1974, with a stable of notable clients, he was able to leave his store-front digs and move into a suite of offices in Columbus Circle. As head of his own company, Guinard Enterprises, he led a capable, energetic staff of talent agents, business managers and deal negotiators.

He and Lori remained close in friendship as well as in business matters, and he never neglected her interests; he gave them the highest priority, even though this sometimes drew gripes from some of his haughtier clientele.

One day Lori asked him exactly what he had done to lose weight and get himself in such excellent shape. "I did it for you," he said. "You were my motivation. I wanted to show you I could make myself reasonably attractive."

She realized he was blushing, and she had never seen his face redden before except when he was in the midst of one of his boisterous enthusiasms or bombastic tirades.

And she was blushing too.

Could it be that he was infatuated with her? And why did that thought cause a warm glow to come over her all of a sudden?

CHAPTER 20

Cletis Barrett and Albert Crane were cleaning their hands with gasoline-soaked rags when Conrad Pryzor stopped off at their garage. He was dressed in tan chinos and a light blue golf shirt and he was carrying his lunch in a brown paper bag. He could hear himself talking on a portable radio in the garage -- one of the prerecorded speeches he relied on to fill airtime when he wasn't actually at radio station ARYN.

"We didn't bring no lunches," Cletis told him. "We's gettin' ready to hit Scotty's Place for a beer and a sandwich or sumpin'." He and Albert tossed their gasoline-soaked rags into a large steel barrel.

"I don't have time for that," Pryzor said. "Gotta get back to the station before the recording runs out."

"What's up?" Albert said warily. Often when Pryzor showed up unannounced in the middle of the day it was because of some crisis or other, or to tell Albert and Cletis to do something dangerous or unpleasant.

"Well," said Pryzor, "I asked you both to try to think of a solution to our little problem up North, and I want to know what you've come up with."

"She has a teenage brat we could kidnap and hold for ransom," Cletis Barrett said. "Me and Albert been doin' us some research."

He went over to a workbench strewn with assorted tools and machinery parts, and picked up a grease-stained tabloid opened to an article on Lori McCoy and her daughter Missy. "Looky here," he said, and held it up so Conrad Pryzor could see the accompanying photograph, which had been taken by a paparazzi with a telephoto lens, catching Lori and Missy unaware in their bathing suits.

"Like to pork the daughter," Albert said. "Helluva body on her for a thirteen-year-old."

Conrad Pryzor said, "It's hard to believe it's been eleven years since you two let them get away."

"I'd love to make amends for that," Albert said. "But I ain't on the same page with Cletis when it comes to doin' a high-profile kidnappin'.

We could get our asses shot full of holes and burnt to cinders just like that fucked up Symbionese Liberation Army got done to them after they kidnapped that other spoiled rich bitch, Patty Hearst. "

"They got their asses shot off 'cause they was dumb asses," Cletis said. "They was paid a couple million bucks of ransom money and spent it handin' out free food!"

"Feed the masses!" Pryzor scoffed. "They were communists and they behaved like communists and it was their undoing."

"Yeah, there was only seven or eight of 'em," Albert said, "and they had the nerve to call theyselves an *army*! Warn't enough of 'em to make one lousy squad! They coulda used all that cash to get a lotta new recruits and arm themselves with grenades, mortars and machine guns, mebbe even tanks. "

"Nobody is more in need of recruits and weapons than we are," Conrad Pryzor said. "We have to take serious action. The conclave in Baltimore takes place next month. I want us looking sharp. I don't want to be embarrassed."

A Ku Klux Klan and American Nazi rally was scheduled for May 15, 1975, the third anniversary of the shooting of George Wallace by a twenty-one-year-old drifter and malcontent named Arthur Bremer. Wallace, a former governor of Alabama who was running for the Democratic presidential nomination on a States' Rights and Segration Forever platform, was turned into a wheelchair-bound paraplegic by a bullet fired by Bremer that destroyed his spinal cord. Since then he had been held up as a martyr by white supremacist organizations everywhere.

Conrad Pryzor's Aryan Confederacy, seventy-eight members strong, was going to march in the upcoming parade in tribute to George Wallace, whose leadership of a get-tough stand against integration was highlighted by the unleashing of attack dogs upon demonstrators in Birmingham in the early sixties. Cletis Barrett and Albert Crane didn't want to miss out on the parade, but they and their leader Conrad Pryzor were afraid they'd be seen on television and recognized by Lefty Lori McCoy.

They did not want to don white sheets and hoods to hide their identities, this was at odds with the image they wished to project. They were more interested in recruiting new members for their fledgling but highly militant Aryan Confederacy than for the Klan, which in their view had become too tame. They wanted to march proudly with their faces in full view, goosestepping down a broad avenue in their tan shirts with swastika armbands and carrying blood-red Aryan Confederacy banners.

"What about Herschel and Horace? What do they think?" Cletis Barrett asked Conrad Pryzor.

"They don't believe there's a snowball's chance in hell any of you are going to be recognized after all this time, especially not them, because they were in police uniforms."

"They's prob'ly right," Albert Crane chimed in. "It all went down so fast that singer gal never got a real good look at none of us."

"I don't want to take that chance," Pryzor said sternly. "I prefer to eliminate her. I think it might actually be a little easier for Herschel and Horace to be picked out because they were in uniform the first time she saw them and they're going to be in uniform again even though it's a different kind of uniform."

"You might be right," Cletis said. "That gal ain't dumb, she proved that before. She's sure turned out to be pretty damn famous and she's out there talkin' against everything we stand for."

"Ignorant people are being swayed by her, too. Which disgusts me," said Pryzor. "If we don't take action against her we lose credibility and self-respect."

"I like the idea of a kidnappin'," Cletis said, "but it's gotta be well planned and financed. And we can't do it down here, don't wanna shit in our own nest and draw cops to us like flies on a turd. "

"If we're aimin' to kill her, how the hell is she gonna pay us to get her daughter back?" Albert said. "Cain't figger that one out, fellers."

"Use your head," Conrad Pryzor told him. "You have to insist that she comes to you all alone and delivers the ransom money in a lonely spot that you're going to pick out and thoroughly scout. Then you don't keep your end of the bargain. Her daughter's already dead by that time but she won't know it. You kill her and make a well-planned exit by a pre-established escape route."

Cletis said, "To do all that and do it right, so's it comes off without a hitch, we're gonna have to spend considerable time up North. The plan's gotta be bankrolled and done in two stages, and we can't use our own vehicles, we gotta use stolen cars. First we gotta pull off maybe an armored car or joolery store heist up North somewheres pretty close to Jew Town, New Yawk, 'cause that's where Lefty Lori lives. Then with a lotta cash under our belts we lay low and scope on her for as long as it takes to figure how we're gonna snatch the little girl without gettin' our asses caught in a sling."

"Don't go on a spending spree when you make the initial score," Conrad Pryzor warned. "Spend what you have to spend, and spend it well but don't waste it. Stash the bulk of it in a Greyhound locker and send me a duplicate key. That way if stage two gets fouled up or delayed, we'll still have plenty of money to carry out our other operations."

Looking at Cletis, Albert asked, "You think we need Horace and Herschel Stoddard to help us?"

"I'd feel better if they were in on it," Cletis replied thoughtfully. "Especially if we have to use any dynamite or pipe bombs, that's what they're good at."

"I want to approve all your plans before you head North," Pryzor said. "I'll help you eliminate any chance for failure, even if you get hit with some unpredictable bad breaks."

"Gonna bang that little teenage pussy afore we kill her," Albert Crane said with a lip-licking leer.

CHAPTER 21

On the day my partner got killed, I was thinking about resigning from the FBI and I talked it over with him at lunch in our favorite Manhattan deli. He was having a pastrami sandwich on dark rye with a side of potato salad, and I was having a bowl of mushroom barley soup and a corned beef on marble rye. We were drinking Amstel, just one bottle apiece, because we thought we should refrain from drinking more than one in the middle of a work day. Funny how so many otherwise insignificant details burn themselves into your brain concerning the day someone you have been close to dies.

Cyrus Lumley and I were working out of the Bureau's New York City office and had been partners for over three years, long enough to know we could depend on each other in trying or dangerous circumstances. He had been raised in a Detroit ghetto and had gone to Michigan State on a basketball scholarship, so we could relate to each other because of our experiences in college athletics, but we had much more in common besides just that. We both had strongly developed social consciences that manifested themselves in similar ways. We were both Army veterans too; he had risen to captain after going in on an ROTC commission, while my highest rank had been Spec Four. Neither of us had served in Vietnam. He got out a half year after I did, and like me he managed to complete his term of active duty before things over there really heated up.

His first post was Fort McClellan, Alabama, and I had spent four weeks there before the Five-oh-worst was redeployed to Fort Bragg. So I knew what the hot, sleepy town of Anniston looked like and could easily picture what had happened to him when he first got there. He told me about it one day when we had been partners for a couple of months. "I was dropped off in the business district," he said, "and had to wait a couple of hours for a jeep to come and take me to my duty assignment. I was sweaty and tired and there was a saloon across the way, so I went in, sat down and a woman came over and I said I'd have any kind of beer they had on tap. She said she was sorry but she couldn't serve me. I said if there was no draft beer she could give me bottled beer, and she said no, it's not that, and looked at me funny so it dawned on me she meant the color of my skin and I slowly got up and walked out of there. I stood on the sidewalk trying to think where else I could go, and I realized I couldn't go anywhere."

"Man, that must've been hell," I said. "It's weird that the Army was getting desegregated at that time but the Southern towns where most of the posts were situated still had Jim Crow. They should've made them desegregate or else relocate the posts."

"Fat chance," Cyrus said. "It would've cost billions and billions of dollars."

"Not only that," I said, "President Johnson had already lost the South for the Democratic Party when he went ahead and signed the Civil Rights Act. If he had tried to take the Army posts away from them he probably would've been impeached."

"Or else shot," Cyrus said. "Anyway, I'm standing in that hot, dusty street in Anniston and I'm homesick for Detroit. I'm even homesick for the ghetto. Up North, white people might've hated me on sight but they couldn't keep me out of stores or bars or most places I wanted to go. I had more freedom and less fear in the mean streets of Detroit than what I had in that peaceful-looking, so-called god-fearing little redneck town."

"Klan's up North, too, though," I said, and then I told him about my family's experience with the Ku Klux Klan in Pennsylvania. He already knew about the murders in Mississippi because they had been dredged up and dwelled on to a large extent once Lori McCoy achieved fame. He also knew of my connection to Lori and to the murder victims.

Over the next three years, Cyrus and I became fast friends as well as symbiotic partners. By May 1975, working together on the FBI Anti-Terrorist Task Force, we had gone up against hard-case fanatics such as the Black Panthers, the Weather Underground, and the White Liberation Army. Sometimes they were better armed than we were but Cyrus had good instincts and seldom let them get the drop on us. His quick reactions saved lives. Local policemen and SWAT team members had been killed or wounded in some of our operations but so far nobody in our task force had been hit; still, it was luck as much as anything else, and we all knew luck like that couldn't hold.

Cyrus had an attractive young wife he had married while he was still in the Army, and they had two children, a boy and a girl ages four and two. My wife Alice and I had been married six years at this time, but we didn't have any children. Fewer people would have been left to grieve if I had been the one killed instead of my partner.

As I said, over lunch I was telling him why I had to consider leaving the Bureau. This morning the Agent in Charge of the New York Office had asked me to help compile dossiers on Lori McCory, Arlene McCoy, Keith Santone and Charlie Guinard. When I first became an agent, I learned through the grapevine that the FBI was conducting covert investigations of Martin Luther King and many other civil rights and antiwar activists whom they considered "subversives." I couldn't say anything about it because I wasn't supposed to even know it, and the fact that it was happening just ate at me. I had hoped this unsavory practice would be terminated with the death of J. Edgar Hoover in 1972. But no. Now I was being asked to contribute to it.

Cyrus said, "They can't make you do it. You can simply refuse. Tell the AIC your morale would be irreparably damaged if you had to rat out your friends."

"I tried that and it didn't work. He told me that I took an oath to protect and defend the United States of America, not my old college pals."

"Well, I don't think he's going to push you into a corner and risk that you'll resign and become a whistle-blower. Tell him if you quit I'll go with you."

"You'd do that?"

"I might and I might not," he said with a wry smile. "But the AIC doesn't need to know that. I think it's a fine little bluff and one we'll probably never have to put to a test."

While we were talking, an armored truck was parking at a strip mall seventy-five miles away in Belmont, New York. A robbery was going to take place there and I found out later that the location had been picked because of its connection to Lori McCoy.

The driver of the black-and-red Dunston Security vehicle remained behind the wheel and put the blinkers on while two other guards in black and gray uniforms got out. One of them went into a department store for a cash pickup while the other one unlocked and opened the back door of the truck, then stood watch, his hand on the butt of his holstered pistol. He and the driver kept scanning everybody and everything around them while continuing to watch for their buddy to come out of the steel security door of the department store.

Meanwhile two uniformed cops got out of a patrol car after pulling into a parking slot about thirty feet from the armored truck. Both the driver and the other guard cast a momentary glance at the two cops crossing the street, then relaxed a bit when they saw the cops chatting idly and seemingly headed for a nearby donut shop.

By this time, the guard doing the cash pickup came out of the side door of the department store wheeling three canvas money sacks on a two-wheeled dolly. He tossed the three sacks into the back of the armored truck and started to collapse the dolly so it could be stowed away and locked in with the cash.

The two cops spun around, crouched and starting blasting away with 9mm Beretta automatics. The guard who had wheeled out the cash was shot in the throat and went down, gushing a geyser of blood from a punctured artery. The guard next to him was shot three times in the chest and twice in the stomach and was dead before he hit the ground.

The driver drew his revolver but never fired a round, never even made it out of the armored truck. While Horace and Herschel Stoddard grabbed two canvas sacks apiece and ran for their phony police car to toss the sacks into the trunk, Albert Crane and Cletis Barrett jumped out of a red Dodge minivan and used M-16 rifles to pump more than a dozen steel-jacketed armor piercing rounds through the "bulletproof" windshield of the Dunston Security vehicle and into the head and torso of the driver.

An elderly security guard ran out of the department store with a little .32 revolver in his hand and was instantly gunned down by M-16 fire from Albert and Cletis. They hotfooted it for the red van, jumped in and peeled out, following the flashing lights of the patrol car, which was leading the way like an official police escort.

They didn't know that before running out of the department store and to his death in a hail of bullets, the sixty-seven-year-old, five-dollar-an-hour security guard, himself a retired ex-cop, had made an emergency call to his former colleagues at the Belmont Police Station. He managed to spit out that the strip mall was within a half mile of a ramp to Interstate 95 and his gut told him that the robbers would probably get on it after quickly ditching the vehicles used in the heist and piling into some other kind of transportation.

He turned out to be right. About twenty minutes after he made his phone call, a medium-sized white U-Haul truck on I-95 South crashed a roadblock set up by the New York State Police. The U-Haul totaled one of the police cars that was attempting to block the highway, but two state troopers in another car sped off in hot pursuit of the U-Haul and radioed for backup.

The U-Haul took an exit ramp that led onto a semi-rural highway, pulled off into a grassy field and stopped. The pursuing car stopped close behind it, and the troopers got out, drawing their revolvers and crouching behind their vehicle for cover.

They didn't have to order the fugitives to come out because that's exactly what two of them did. The back door of the U-Haul lifted straight up and all the way open and Albert Crane and Cletis Barrett jumped down to the ground and started shooting without bothering to take cover. They brazenly came right at the two troopers, firing their M-16's.

The troopers fired back with no effect whatsoever. They were totally outgunned, and the robbers were wearing body armor. In a matter of seconds the officers' bullet-riddled bodies were twisted into grotesque shapes on the ground, puddles of blood soaking into the grass.

Looking at one of the dead troopers, Cletis said, "Half a face is better'n no face at all, right?"

He and Albert both laughed.

They climbed back into the rear of the U-Haul, pulled the door down and yelled at Horace, who was sitting behind the wheel, to hit the gas and take off. Herschel Stoddard was in the cab with his brother. They had shed their police disguises while making the switch from the phony squad car to the U-Haul, and both were now wearing ordinary work clothes.

They laughed and joked about how easily the robbery had come off and were so elated about it that Horace said it was like a fucking blitzkreig and Herschel said, "Yeah, we hit 'em like a bunch of reg'lar goddamn storm troopers!" They agreed that Conrad Pryzor would've been proud if he had seen them in action.

Perhaps they wouldn't have been so smug if they had known that within five days we would track them down at their supposed "safe house." Sometimes I wish somebody else had found them so things would've gone down differently. Perhaps nobody on our team would have been killed and Cyrus would still be alive.

On the day of the robbery, not long after killing the two state troopers, the armored car robbers slaughtered a family of three in a rural home about fifteen miles south of Belmont.

They could have left the man and wife and their seven-year-old daughter tied up and gagged, which would have given them plenty of time to make their getaway, but instead they slit their throats just to steal the family car.

Fewer people would have died that day if the department store security guard hadn't managed to alert the police department before he got killed. There would have been no emergency roadblock and no one would have tried to stop the U-Haul. The security guard's phone call is what caused the robbers' ruthless heavy-handed plan to come apart at the seams.

They managed to steal more than three million dollars, but their use of military weapons and terrorist-style methods meant that our Anti-Terrorist Task Force would be put onto the case. The utter viciousness of the murders and the fact that they were committed against innocent citizens as well as police officers galvanized not only the various law enforcement agencies but also the general public. Virtually everybody wanted these scary bastards caught and therefore we had hope that we might eventually get some kind of a tip.

The Belmont police and the New York State Police didn't have much trouble locating the red van and the fake police car used in the initial phase of the robbery; this was done on day one. But we didn't find the U-Haul till the young family of three was found murdered by a worried relative who hadn't heard from them for several days. By this time Cyrus Lumley and I were the lead officers on our team, and we helped search and analyze that particular crime scene. But we didn't learn much of value other than the make, model, and license number of the car that had been stolen there. It was a blue 1973 Buick Regal with Jersey plates and its place in the garage had been taken over by the abandoned U-Haul.

All the vehicles we discovered were scrupulously examined by our forensic specialists. They came up with some reasonably unsmudged fingerprints, but it was going to take a long time to process them and look for matches. This was before the advent of the Automated Fingerprint Identification System, or AFIS, which is a computerized method that can compare millions or fingerprints in a few minutes.

What we had to work with were vague descriptions of the four robbers and the info on the stolen car. Plus anything we might be able to find out about the abandoned red van, the automobile dummied up to look like a police car, and of course the U-Haul truck -- which looked like our best possibility. Maybe it wasn't stolen, maybe it was rented, and one of the robbers might have signed the rental contract. Since they had expected to get away clean after transferring themselves and the stolen money from the vehicles used at the scene of the robbery, they might not have used fake ID to obtain the U-Haul.

If their plan would have gone smoothly, nobody would've seen them escape in it, therefore turning it back in wouldn't have been much of a risk.

We released the description and license number of the U-Haul to the media, complete with actual photos to be run on TV, and three days after the robbery we got a phone call from a truck rental outfit in Keyport, New Jersey. The owner said, "I rented a truck with that license number to a guy named Herschel Stoddard. He had mean written all over him, I didn't trust him one bit, in fact I was sort of scared of him, but I had no real reason not to rent him a vehicle since his ID and everything were in order and he paid a hefty deposit. He kept sounding off on 'cops and niggers' in the vilest kind of language. I'm Jewish, that kind of naked bigotry made my hair stand on end, it sounded like Nazi talk. I couldn't wait till that man got out of here."

Cyrus and I promptly drove to Keyport to look over the rental contract and interview the tipster and any of his employees who had contact with the man who had rented the U-Haul. Meantime back at our office, FBI personnel gathered information about Herschel Stoddard from the Mississippi Bureau of Motor Vehicles and from other sources deriving from their initial queries.

The net result was that we uncovered some vital statistics on Stoddard such as the year and date of his birth, his weight and height, current home address, place of employment, and so forth. We obtained a driver's license photo that had to be enlarged and reworked into a more current likeness by an FBI artist utilizing descriptions given to him by the people at the truck rental place. The updated rendering was published the following day in New York and New Jersey newspapers.

We didn't think the killers would have rented the U-Haul anywhere close to their safe house, but again we were surprised by their cavalier overconfidence, otherwise known as stupidity. It's often what causes people like them to commit mindlessly heinous crimes, and it also often enables us to catch up with them and put them out of action.

In this case, it developed that Herschel Stoddard got spotted by a postman in a quiet little community less than thirty miles from Keyport. He saw our artist's rendering on the front page of a newspaper he was slipping into a mailbox on his delivery route and recalled that the day before he had seen a similar looking man coming down off the porch of a house that had been vacant until recently. He called our hotline, said he had important information on the Dunston armored car robbery, and asked if there was a reward. Cyrus, who had taken the call, told him we'd need to interview him in person to ascertain all the facts and if they led to an arrest we'd make sure he got everything that was coming to him. What was coming to him in the way of money was zilch but he didn't need to know that right away; it might interfere with his willingness to do his duty as a decent law-abiding citizen.

On our way to see the postman we wondered if his info would pan out. Lots of phony tips came in on almost every case, especially those that were high-profile, but this time we found the informant credible.

He said, "When I first saw this fellow he was stepping off the front porch and heading toward a Buick parked in the driveway. Next time I saw him the Buick was gone and a brown car of I don't know what make was sitting behind the house partly hidden under some trees. I figured he must've made a trade -- now I see he had to do that because the description of the Buick was in all the papers."

Cyrus and I had already figured that the Buick Regal would be dumped and torched somewhere and replaced by yet another stolen car or maybe even a bought one, and what the postman said confirmed our reasoning. But if the killers got away this time we wouldn't know anything about the kind of vehicle they were riding in except that it was brown. We asked the postman if the car he had seen was a convertible and he said no but he didn't know the make or model. He gave us the street and number of the house where he had spotted our suspect, and Cyrus and I went to check it out.

It was a modest two-story white frame house with blue trim, in a pleasant, innocent-looking neighborhood. Knowing what kind of firepower the suspects had employed, we didn't want to do anything to alarm them. We drove by once, waited a few minutes, then drove by yet again and kept going.

"Brown car's still behind the house," Cyrus said. "Looks like a Chevy or a Pontiac, maybe a LeMans -- all I saw was the hood, couldn't make out the insignia."

I said, "If it's their only car, they're probably all inside the house. But who knows for how long. If we let them out of our sight they might be long gone before we can get some backup. "

"And they're not gonna head for Mississippi," Cyrus said, "because they know we've ID'd one of them. Probably the only reason they're still here is they have to figure out where they might be able to go that'd be safe. They're probably all shook up. They gotta realize that we know who one of them is and it won't be long before we ID all of them."

"There are some woods behind the house," I said. "Maybe we could sneak close enough to the car to get the exact make and the license plate number. That way if we lose them we'll at least have something to go on."

"Yeah," Cyrus agreed. "Before we do that we can give the AIC a heads up and ask him to assemble an assault squad and send them out here ASAP."

It took two hours to scramble sixteen members of our team and get them deployed in the woods. They landed a mile away by helicopter, making an approach that didn't necessitate circling anywhere near the robbers' hideout. Then they had to get to us on foot, in some places using machetes to cut through weeds and bramble.

We surrounded the house, all of us wearing Kevlar vests and armed with assault rifles. Once our operation got into full swing, four members of our team would position themselves to head off civilian traffic into the area, both vehicular and pedestrian.

This was a dense housing area and our greatest fear was to cause innocent men, women, and children to get hurt or to be taken hostage. The time of day helped us a bit. It wasn't three o'clock yet and kids five and older were still in school. I had a megaphone and once we moved in close enough, taking cover wherever we could -- behind trees, behind the posts of a picnic shelter, behind overturned benches, et cetera -- I clicked a button and my voice boomed out. "This is the FBI. You are surrounded. Your situation is hopeless. We order you to come out with your hands up!"

There were long moments of silence during which I could hear my speeding pulse pounding in my ears. My mouth was bone dry and I was perspiring heavily. I looked toward Cyrus and saw him edge forward and station himself behind the fugitives' brown car. Earlier when we had sneaked in from the perimeter of the woods, we had confirmed that it was a Pontiac LeMans.

Suddenly all hell broke loose.

Window panes shattered, gun barrels poked through, and we were hit with a terrific fusillade. I dropped the megaphone and peeked out from behind a tree to see if any of our guys got hit -- but I couldn't tell for sure. I opened up with my assault rifle. Our entire team went into attack mode just as we were trained to do. We started shooting the house to splinters. And at the same time two of our guys with grenade launchers fired teargas grenades through the shattered windows.

The shooting from inside the house subsided to a sputter, then stopped. We could hear muffled coughing and gagging, then the back door flew open and the four killers came out in body armor, wielding M-16's and Uzis, panning their weapons back and forth in what was intended to be a lethal blanket of bullets.

But it was a de facto suicide assault. They couldn't hope to make it to the LeMans -- maybe they thought they might make it into the surrounding woods -- but they didn't stand a chance. We had them drastically outnumbered and our weapons were comparable to theirs, we weren't outgunned the way the Belmont police and the state troopers had been.

The hellish firefight felt like it lasted a half-hour but in reality it was over in less than five minutes. There were more of us than there were of them, so we riddled them. We fired high and we fired low, hitting them where they had no protection from bulletproof vests. They all went down. Only one of them succeeded in penetrating our encirclement -- he got halfway to the woods before he was hit. He flung his rifle aside and sprawled down hard. I saw him screaming and writhing in a patch of weeds. I didn't want him to be finished off, so I picked up the megaphone and yelled, "Hold your fire! Hold your fire!"

Scanning our perimeter, I saw that three of our men had also been shot. Two of them weren't moving, half their skulls blown away. The third man had a thigh wound but it didn't look to be arterial; he was lying back groaning while another of our team members was starting to administer first aid.

We still had to clear the house. We couldn't take it for granted that nobody else was in there. But before we collected ourselves to do that, I told one of our men to subdue the fugitive who had been shot in the legs and get him medical attention.

"I know you'd like to put him out of his misery," I said, "but don't do it. Don't go too close either, till you make sure he can't reach for his weapon. We need to interrogate him. It's a good break for us that he's still alive."

Cyrus and I crept toward the house with two of our team members. We didn't want to fill the place up with more agents than that because it would increase the danger of a friendly fire accident -- one of us getting shot by another of us as we bumped into each other rounding a corner. We exercised utmost caution and we knew the drill, so in a few minutes the house seemed to be cleared from basement to attic. The four of us met up back in the living room where we had first entered, and we yelled, "All clear, all clear," to the men outside.

Cyrus said, "I saw the sacks of money in an upstairs bedroom all by their lonesome. I'll go up and retrieve them."

I nodded and he climbed the stairs.

We heard his footsteps on the landing -- then a powerful explosion rocked the house.

When we recovered our senses and dared to go upstairs, we found the staircase full of acrid smoke, and when we reached the landing we saw Cyrus's body sprawled there, torn to shreds by a booby-trap. I stepped backwards, stumbled and almost fell backwards down the steps. My eyes were blinded by smoke and tears. I wiped my hand across my face and tried to pull myself together. One of the agents who had gone up there with me put his arm around my shoulders to steady me. We stared at the god-awful devastation and tried to think analytically.

The bomb obviously had been rigged to go off if anyone tried to enter the bedroom where the money was kept without knowing how to disarm it. Part of a wall was blown open, revealing gaping ductwork -- the bomb had been hidden inside a furnace vent. The force of the blast was thereby contained in such a way that none of the money bags on the bed got any damage. All of the damage had been done to Cyrus. We saw bent and half-melted nails, screws and bolts all mixed up with bone fragments and chunks of flesh soaking in pools of blood. There were hundreds of puncture wounds not only in Cyrus's body but in the blood-splattered walls and ceiling. Jagged fragments of galvanized pipe were lying in the hall, which told us that the explosive device had been a pipe bomb packed with shrapnel consisting of ordinary metal items that could be bought in any hardware store.

Simple but extremely lethal.

Welcome to the modern terroristic world.

CHAPTER 22

Ambulances arrived, and the FBI agent who was shot in the thigh was taken to a hospital and successfully treated. The bodies of the three dead agents were taken to a morgue. I kept thinking about the mutilated body of Cyrus Lumley inside one of the body bags. Thinking about it depressed and angered me but it made me want to go on, to avenge him.

Albert Crane was the fugitive who had gone down wounded in a hail of bullets in the backyard of the safe house. Before he was lifted into an ambulance he gave us his name and we confirmed it by fishing a Mississippi driver's license out of his blood-soaked hip pocket. He gave up the names of his three accomplices. Cletis Barrett was dead and so were the Stoddard brothers, Horace and Herschel. Good riddance to bad rubbish.

From the "safe house" that had turned out not to be so safe for them, we confiscated four M-16 rifles, four 9mm Berettas, four Uzis and a cache of gunpowder, wire, batteries, timers and other bomb-making paraphernalia. It appalled me that this kind of firepower could be appropriated by the most vicious of criminals, and I wanted to find out where it all came from and shut the places down if at all possible.

I interrogated Albert Crane in a hospital room where he lay all bandaged up and pumped full of pain killers. His legs were so badly shot up that they had to be amputated. He also had a shattered right hip that was repaired with screws and a steel plate at taxpayers' expense.

His court appointed attorney was present for the interrogation and so was the federal prosecutor. The attorney tried some mealy-mouthed talk about a plea bargain which showed how young and inexperienced he was because a life sentence was obligatory in these kinds of cases. The United States Supreme Court had recently ruled the death penalty unconstitutional and the New York legislature was scrambling for ways to get around the ruling, but in the meantime Albert Crane was going to slip through the cracks, which totally disgusted me.

The defense attorney said, "Have some pity, Mr. Crane can't go to jail. He's in no condition. "

"I don't care," I told him. "He put himself in the condition he's in. He has only himself to blame. "

"As soon as your client is well enough to be taken from this hospital," the prosecutor said, "he's going to prison to await trial. No bail will be granted and the trial could be months away. I don't give a damn if he rots in his cell or takes a shiv in his back. Some of the other inmates will despise him as much as we do and we can all picture the things they'll probably do to him of an indecent sexual nature. Maybe I can see that he isn't put in the worst kind of hell-hole if he spills everything he knows without lying to us and wasting our time."

Crane was so frightened over how helpless a man with no legs would be among a bunch of vicious sex-starved convicts that the possibility of being held in protective custody caused him to cave. He agreed to be cooperative and this made my interrogation go easier but it still didn't mean he was always telling me the complete truth.

I started out by asking him where he and his accomplices had gotten the arsenal that we had confiscated. I pretended to be impressed by their ability to pull this off, in hopes that he'd start bragging.

"Gun shows," he said proudly, "in Virginia and North Carolina. We coulda got even bigger stuff. Coulda got a mortar and a .90 caliber machine gun." He smirked at me in spite of his pain. "Feller at one of them shows was sellin' damn near every kinda weapon the U.S. Army has. Russian army too."

"How about the bomb-making stuff?"

"That's simple to do. Just pipes, wires and batteries. Gunpowder can be bought or made. You can make it from potassium nitrate mixed with carbon or even sugar -- or you can just empty a pile of cartridges, which is a pain in the ass."

"Did you make the bomb that killed my partner?"

His eyes darted nervously. "Naw, I ain't no bomb maker, but I watched it being done, that's why I basically know how."

He said the Stoddard brothers had rigged the bomb, not him, but that didn't make me hate him any less. I was still reeling over Cyrus's horrible death and wanted to strangle Crane with my bare hands. But I had to stifle my rage. I had to be a good listener. Criminals often can't resist trying to impress others with their exploits, even when it would serve them better to keep their mouths shut. So I let him talk. His attorney tried to stop him but he was too dumb to heed good advice. He boasted that he and his pals didn't intend to stop with the armored truck robbery.

"Small potatoes," he said. "Just a setup fer somethin' a lot bigger." He actually winked at me.

"What was this big step going to be?" I asked him.

"We's gonna kidnap that rich bitch singer's thirteen-year-old daughter."

"What rich bitch?"

"Lefty Lori McCoy. You done heard of her, everyone has."

He had caught me totally off guard with this, and I hoped it didn't show on my face.

"We wasn't gonna hurt the little girl," Albert Crane said defensively, as if he would never sink that low. "We was just gonna hold her for ransom."

Calmly I said, "If your escape from the strip mall in Belmont had come off without a hitch, the four of you would've gotten away with more than three million dollars. Why wouldn't that have been plenty enough for you?"

"Guess we was greedy, wanted more. We wasn't sure how much we'd get from the armored truck neither. We thought mebbe more checks than cash. It was s'posed to bankroll us so's we could get set up to snatch the girl. We figgered that's where we'd make the biggest score."

"Who else helped you plan it all?"

"Nobody. We didn't want nobody else. We didn't care to split up the money more 'n four ways."

"Why'd you pick Lori McCoy?"

He hesitated, licked his lips. "No special reason ... other 'n her bein' rich and famous."

"You're lying, Albert."

"Naw. I know if I lie to you I'll be ... uh ... I'll ... be screwed. "

"Screwed good," I agreed. "And we both know what kind of screwing we're talking about. You know, Albert, we once got a timid little banker sent up on federal embezzlement charges, and his big black cellmate used him as his little white bitch. How you feel about going homo, Albert? I can make sure you find just the *right* cell mate?"

Crane went totally wide-eyed, a trembly look on his face. "Look ... please ... I'm tellin' you the god's truth," he whined at me.

"I don't believe you," I said flatly.

"I don't believe you either, Albert," the federal prosecutor said. "And if I think you're lying our deal is off."

"You've got to tell the truth, Albert," his attorney told him. "This is your best chance to help yourself."

118

He squirmed and perspired, his face pale and drawn, the stumps of his legs outlined under the white sheet. I thought about taking hold of one of those stumps and squeezing it till he told me everything he knew. Of course he might still lie, but at least he would suffer. Sometimes when I was faced with the worst kinds of scumbags it almost seemed a shame that our society didn't condone torture.

"Albert," I said, "you zeroed in on Lori McCoy for some special reason and I want to know what it is."

"Didn't like her music or her politics, that's all. And it had to be somebody who had a lot or money and a kid we could kidnap. To boot, she's a nigger lover and a traitor, so we figgered we'd give her what she had comin'."

His eyes darted from me to the prosecutor to the defense attorney as if maybe one or two of us might secretly approve of giving a "nigger lover and traitor" her just desserts.

Certain things were starting to come together in my mind, or at least I thought they were. I wanted to find out if they were mere hunches or real insights, so I started pursuing a different line of questioning. "Albert, tell me, what gave you fellows the idea to use a phony police car? That was a damn clever way to get the jump on the guards."

He gave me a smug little smile. "Just 'cause we ain't perfessors with alphabet soup after our names don't mean we ain't purty damn smart in our own way. We done some research and found out that some of this singer gal's nigger friends was kilt a ways back after they was stopped by some cops down where we's from. We figgered they mighta been phony cops 'stead of real cops and that's what give us the idea."

"Well, isn't it just a hell of a coincidence," I suddenly barked at him, "that you and your asshole buddies come up here from around Oxford, Mississippi, where rednecks of your ilk pulled off some murders a decade ago, and two of the rednecks were cops, or, as you say, phony cops, and they tried to kill Lori McCoy and her little girl back then, and now you four assholes use the same M.O. to rob an armored truck and come after Lori and her daughter just as if you're trying to take up where those other four assholes left off."

"Helluva bunch of coincidences," Crane said shakily. "But that's all they is, just coincidences."

"Bullshit! I don't believe in coincidences, Albert. Not in my line of work. I think we're dealing with two cases and four rednecks, not two cases and eight rednecks, and if you don't start leveling with me I'll make sure you get put in the kind of prison where somebody will tie what's left

119

of you to the bars of a cell with your naked ass waist high to all the white guys and the black guys with both their legs so they can screw you standing straight up."

"Look," he said pleadingly, "the kidnappin' part was gonna be called off. After we seen how much we got from the armored truck we didn't wanna take no more risks, didn't feel like we needed to. Cost of livin' in Mississippi is dirt cheap. We was all gonna live down there like millionaires with niggers waitin' on us hand and foot and callin' us boss and massa like they oughta still be doin' if'n you Yankees never come down and set 'em free. "

"You disgust me," I told him, eyeing him with undisguised contempt.

"Wait till one of 'em marries your daughter or rapes your wife," he said. "Then you'll change your tune. You oughta be stickin' up for your own race before it's too late."

Shaking my head, I turned toward the prosecutor and said, "Let's get out of here. I can't stand to look at him any more today. I need a breath of fresh air. "I wanted everything we had said to Crane, especially the threat of putting him in with the general prison population, to prey on his mind for a day or so. Then maybe he'd tell me fewer lies when I came back to pry more information out of him.

But I never got the chance. He got a staph infection from his wounds and died a few days later without ever leaving the hospital.

CHAPTER 23

I went to see Lori at her lovely Fifth Avenue apartment, and brought with me enlarged photos of Albert Crane, Cletis Barrett and the Stoddard brothers. The uniformed doorman greeted me. I told him who I was and showed him my badge and he dialed a number so somebody up there would let me in when I stepped off the elevator.

Charlie Guinard opened the apartment door for me. He and Arlene Shoaf were with Lori, and whatever the three of them had been talking about before I arrived seemed to have put them in a sour mood. I didn't think it had anything to do with me because I hadn't told Lori the precise purpose for my visit.

"Is everything okay?" I asked. "How's Missy?" She gave me a hug, then sat down, looking stressed.

"Oh, she's doing great," Lori said. "Taking guitar lessons. That's where she is now. All of a sudden she's decided she wants to be a singer and song writer, like her mother. I don't know whether to be flattered or upset. It's a hard life if you don't manage to succeed in a large enough way."

"We're glad to see you," Charlie said, shaking my hand, "but we're very sorry about what happened to your partner."

"You have my condolences," Arlene added. She gave me neither a hug nor a handshake but remained seated on a black leather sofa at the opposite end from Lori.

Charlie sat down between them, and they all eyed the manila envelope I was holding.

"Please, Frank, have a seat," Lori said. "You're in such a dangerous line of work. I worry about you all the time. I wish you had become a writer. That's what I thought you always wanted."

"Maybe I'll get back into it someday," I said. I sat in a black leather armchair but didn't relax. I didn't know how Lori was going to react to the photos in the envelope; if she was truly able to recognize any of the four men, perhaps she'd have panicky flashbacks.

"Maybe one writer in the family is enough." Charlie said, referring to my wife Alice who was a freelance journalist.

"I liked her *Cosmo* article," Lori said. "For once I didn't feel maligned or misquoted."

"Thanks, I'll tell her," I said. "But I guess she already knows. She told me you sent her a nice note."

"Can I get you something?" Arlene interjected. "Soda? Something stronger?"

"No, thanks. I seldom drink alcohol when I'm on the job, and I'm afraid with what happened to Cyrus if I got started I'd have a hard time stopping. The funeral was Friday and I did get a little blitzed at the wake."

"I don't blame you," Lori said.

Charlie got up and said, "I'm having coffee, it's done brewing, I can smell it. Want some?"

"Thanks but I'm coffeed out. Had at least four cups this morning at the office."

"Made from fresh-ground beans," Lori coaxed. "Imported from Colombia. Umm, doesn't it smell good?"

"Well, I guess you talked me into it."

"Sit down, Charlie," Arlene said. "I'll do the honors."

She got up and went toward the kitchen, her high heels making little indentations in the plush white carpet.

The chit-chat was almost over. I could see they were all curious and a bit worried about why I had come here. I hadn't seen any of them since we all went to dinner together about six months ago when Alice finished writing the *Cosmo* article.

I still couldn't get over how debonair looking Charlie was these days, a complete turnaround from the scruffy behemoth I remembered from college. He was wearing a red silk shirt with puffy sleeves and tight cuffs, black trousers and black patent leather shoes. There were several bejewelled rings on his fingers, and at his much thinner but still not flat waist was an ornate gold-and-silver buckle. His beard, which used to be so wild and woolly, was now down to a neatly trimmed dark brown goatee flecked with gray.

When I took note of the gray, it reminded me that we were all growing older. I was thirty-six now and my wife had called my attention recently to the fact that I had developed a bald spot at the crown of my head. I hadn't wanted to believe her, but it was there; I saw it reflected from the bathroom mirror to a hand mirror, and it was a sobering sight. I never considered myself a particularly vain person but I hoped I wasn't going to lose much more of my hair.

Arlene came back bearing a tray holding a silver coffee service. She set it on a glass-topped table, distributed dainty cups and saucers, and we leaned in to help ourselves to cream and sugar while she poured. She still looked a lot like Lori but her hair was up and she wore a slinky green pant suit with a touch of jewelry, looking every bit the urban sophisticate, her humble past seemingly far behind her.

As ever, Lori was a nearly perfect representation of simple homespun beauty. In tight jeans and a pale blue blouse, she was curled up on the leather couch, her long legs tucked under her. I momentarily flashed back to the days when I used to secretly lust after her while we were studying for exams.

After a sip or two of my coffee, I set the cup and saucer on the table and said, "Well, there's no use beating around the bush. I have some mug shots that I'd like Lori to take a look at. We have reason to believe that the four men who robbed the armored truck in Belmont might be the same four who committed the murders in Mississippi eleven years ago. I hope to God it *is* them. They're all dead. They can't hurt anyone anymore."

While I was talking, Lori tensed up, her eyes widening with apprehension, and Charlie comfortingly put his arm around her. It was my first indication that their relationship must have evolved beyond a lawyer to client arrangement and an old friendship built on a commitment to social issues.

Charlie said, "What Frank said is true, honey. Let's hope you can identify them. It'll bring closure."

I moved the coffee tray aside and laid the four photos out on the glass-topped table. Charlie held Lori's hand while she leaned forward to look. She trembled and sucked in her breath, covering her face with her hands. Then she slowly pulled her hands away and looked again.

"I think it's them," she said, pale and shaky. "The only close look I got was when I was desperately trying to get away, trying to run them down in that old Plymouth. It all happened so fast, and it was close to eleven years ago, but I still see them in my nightmares. I thought at the time I possibly could have picked them out of a line-up. But they were never caught and no line-up ever happened."

"How about now?" I asked gently.

She said, "If the men in these photos were still alive and they were lined up in front of me with a dozen other men who looked similar, I don't know if I could pick them out. But at my first cold glance at their images a déjà vu thing hit me, a chill went up my spine. Maybe it's more

123

of a gut feeling than anything else, but I think it's them. I'd bet on it if I had to. "

"Yeah, I would too," I said. "I know some other facts that fit right in, that's why I came here. I won't go into details till I know more though, then I'll fill you in. I'm going to dig up as much background information as I can about these guys, and I'm pretty sure that we'll end up satisfying ourselves that a belated, roundabout form of justice has taken place at long last."

"Maybe your nightmares will stop now, honey," Charlie said to Lori, once again taking her hand in his. He noticed me observing this and said, "We're getting married in July, Frank, and you and Alice are going to be invited."

"Well, congratulations," I said, smiling. "I had no idea that Cupid had struck you two. Are you still going to live in New York?"

"Yeah, I'm giving up my place," Charlie said. "Putting it on the market. Lori and I will both stay here. We both love this place."

"I'm moving out," Arlene said. "Maylon is already gone. We had to fire him. We didn't want to do it but …"

"That's what we were discussing just before you got here," Lori told me. "I feel awful about it. I tried so hard to help him, but nothing worked. My own brother! I didn't want to ask him to leave. My mom and dad are probably gonna jump on me about it. But he's completely changed ever since he came back from Vietnam. "

"The war really messed him up," Arlene said. "He killed people over there and saw some of his buddies get killed. But he's gotta pull himself together, and he's not going to do it so long as we keep bailing him out. "

"He's done some good things," Charlie put in. "We've been keeping him in the loop. We've had him marching with Vietnam Veterans for Peace."

"Maylon's been in therapy off and on," Arlene continued, "but he always relapses. One of his psychologists told us we're enablers -- we're always there to support him and give him a roof over his head, so he doesn't have enough incentive to pull himself up by his bootstraps. "

"He had desperate hopes while he was in the war that he'd be able to come back and play lead guitar in my band," Lori said. "But he's not good enough, that's the unfortunate truth. Arlene and I had to try to let him down easy, but he took it hard. He used to accompany me sometimes when we were in our teens, but the musicians I work with now are on a whole different level, and I need them to be. We gave

Maylon the best job we could, supervising the roadies and the concert setups, but he said we turned him into a flunkie. "

"What about his wife and his little boy?" I asked. "Where are they?"

"Roseanne already left him and took little Delbert with her," Charlie told me. "They disappeared one day, didn't tell anybody where they were going. Maylon said they must've gone back to West Virginia, maybe to stay with his in-laws. But he didn't chase after them like I thought he would -- he just got drunk and wallowed in self-pity. "

"He has what they used to call combat fatigue," Arlene said. "He shouldn't drink at all. He has crazy fits, flips out and thinks he sees Viet Cong all around him. One night I heard Roseanne screaming -- she woke up and Maylon was trying to choke her. He didn't even know who she was, he was in some kind of wild trance."

"I had to sit up with him half the night and keep an eye on him and try to get him calmed down," Charlie said. "And it wasn't easy, it was touch and go -- I was afraid he was going to turn on me."

"Somehow he's even scarier than Truman was," Arlene said. "Truman was a mean drunk but he knew exactly what he was doing, just didn't have sense enough not to do it. He thought he could control the world with his fists."

I nodded in agreement. My memories of Truman weren't exactly jolly ones. He would've beaten me senseless that day at the McCoy farm if Lori's father hadn't hit him over the head with a shovel.

"Maybe if Maylon comes back or gets in touch, I could try talking to him," I offered. "I like him even though I've only been with him a few times. He's intelligent and basically he has a good heart. "

"He's my brother and I'll always love him," Lori said despairingly. "I just don't know how to handle him anymore. If you could help him, Frank, that'd be great. Maybe he'll listen to you more than he'll listen to his own family."

"It works that way sometimes," Charlie said.

I said I'd be willing to give it a shot, but I couldn't promise any miracles.

"We know, we know," Lori said with a sigh.

As I left her apartment I wondered if I was correct in not telling her yet about the kidnap plot. Luckily it wasn't going to take place now. I thought about Missy taking guitar lessons, attending school, doing any number of things that the would-be abductors would have been tracking if they had survived to carry out their sick plans. I knew that a couple of bodyguards were a part of Lori's entourage, but that still didn't necessarily mean that she and her family were as well protected as they possibly could be. I wanted to ask her some questions about that and make some suggestions. But I decided to wait a few days so she wouldn't connect my comments to this particular visit. I didn't want to shake her up any more than I had to. The immediate danger was over. But it was a treacherous world out there, and if the bad guys were of a mind to hurt you, sooner or later they would get you no matter how safe you tried to make yourself.

My wife always had a lot of trouble living with the fact that my job was often very dangerous, and going to Cyrus's funeral and seeing how his death affected his wife and children didn't make it any easier for her. Over lunch on our last day together, I had not told Cyrus that my thoughts about leaving the FBI were partly motivated by a desire to save my marriage; I had mentioned only the pressure that was being put on me to contribute to dossiers on some of my closest friends.

I was reluctant to tell anyone that my marriage was on the rocks, as if saying it out loud would make it a fait accompli. When Alice's name had come up at Lori's apartment I had blithely carried on with the conversation, pretending everything was okay between us, probably because I still found it hard to admit how much our relationship had deteriorated. And it had started out so rich and promising.

I first met Alice Kenton in an Irish pub of her choosing, near Times Square, after she had phoned the FBI office to set up an interview for an article she was writing about our Anti-Terrorist Task Force. I was surprised by how attractive she was, not stunningly beautiful, but slim and perky with good legs, shoulder-length brown hair and alert, inquisitive green eyes. We ordered Guinnesses and she started asking questions and taking notes. After a while she looked up at me and said, "You talk like a writer, I can feel you composing your sentences."

"Trying to give you good quotes," I said. "And trying not to make myself sound stupid."

We both laughed.

I told her I had wanted to be a writer before I became an FBI agent, and when she asked how I had gotten sidetracked in such a strange way, I ended up telling her how I had been motivated by the murders of four of my friends.

"Hate crimes disgust me," she said. "That's why I'm writing this article. It's a shame you got pushed into a career you maybe didn't really want."

"Oh, I ended up wanting it. And I think I'm actually doing some good in the world. Like they say, 'Life is what happens while you're making other plans.'"

She fell silent for a while, then said, "Maybe you'll get back to your writing someday."

"I didn't stick with it long enough to find out if I'm any good."

"Sticking with it is what makes you get good," she said. "Assuming you have talent to begin with."

She shut her notebook and put her pen in her purse.

"The interview's over already?" I said. "I didn't think I gave you enough material."

"You didn't," she said. "Can we get together again, maybe tomorrow?"

"Sure. I've enjoyed talking with you. "

She smiled and said, "Let's have another Guinness."

I lifted my mug, signaling the waiter.

Alice and I started talking earnestly and revealingly about ourselves. Our conversation was intense and absorbing. I had never before opened up to anyone so easily, so quickly. A couple of hours sped by, and the waiter had to come and tell us the bar was closing. I walked her to the subway station and saw her safely on board. I couldn't wait to see her again, and was glad she had said that the interview wasn't over.

Alice and I were married on July 12, 1969. I was almost thirty years old and she was twenty-five. It was a small wedding, about twenty guests. A magistrate performed the ceremony at a lakeside restaurant in Old Bridge, New Jersey, where Alice grew up and where her father and mother still lived. Her parents paid for the celebratory meal, and I paid for the booze.

Outside of a couple of her aunts and uncles, most of the guests were friends and associates of ours from New York City, including Keith, Lori, Arlene, and Charlie. I had no family members to invite.

The only arrangement I made for the honeymoon was to buy two one-way plane tickets to Boston. When we got there we'd rent a car and head for Martha's Vineyard, a place I had always wanted to see after a lieutenant at Fort Bragg had raved about it. From there we'd go wherever we wanted to, on whim, renting cars and buying plane tickets as needed. Alice loved the flamboyancy of it, the lack of a specific itinerary. We were both endowed with a spirit of adventure and we believed in serendipity.

Serendipity was what we got, in spades.

From Boston we drove to Falmouth where an ocean-going ferry took us to Edgartown on the island of Martha's Vineyard. We were blindly lucky because this was a Thursday and we got there ahead of the massive influx of weekenders, which we hadn't even considered. There was one room available at a charmingly quaint seaside inn. When we walked down to the beach to go swimming, we passed horses grazing in tall grass. The beach had a picturesque jetty and lighthouse, and some years later we amusedly recognized this gorgeous setting when we went to see the movie, *Jaws* -- it was used for the scene of bathers stampeding and trampling each other to get away from an imagined sighting of a huge, vicious shark.

With Alice I realized that although I had made love with other women, particularly during my football-playing days, I had never really been in love until now. We did what most people do on their honeymoons; we made love as often as possible. We also swam and bicycled and wined and dined in excellent restaurants. The weather remained sunny with beautiful blue skies, and the ocean breezes were delightfully refreshing and invigorating.

The Montreal World's Fair was happening, and we decided we wanted to go there before the weekend crowds poured into Edgartown. This would necessitate taking the ferry back to Falmouth and then driving north. We left on a Saturday, and afterwards we found out that Ted Kennedy's car had gone off the bridge at Chappaquiddick on that very day and that Mary Jo Kopechne was drowned. The other thing that had resonance for us was that the inn we had stayed in was only a block from the Kennedy compound and we used to pass by it when we walked to some of the nearby restaurants.

Since we were headed back toward Boston, I decided to call Jerry Patterson, a former guard on our Belmont football squad who was now working as a flight engineer for Transworld Airlines. He was glad to hear from me -- and very surprised when I told him that my wife and I were heading to the World's Fair.

"Cripes! We're going there, too!" he exclaimed. "Me and the wife and kids. We're leaving tomorrow morning. Why don't you come and stay here overnight, and we'll all go together, I mean in separate cars, but we can follow each other."

I got lucky again and was able to make a room reservation at the Queen Elizabeth Hilton. Jerry's wife had already reserved a hard-to-get table at the oldest French restaurant in Montreal, a magnet for tourists, where we enjoyed a marvelous meal of wine and chateau briand -- we wouldn't have been able to eat at that charming little place if we didn't go with the Pattersons because, as I said, I made no such arrangements in advance. We spent a day at the Fair, mainly to entertain the two kids, and we toured the government buildings and the British colonial log fort in Old Quebec.

When Jerry and his family drove home to Boston, Alice and I headed to Provincetown, another place I had wanted to see ever since I learned of its status as an artists' colony back when I was reading a lot of Jack Kerouac. We happened to get there on the very day that the first man landed on the moon. Horns and sirens were blasting and confetti was raining down onto our rented car, as if we were the recipients of a massive community welcome. Even after it dawned on us what the celebration was really all about, it struck us as yet another of the timely events that seemed to make our honeymoon magical.

But that kind of magic can't last forever.

Living together on a permanent basis requires many adjustments, some easy and some jarring. But most couples don't have to contend with long separations fraught with danger. Alice was adventurous but not masochistic. She wanted our home life to be calming and peaceful. I did too. But I couldn't have it that way and still do my job.

And I wasn't ready to leave the job yet. I suppose I was still addicted to the adrenaline highs. And I didn't want to give up my pursuit of the bad guys, especially my pursuit of that gang of bigoted thugs that killed my friends. They were unfinished business. Walking away from them right now would be like closing a book before the final chapter was read. I wanted to be there when they were put in a prison or a morgue.

I conceded to myself that I was nursing an obsession. But at bottom, I didn't believe that I would lose Alice over it. I thought that somehow we would work things out because we loved each other too much not to.

But I turned out to be wrong.

CHAPTER 24

A few days after showing Lori the mug shots, I went down to Mississippi. I hadn't been assigned a new partner yet, so I went by myself, authorized by the AIC. He knew what I was after and hoped I'd find it. I was going to try to uncover any and all persons or organizations who might have aided or abetted in the Belmont armored truck robbery and murders. I would also be looking for any connections between the culprits and the murders of eleven years ago.

I hooked up with a state trooper from the Oxford barracks.

His name was Al Mayfield, and he seemed to be a decent and competent law officer. His rank was lieutenant and when the first murders went down he was a sergeant and helped investigate them. He had stayed in pretty good physical condition. Right now he was in his late forties, but still solid looking, without the usual big belly of local cops everywhere. He was genuinely enthused about helping to uncover anything that might connect the dots between two murder rampages that were separated by more than a decade.

He filled me in on all that he had discovered before the first case went cold. It wasn't much. Albert Crane, Cletis Barrett, and the Stoddard brothers hadn't even come under suspicion.

"A colored preacher and his daughter were killed around that same time," Mayfield told me. "Fellow who murdered them was retarded. He set fire to their church, too. Burned it to the ground with them and himself in it. "

"I knew about that back then," I said, "and I always wondered about it."

"Well, what you might not know is that this retarded black boy that the murders were blamed on, rightly or wrongly, he was workin' at a general store that was owned by one of Crane's asshole buddies -- Pete Jones was his name. We questioned him but he had a solid alibi. We can't go and question him again now, he died of cancer a couple years ago."

"Is it true you ran out of leads, or was the investigation being intentionally hampered?"

"Somebody knew somethin', prob' ly more than just one somebody, but nobody was talkin'. We couldn't figure out who might be in on it or who was just afraid or sympathetic ... sympathetic to the killers, I mean."

"How much have things changed around here?"

"Well, this is s'posed to be the New South. But a lot of folks still act like they're livin' in the Old South. We got the Klan and we got neo-Nazis. Wish we didn't but I can't deny reality. "

"What about Barrett, Crane and the Stoddards? Any of them belong to the groups you just mentioned?"

"If they did we'll prob'ly find it out," Mayfield said.

He took me around to see the crime scenes from long ago and to interview all the known associates of Barrett, Crane, and the Stoddards. Nobody seemed to know much about them, other than unhelpful gossipy details. We were told over and over that they were loners who kept to themselves pretty much, the Stoddards on their hog farm and Barrett and Crane in their garage where they repaired heavy machinery. If they had been living secret lives all these years, they had succeeded in hiding the fact pretty well -- either that or nobody wanted to tell us about it.

When we went to their garage we saw a big For Sale sign in front, and we phoned the realtor to see if he could tell us anything of note and if he could let us inside the place so we could examine it for evidence. We waited for him in Mayfield's unmarked car, and within twenty minutes he pulled into the gravel lot.

His name was Ed Phillips. We introduced ourselves, and he took some keys from his pocket. "Lots of Nazi shit in there," he said angrily. "Not out in the open, but in a back room with no windows and a heavy steel door with a lock and hasp on it. I had to take a complete inventory for a possible Sheriff's sale, so I had my man use his bolt cutters. Shit I saw in there made my blood curdle. Flags, weapons, and uniforms -- Nazi shit and Aryan so-called Confederacy shit! That fuckin' Conrad Pryzor, he's on the radio, acts almost like a preacher except he's preachin' hate. Gives the South a bad name. He's an embarrassment for the state of Mississippi. We don't need to hear shit like that no more. We're tryin' to move out of the Dark Ages. "

"Let's go have a look inside," I said to Mayfield. "Then you can tell me where to find this bigot. What did you say his name is?"

"Conrad Pryzor," Mr. Phillips said. "Conrad fucking Pryzor."

CHAPTER 25

We went unannounced to see Conrad Pryzor at his radio station. The sight of the big red call letters, ARYN, on the front of the yellow concrete block building sickened me.

Trooper Ed Mayfield and I were let in by a gangly teenage kid in a brown and tan Aryan Confederacy uniform. I showed my badge and said, "I'm FBI and my partner here is with the Missisippi State Police. We're here to see your boss, Mr. Pryzor."

The punk kid said, "Yes, sir, he's on the air, I'll take you back there." He backed away, looking sheepish, then turned and we followed him.

We passed through a foyer where there were racks of hate pamphlets free for the taking, and then through a moderately large meeting room with folding chairs facing a podium flanked by a Nazi flag and an American flag. The walls were decorated with huge photostats, mounted and framed, of National Socialist triumphs, such as their troops parading past the Eiffel Tower or their massive rally at Nuremburg.

That anyone would take pride in this stuff was appalling. The ambiance was blatant and unimaginative, yet weird and scary. I was reminded of the fascist trappings I had seen in nonfiction books and documentary movies. Images came to mind of the bloatedly uninspired, monolithic buildings that Albert Speer had designed according to his Furher's vainglorious vision of a Thousand Year Reich.

Our young Nazi usher led us back to a small broadcasting booth where we could see Pryzor through thick glass wearing a headset and babbling into a microphone. We could also hear what he was saying over exterior speakers. I waved my badge in front of the soundproof glass, and he grimaced, mouthed a few more sentences, then pushed a button on a console. A canned speech came over the speakers in an almost seamless segue from the bigoted diatribe he had been spewing out live over the airwaves, polluting the minds of his listeners.

He took off his headset and came out of the booth. I introduced myself and Ed Mayfield. Pryzor was in blue slacks and a yellow golf shirt. He ushered us into his office where there was a portrait of him in his Aryan Confederacy uniform with a fierce scowl on his face, trying to come off like a twentieth century warrior and a born leader. But in real life he was a potbellied, baldheaded, unimposing little man who reminded me of the paper-pushing petty bureaucrats who made the trains run on time for millions of people carted to the gas chambers – and later claimed they were only following orders.

Pryzor's portrait of himself mimicked the style of the Hitler portrait that was on the wall to the right of his gray metal army-surplus desk. The wall opposite the desk was covered ceiling to floor with a huge neo-Nazi flag in black, red and blue, the banner of the Aryan Confederacy.

Pryzor sat down behind his desk while Ed and I remained standing. We had no choice because there were no other chairs. Perhaps this penny-ante führer thought that leaving his underlings standing would allow him to more easily intimidate them when he called them on the carpet. Except the floor had no carpet, just cheap linoleum in swirling gray patterns, good for hiding dirt -- which made me wryly think to myself that the real filth was behind the desk.

"Gentlemen, what can I do for you?" Pryzor said, a small smirk on his lips, intended to convey how impervious he was to our unwanted intrusion.

I didn't want any of his bullshit. I wanted to knock him off his high horse before he knew what hit him. With a cold stare I said, "You can tell us everything you know about Albert Crane, Cletis Barrett, and Horace and Herschel Stoddard. And don't try to claim you don't know who I'm talking about."

"Of course I knew them," he said. "They were four of my bravest men. I'm planning a memorial tribute for them and a two-hour eulogy to be delivered this Sunday on ARYN. They deserve to be honored for fearlessly standing behind me in my battle for the survival of the white race."

"Hmph!" Ed Mayfield snorted. "The white race doesn't need any saviors, especially your kind. What makes you think whites are so persecuted? We hold just about all the high offices and positions of power in this country."

"The whites who hold those positions are nothing but puppets!" Pryzor scoffed. "Puppets dancing on strings controlled by the international Jewish conspiracy. When we take over, we'll finish the job Hitler started."

"I didn't come here to listen to your sick rhetoric," I barked at him. "We have reason to believe that you incited Albert Crane and the other three scumbags to go up North to rob, kill and kidnap innocent people."

"Does your 'reason to believe' include proof?" Pryzor inquired snidely, and when I didn't come up with a quick answer he continued, even haughtier. "I thought as much. You don't have proof of any involvement on my part. I can't be held responsible if some of my followers get carried away in their zeal to contribute to the great *Kampf,* the great Struggle."

"The great abomination," I corrected him. "Your speeches, your filthy broadcasts, your poisonous little pamphlets, are all part of a concerted effort to instigate others to commit hate crimes. That's criminal conspiracy. I'm going to keep digging till I can put together enough evidence and enough testimony to indict you for murder."

"Good luck," he said curtly. "And good riddance until you can come back here with a warrant. In the meantime if you have anything further to say, say it to my attorney. I'll be happy to give you his name and phone number."

I stared at him coldly and said, "I'm going to bring you down, Pryzor. I'll be on your ass from now on. Albert Crane confessed that he and his cronies were planning to kidnap Lori McCoy's daughter. They're personal friends of mine. If any harm comes to either of them from this day forward, I'll hold you responsible -- with or without proof. And I'll come after you, and I won't bother with a warrant. You'll disappear from the face of the earth. Nobody will ever know what happened to you, I mean how you died and how you suffered. But I will know, and remembering how it went down will give me a great deal of satisfaction."

"You're trying to scare me," he said, "and you're not succeeding."

But I saw the perspiration on his upper lip and was satisfied that I had shaken him up about as much as I was going to be able to. "Let's go, Ed," I said, and we pivoted and left Pryzor standing there trying to look unfazed.

Out in the parking lot, Mayfield said, "Would you really torture and kill that scumbag?"

"Yeah. I think so. And I don't believe I'd lose any sleep over it."

"Well, I would," Mayfield said. "I'd know you did it, and I'd sure as hell have to come after you."

PART FOUR
CARTER

"I don't feel society needs to welcome me back. Just give me help.
If society doesn't want to help me, I want to die, because
death means the nightmare will be over. "
-- Wayne Felde, Vietnam vet

"Young intelligent Aryan people realize the extermination of
our race is at stake. Damn right we're preaching violence!
It's about time somebody is telling you to start getting violent, whitie!"
-- Conrad Pryzor

"This country has sunk into a deep malaise of the human spirit."
-- President Jimmy Carter

CHAPTER 26

Immersed in the drone of its engines, the riveted wing inched forward, slowly uncovering the land. I was seated behind the wing, looking down. Snaky black highways, brown tarpaulin fields and clumps of budding trees were miniaturized far below. I choked back the acid in my gut, chewed two chalky antacid tablets, swallowing them without water, and hoped the FBI Cessna would get me where I needed to be, and on time, before people started to die.

Maylon McCoy was holed up in a bank in Cherry Hill, West Virginia. He had taken hostages, hometown folks whom he had probably known his whole life. After sixteen hours of standoff, he told the negotiator that he wouldn't talk anymore to anybody except me. And if I didn't get there by five p.m., he'd start shooting one person every fifteen minutes.

An hour ago the lead negotiator had put Lori McCoy on the phone with me. She was in Cherry Hill with Charlie, Arlene, and Missy to celebrate her mother's birthday. It was Mama McCoy's first birthday without her husband. Last winter she had found Tillman lying dead in the barn, sprawled halfway into the stall occupied by Jed, the mean old plow horse. Cause of death was a skull fracture. It looked as though Jed must have snorted and bobbed his angry head at Tillman, cracking him in his forehead while he was trying to attach the horse's feed bag. Perhaps it was done out of malice; who could know the mind of a horse?

My wife Alice and I had gone down there for Tillman's funeral and now I was going back to try to save Tillman's son.

"Please, Frank, he's asking for you," Lori had pleaded on the phone. "We invited him to Mama's birthday dinner, but he didn't come. And now he's gone off the deep end. We have to be able to tell him you're on your way or else he's going to do a lot worse than he's already done."

"Try not to panic," I told her. "You may yet be of help. I'll do my best to get there. In most cases, those kinds of threats don't really get carried out."

There weren't any statistics to support what I had just said. I was trying to ease her mind and give her hope, but the truth was that I had little faith in the capacity of human beings to behave rationally. I had seen too much of the other kind of behavior.

Today was Wednesday, April 14, 1977. Grisly highlights of the past decade included the Martin Luther King Assassination, the Watts Riots, the Charles Whitman sniper killings, the assassination of Robert F. Kennedy, the Kent State Massacre, the Mi Lai Massacre and the Manson Family Murders. Evidence kept on piling up for what I had come to believe: that the country had gone nuts and had gotten nuttier and nuttier ever since the assassination of John F. Kennedy.

Maylon McCoy wouldn't be freaking out if he hadn't had his mind screwed up in Vietnam. And he probably never would have been sent there if President Johnson hadn't kept asking for more and more troops, in a vain effort to end up with something that could be labeled a victory.

Maylon was 31 years old now, and his life was a mess. He had come home suffering from post-traumatic stress syndrome and probably Agent Orange poisoning. He had been in an artillery company responsible for taking ammunition to troops in the jungle, and almost every day he had to drive truckloads of ammo through Agent Orange-drenched territory, inhaling its tarry fumes and the dust from dead and crumbling bushes and trees.

The last time I saw him, at his father's funeral, he looked emaciated. He stayed apart from his two sisters and talked to me in a corner. He told me he was getting painful oozing rashes on his arms and legs and the VA doctors didn't know why. "I know what it is," he said sadly. "It's that stuff they used to spray. I used to cheer when I saw our planes sprayin' the jungles and rice paddies, killin' the foliage so the slopes wouldn't have so many places to hide. I figured anything bad for the Viet Cong had to be good for me. But I started not bein' able to breathe so good, and when I got my discharge physical I didn't dare tell nobody. I wanted to go home, not into an Army hospital."

Over a year had gone by since he quit the job Lori had given him, and I asked him where he was working now. "Nowhere, 'cept they gimme a little part-time stuff at the saw mill," he said ashamedly. "I get shaky and they don't want me on the machinery. I oil it and clean it and sweep up, that's all they trust me to do."

Looking at him, I felt sad. Alice came over and put her arm around me and I thought how lucky I was not to have had to go to Vietnam. Maylon's marriage had busted up and he had lost custody of his son. Roseannne had a protection order against him, and there was little doubt that she needed it. At the funeral he seemed calm, but I knew he was a walking time bomb, especially when he was stoned or boozed up. He was probably stoned or blitzed out on pills when he tried to pull off a bank robbery and bungled it. Now he was threatening to kill a bunch of innocent people. And there was a good chance he'd follow through on the threat.

If the Cessna got me there on time, I had to try to talk him out of it. I wasn't a well-trained hostage negotiator. It wasn't my specialty. I didn't know why Maylon wanted to talk to me instead of his own kin. Maybe it was because he viewed me as friend as well as an authority figure; maybe he thought that since I was FBI I could get him some special favors if he surrendered to me. Years ago on the day we had our wild and woolly fight with Truman Shoaf, Maylon had told me that he was thinking about joining the infantry and volunteering for Vietnam, and I had tried to talk him out of it. Maybe he wished he had listened to me. Maybe he was ready to listen to me now.

The Cessna landed at a small airport in Charleston where three patrol cars manned by state troopers were lined up waiting for me on the tarmac. I got into the backseat of one of the cars and we were escorted by the two others, one ahead of us and one behind us, as we raced toward Cherry Hill with our turret lights flashing and sirens screaming, at speeds in excess of ninety miles per hour.

We got to the center of town at twenty-three minutes to five, and the troopers cleared our way through a thick, noisy crowd of gawkers, cameramen and reporters -- a media circus amplified and made worse by the fame of Lori McCoy -- and we had to plow through it to let the lead negotiator know I was finally here so he could tell it to Maylon and stop him from selecting somebody to kill.

I caught a glimpse of Lori standing on the stoop of a hardware store, well back from the yellow crime scene tape. She was huddled there with her family. She and her mother were hanging onto each other and Charlie had his big arms around them. Arlene and Missy were holding hands. Maylon's ex-wife Roseanne was standing off to one side with her little boy, Delbert, whose face was buried in her skirt.

The command post was set up in a clothing store opposite the bank, behind a barricade manned by local police officers. The hotel where Keith and I had shared a room over a decade ago was down the street in the same block. A wide area was cordoned off with crime scene tape, and armed cops and SWAT team snipers were stationed in strategic positions, alert for anything that might all of a sudden happen.

The lead negotiator, Special Agent Joe Flaherty, was glad I had made it on time. He immediately dialed the bank's business number and got Maylon on the phone. After a brief conversation Flaherty turned to me and said, "He's going to let you come in. He wants to talk with you face to face. It's your decision. I'm sure you're aware of the risks. "

I nodded and said I'd go in. There was some discussion about whether I should wear a wire or a hidden weapon of some sort, but I decided to go in unarmed. If I tried to be tricky, it might set Maylon off. I had to get him to trust me. It was the only way to finesse the situation. I tried to steel myself for the confrontation and hoped I would be able to say the right things.

Maylon made one of the hostages, a girl about twelve years old, open the front door of the bank while he stayed back and held his gun on her. I stepped inside and he called out, "Run honey, you're free!" The little girl took off and the door went shut and automatically locked itself. Maylon motioned me forward and I saw that his weapon was a .32 revolver that looked old, its bluing worn patchy and thin. If that was all he had, he wasn't heavily armed. I had a fleeting notion of trying to overpower him. But I rejected it because if I failed too many others could die.

His pupils were dilated, his eyes darting around with an odd gleam, as if hopped up on something. Once he had been a lanky, rawboned, rather handsome young man. Now his face was gaunt, his sandy hair limp, ragged and partially bald, the scraggy remnants of it tied back in a ponytail. His teeth were bad; some were missing and the rest were brownish yellow.

He backed up with his gun on me, leading me into some kind of storage room. It was a large room lined with floor-to-ceiling shelves, and eight hostages were lying face down on the floor with their wrists and ankles bound. There were two folding chairs on one side of the room. "Have a seat, Frank," Maylon instructed, and we both sat down. We were facing each other about six feet apart. If I tried to charge him I wouldn't be able to get to him before he drilled me.

On the far side of the room, at the foot of the shelving, there was a canvas bag with lots of money spilling out -- and I could see that it was stained red. Maylon's hands and forearms were splotched red too. He saw me looking and said, "Guess this little hick town ain't so far behind the times. The dye exploded when I was on my way out loose as a goose thinkin' I was a slick sumbitch. But nothin' I do ever goes right. I shoulda known. "

I didn't want him to lock into self-pity which could lead to self-destruction of the destruction or others, so I changed the subject. "Why wouldn't you talk to Lori? I always thought you two were extremely close. "

"When we was growin' up," he said. "But not now. I got tired of acceptin' her handouts, tired of my shitty job, my shitty fucked up life. Somethin' inside me just blew like a popped circuit breaker. Lori coulda let me play guitar in her back-up band, but she didn't. I figured I hadda get my own pile of money, my own stake in life and all of a sudden didn't care how I got it. I'm real sick inside. Crazy rashes and crazy thoughts. Fucked up lungs, liver, kidneys and who knows what else. The doctors don't know a fuckin' thing about it and don't wanna know. The gov'ment's scared they might have to pay out billions of dollars to us fucked up veterans. But they're the ones fucked us up in the first place. Now they don't wanna look at us no more. We did their dirty work. Now they just want us to go away. They figure if they can just stonewall for a few more years we'll all be dead from the diseases we got over in them fuckin' rice paddies and jungles."

"I don't know," I said. "Maybe you're right. A lot of what you're saying makes sense. "

"I can think better'n I was able to before, I'm on a new kind of drug. Powerful shit. Makes my brain work sorta better but fucks me up in other ways. They call it psycho-somethin'."

"Psychotropic?"

"Yeah. I got a bottle of it right here." He patted his pants pocket. "Got a long, funny name to it. I took a triple dose -- not s'posed to but who gives a shit. I used to drive down the road and see slopes in black pajamas hangin' outta the trees. Saw 'em everywhere. Tried to kill 'em. Even tried to kill my wife. That's why she left me. She done right. By now I mighta killed her and my little boy."

"They're both outside waiting for you to come out. Delbert loves you, you're his daddy. Roseannne still cares about you too."

"No, she don't. I did too many bad things to her. Done bad things to my whole family, even my dad. And now he's dead and I can't tell him I'm sorry."

"Why am I here? Why did you ask for me?"

"I always liked you, Frank. You put your ass on the line. You didn't go to Nam but you woulda gone if you got sent. You didn't run away to Canada. When us guys come home, people spat on us. They called us baby killers. Most of them fuckin' so-called peaceniks didn't really care how many yellow-skinned people we killed. All they wanted to do was end the draft so they pretended to be so fuckin' concerned about their quote fellow human beings. Well, what about *us* fellow human beings? Now the draft's ended and they don't ever have to worry 'bout gettin' their own asses shot up, so you don't hear a peep from 'em no more. Even when a couple million people was exterminated in Cambodia just like Nixon said was gonna happen if we pulled out. "

"What about Charlie Guinard? He cares deeply."

"Charlie's different. I think he's sincere, he really means it. But he never put on a uniform neither. Stayed here and got rich ridin' my sister's coattails."

"No matter what you think of him, he and the people who marched with him did finally get you out of there."

"But they didn't need to crucify us grunts. They shoulda stuck to crucifyin' the politicians and the generals. Body count, body count, body count -- that's all they wanted -- they figured if we wasted enough slopes they'd throw their hands up. If we couldn't tote back the bodies we was told to bring back the ears -- I had a string of 'em one time. Fuck it, they was stinkin' rotten and I threw 'em away and got cussed out for it."

Out of the corner of my eye, while we were talking, I saw that some of the hostages lying on the floor with their faces sideways were trembling or shedding tears. Their eyes darted as they wondered how what they were hearing was going to affect them. Would they be saved or would they die?

"You know your mother's outside crying," I said to Maylon. "She lost your father and she doesn't want to lose you. Today is her birthday. The best present you can give her is to come out of here alive. "

"I can't stand to be locked up," he said flatly. "That's the other reason you're here. What can you do for me to bail me at least partway outta this mess?"

Trying to tread carefully, I said, "I'm not going to lie to you. You're going to have to do some prison time. There's no way out of that. But I can recommend the minimum, providing none of these people gets hurt. I think the prosecutor and the judge will listen to me. In a couple of years, with good behavior, you can go up for parole, and I'll come to your hearing. That will carry a lot of weight."

"I was thinkin' maybe because of my mental condition I'd be able to plead temporary insanity and get put into a hospital. That's where I really belong. I got doctors who can testify. Maybe if I was in a hospital they'd eventually find out what's wrong with me, find somethin' that can fix it a lot better than what I'm takin' now."

"If you got a good lawyer, which I'm sure your sister Lori would be willing to pay for, he could make a pretty good case for hospitalization and rehab."

There was a long silence while he thought about it. While I had him thinking, I wanted to put some icing on the cake. "The best possible scenario in your favor," I said, "would be for you to give me the gun, then we can both untie these hostages and walk out with them, me with my arm around you, like a true friend, you hanging your head, looking penitent. That would get on television. It would play and play, and people would start to forgive you."

A chubby fortyish lady tied up on the floor murmured, "I would be willing to speak up for you, Maylon."

"Thanks, Melva," he said. "Sorry I had to tie you up."

"That's okay," she replied. "But please don't ... please don't hurt me."

"She's a teller in here," he said. "Always cashes my disability checks for me."

I hoped the bizarre exchange would help mellow him out.

After another long moment he said, "I'll come out, but I'm not turning over my gun yet. Not till I'm sure the SWAT team ain't gonna storm this place. You go out first, Frank, and tell 'em I'm gonna set these folks free. When they see that, they'll know I'm serious, I mean business. The folks'll walk out first, then I'll come out unarmed with my hands up. You tell 'em not to shoot me, and you be at the door to meet me as I open it up, and shield me with your body."

I didn't like some aspects of what he was proposing, but I accepted that it was probably the best I could bargain for. "I'll do it your way," I said, "as long as you assure me that you'll follow through."

"You have my word," he said solemnly. "I'll even let you untie the hostages, right now."

I asked him if I could use my pocket knife. He nodded and while he held his gun on me I used the knife to cut through the duct tape around the peoples' wrists and ankles. This took what seemed like an unbearably long time. Maylon didn't want them to stand up. He made them remain sitting on the floor, against a bank of shelves.

I went to the front door of the bank and opened it a crack, keeping my body back from the glass.

Someone yelled, "Don't fire!"

I let myself out and started walking in the direction of the command post so I could tell lead hostage negotiator Joe Flaherty what the deal was. The crowd was fidgeting and muttering.

Just as I was ducking under the crime scene tape, I heard a muffled shot from inside the bank.

Someone gasped, but other than that everything was hushed.

I was frozen in my tracks.

Nothing happened in the next few moments.

Then the door of the bank slowly opened and an elderly man in a disheveled suit and tie stepped out with his hands up.

Somebody yelled, "Hold your fire!" It sounded like the same person who had yelled before.

"We're all coming out!" the man with his hands up said. "We're all okay! The gunman shot himself! He's dead!"

Somebody called out, "Thank God!"

I looked up the block and saw Lori burst into tears.

CHAPTER 27

After her brother's suicide, Lori McCoy couldn't sing any more. All the joy went out of her. She struggled through the last few dates at the tail end of a concert tour, then retreated into seclusion. She blamed herself for Maylon's death and for everything that led up to it.

It seemed to her now, when it was too late, that she could have relented enough to let him play guitar in her touring band. It was true that he wasn't up to the level of the other musicians but maybe that fact could have been concealed with the right kind of orchestration. In recording sessions musicianship mattered more than it did on tour. Ringo Starr didn't always play drums on the Beatles' records, but he always played during live appearances. At concerts the fans were totally crazy and loud. They clapped and sang along, so drunk, stoned and excited that the happening was what really mattered to them, not so much the quality of the music.

Charlie, Arlene and even Missy tried telling Lori that she needed to keep working, but she refused to allow them to penetrate her depression. She worked with Charlie on various social problems and causes, going through the motions without much of the old passion. She was thirty-six years old now, and felt as if her happiest, most gratifying days were behind her. Celebrity seemed to have brought her a load of grief. She looked back on her growing-up years, when her family in Cherry Hill had all been together, with wistful nostalgia and painful regret.

She felt guilty that her mother was all alone. She tried to talk Mama McCoy into coming to live with her and Charlie, but Mama said she was born and raised and spent all of her married life in the valley and she intended to die there. When she said that, she wasn't showing pluck and resilience, she was just plain giving up. She still had two daughters, a granddaughter and a grandson to live for, but she was letting herself become a basket case over the loss of her husband and her son. She made lengthy phone calls to Lori four and five times a week -- calls that Charlie and Missy had come to dread. If Lori ever managed to drum up a spark of enthusiasm or ambition, her mother was sure to squelch it with bottomless self-pity and deadening pessimism.

Lori's record sales began to drop off, too. Folk-rock was out; disco was in. She was so down on herself she almost didn't care. The A&R men and top executives at her record company, who used to fawn over her and Charlie, now started giving them the cold shoulder and hinting about cutting the promotional budget for her next album. They complained that she could have bolstered her sagging sales if she had kept on touring and making TV appearances.

But the truth was that she had developed a form of agoraphobia. It was a relatively mild form, but still debilitating. She wasn't afraid to go out, but she second-guessed every step that she took, every direction she chose to walk or drive. It was a symptom she recognized because she used to have it when she was a teenager. At age fourteen she was riding her bicycle on the dirt road through the valley when a speeding car roared around a curve and fishtailed into her, knocking her off her bike, sending her flying head first over the handlebars while whoever was driving the car just hit the gas and sped off in a cloud of dust. She landed in the dirt on all fours and somehow didn't get any serious injuries, just a few scrapes and bruises.

But after that she acquired a fear, not so much of death itself but of how, when and where it might be lurking for her. She dwelt on the notion that if she had turned right or left at the crossroads she had passed moments before the bike accident, she and the car would never have fatefully occupied the same space at the same time. She fell into a habit of deliberating excessively over every decision that she had to make, worrying and wondering which one might end in tragedy.

She confided in no one about this, merely endured the torment internally. She knew it was a form of obsessive-compulsive behavior, and she understood what had caused it, but that didn't help her get rid of it. Somehow it went away by the time she got married, maybe because she was so much in love with Keith at that time. Maybe love really had the healing power that people said it did.

But the death fear came back after her narrow escape from the murderers in Mississippi, and it got worse after the split-up with Keith. In the midst of every moment of happiness or achievement in her career or in her personal life, a shadow of dread hung over her, telling her it wouldn't last, it all had to end and might very well end soon.

Eventually, after a few years, the affliction slowly dissolved, and she thought she might have burned out all of its circuits. But now here it was once again, full blown, as if the dark shadow had crawled out of the woodwork.

Terrified of the subway trains and even the taxis in New York, she started carrying a loaded pistol in her purse. She didn't have a license for it. One of the musicians in her band gave it to her. It was a .38 Colt Special. She was an excellent shot, and reconfirmed this on an indoor firing range, then started going back to the range every few months for more practice.

Her father had taught her to shoot down on the farm with a .32 caliber Smith & Wesson once owned by her grandfather. She shuddered when she thought about that old gun. It was the one Maylon had used to kill himself.

The only positive thing to come out of Maylon's death was that Lori and Keith were getting along much better these days, which was good for Missy's sake. Lori had mellowed toward her ex-husband after he had surprised her by showing up for Maylon's funeral, making the drive by himself all the way from New York. It was more than what some of her childhood friends and neighbors had done. They shunned the church service and the wake because of the "sinful and disgraceful" way that Maylon had died. But Keith hugged Lori and Missy, shook hands with Arlene and Charlie, and gave Lori's mother a sympathy card containing a check for five thousand dollars.

Now, nine months later, he called up with an offer to take Lori, Charlie and Missy out to celebrate Missy's seventeenth birthday. He had front-row tickets for Doug Henning's Magic Show which was playing on Broadway. "Afterwards we'll have a late dinner at Jilly's," he said on the phone. "I've gotten to know some of the Sinatra people who hang out there. The Chinese food is great. Michele's graduation is coming up fast, too. Let's talk it over. I'd like to give her a party."

"Well, Charlie and I can help pay for it too," Lori said.

Although their relationship had remained decidedly frigid in the first few years after their divorce, Lori and Keith had never had any knock-down drag-out fights over Missy. They had lived as estranged equals in their daughter's life, both deeply concerned about Missy's welfare and able to cooperate when situations called upon them to do so. If either Lori or Keith had been struggling financially, maybe they would have fought more about everything, including their daughter, but one thing their wealth was good for was to enable them to give Missy all of life's necessities and advantages without very much stress or antagonism.

In the coming fall Missy was going to go away to Belmont University, and both parents were gratified that she had chosen their alma mater. Being able to picture every detail of the campus made Lori feel a bit less overwrought about her daughter's safety, but she still worried a lot and kept it to herself so it wouldn't upset anyone but her.

Missy took after Keith in her choice of majors, which was broadcast journalism. Just a few short years ago she had seemed intent on pursuing a singing career, following in her mother's footsteps, but the fire had gone out under that impulse. She had turned out to be as changeable as any other teenager. Although she had a nice little singing voice, she didn't cultivate it anymore, and she gave up her guitar lessons. But sometimes she still sang to herself while doing chores or taking a shower.

Lori had never tried to force her daughter in one direction or another, and she allowed Keith to take pride in the fact that he knew how to give Missy pointers and to act as her mentor in what was now her chosen field. He let her work in the summers and on weekends while she was still in high school as a production assistant on commercials for Natural Life products. And he often promised her that someday he would use her as on-camera talent.

On the evening of Missy's birthday, Keith made a grand appearance in front of Charlie and Lori's apartment building, stepping out of a shiny, black, exorbitantly long stretch limo as a uniformed chauffeur held the door open for him. Devilishly handsome as ever, his wavy blonde hair showing just touch of gray, he hugged Lori and Missy, kissed them both on the cheek, and shook hands with Charlie. Mother and daughter were both wearing cocktail dresses. The men were wearing leisure suits with wildly colorful shirts.

There was no denying the fact that Missy -- or Michele, as Keith preferred -- had to be thought of as a mature young woman now. She was not only beautiful physically but she had a quiet reserve about her that spoke of a high degree of perceptiveness and intelligence. With her blonde hair, blue eyes and dimples, she was a combination of the best features of her mom and dad.

After embracing Keith she turned and said, "Daddy, I can't believe you came here in this."

She was referring to the limo, which was so overblown and overdone it was almost a parody of itself. It had three sets of fat white-walled tires to support its exaggerated length -- all twenty-two feet of it -- and it gleamed with heavy ornamental chrome even in places where one wouldn't expect chrome to be. "I rented this thing for the hell of it," Keith said with his old charming grin. "It's completely tacky and gaudy. Liberace rented it to take him to Carnegie Hall every night when he was appearing there. Wait till you see all the gimmicks. I came early just to show you. "

The chauffeur pressed a button and the trunk opened with a soft purr, revealing a rumble seat plushly upholstered in purple velvet. "On nice days," Keith said, "Liberace would ride here standing up in the open air, wearing his bejewelled cape and waving grandly to onlookers like a pope or an emperor."

"He loves making a huge spectacle of himself," Charlie said. "That's his schtick, and he makes it work for him, but who in the world can take him seriously?"

"I can take his cash seriously," Keith said. "Matter of fact I do take some of his cash. He's a big Natural Life customer. Thinks our stuff is gonna make him live forever."

"You mean the junk you sell in supermarkets?"

"No, we have top-of-the-line Natural Life products now, very expensive and available exclusively through our special staff of personal health consultants."

"You call it top-of-the-line and I call it a sleazy moneymaking gimmick," Charlie said, laughing. "But at least the sleaziness is directed at gullible rich fools."

"I'll take that as a compliment," Keith said. "You're not gonna refuse to ride in this resplendent vehicle, are you Charlie? Just to uphold your status as a champion of the proletariat?"

Just then the chauffeur pressed another button, and with a soft electronic whir the lid of a compartment adjacent to the rumble seat slowly lifted.

"My god!" Lori exclaimed.

Missy giggled.

They were looking at a self-contained hot tub inlaid with colorful ceramic tile. There was a mirror above the tub, plus holders for a towel, wash cloth, shampoo, soap, perfume, hair brush and various other articles for pampering and primping.

"According to the brochure," Keith said, "it holds ninety gallons of heated water. The tile patterns were copied from a Roman villa in Pompeii."

"I suppose you'd have to park in order to use the thing," Missy said. "Otherwise the water would slosh out. Plus you'd have other drivers gawking at you and cracking up all over the highway."

"Cracking up in both senses of the word," Charlie said.

"You could park it in a sunny little meadow," Lori mused, "have yourself a wine and cheese picnic, go hiking or toss a Frisbee, and then freshen up in the hot tub."

"See, you're starting to get the hang of it," Keith said. "I'll turn you into an aristocrat yet, Lori."

After the chauffeur closed down the rumble seat and the hot tub, Keith whimsically bowed to his guests and said, "Please let me escort you into the passenger lounge."

Calling it a lounge was not an overstatement. It was lavishly upholstered in plush purple matching the interior of the rumble seat. There were two luxuriant couches, a well-stocked cocktail bar, a stainless steel sink, a radio/cassette player and a television.

"Holy shit, what else?" Charlie said.

"Well, there's a microwave oven under the bar," Keith replied with a twinkle in his eyes.

Everyone laughed.

Missy said, "Wouldn't it be a hoot to arrive at my prom in this thing!"

"Either that or I'll rent it for you on your graduation day," Keith told her. "You can ride around in it honking the horn, you and your friends. I think it's kind of a fun thing. Some limo company from California built it originally for a movie premiere, out of a converted a 1967 Cadillac. It only costs a hundred bucks an hour to rent, and that includes the chauffeur. "

Shaking her head in amusement, Lori said, "Leave it to you, Keith."

"What do you mean?"

"Always wanting to make a show, or to be the show. I'm not putting you down for it, mind you. It's nice that you want to make the people around you enjoy themselves."

Suddenly he got very serious and said, "You're the one who gets to be the show in a really big way, Lori. I really wish you wouldn't give it up, toss it all aside. It's kind of fun having everybody know I'm the ex-husband of a big star."

"An ex-star," she corrected.

"You'll be back on top again as soon as you make up your mind you want to be there," Charlie said.

As the limousine pulled away from the curb, Keith said, "Well, hell, let's all have a drink on our way to the theater. I'm paying for this monstrosity; we might as well enjoy it. "

Lori patted her little satin cocktail purse and felt the comfort of the revolver, snugly concealed.

CHAPTER 28

A tiny smirk on his face, Conrad Pryzor worked his way in among the crowd in front of the courthouse in Skokie, Illinois. He relished the boos and hisses that were greeting the speech that Pinko Charlie Guinard was giving with his wife and stepdaughter at his side. He was so close to Charlie, Lori, and Missy that if he had a gun he could easily shoot all three. This bunch of stupid kikes, niggers and kike-and-nigger-lovers would probably damn near give him a medal for it. But of course he didn't dare carry a gun; although he hadn't spotted asshole Frank Williams lurking anywhere, he knew that other FBI agents must be monitoring the crowd. And there were two guys up on the courthouse steps who looked like bodyguards for Lefty Lori.

Pryzor could not get over the sweet, rich irony of it. The American Civil Liberties Union was defending the First Amendment right of American Nazis to march in Skokie. And Pinko Charlie Guinard had felt obliged to come here to deliver a mealy-mouthed speech explaining why it was important for every American, even American Nazis, to be able to exercise freedom of assembly.

Conrad Pryzor got a good belly laugh out of the situation, which was already a glorious triumph as far as he was concerned because the ACLU had already lost 30,000 members who were foaming at the mouth over the idea of defending Nazis. Guinard and his wife and stepdaughter were at considerable risk of being stoned by the angry mob whose hatred of National Socialism was making them toss aside their so-called democratic principles

Skokie had cleverly been chosen for the upcoming march by Pryzor and other neo-Nazi leaders precisely because out of the city's population of 70,000 people approximately 40,000 were Jewish. And one out of six of these Jews claimed to be either a survivor or a relative of a survivor of the Holocaust -- which of course was a pack of bald-faced lies because the Holocaust never happened.

Pinko Charlie's speech was full of bleeding heart, tearjerking blather about how these "victims of diabolical terror" had fled Hitler's Germany to come to America, where they "hoped to lead peaceful, productive lives free of mad, tyrannical persecution and butchery." This was a sop for the slavering mob, because his true purpose was to convince them that they had to be tolerant of free speech even when it aired ideas they found repugnant.

Talk about politics making strange bedfellows! Zionist pig lawyers like Charles Guinard had been forced to either defend the right of free speech and free assembly for their enemies or else admit that their vaunted belief in universal democracy was a sham!

On the other side of the issue, wanting to almost tear Guinard's throat out, were the kikes who had shown their true colors by petitioning the courts to deny Nazis the right to march in Skokie!

Jews were never brave enough to fight their own battles. They always ran to the police, the shysters and the courts with their sob stories and bulging bags of bribe money. But this time they were divided against themselves.

Pryzor hoped the furor would lead to a bloodbath.

Guinard got more hisses and boos when he said that the Constitution and the First Amendment "were designed to protect even the most abhorrent and righteously despised views from being censored." He said it was the price we had to pay for our democracy.

Conrad Pryzor scoffed at this. He knew that it was the very freedom that democracy gave its citizens that would cause them to run amok with greed and corruption, milk the country of its riches, and ultimately cause it to decay and collapse.

On May 22, 1978, thanks to the efforts of the Zionist pig lawyers who stupidly chose to go against their own best interests, the United States Court of Appeals ruled that it was unconstitutional for the Skokie Village Board to try to prevent Nazis from assembling and marching in their city.

Having scored this victory, Pryzor and his colleagues basked in triumph for a while, keeping their enemies on edge, and then made a decision to move their scheduled march to the city of Chicago, which belatedly had granted them a permit to march in Marquette Park.

Pryzor and the other Nazi leaders were swayed by the idea that the much bigger city would mean larger crowds and a more impressive parade of marchers. But to Pryzor's chagrin, the Chicago march turned out be an embarrassment. Besides himself and eight of his own followers, only twenty-five other Nazi marchers showed up. The rest were scared off by the massing in the tiny park of over three thousand misguided but highly vocal protestors. Like dumb oxen the stupid oafs were herded and kept back by hundreds of armored policemen, but yet they kept threatening to break through the barriers and attack with rocks, clubs and bare fists.

Pryzor had two of his people shooting eight-millimeter footage of the angry mob, hoping they would go stark raving mad and launch an attack. Although this did not materialize, the film footage still made excellent propaganda. It let white people see the undeniable urgency of banding together to protect and preserve their own race against the "garbage races" of kikes and niggers.

CHAPTER 29

I would have liked to have gone to Skokie to keep tabs on Conrad Pryzor, but I was going through a divorce at the time and so I stayed in New York. Ironically, the divorce was partly caused by my obsession with destroying Pryzor and everything he stood for.

I had tried to talk my wife into giving me another chance, but I knew she wouldn't, and she didn't. It was too late. Most of our friends were already divorced, and we joined the trend.

The divorce craze of the seventies was part of a hedonistic pastiche of pot, pills and promiscuity, but our breakup was more mundane than that. After a prolonged period of marital erosion, the end finally came when I intentionally got myself transferred to the FBI office in Pittsburgh. Alice considered New York the center of everything, not just the center of writing and publishing, and she couldn't bear not being where the action was.

I didn't tell her about the transfer until the day it came through. I had applied for it as soon as I learned that Conrad Pryzor was relocating, setting up an Aryan Confederacy compound on a farm in southwestern Pennsylvania. That part of the state was known as "Klan Country North" and it was being monitored by the FBI Anti-Terrorist Unit operating out of Pittsburgh. It was the unit that had the best chance of bringing Pryzor down, and I wanted to be part of it. Plus, I hoped that the reassignment would let me squirm out from under my AIC's attempts to make me contribute to the dossiers being kept on my friends in New York.

As I said, things were rocky between me and Alice even before I got the transfer. For over a year she had been trying to become pregnant, and when it didn't happen she felt like a failure. My test had shown that I had a good sperm count, but hers had revealed a slight uterine abnormality. Frustrated and determined, she resorted to taking fertility pills and charting fluctuations in her body temperature in an effort to pinpoint the days when she might be ovulating. Month after month, we'd refrain from having sex for three-and-a-half weeks -- then I'd have to perform like a satyr for three or four days in a row.

All the spontaneity went out of our lovemaking and it got to be almost a chore. I ended up with a severe prostate infection, and the urologist said, "You know who gets prostate infections? Priests and sailors. They go through long periods of sexual abstinence because of sea duty or a commitment to celibacy, and the fluids clog up inside that important little walnut-sized organ, and it turns into a happy playground for all kinds of germs."

In the worst stages of the infection, instead of having sex like mad on Alice's ovulation days I was taking antibiotics and not having sex at all because it hurt when I ejaculated. In the urologist's office I had seen blood in my semen, and the thought of it was enough to kill an erotic mood before anything could get started.

When I came home and told Alice about my transfer, instead of yelling and crying and slamming the bedroom door shut on me like she used to do when she got mad, she merely said, "Fine. Do what you want. What I want doesn't matter to you anyway."

The next day I was served with divorce papers. So she must have had them already in the works. I was stung by this. I had been arrogant enough to believe that she still loved me enough to stick with me in spite of my own selfishness, my obsession with my job. I should have known she wasn't the type to be a handmaiden to her husband's whims and desires. She had her own ambitions, her own career.

These realizations came too late, of course. Maybe the truth was that I wasn't cut out to be married. Maybe an inner part of me wanted to be free. Free to pursue the kinds of people I hated. Free and unencumbered enough to keep coming after them till I hunted them down.

CHAPTER 30

Conrad Pryzor bought his ninety-six acre farm in southwestern Pennsylvania with money stolen from Jonestown, Guyana, a commune run by Father Jim Jones, founder of a church called the Peoples Temple. "Dad" Jones, as he preferred to be called, was a master at controlling people and making them do whatever he wanted. Everyone knew this after he made nine hundred of his followers kill themselves by drinking poison. What they didn't know was that Conrad Pryzor, from a distance, had helped set the horrific event in motion.

Pryzor admired Jim Jones in the way that Hitler admired Stalin. He felt they were kindred spirits even though ideologically they were polar opposites. It was a truism that the means and methods of controlling people and molding them into a cohesive, obedient mass did not vary from ideology to ideology, system to system. Pryzor called Dad Jones "a commie in a clerical collar," but he knew that Jones could have become an asset to the New Order if he hadn't chosen to go in the opposite direction.

Jones first attracted national attention by taking four busloads of his followers from his home base in San Francisco all the way to Washington, D.C., to pick up trash from around federal buildings and monuments. Politicos gushed about it and the *Washington Post* did a big, splashy story on Jim Jones and his "church for poor people." Jumping on the bandwagon, the mayor of San Francisco appointed Jones to the Housing Authority, the governor of California gave him a citation for outstanding citizenship and the lieutenant governor, accompanied by huge media razzle-dazzle, paid a fawning visit to the sprawling plantation Jones acquired in 1974 as the site for his Guyana commune.

Due to all this hype, the Peoples Temple grew to over twenty-thousand members, and Dad Jones started calling himself the Reincarnated Jesus. By requiring his followers to donate all their money and worldly possessions to the Peoples Temple, he amassed a huge fortune. In a magazine interview he bragged that he was taking three million dollars in cash to Guyana to begin construction of "a community ruled by God through me as his earthly incarnation and Savior."

Conrad Pryzor was envious of the wealth Jones had accumulated by pushing a perverted form of religion. No wealthy person had ever turned his entire estate over to the Aryan Confederacy. But Jones had proven that you didn't need the wealthy people; you could do it on the backs of poor people. If you got ten fools to follow you and each of them signed a fifty-thousand-dollar home over to you, the property value would amount to half a million bucks. Jim Jones had over twenty-thousand fools believing he was Jesus come back to earth. The three million he took to Guyana was probably only a fraction of his total net worth.

Pryzor dwelt upon all that money down there in the sticky-hot jungle. He pictured it being chewed on by rats, as had happened to currency hoarded in tents by Arab oil sheiks. For sure there was no bank vault down there. The money was probably being kept in a footlocker or a safe or maybe even a cardboard box. Those poor deluded religious folk were probably relying on God to watch over it for them. When Jim Jones announced publicly that he was going to finish building his colony and then ship the vast bulk of his fortune to the Soviet Union, Pryzor was incensed. He thought of how he could use that nest egg to found a Nazi colony right here in the United States. He pictured it starting small, then growing and growing, like Hitler's little band of Brown Shirts that at first had seemed so harmless, so insignificant. In time the Aryan Confederacy would become a force to contend with in national politics. Pryzor entertained visions of getting himself elected to Congress or even to a governorship, which would be better because then he would control an entire state and he would have the still-potent doctrine of "state's rights" working for him in a big way.

When he had that kind of power, no longer would he be tormented and embarrassed by poor showings like the one in Chicago's Marquette Park. Having established the legal groundwork in Skokie, he would build a vast army of storm troopers who would proudly and defiantly march in any American city of his choosing.

In accordance with his thinking on these matters, in early 1978, he had sent two of his henchmen, Mickey "Curb" Burton and David "Bash" Halsey, to South America to infiltrate the Peoples Temple colony. A dozen years ago when they were still in their teens, Curb and Bash got their nicknames from going around together "curbing and bashing faggots." They'd loiter outside of bars frequented by gays, lure them into dark alleys, then attack them, stomp on them, and bash their heads against a curb. This was a favorite recreation of young neo-Nazis. It toughened them and helped turn them into strong, unfazable warriors.

And it showed the faggots that they didn't belong in an Aryan society. They'd be disposed of in a Final Solution when the New Order took over.

To ingratiate themselves with Jim Jones, Curb and Bash showed him their swastika and SS double lightning tattoos and portrayed themselves as repentant Nazi thugs who wanted to give up the Iron Cross and take up the Christian Cross. Jones had a need for two big, beefy bodyguards and enforcers, so he turned them into thugs for Jesus. Their job was to whip the colonists into line and strike fear in the hearts of any who might be tempted to betray Dad Jones by defecting from his Jonestown settlement.

In spite of his dark good looks and his charismatic power over women, Curb and Bash thought that Jones might be a closet homo. Behind his back they joked about bashing his head against a curb. His eyes had a nervous dart to them and he was full of the kind of false heartiness and braggadocio some faggots got into when they wanted to seem manly.

Like gladiators of old, Curb and Bash were given young, nubile concubines when Dad Jones felt like rewarding them, and one night when they shared three women with Jones in his own bedroom they thought that his eyes lingered too much on their male organs. And although he did things with the young women, he seemed to like orgiastic positions that caused the men's bodies to "inadvertently" rub against his.

When the women left and Jones fell asleep, Curb and Bash tiptoed around a bit. They spied a safe halfheartedly concealed beneath a pile of linen in a closet. They winked at each other when they saw it was a piece of junk, easy to crack, even without dynamite. They could probably pry it open with a crowbar.

But how to steal it and make a clean getaway? There were too many people always around Jones's bungalow and all through the compound. Curb and Bash didn't want to be chased into the jungle by a horde of religious fanatics heavily armed from the colony's sizable cache of weapons. If they were caught, Jones would probably have them crucified. Totally paranoid and obsessed with the absolute power he enjoyed down here, he always kept his hawk eyes on everyone, watching everything that went on, trying to catch someone breaking one of his "Commandments" or, worse, planning to escape from under his thumb.

Two or three nights a month he would hold what he called "White Night Exercises." His voice would blast from loudspeakers all over the compound, waking everybody up and herding them into a pavilion where he'd lecture them on the "beauty of dying." Then they'd be given poison to drink, mixed with grape Kool-Aid. Like stupid sheep, they'd drink it. And then Jones would say, "This time what you all just drank *wasn't* really poison. But if evil government agents ever descend upon us to take us away from here, we'll have to commit revolutionary suicide. When that time comes, our deaths will be glorious and will show the entire world how dedicated we are to our beliefs."

Curb and Bash wished these "glorious" deaths would hurry up and happen so they could get their hands on the cash without having to worry about getting caught. They discussed ways to hasten the event and couldn't come up with anything that seemed workable and foolproof.

Finally, though, they got an unexpected opportunity when the colony was visited on a fact-finding mission headed by California Congressman Leo Ryan.

Several defectors from the Temple in San Francisco had told the congressman that a young man had been murdered last year in the railroad yards when he attempted to convert to Judaism. It was an "accidental" murder, they said, the result of torture with a cattle prod that apparently set off a heart attack. The autopsy showed the heart damage but did not reveal the underlying cause of it, therefore homicide was never suspected.

The snitches also told Congressman Ryan that people were being held in Guyana by force and were whipped or tortured if Jim Jones caught wind of their plans to leave. They accused Jones of sexual deviancy, saying that he took his pick of all the young females, even those as young as twelve or thirteen, while no one else was allowed to have sex without his permission, and when they did have sex he had to select their partners for them.

At the urging of Congressman Ryan, the U.S. State Department looked into these allegations. They interviewed some of the members of the Guyana colony, but none of them would openly testify against Jones, and nobody would admit to wanting to leave the place. Suspicious that they were being coerced, Ryan wrote to Jim Jones on behalf of their concerned relatives and got a reply from Jones's attorney, who said that the members of the Peoples Temple who were now in Guyana had to flee the United States because of "religious persecution by the federal government." However, the attorney said he would be glad to make arrangements if Congressman Ryan wished to personally inspect the commune at Jonestown.

Curb and Bash helped Jim Jones and his people get ready for the congressman's visit. It was a dumb show, like the sham of a "lovely camp for Jews" at Thereisenstadt that the Nazis set up during World War Two to smooth their way past Red Cross inspections. Nothing was left to chance. In the week preceding the all-important visit, everything was spiffed up and all the colonists were thoroughly indoctrinated and drilled on what they should do and how they should behave.

Two days before the visit, Curb and Bash had the good fortune to catch wind of a defection in the making. A snitch led them to a cache of canned food, water and clothing buried inside a plastic garbage bag under a tree about thirty feet off of one of the trails through the jungle.

The would-be defector was a skinny twenty-two year old redheaded kid named Skip Johnson. "Skip was about to skip out on us but he ain't skippin' no more," Curb joked.

"I think we can use him," Bash said slyly.

"How?"

"Make him do a little somethin' for us."

Bash told Curb his idea and they both agreed that it was workable.

They dragged Skip Johnson out into the jungle and showed him where they had uncovered his cache of supplies. Then they told him what he had to do if he didn't want them to kill him. He tried to resist the suggestion, and they had to burn his testicles with lit cigarettes and threaten to cut his tongue out. But he didn't give in until, sobbing and moaning in pain, he said, "Please ... don't hurt me anymore ... I have a young son."

This was perfect. With a little more torture, Curb and Bash found out who the boy was and how to get to him and made it clear that Skip Johnson's son would die if Skip didn't do exactly as he was told. They had to take the chance that he was too scared to turn on them and that he would accomplish his mission.

On the appointed day of the congressman's visit, the dumb show unfolded with all its artificial mimicry. All over the compound there were smiling, happy colonists cheerfully engaging in pleasant chores and politely bowing and scraping for Congressman Ryan and his entourage. After their thoroughly chaperoned and timetabled tour, the distinguished visitors were served a lavish banquet. While they were having coffee and dessert, they were entertained by adults and children singing and dancing and performing skits.

In guarded whispers among themselves, the congressman and his people voiced their skepticism. They weren't entirely fooled, but they didn't know what to do about it. They had seen nothing offensive, nothing they could put their finger on. There was no overt evidence of sexual abuse or any other kind of abuse to report back to America.

Jim Jones beamed at them, satisfied that his well-orchestrated charade was working.

Then suddenly it all went to pieces.

With sudden fury one of the colonists who had been serving as a waiter charged at Congressman Ryan with a steak knife.

The wild-eyed young man slashed and jabbed with the knife and the congressman tried to fight him off.

Perhaps Ryan would have been killed if it weren't for two of the men in his party, who jumped the attacker from behind, knocked him to the floor and took his knife away.

He curled up in a ball and started crying. "They made me do it!" he whined. "It was --"

He never finished whatever he was going to say. Bash hit him on the head with a leather blackjack and he went totally limp.

"That's Skip Johnson!" an excited waitress said. "I knew something was wrong about him. He's been sneaking around a lot lately."

"Don't worry, we'll take care of him," Curb said.

"You haven't heard the last of this," Congressman Ryan snarled. "This kind of thing never should have happened. Now I've got grounds for a more thorough investigation. And this time I'll be calling in the FBI or the military."

The congressman was bleeding, but the defensive wounds on his arms weren't life-threatening. Skip Johnson hadn't been committed enough to his attack. Ryan kept making a big fuss while a couple of women cleaned his cuts with alcohol-soaked cotton swabs and applied sterile bandages. Dad Jones tried to calm him down and talk to him, but he wasn't having any of it.

He kept ranting about sending armed soldiers down here. Members of his entourage backed him up, vehemently agreeing that tough measures were called for and giving Dad Jones and his followers stern, angry looks.

Curb and Bash handcuffed the semi-conscious Skip Johnson and dragged him out of the banquet room. As they were leaving they heard Dad Jones saying, "Congressman Ryan, if you follow through on what you're threatening, it will mean the end of my ministry. All our good works here will go up in smoke. None of my flock will want to live, and neither will I. I'm warning you, there will be many deaths on your hands."

This was exactly the outcome that Curb and Bash had hoped to instigate. Before Skip Johnson could blab, they hustled him out of sight at a prearranged spot in the jungle, put a noose around his neck and hoisted him up, hanging him from a stout banyan tree. Then they removed his handcuffs. If and when his body was discovered, they would say he must have killed himself in remorse for his attack on the congressman.

They returned to the banquet room and confessed to Dad Jones that they had let Skip Johnson get away from them. "He ran into the deep part of the jungle," Curb said. "He ain't gonna last long in there, especially not after dark. He'll get snakebit or some kind of animal will chomp on him."

Dad Jones was frantic -- but not about Johnson. Flailing his arms, he said, "The congressman and his party are heading for the air strip. They have to be stopped. They're going to bring soldiers down upon us."

This was more good luck for Curb and Bash. "We'll stop 'em," Curb promised. "Don't worry, Dad, we'll take care of 'em for you. They'll never get outta here and nobody'll ever know what happened to 'em. We'll say their plane went down in the jungle."

"Like Amelia Earhart," Bash said with a snicker.

"It's not funny," Dad Jones said. "This is serious business. While you were dealing with Skip Johnson, I was dealing with Leo Ryan. He insisted on taking some defectors out of here, and I let him. But he doesn't know that some of them are plants. And they're armed with automatic pistols. They're going to open fire soon as they get on one of the planes. There are two planes, an Otter and a Cessna."

"Good thinking, Dad," Curb said. "Let us take some guys we can trust to join in the ambush. They'll never know what hit 'em."

"What you're doing is fully authorized," Dad Jones said. "The Guyanese government has granted me authority to shoot anyone who tries to leave without my blessing."

Curb and Bash did not believe this. It must be another of Jones's delusions. No way did he have the right to shoot anyone, especially a congressman. But let him think it. It perfectly suited Curb and Bash's plans. When they got out of earshot of Jim Jones, Curb said, "The idea is gonna be to shoot the congressman and maybe a couple others, but let the plane take off, let the rest of 'em get away."

"Why?"

"Because once Ryan is killed and the other people escape to tell about it, the jig is up for Dad Jones. For him it'll be whatchamacallit-- Armageddon. He'll hold one of his White Nights for real."

Curb and Bash got into a two-man jeep and two other men armed with automatic rifles climbed onto a flatbedded trailer pulled by a tractor. They headed down a muddy, rutted road to Port Kaituma, where the Cessna and the Otter were standing by on the little air strip.

They caught Ryan's party just as they were boarding -- and they opened fire. A reporter from the *San Francisco Chronicle* was hit in the shoulder and crawled behind a plane wheel. A TV cameraman tried to stay on his feet, keeping his camera rolling, but he took a bullet in the chest, and then Curb ran up to him and blasted him in the face with a shotgun, blowing his brains right out of his head.

At the same time, the fake defectors began firing at people inside the Cessna. There were fourteen genuine defectors -- some were killed and some were wounded trying to get out of the plane. The ones who managed to get out ran straight into a hail of gunfire from Curb and Bash and their accomplices.

The Cessna's engines roared to life and it started taxiing. Curb and Bash didn't shoot at it because they wanted a few people to live to tell the tale that would doom Dad Jones.

The other two assassins did fire at it, but luckily they didn't bring it down. Nobody tried to start up the Otter. It looked as if it was too shot up to be able to fly.

Bodies were strewn all over the little landing strip. At least half a dozen people from the visiting party were dead, including Congressman Ryan.

There was a sudden roar and Curb and Bash spun around to see their Jeep taking off in a cloud of dust with the other two gunmen in it. "This is perfect for us," Bash said. "They're in an all-fire hurry to tell Dad Jones some of the congressman's people didn't get killed."

Satisfied with how things had turned out so far, Curb and Bash climbed onto the flatbed and headed back to the Jonestown colony.

When they got there they were embraced by two young black men carrying rifles. They had beatific smiles on their faces.

One of them said, "We're gonna die in revolutionary suicide, with dignity and honor, like the Jewish rebels at Masada." And the other one added, "We're gonna give our lives in the battle against fascism and racism."

Dad Jones came out of his bungalow looking totally haggard and depressed and put his arms around the young black men, embracing them for their loyalty. "I can't believe fourteen of my people wanted to betray me," he lamented. "They might as well have nailed me to a cross. It's a repudiation of all my work here on earth. I don't want to live any longer in this world of sin and corruption. I've already ordered preparations for mass suicide. "

They all headed for the pavilion. Jones took up a microphone and ordered nurses to hurry with the potion and take care of the little babies first. He said everybody had to die because any survivors would be tortured and castrated by the Guyanese army.

Curb, Bash and the two young black guys with rifles started making people drink the Kool-Aid laced with potassium cyanide and potassium chloride. It was surprising how many of them did it willingly, without any hassle. Maybe they thought it would turn out to be another dry run.

Many of the mothers gave the poison to their children, then drank it themselves.

Dad Jones was seated on a high, throne-like wicker chair, urging everybody on. "We'll all meet in a much better place!" he shouted. "We'll all be reunited in Heaven!"

Babies were bawling, children were screaming, and adults were crying and praying. Everywhere there was mass confusion.

Entire families filled their plastic cups from a vat in the center of the pavilion, then wandered off to die together, lying down arm in arm. The passage from life to death only took about five minutes.

Of course there were some recalcitrant people who refused to drink the Kool-Aid. Dad Jones called them "dissenters" and said they must comply or be shot. That task fell to Curb, Bash and the two armed black men. They had to shoot about two dozen people, and they also shot the commune's two pet monkeys and a pet gorilla named Mr. Muggs. The panicked animals screeched and roared when they were hit with the first bullets, which did not kill them, then scampered and crawled, trapped in their cages, till succeeding shots proved to be fatal.

In the end, dead bodies were lying everywhere. Nothing moved. Freshly washed clothing hung in breezeless silence on clotheslines strung throughout the commune, while patches of color among the surrounding trees and bushes showed where people had huddled together to breathe their last.

It was an awesome and eerie sight, even for Curb and Bash, the hardened Nazis who had helped cause it. The two young black men, who had never killed anyone before, both had tears streaming down their faces.

"You can shoot us now," one of them said. And they both threw down their rifles.

They knelt to pray, and Curb and Bash shot each of them in the back of the head.

Then they went to find Dad Jones, whose voice was still droning over the stillness. He finished reciting the Lord's Prayer as Curb and Bash entered the pavilion. Then he said, "Lord forgive them, for they know not what they do."

These were his final words. Curb walked up to him and shot him in the temple.

"You see the way he looked at us?" Bash said. "I think he musta known exactly what we was gonna do."

"He was stark ravin' nuts but he wasn't no dummy," Curb said.

Then they went to Jones's bungalow to bust open the safe and take three million bucks in cash back home to their leader, Conrad Pryzor.

CHAPTER 31

One day in the spring of 1980, after Lori's depression and withdrawal from life had gone on for about two years, Charlie phoned her from his office and told her he had just gotten an offer of a three-week engagement for her in one of the new Atlantic City casinos. "I asked for twenty-thousand a week and they didn't balk," he said. "They want to make a big splash out of bringing you back, like Sinatra."

There was a long silence from Lori's end of the line.

"Well, honey?" Charlie said.

"I'm not as big as Frank Sinatra. Never was, never will be. "

"Same goes for everybody else in the biz. But you're still plenty big and twenty thou a week proves it. They know you have tons of fans who will come and see you. "

"They've probably all forgotten about me. In any case I'm not ready to sing again right now. I'm not sure I'll ever be. If that's what happens will you still love me?"

"I'll always love you, honey."

"I love you and appreciate you for not trying to push me into it," she told him.

They talked some about a fund raiser they were putting together for Jimmy Carter who was running for a second term as president against the former actor and governor of California, Ronald Reagan. Charlie called Reagan a "photogenic empty suit" and was stunned that the star of such folderol as *Bedtime for Bonzo* had actually won the Republican nomination. But Carter was in big trouble and might actually lose, because of his ongoing failure to negotiate the release of fifty-two American hostages being held by the religious fanatics in Iran who had overthrown the shah.

"You could raise more money not only for Carter but for the ACLU and the Anti-Defamation League if you'd agree to sing again," Charlie told Lori.

"There are lots of singers with more hit songs than I ever had," Lori said.

When Charlie got off the phone with her he placed a couple of calls designed to put in motion a plan that he had been pondering for several weeks. And he hoped it wouldn't blow up in his face.

Come Saturday morning, as they were lying in bed, he offhandedly told Lori that Tammy Wynette had phoned the day before to personally invite them to her show at the Grand Ole Opry.

"How come she called you instead of me?" Lori asked.

"She misplaced our home number," Charlie lied.

"I used to want to go to the Ryman Auditorium," Lori said regretfully. "Almost made it, but you know what happened."

She was referring to the murders in Mississippi and they both knew it and they refrained from commenting further.

After some long moments of silence, Lori said, "The Grand Ole Opry isn't at the Ryman anymore; it's in some kind of brand new place."

"Not exactly brand new," Charlie corrected. "The Opry's been out of the Ryman since 1974. They call the new place the Grand Ole Opry House."

"Call it what they like, it's not the same," Lori said. "It's not even in Nashville, it's on the outskirts."

"So what should I tell Tammy Wynette?" Charlie pressed.

"I love Tammy. Tell her I'll go," Lori said.

"While we're there we can visit the Country Music Hall of Fame," Charlie said.

He was greatly relieved that the first part of his plan seemed to be working. It had been he who had gotten in touch with Tammy Wynette, not the other way around as he had portrayed it. He wanted Tammy to help him talk Lori into a career change that might lift her out of the doldrums.

Lori and Tammy had hit it off from the time they first met, when they were both on *The Tonight Show* with Johnny Carson back in 1975. They had lunch together twice during the following week. Tammy at the time was going through a divorce from George Jones who was not only her husband but her singing partner on a string of hit songs. Lori of course had already been through a hurtful divorce and readily commiserated.

Another thing they both shared besides growing up on dirt-poor farms in the South, was being attacked by cruel, brutal men. Tammy didn't manage to get away clean. Just two years ago, in 1978, she was abducted at gunpoint at a Nashville shopping center. She was forced into the passenger seat of her own car and taken on a harrowing eighty-mile ride, under the threat of being raped or having worse done to her, until the car was pulled off to the side of a lonely road where she was badly beaten and finally turned loose. The man who did it was wearing a mask and was never identified. Tammy told Lori that his amorphous face was still haunting her in her sleep. Lori told of her own nightmares -- one other thing that they had in common.

The tabloids had lambasted Tammy, too, claiming it was her own husband who had beat her up. But Lori totally believed in Tammy's version because she had felt her honest sincerity and outrage.

In spite of a stormy life that included a string of failed marriages and constant battles with serious health problems, Tammy had seventeen hit songs during the sixties and seventies, including one of the biggest and most controversial country songs ever, *Stand by Your Man* -- women's lib groups hated it and she stuck it to them by choosing to sing it on *The Tonight Show*.

Charlie knew that Lori had bought all of Tammy's records and had been delighted to actually meet her and become her friend and confidant. He hoped that because of the intense bond that had so easily developed between his wife and Tammy Wynette that Tammy could help him influence Lori in the direction that he thought she ought to take. After all, he had been the one to suggest the folk rock style for Lori's first hit album, including her Vietnam anthem, *A Soldier's Song*. He wanted to try once again, from behind the scenes, to point her toward a goal that he believed would lift her out of her depression and help her truly fulfill her childhood dreams.

CHAPTER 32

"Ever hear of a song called *Lucille*?" Tammy Wynette asked. She was being flippant. Anyone who hadn't heard of that song had to be either dead or living in outer space.

Charlie looked on with a big smile as Lori started singing it and Tammy joined in, in perfect harmony.

"You picked a bad time to leave me, Lucille ... with five hungry children and a crop in the field ... "

They broke it off, laughing and toasting each other.

Tammy asked, "Who sung it?"

"Duh ... Kenny Rogers."

"That song was a smash hit for Kenny, made him a megastar after everybody thought his career was in the toilet. He came home to country music. It's what you oughtta do."

Lori blinked.

Charlie perked up. Tammy wasn't wasting any time making the pitch that he had asked her to make.

Charlie, Lori and Tammy were unwinding after Tammy's show at the Grand Ole Opry House. They were in a restaurant hideaway on the sixth floor of the hotel where they were staying. It was a special place, a retreat for performers, where they and their friends and associates were discreetly protected from unwanted intrusions.

Walking the streets of Nashville, where so much of the music that she loved had been created, had softened Lori up for Tammy's pitch. All the right vibes were at work. Being in the Grand Ole Opry House, even though it wasn't as venerable as the Ryman, had affected Lori more powerfully than she could have imagined. The emotional high point was when the spotlight fell upon Tammy, standing in a six-foot circle of dark oak in the center of the Opry House stage and singing her heart out. The circle was cut from the stage of the Ryman Auditorium so that current performers could feel that they were standing on the very spot where the old-time legends once stood: Hank Williams, Ernest Tubb, Minnie Pearl, Patsy Cline, Elvis Presley, and on and on, down through the dusty decades.

Overcome by a sense of nostalgia and tradition, and remembering her fretful, restless longing to come to Nashville when she was a little girl listening to a staticky radio, Lori wept during Tammy's performance. She'd never forget how Tammy had been one of the few to call her up and console her when the tabloids blasted her with hateful headlines like LORI McCOY RESPONSIBLE FOR BROTHER'S SUICIDE.

She had her doubts about the advice that Tammy was now giving her but she felt obliged to listen with all due respect.

Tammy went on making her points, using Kenny Rogers as a role model for what she thought Lori ought to do. "Back in the sixties, Kenny sang with the New Christy Minstrels and the First Edition, and you might not know that before that he was a bass player in a jazz combo. He went from jazz to folk to pop. He was floundering, trying this and then that, not finding any kind of niche and not able to figure out what was best for him. Somehow or another he got signed by Mercury records but everything he recorded totally flopped. He was darn near dead meat till he came out with *Lucille* three years ago and it went through the roof. He found a home in country music, where he always belonged in the first place. The same thing can happen for you, Lori."

"I'm not sure I want it to."

"Bullcrap. You got it in your blood. Denyin' it to yourself and lettin' other people beat you down is why you're so goldarn unhappy. You know my life hasn't been any walk in the park, but I always have my music, and it's the kind of music I grew up with. It's what gets me through."

"Lori, you have a treasure trove of great material that you've never touched," Charlie chipped in. "I guess it's my fault. Pushing you into the folk-rock thing was a double-edged sword. Sure, it worked at the time, but it's not really where your heart is."

"Country music is forever," Tammy said. "It tells it like it is. It speaks to poor, downtrodden, hard-workin' folks like the ones you and me grew up with. They know we think and feel the same as they do. Who else is gonna tell their stories if we don't? Nobody can tell it better neither, 'cause we lived it, we know what it's all about."

"Nobody can argue with that," Charlie said. "If anybody has the right to speak for them, it's you."

Charlie and Lori knew that Tammy had grown up on a Mississippi farm, picking cotton out in the fields when she was in grade school. Her father was a struggling musician who died of a brain tumor less than a year after she was born. Married at seventeen, she gave birth to three children, and one had spinal meningitis. When she was divorced after only three years of marriage, she taught herself how to play the piano and guitar and took gigs in bars to help pay her sick little girl's medical bills. Along the way, she hooked up with an agent who changed her name from Virginia Wynette Pugh to Tammy Wynette, saying that her long, blonde ponytail reminded him of Debbie Reynolds in the movie *Tammy and the Bachelor*.

Today, at age thirty-eight, she no longer had the ponytail but still looked beautiful and younger than her years. Her hair was close-cropped. She showered and took off her makeup right after her show and was now in tight-fitting jeans and a pink blouse. Her fresh, perky, clear-eyed appearance was remindful of her honest homespun roots.

"What do you think?" she asked Lori.

"I don't know. I'm not saying you're not making sense, but ..."

"But what?"

"Charlie put you up to this, didn't he?"

Charlie put both palms up in denial. But Tammy burst out laughing. "We're caught red-handed, Charlie," she said. "No use tryin' to lie our way out of it."

"What exactly is going on here?" Lori said.

"Your husband loves you," Tammy said. "He asked me to talk to you, Lori, but what I been sayin' is my own truthful thoughts. You're my friend, and I only want what's best for you, same as Charlie does. If I can help you in any way I'd be darn glad to do it."

"You're doing it right now," Charlie said.

"Why didn't you just tell me these things yourself?" Lori asked him.

"I did but you weren't listening. I couldn't crack through. You were so depressed all the time. I wanted to get you down here so you could hear it from the horse's mouth."

"Well!" Tammy said. "I've been called a horse's ass before but never a horse's mouth!"

They all laughed.

Lori said, "Well, you two have given me a lot to think about, but I'm not sure what I'm gonna do about it."

"Think about it some more," Tammy urged. "Picture us doin' one of your own good ol' country songs as a duet some day in front of a whole lotta people."

CHAPTER 33

In a process that began five years ago, after Lori and Charlie got married, Arlene Shoaf slowly pulled herself out from under Lori's shadow.

It began when she got her own apartment. At first the mere thought of being totally on her own and living by herself was scary. Often, when she had to come home to silence and empty rooms, she was overcome with loneliness. She had to get out. To ward off dejection, she plunged into the task of furnishing and decorating, and found herself automatically doing it according to her own unique tastes instead of her sister's -- in fact, surprisingly, she had a genuine flair for such things, and pulled it off in a style that was as charming as it was functional. The shining success of it made her quite proud of herself. When she had Charlie, Lori and Missy over for dinner, they showered her with compliments.

For over two weeks, she had looked forward to this first social occasion in her own apartment, and the evening turned out to be a delight, yet she was glad when it was finally over and she could totally relax. She realized she was beginning to enjoy not having people around all the time, even though she still sometimes felt very lonely without them. It was so nice to be able to do exactly what she wanted to do, when and how she wanted to do it.

All during her growing-up years she and Lori had to take great pains not to ever display any trace of nakedness around the two men in the house, Tillman and Maylon. When Arlene got married, she found that Truman Shoaf was similarly inhibited from growing up with his three younger sisters. He was so mean and pent-up that Arlene's sex life with him had never been one of spontaneity, much less of joy. And after he died her sex life became nonexistent.

When she was living with Lori, Charlie and Missy she used to at least put on a housecoat before coming out of her room, but now she could prance around naked if she chose to. Sometimes the first thing she did after she came home and bolted the door was to strip down to panties and bra so she'd feel free and unencumbered. But she didn't like seeing her own chubbiness when she passed one of her full-length mirrors, so she began to think of doing something about her weight.

Her personality was changing too, or else it was simply re-emerging. She definitely liked her new freedom and independence. She became able to smile and laugh more readily. Sometimes when she went shopping with Lori and Missy or met them for lunch, she caught them smiling at her, amazed and pleased by her displays of vivaciousness. Now and then she was almost giddy, like a teenager cutting loose from the restraint of her elders for the first time, and she had to reign herself in for the sake of decorum.

She was in her thirties now, belatedly realizing how sad it was that she had been bottled up, first under the thumb of Truman Shoaf and next under the heavy load of guilt she carried for helping to break up her sister's first marriage. Playing these circumstances over and over again in her own mind, she realized she had been living inside a shell of her own making. She even came to an understanding of why she had put on so much weight -- subconsciously it was a way of covering up her own natural attractiveness so it wouldn't get her into any more trouble with men, especially any man who might show an interest in her sister.

In the months following Maylon's death, when Lori sank into a lengthy bout with depression, Arlene found herself without nearly as much work to do in furtherance of her sister's career because the career had lapsed into a holding pattern. She kept up with her accounting and other business managing chores plus her maintenance of Lori's fan club, and she drew a nice salary for doing so, working either out of Charlie's offices or out of her own apartment. Because of the quiet, withdrawn lifestyle she had led for all those years previously, she now had a substantial bank account and lucrative investments.

The notion of starting to lead a more satisfying life began to appeal to her. She was still young, and she had the means. She could travel overseas, she could enjoy New York as she had never done before, and she might even find a man that she liked. She thought she would know what not to look for in the opposite sex. Hadn't she had enough bad experiences?

She began dieting and going to a gym. In the first month or so of this, she couldn't help but notice that her youthful good looks were beginning to return, which elevated her sense of pride, self-assurance and determination.

One day during her workout, an older woman who was in better shape than she was asked, "Would you mind spotting me while I do some bench presses?"

"I wouldn't mind but I don't know how."

"Oh, it's just you stand over me and keep your hands on the bar as it goes up and down so you can catch it in case I drop it or pass out or something. It's not going to happen, but still it's just a precaution."

"Oh, I can do that."

The woman extended her hand. "By the way, I'm Jane Hawthorne. I've seen you here before."

"I joined three months ago," Arlene said. "But I've only been coming in for about a month and a half."

"Why, were you travelling?"

"Not exactly, no."

Arlene didn't want to admit that it had taken more than a month for her to work up the nerve to actually go to the gym and let all the fit and trim people, like Jane Hawthorne, get a good look at how fat and out of shape she was. A tall, winsome brunette whose softly-lined face seemed to put her in her mid- to late-thirties, Jane was so enviously trim and physically fit that Arlene wanted to sink into the woodwork.

For the next forty-five minutes, after helping Jane with her bench presses, Arlene continued with her own exercise routine, which was pathetically undemanding compared to Jane's. The workout room had walls full of mirrors reflecting the bodies of both women in multiple images, and Arlene was embarrassed by the unwanted comparison. She noticed how many exercises Jane was doing and how quickly she was able to zip through them.

After they were done with their workouts Jane asked Arlene if she'd like to go for a cup of coffee at the Chockfull O' Nuts a few doors away. They took a booth and Jane ordered a strawberry danish with her coffee, but Arlene forced herself to have just coffee and decline the pastry.

"Yum!" Jane said, biting into her danish. "One of the reasons I exercise every day is so I can eat stuff like this without gaining. If I ate everything I want to eat I'd weigh four-hundred pounds."

"I can't believe you have to watch," Arlene said. "Isn't the main factor your metabolism?"

"Hmph!" Jane scoffed. "Fat, lazy people like to believe that 'cause it lets them off the hook. But unless you have some kind of glandular disorder, if you don't get enough exercise and don't push yourself away from the table, your ass is gonna get fatter and fatter and fatter."

"Like mine," Arlene said, her face reddening.

"Well, yours is actually getting thinner," Jane told her. "You're making an effort and the results are beginning to show."

They fell silent for a while. Then Jane asked Arlene what she did for a living. "I'm sort of a business manager for my sister," Arlene said. "She's the singer, Lori McCoy."

"Oooh, I love her songs!" Jane said. "I haven't heard anything new from her lately."

"She's still bummed out over what my brother did to himself," Arlene said. "Not to mention the scandal."

"Well, I wish the tabloids would leave her alone, but I guess that's too much to hope for."

"What do you do, Jane?" Arlene asked.

"I'm a book editor for Kaiser Press."

"That sounds pretty interesting, especially if you like to read a lot."

"Yeah, I was an English literature major, so it's a good niche for me, and what else could I do since I don't really want to teach? But let me tell you, I had to read a ton of garbage when I first got hired. My gig was the slush pile -- bottomless stacks and stacks of unsolicited manuscripts that come in every week. I was supposed to try to find unexpected treasures. It was like looking for a gold nugget in a heap of manure."

They both laughed.

"How many years ago was that?" Arlene asked.

"I started eleven years ago, and I lived like a worm burrowing through the slush pile for three years. They gave my job the title 'first reader' to make it sound a bit glamorous, and actually I did discover two bestsellers that came in over the transom. That's what got me promoted to associate editor and then editor. "

Flashing a bright smile, Arlene said, "Maybe you can clue me and my sister in on some good books that aren't in the stores yet."

"Well, I'm working on one right now that's utterly fascinating and disturbing," Jane said. "Sometimes it makes me so mad I want to scream. It's called *Satan's Vessel* and it's about how women have been blamed for all the world's evils from Adam and Eve on down. Most of the thousands of so-called witches burned at the stake were women. And today we're called witches for wanting to determine the course of our own lives and to be considered equals with men. "

"Are you a feminist?" Arlene ventured hesitantly.

"I belong to the National Organization for Women. You should come to a meeting with me, find out what it's all about and then join."

"I've heard of Betty Friedan."

"So what do you think of her?"

"I'm not really sure."

"Come with me next Tuesday night and I'll introduce you to her. Meantime I'll send you a copy of *Satan's Vessel*. The proof sheets should be in my hands in a couple of days."

Several days later, true to Jane's word, the proofs were delivered to Arlene via FedEx. She read them that evening and found the material as intriguing and maddening as Jane had said.

A quote in the foreword, taken from a medieval religious tract, totally infuriated her:

"All wickedness is but little to the wickedness of womankind. What else is woman but a foe to friendship, an unescapable punishment, a necessary evil, a natural temptation, a desirable calamity, a domestic danger, a delectable detriment, an evil of nature painted with fair colors!"

Reading further, Arlene discovered that Saint Paul had referred to women as "the vessel of dishonor." And in 1486, Pope Innocent VIII had sanctioned as dogma a book called the *Malleus Maleficarum*, written by two friars, which stated that any woman who used contraception, performed abortions or "robbed a man of his virility" should be burned at the stake for witchcraft. This was the authorizing document for the Inquisition, under whose auspices millions of innocent people, most of them women, including Joan of Arc, were brutally tortured and executed.

It seemed to Arlene that in many ways our so-called modern world hadn't progressed much beyond the Dark Ages. Abortion and contraception were still being condemned, women were still being denied the right to make decisions concerning their own bodies and they were still being caricatured as "witches" and "bitches" for wanting to be on an equal footing, politically, economically and socially, with men.

Arlene thought she might like to help the crusade for women's rights in some way, but she was rather hesitant about getting involved with an organization that many people associated with lesbianism. She played over and over again in her mind the way she and Jane Hawthorne had met and wondered if it had been a gay come-on. But it didn't seem like that to her. She wanted to believe that Jane liked her in a friendly, nonsexual way and she was pretty sure that was the case. So she ended up phoning Jane Hawthorne at Kaiser Press and making arrangements to go with her to the next NOW meeting.

PART FIVE
REAGAN

"Women are getting raped all the time. And I don't need to get raped because I'd never get over it. That's when my songs would stop. That's when my belief in the world would die. "
-- Stevie Nicks

"Why are people so afraid to admit they have it in them? I could pull a trigger. Am I crazy?"
-- Jodie Foster

"The problem that has no name -- which is simply the fact that American women are kept from growing to their full human capacities -- is taking a far greater toll on the physical and mental health of our country than any known disease. "
-- Betty Friedan

"Soon there will not be a Jew in the United States -- and by that I mean a Jew that will be able to walk or talk. "
-- Klan leader Wesley Swift

CHAPTER 34

By the early 1980's, thanks to effective use of the money appropriated from the Peoples Temple colony in Guyana, Conrad Pryzor's Aryan Confederacy was firmly established in southwestern Pennsylvania. His ninety-six-acre compound was thirty miles south of the small town of Washington, sometimes called "Little Washington." Pryzor liked to point out that it was named after George Washington of cherry tree fame, not George Washington Carver the ex-slave whose "shitty little experiments with peanuts got gushed over to high heaven by all the stinkin' commie perfessors and nigger lovers."

As a young man, George Washington had roamed these parts while surveying for the Mason-Dixon Line, and had invested in an iron forge and various other enterprises round about. When Conrad Pryzor made his scouting trips here, planning his move from Mississippi, he felt as though he was following in Washington's footsteps, laying the groundwork for an even grander legacy of his own. He pictured himself being recognized as the true Father of His Country for helping it to complete its predestined evolution into an Aryan Nation.

There were heartening signs of progress already. In June 1980, Tom Metzger, the chief of the California Ku Klux Klan, defeated Ed Skagen, the Democratic Party Chairman of San Diego County, in a primary election in the 43rd Congressional District. This was America's most populous District, with over one million people! As the primary winner, Klan Leader Metzger earned the right to install several Klansmen onto the state and county Democratic Committees. Ed Skagen, humiliated in defeat, said, "It seems like Riverside and Imperial Counties want to be represented by the Ku Klux Klan. I don't like being beaten by the Klan, but if that's what the people want, give it to them."

Music to Conrad Pryzor's ears. He could picture himself staging a similar coup someday.

He had been attracted to this part of Pennsylvania because it was known as "Klan Country North" but initially he found that its reputation on that score was exaggerated. True, there was some Klan and neo-Nazi activity here, but it was sketchy and sporadic, not strongly organized and led -- which was the opening Pryzor was looking for. He used his money to set himself up as a force to be reckoned with and launched an intensive indoctrination and recruitment campaign. Within a few years, his Aryan Confederacy had absorbed the smaller, less dynamic groups, and had grown to over three hundred members.

He believed that as his army of soldiers and worker ants grew, he might well acquire enough clout to get himself elected mayor of Little Washington. As the county seat of Washington County, the town already had a courthouse modeled after the United States Capitol, which could fittingly serve as the capitol of the Aryan Confederacy. Pryzor could picture his troops goose-stepping down the avenue in front of "his" capitol, striking awe and fear in the hearts of non-whites and inspiring whites to join the Movement in such large numbers that it would rapidly spread across the county, across the state and across the nation.

For now, the scope of his ambitions, plans and activities must be kept secure from the prying eyes of unwanted visitors. If you didn't know exactly how to get to his compound you would be hard-pressed to find it. The mouth of the rude yellow-dirt road was obscured by tall, thick weeds as you rounded a tight curve on a sparsely travelled rural blacktop. If you managed to spot the unmarked entrance instead of shooting right past it, it would take you on a discouragingly rough, rocky ride for three twisting and climbing miles through dense woods devoid of any signs of human life, and by that time you would be quite likely to give up and turn back. Even if you kept on going in spite of your misgivings and finally reached the outskirts of the compound, you must then get past a concrete guardhouse and a chain-link fence topped with razor wire.

At each corner of the fence were watchtowers manned by sentries with automatic weapons, and at night the inner perimeter was patrolled by vicious Rottweilers. A large rudely painted sign asked those who wanted to risk climbing the fence to please first remove their watches, eyeglasses and false teeth so that those small hard articles wouldn't stick in the dogs' throats or upset their stomachs.

The ten-foot-high fence encircled the main installations of the compound: the original farmhouse which had been completely renovated, rewired and re-equipped as an administrative headquarters; the newly built broadcast tower and studio of ARYN radio; two low-slung military-style barracks; a large mess hall; and a charmingly quaint little white church with a steeple, built in the image of the proverbial "church in the wildwood," except the marquee said that it was called the

Church of the Aryan Savior, Conrad Pryzor was its pastor, and the topic of his upcoming sermon was, "Is it a Sin to Kill Jews for Jesus?"

In founding his church, Pryzor had been inspired by Jim Jones's successful manipulation of religion for his own ends. From the pulpit of his church and the microphone of his radio station, Pryzor preached more vehemently than ever that Jesus Christ was an Aryan, not a Jew, that the biblical lost tribes of Israel were Aryans, that the Aryans were God's Chosen People, that America was the Aryan Promised Land, that Jews were Satan worshippers who must be destroyed, and that all non-whites must be subjugated and enslaved.

Conrad Pryzor's mother and father had been sharecroppers in Mississippi, which meant that the entire family including the ten children had to work in the cotton fields. Three of the children died without making it into their teens. Ellie Pryzor, the mother, died of pneumonia when she was forty-seven, weakened and shriveled beyond her years by all those episodes of childbirth and the daily grind of hard work and poverty. In the absence of her gentling influence, the seven surviving children grew up ragged and wild, yet too helpless and weak to squirm out from under the cruel thumb of their drunken and abusive father.

Harry Pryzor, Conrad's father, hated Jews and "Nigras" with the passion of the downtrodden against those he could blame for his misfortune. He was an unexceptional man whose life was a failure, yet he was proud of his membership in the Ku Klux Klan and liked to put on his white sheet and hood and go to Klan rallies and get plastered and mean. He absorbed enough Klan rhetoric to call the First and Second World Wars "Jew War One" and "Jew War Two" and to blame the "world-wide Jew conspiracy" for the defeat and humiliation of Germany and for the Great Depression of the Thirties that had caused his own father to lose the family farm, plunging him into poverty and sharecroppery. Harry Pryzor considered Negroes a "garbage race" who should still be chained up and picking cotton in the hot sun while he stood over them sneeringly with whip and pistol.

"Atsaway t'was," he said, "afore the damn Yankees come down here and spoilt ever 'thing. "

Since he couldn't tyrannize blacks as freely as he would have liked and, for that matter, since he was financially inferior to and disrespected by all the whites that he worked for, Harry Pryzor chose to tyrannize his own children. He abused them with his heavy leather strap and his engorged penis. His perverted lusts were slaked on the bodies of each of the four girls before they reached puberty, while the three boys were successively sodomized one by one while they were still in elementary school. They were too terrified to tell anyone what was being done to them, even if they could have convinced themselves that anyone would care.

When he was fifteen, Conrad and one of his older sisters, Jasmine, decided to club their father to death while he was in a drunken stupor. But he wasn't as stupefied as they thought, and when Jazzy raised her club to hit him his eyes popped open and he rolled aside with startling agility, receiving only a glancing blow to his shoulder. Jazzy dropped her club and ran out the back door. Conrad banged his father in the shin with a coal shovel, but the old man didn't go down and Conrad panicked, dropped the shovel and ran after Jazzy. They fled deeper and deeper into the woods with the old man panting after them, ranting and cursing, stumbling and crashing through the underbrush.

When Connie and Jazzy were too tired to run anymore, they hid in a ravine covered with thick, leafy vines, a hidey hole growing darker and darker with approaching nightfall. Not more than fifty feet away, Harry stopped, out of breath, his eyes seeking them out as he cursed and yelled at them intermittently between gasps. They shuddered at the sound of his hoarse rasping, expecting to be spotted at any moment. It took a long time for him to catch his breath and calm down.

Then, in a tone that was eerily soft and seductive, he said, "Jazzy ... Connie ... I'll sure's hell be waitin' up fer ya when y'all come slinkin' home hungry. I'll feed ya after I make ya pay fer what ya done to me. So come on home, ya hear me, when y'alls ready to take what's comin' to ya."

They heard him leave, or at least they thought so, but they were still too afraid to come out of their hiding place. They stayed there all night, hugging each other for warmth, shivering with coldness and fright, sleeping but little in the leafy ravine. When rays of sunlight started poking through the leaves they crawled out and hastily started working their way out of the woods. They didn't even discuss any notion of heading home; they both knew it wasn't an option any more. As soon as they made it to a paved road they started hitchhiking and didn't stop till they got to Jackson, Mississippi, over two hundred miles away from their father's rage and lust.

But they hadn't really escaped him after all. They found that they had to survive by doing what he had taught them to do with their bodies. They had to resort to trading sex acts for favors and for money, living on the streets and in tumble-down shacks in the city's slums.

Though she was a young female, barely seventeen years old, Jazzy wasn't very pretty and couldn't attract high-paying customers; she had big breasts but also a big belly, a fat ass and a double chin. A constant tic and a blank look in her watery gray eyes made her seem stupid or retarded, easy to victimize.

Connie found that he could score easier than she could. He was lean and lanky with a handsomely chiseled face, deep-set blue eyes and blonde hair. Gay men flocked to him. He earned three times as much as Jazzy did, which eventually enabled them to stay in flophouse hotels instead of in the streets. And one day by a stroke of luck his good looks became their key to an improved situation.

At first it seemed like bad luck when he got busted for prostitution, but his court-appointed attorney, Jim Richards, got him off with a fine and probation, and then made him an offer that included Jazzy. Jim wanted Connie to himself as a kept lover, so he gave him a job in his law office, filing papers and running errands. He also got Jazzy a waitressing job in a place where she made a decent hourly wage topped off with good tips. She didn't have to sell herself any more.

The arrangement lasted for several years, till Connie got older looking and lost his attractiveness for Jim Richards, who preferred boys so young that he could fantasize they were still virgins. Jim, Connie and Jazzy parted amicably. Jazzy landed a better paying job in a fancier restaurant and Connie became a clerk for yet another lawyer, this time in Oxford, where he was able to finally afford a fairly nice apartment. His new boss handled all the legal work for a local branch of the White Warriors, and he urged Connie to become a member.

When Connie attended his first meeting of that neo-Nazi organization, the leader ranted against Jews, niggers and faggots -- and Connie was so horribly humiliated that he almost ran out of the Chamber of Commerce hall. He felt as if people were staring at him, seeing into his soul with contempt and disgust.

He had never considered himself a faggot even while he was selling himself on the street, and especially not while he was being abused by his father. He never willingly accepted another man's penis. His customers paid to perform fellatio on him or to feel his penis inside them, not the other way around. That's the way it had been with Jim Richards, too; it was part of their deal. And the deal was over. All of that was behind Connie now. He wasn't having sex with men anymore and nobody was coercing him to do it and he was prepared to kill anyone who tried.

185

He was attracted to women, but only mildly. He believed therefore that he was basically heterosexual but his natural sex drive had probably been burnt out. In this he felt yet another form of kinship with Adolf Hitler, whose sexual tastes were unorthodox or perhaps largely dormant. It was rumored that Hitler was infatuated with his teenage niece and that the relationship was well hidden and eventually covered up after the girl was murdered or committed suicide. No one could testify that there had ever been sex between Hitler and his mistress Eva Braun even though he had married her before they ended their lives in a Munich bunker (or before the Red Army set it up to appear that way).

In any case, the Führer had made it amply clear that he was "wedded to the Reich." And Conrad Pryzor felt the same way about himself and his Aryan Confederacy, which was now carrying the torch for the White Race in its rightful drive toward world dominance.

Nobody was allowed to call Pryzor "Connie" anymore -- the name under which he had been victimized and abused. He was no longer a handsome youth, ignorant and callow but unusually sexually attractive -- which had proved to be a curse more than a blessing. Ashamed of his past and preoccupied with the pressures of leadership and hard work, he had gone soft and bald at an early age.

He was mindful of how the Führer had become a pitiful shell of himself as his health and his prospects of winning Jew War Two had deteriorated, and he was determined not to end up the same way. He scrupulously cultivated and preserved his image of strength, wisdom and unshakable conviction. He kept himself always fastidiously groomed whether in his uniform or in his pastoral robes. He took pride in his appearance as well as in his accomplishments.

In the fields and forests of his converted farm, squads of Aryan soldiers were being trained in modern guerilla tactics employing rifles, grenades, machine guns and mortars. They were learning efficient sabotage techniques such as how to build homemade bombs, how to plant explosives on bridges and railroad tracks, and how to ignite gasoline fires in tunnels and sewer systems.

Lately Pryzor had come up with the audacious idea of building his own air fleet. He urged his two best recruiters, Curb Burton and Bash Halsey, to try to enlist men who could fly airplanes.

Three pilots had already joined the Aryan Confederacy and one of them owned a Piper Cub. The other two did not have their own planes at the moment, but they could be called upon to fly rented crop dusters to disperse toxic chemical or biological vapors down upon chosen targets.

Conrad Pryzor was not so shortsighted as to confine his recruitment efforts to adults only. He was a man of unique vision and foresight, and so he had established an Aryan Youth Brigade. Kids liked to wear uniforms and be accepted and organized into troops, as in the Boy Scouts or the Hitler Youth.

They liked shooting at things with peashooters, slingshots or bebe guns. They liked setting off firecrackers. And their little minds were perfectly malleable, which is why Adolf Hitler had said, "Give me a child before he is five and he will be mine forever."

Pryzor's Aryan Youth Brigade was divided into four platoons. Cubby Platoon was for ages four to six; Cub Platoon was for ages six to ten; Bear Platoon was for ages ten to thirteen; and Lion Platoon was for ages thirteen to seventeen. As they progressed through these ranks, the enlistees were methodically taught obedience and discipline, endurance and teamwork, stoicism and stealth.

The intensity and severity of their training was stepped up progressively as they grew older and more mature. When they were kindergarten age, their crawling and hiding exercises were easy and fun, like the make-believe games played by ordinary children. But by age six, calisthenics, sprints and endurance runs were introduced. Eventually they were learning ju-jitsu, karate and more lethal forms of hand-to-hand combat. By the time they were in their early teens they could assemble and disassemble the rifles and handguns that they used with impressive expertise on the firing range. And when they graduated from the Lion Platoon, by age eighteen or nineteen, they were well-schooled in disguise and deception, escape and evasion, clandestine communication and spy tactics, methods of sabotage, and strategies of assassination and murder.

The instructors and squad leaders under Pryzor were hardened true believers in the Aryan Confederacy and its avowed goal of white supremacy. Most were not only veterans of official hostilities such as the Vietnam War, but also had Special Forces, SEAL or CIA training, including experience in carrying out clandestine search-and-destroy or kill missions.

Just as Conrad Pryzor's Aryan Confederacy was growing and thriving in the United States, the decade of the 1980's so far was heralding a symbiotic rise in world-wide Naziism. In Paris a few months ago a bomb blast rocked 350 Jewish worshippers in a synagogue not far from the Arc de Triomphe, wounding dozens and killing three -- a delicious irony, as far as Pryzor was concerned, for this same synagogue had been blown up by Hitler's troops back in 1944.

In Munich a bomb planted in a trash can during Oktoberfest killed thirteen and wounded more than 200. And in the previous August Italian neo-Fascists blew up the Bologna train station, killing eighty-four and wounding 180. The Armed Revolutionary Nuclei, who claimed responsibility for the Bologna bombing, followed it up by assassinating Mario Amato, a magistrate who had tried to bring them to justice.

In the small Italian town or Predappio, the birthplace of Benito Mussolini, preparations were underway to celebrate the one-hundredth birthday of Il Duce, with a gigantic festival and a high mass led by the pastor of a local church. Millions of Italians were now waxing nostalgic over the grandeur of Rome that Mussolini had attempted to revive, and were hoping for it to happen all over again but with greater success.

As heartened as he was by these kinds or developments, Pryzor knew that he must exercise caution and not try to move too quickly. Like young braves too hotheaded to listen to the old chiefs, the young Nazis who blew up synagogues and train stations were likely to bring a terrible backlash down upon themselves. They might easily be wiped out before they were strong enough to resist the powerful police and military forces wielded by the established governments of their countries.

Here in the United States hotheads were also on the loose. Many of them were inspired by a novel called *The Turner Diaries* in which an army of super-patriots overthrows the American government, massacres Jews and other non-Aryans, and annihilates Israel with nuclear weapons, thereby ushering in a Christian Paradise. It would be nice if it could actually happen. But it was a pipedream. A novel! Written by a former physics professor! Yet young zealots were taking the book to heart, forming their own militant splinter groups, and going out and blowing up schools, police stations and synagogues. While he might find their zeal commendable, Conrad Pryzor repudiated their methods. He wanted to rein his followers in and teach them patience. He wasn't against violence when it was used judiciously. But right now he needed to bide his time and build his strength without prematurely risking everything he had worked for.

ZOG -- the Zionist Occupation Government of the United States -- had gone a long way toward bleeding itself out in Vietnam. Its wasteful spillage of American blood had turned millions of its subjects against it. Widespread alienation had given rise to many small, fanatically militant groups such as the Black Panthers, the Weathermen and the Symbionese Liberation Army -- but none of them ever had a real chance of gaining power or starting the revolution they hoped for. They were all pathetically weak and inept, and if they hadn't been blasted out of existence they would have fizzled out in their own good time. Pryzor did not want his Aryan Confederacy to suffer that same fate. Right now he was growing stronger every day. From the microphone and the pulpit, he was winning hearts and minds and making political inroads. He was building up a broader and increasingly disgruntled base of like-minded supporters for the time of the Big Push that was surely coming.

He was willing to wait for the time to be ripe, for ZOG to grow weaker and weaker as it kept on turning millions of its own citizens against itself. Poverty, despair and the loss of national pride were the fertile soil of rebellion. When the people were made totally ready for a strong leader, exactly as the political and economic collapse of Germany after World War One had made the populace ready for Adolf Hitler, then the American people would embrace Conrad Pryzor and bring him to power.

CHAPTER 35

On Easter Sunday in 1981, Roseanne McCoy beamed proudly as her eight-year-old son Delbert knelt at the altar of the Church of Our Aryan Savior to be inducted into Conrad Pryzor's Aryan Youth Brigade.

After Maylon's suicide back in 1978, Roseanne had desperately needed to get away from Cherry Hill, where she and her son were treated like outcasts. Delbert was constantly being picked on by other boys because of what his father had done. Just about everybody in town was either a friend, relative or acquaintance of somebody who had been held hostage in the bank, and even though none of them had been killed, they and their loved ones had been thoroughly terrified. People who had been warm and friendly toward Roseanne from the time she was a little girl, now brushed past her without a word, pursing their lips and giving her disapproving, scornful looks.

She thought the town's attitude toward her might soften and she might even get some sympathy and understanding after her mother-in-law died in the winter of 1980. It was a bitter cold February, and on Groundhog Day Mama McCoy was found lying in the snow by the postman delivering mail in his Jeep. Mail from the day before was lying beneath her, a couple of seed catalogues and a letter from her daughter Arlene. People clucked their tongues and said she must've died of a broken heart. But they were a bunch of hypocrites. While she was living they had shunned Mama McCoy just as much as they shunned Roseanne. But they came to the funeral home and the burial just to stare at or sidle up to the only celebrity who ever came out of Cherry Hill -- Lori McCoy. It was sickening how the bigwigs of the town and all the other two-faced jerks groveled around Lori and her sister Arlene, Lori's daughter Missy, and Lori's husband and ex-husband. Lots of them were hoping they'd get some money from being interviewed or peddling old pictures of Lori in grade school or high school to the tabloids. Meanwhile they continued treating Roseanne like dirt. It made no never mind to them that poor little Delbert had lost his grandmother same as Missy had, yet they mooned over Missy and acted so damn sorry for her, as if butter wouldn't melt in their mouths.

Roseanne and Delbert and Roseanne's ma and pa were treated nice, like part of the family, by Lori and her entourage, and when some of the folks saw that, they forced themselves to be kind for a little while, too. But right after Mama McCoy was laid in the ground, they went right back to their hateful ways. Their meanness against Roseanne got worse and worse, till she started to feel as if Gene Pitney's hit song *A Town Without Pity* was written with her in mind. She got laid off from her job at the only dry-cleaning store in town, her boss using the excuse that his daughter was coming to work for him without pay, when any fool knew that the daughter, who had given birth out of wedlock and yet was considered a better person than Roseanne, would be paid under the table so she could still collect food stamps and welfare checks, same as Roseanne had been doing.

Totally demoralized and depressed, Roseanne couldn't fight the whole town. She knew she was never going to get her old job back and no other place in Cherry Hill was going to hire her. She couldn't sponge forever off of her ma and pa; they could barely make ends meet even before Roseanne and Delbert came to live under their roof. She chipped in out of her food stamps and welfare checks, but it wasn't a drop in the bucket. Somehow she had to find a decent-paying job, and that meant she had no choice except to get out of town.

But where to go? South to Charleston or maybe Parkersburg? Or north toward Wheeling or Weirton? Where would she find some kind of silver lining? Where would her streak of bad luck end?

She wished she could find herself a man. True, she'd be asking him to accept a ready-made family, but that hadn't appeared to be much of an obstacle before Maylon went off the deep end. Some of the guys in Cherry Hill were starting to get extra friendly while she and her husband were separated.

But now none of them would come near her; they acted like she was some kind of witch. She wished Maylon had never come back here. Things would have been totally different. He'd still be alive and she'd be hooked up with somebody new. Delbert would have nice visits with his biological father, plus he'd have a money-earning stepfather to take good care of him day to day.

Roseanne knew she wasn't a raving beauty but she was still plenty attractive to men. She was barely into her thirties. Her face was plain, like her mother's, dotted with freckles and framed in frizzy red hair. But her body was solid, her best feature. When she stood naked in front of her mirror, she couldn't grab more than a pinch of belly fat -- thanks partly to the fact that she held back from eating too much when she was at her parents' table. Her breasts were small but perky, her thighs maybe a bit thin but lithe and muscular. Maylon used to tell her she had a nice butt. If she got her nice butt out of Cherry Hill, maybe she'd find herself a job and a man. One day when she was mooning about feeling sorry for herself, her pa told her she ought to call up her cousin Mary Rae, who had a good secretarial job with Weirton Steel. "Mebbe she kin git ya hired 'longside 'er, 'at gal's allas been a talker'n' a go-gitter. Take a lesson from 'er 'n' pull yerself up by yer bootstraps. "

Roseanne flushed and almost burst into tears. It was the first time her pa had let her know he was upset with her and probably tired of having her and her son hanging around, putting a drain on his finances. The very next morning she phoned Mary Rae and was told that Weirton Steel wasn't hiring anybody at all right now, but there were lots of other kinds of jobs in Weirton of the low-wage variety, and Roseanne and Delbert were welcome to come and stay with her in her spare room till they found something and got themselves settled.

And so Roseanne and Delbert moved to Weirton, which was up in the northern panhandle of West Virginia, not far from the Pennsylvania border and within thirty miles of Little Washington. About three months after finding under-the-table work at a shot-and-a-beer dive near the steel mill gate, Roseanne took up with a rough-and-tough blast-furnace laborer, Harney Logan, who had joined the Aryan Confederacy a few months earlier and was one of its most ardent new recruits.

Harney had a passion for motorcycles and rode a huge, powerful Harley, so he was called Harley Logan most of the time rather than Harney. He belonged to the Aryan Warriors, a newly formed "mechanized platoon" of the Aryan Confederacy. He loved going on bike runs with a couple dozen of his fellow Warriors, all of them in black Nazi-style helmets and black leather jackets emblazoned with swastikas and lightning bolts. They'd gun their machines, chewing up the highway and scaring dogs, cats, kids and adults with their mighty roar and their brazen, scowling faces, afraid of nothing and nobody.

Harley Logan never missed a Confederacy picnic, beer blast or rally, and he began taking Roseanne and Delbert along with him. She'd ride on the back of his big bike, clinging to his lean, hard hips, and Delbert would ride the same way, hugging onto one of the other Warriors. They always made a wild, raucous, dust-churning entrance to every event, and being included in the romp gave Rosanne and Delbert a spine-tingling surge of excitement mixed with a feeling of being special and important.

When Harley Logan first introduced Roseanne to Conrad Pryzor, of whom she was in awe, the venerated Leader of the Confederacy received her in a warm, dignified way and seemed intensely interested in her circumstances. She revealed that she blamed an FBI agent, Frank Williams, for her husband's death.

"I know Frank Williams," Pryzor said, patting little Delbert on his blonde head. "I've had a run-in with him. He's out to destroy people like us."

"He was supposed to bring Maylon out of that bank alive!" Roseanne said angrily. "But Frank come out by hisself. What it boils down to, he abandoned my husband! Prob'ly on purpose! I think Maylon musta felt like it was a setup -- if he came out he was gonna be shot. So he put the gun to his own head. But he didn't hurt nobody else. He let all the hostages go free. "

"He was the real victim, the only victim," Pryzor said. "He fought for his country and his country betrayed him. That won't happen when the Aryan race is in power and running this country the way it ought to be run. "

"I agree with you," Roseanne said, blushing. "The speech you give at the beginnin' of the rally was wonderful. It made me think about changin' my life. Me and Delbert ... I know he's just a boy ... but we both wanna fight for somethin' we can believe in."

"I can show you the way to do that," Pryzor said. "So can Harley. He's a good Aryan soldier."

Roseanne and Delbert had long felt like poor downtrodden victims of society at large, and so they were primed to accept the Aryan Confederacy's version of who was to blame for their plight and how they could begin to fight back. The little boy idolized Harley Logan and the other members of the mechanized platoon. And his mother felt totally safe and protected when she was surrounded by them.

Harley was rough with Roseanne sometimes but she decided it was the price she had to pay for being with a real man. In retrospect, it seemed to her that Maylon had been too nice, too darn sensitive. He had let people walk all over him. Like that high-falutin' sister of his. In fact, both sisters. If they had loosened their purse strings and treated Maylon the way he deserved to be treated, his life wouldn't have ended in tragedy.

After Delbert and the other little boys kneeling at the altar took their Oath of Allegiance to the Aryan Youth Brigade, all nine of them had medals pinned on them and Conrad Pryzor himself shook their hands.

Then the Easter party got started on the grounds of the compound, where there was a huge picnic shelter and barbecue pit. There was cake and ice cream for the kiddies and beer and hot dogs for the adults.

Sitting at a picnic table with Harley's beefy arm around her, Roseanne felt warm and mellow, getting a buzz on from the beer, and smiling at the way her son totally fit in with the other boys who had taken the oath with him. They were out in the field playing a game of touch football, and Delbert had been chosen as one of the quarterbacks. He was small for his age but surprisingly good at tossing long passes. These new friends of his had recognized that, whereas the boys back in Cherry Hill never let him play at all -- they just refrained from picking him for either side and beat him up if he tried to stay and watch on the sidelines.

One of the kids who picked on Delbert the worst was a boy two years older and much bigger, whose father was an ex-Marine. He made Delbert's life a living hell on the playground and on the school bus. The principle of the school did nothing about it. And when Roseanne went to have a talk with the bully's father in the divey bar where he hung out, he sneered at her, tossed down a shot of whisky and said, "My boy's tough, gonna be a jarhead like his daddy. I raised him up to be a fighter, and you shoulda done the same for your boy steada raisin' him up to be a sissy. Gettin' beat up's good for him, it'll maybe teach him how to fight back steada always runnin' to his mommy. "

The other bar patrons snickered at this. One of them even chimed in, saying, "Your husband was a coward, Rosie, an' at's a fact -- he proved it when he blowed 'is own head off."

"Don't you dare talk about my husband!" Roseanne shouted. "None or you went and fought in Vietnam! *You're* the goddamn cowards!"

"Well, *I* fought over there -- two hitches," the bully's father said. "So whaddayou gotta say to that, huh?"

"All's I want you to do," Roseanne said meekly, "is tell your son to leave my boy alone. If he's as tough as you claim he is, he should at least pick on some kid his own age."

"You don't mind if he beats up somebody else's kid?" the bully's father said with a big, mocking smile.

All the barflies cracked up, and Roseanne turned around and slinked out of the place, totally embarrassed, angry and demoralized. She felt that way all over again each time she remembered the incident.

She looked forward to the day when her son might go back to Cherry Hill, a weakling turned into a warrior. She pictured him bigger and stronger, toughened up and made proficient in Karate, judo, hand-to-hand combat and all the other skills he would learn in the Aryan Youth Brigade. Sure enough he'd kick that damned bully's ass! Revenge would be sweet. His jarhead father wouldn't know whether to shit or go blind.

Roseanne believed that joining with the people here, the people she was surrounded with inside this safe, secure compound, was the best thing that could ever have happened. She thanked God for it. And she knew that Delbert felt just as good about it as she did. He was more confident, more alive. They were both basking in the glow of being part of something much bigger than themselves. They weren't being picked on anymore. They had powerful friends and protectors now. The dark cloud over them had lifted, and they were beginning a bright new life.

CHAPTER 36

When Michele Santone graduated from Belmont University in June of 1982, Keith treated all of us to a flight up there in his private airplane. By "us" I mean Lori and Charlie; Keith and his main squeeze at the time, a tall blonde fashion model named Shannon Cristy; Lori's sister Arlene; Arlene's friend and co-worker in the women's movement, Jane Hawthorne; and of course myself. I had driven from Pittsburgh to New York the day before and had stayed overnight at Keith's penthouse.

We had hotel reservations for the day before the commencement through to the day after. Since we didn't have to get spiffed up for the ceremony yet, we were all dressed casually for the flight, most of us in jeans. I didn't feel very casual, though. I was stressed to the max from spending most of last week in a desperate scramble for leads on some nuts doing a string of bank robberies and bombings in Pennsylvania.

Keith loved expensive gadgets and gimmickry, and his newest toy was the ten-million-dollar Gulfstream Executive Aircraft we had just boarded. "To get this baby I had to trade in two Learjets," he said, grinning proudly. "It's my second home anytime I'm on business trips -- or pleasure trips too, for that matter. Let me show you around, we have a few minutes before takeoff. Meanwhile Melanie will serve cocktails." Melanie was the young rosie-cheeked flight attendant who took orders for drinks while we gawked at the plane's lavish decor. The curved walls in the cigar-shaped hull were paneled in tan suede. The hand-woven carpet was dark brown. The passenger chairs were plushly upholstered in soft burgundy-red leather, and Keith showed us how they could be swiveled, tilted and reclined in multiple ways for maximum comfort. The seating arrangements were quite roomy and equipped with worktables that would rise from the floor at the touch of a button, which Keith demonstrated. Then he touched another button to show us how we could make TV monitors descend from the ceiling in front of our seats, giving us in-flight access to three video and eight audio channels.

He then led us into his plush but compact executive compartment, his private abode, which could be isolated from the passenger cabin by a padded soundproofed barrier that was folded into the fuselage. Pulling it shut so we could see how tightly it could close the compartment off, he said, "See? It's practically soundproof. Most noises won't carry out of here. A handy feature, am I right, Shannon?" He winked mischievously at her and she smiled, unembarrassed. "The sofa converts into a double bed," he continued with another wink, "and the wall over there conceals my foldaway desk, and it has an eighteen-inch color monitor installed above it that's connected to a microcomputer, state of the art. Dig? I can run business programs and transmit data back to my office in New York, even if I happen to be a thousand miles away."

"And we can look at porno tapes too," Shannon added saucily.

"Hey, babe, don't give away *all* my secrets," Keith said.

We all laughed as if they were kidding, but they probably weren't.

Mouth-watering aromas were filling the plane by now, and Jane said, "Umm ... smells delicious in here."

"That's why I told you not to have any breakfast," Keith said jovially. "We're gonna eat like kings -- and queens. I'll show you the galley later. Right now the chef is busy in there."

Once we were in the air and cruising, we dined at two small mahogany tables laden with delicately crafted china and silverware and fine linen napkins and placemats. The diminutive, mustachioed chef appeared in a white apron and tall white hat and with a proud flourish he served us chicken marsala, sauteed asparagus and hot, crusty French baguettes. Throughout the meal, Melanie kept refilling our tall crystal glasses with Dom Perignon, and we all got a bit tipsy, lapsing into light patter and easy laughter.

I was seated across from Jane Hawthorne, and was finding her engagingly witty and vivacious. I could have allowed myself to be smitten, but I fought against the attraction, warning myself not to be overly charmed. I could use a sack partner from time to time, but I wasn't looking to get heavily involved with anyone. Especially, I wasn't looking to get married again. I had learned that most marriages, especially cop marriages, didn't last. My split-up with Alice Kenton was a prime example.

I reminded myself that I was cut out to be a loner, and it was best that I stayed that way. And not just because of my particular mission in the FBI. Something in my nature had made me back away from the social clamor of my football playing days, even before I had thought of becoming a cop. Writing, if I had become a writer, was a largely solitary profession, and so was law enforcement, but of course there was a big difference -- in fact a chasm -- between writing crime novels and immersing oneself in real-life murder and mayhem. I had taken a strange path from one aspiration to another. If I could have made a career writing about tragedies and atrocities, instead of dealing with them in person, would I still have turned into an unfit companion for normal everyday people?

Sometimes I felt like I was actually doing some good in the world, and sometimes I felt like I was swimming in garbage. As a nation, we still seemed to be stuck in a downhill self-destructive spiral. Less than a year ago, President Reagan had been shot and nearly killed by a would-be assassin named John Hinckley. Reagan's press secretary, James Brady, had taken a bullet in the head during the attack, but was miraculously still alive although horribly impaired -- twenty percent of his brain had been removed by surgeons. Hinckley claimed he did it to impress a teenaged actress, Jodie Foster, whom he had seen in *Taxi Driver*, a movie that he had watched over and over, fixating on Foster and identifying with a homicidal sociopath portrayed by her co-star, Robert DeNiro.

America had no shortage of real-life sociopaths for disturbed young men to model themselves after. I kept tabs on all the high-profile FBI cases, even the ones I wasn't directly involved in, because you never could tell when two or more seemingly unrelated investigations might start to mesh. And I still had a powerful passion to see the bad guys put out of business, whether on my watch or someone else's. Black people especially were running scared these days, and with good reason. The Ku Klux Klan and the neo-Nazis were on the rise again. In Buffalo, New York, six black men had been gunned down from ambush. Two of them, both cab drivers, were found with their hearts cut out. And somebody, possibly the same perpetrator, tried to strangle a black man who was recovering from an appendectomy in a Buffalo hospital. "I hate niggers," he mumbled as he tightened his fingers around his victim's throat. He was caught in the act by a nurse and a janitor, and he knocked them both down, running down the hall and getting away clean. Luckily the black man survived.

All around the country there was an epidemic of lynchings, shootings, bombings and church burnings. When young black kids started turning up dead in Atlanta -- fourteen of them – hysteria ran rampant; the black community thought the murders must be racially motivated. When the murderer was caught he turned out to be a mild-mannered, rather nurdish black man named Wayne Williams who had befriended the boys right in their own neighborhood. But to this day, stuck on the racial theory, lots of folks persisted in believing that Williams was framed.

One of the bizarre effects of the assaults and murders unleashed on high-profile people like Ronald Reagan, John Lennon, Sharon Tate and Patty Hearst was that new companies sprung up selling bulletproof designer clothes. The old-fashioned bulletproof vests were so cumbersome they couldn't be worn to chic Hollywood parties, but a breakthrough happened when Du Pont developed a puncture-resistant material called Kevlar, originally intended for automobile tires. The thin, lightweight armor not only could stop nails -- it also could stop bullets. Cops started wearing bulletproof undershirts. Soon Kevlar became trendy. A New York company debuted a line of gunshot-resistant jump suits, safari jackets and vests in pastel earth tones. And a Beverly Hills fashion designer began offering men's and women's suits and fur coats lined with Kevlar.

I was worried that all this bulletproof "finery" was going to find its way into the hands of bad guys, including terrorists. Already many of the criminals that I had to face were armed way better than I was. They had assault rifles, M-16's, grenades and machine guns, whereas most police officers, especially the ones in municipal departments, were carrying nothing more powerful than a .38 revolver.

Lori McCoy confided in me that she was carrying a .38 in her purse that had been given to her by one of her band members. I warned her that more civilian weapons end up being used against their owners than against attackers. But she said, "Don't you worry, I know how to use it. I won't let anybody take it off of me. And even though I can be pretty damned depressed sometimes, I ain't gonna kill myself neither."

My own gun, a 9mm Sig-Sauer, FBI issue, was a nuisance to me a whole lot of the time. Like now, for instance. On the plane, even though I'd have been more comfortable with my jacket off, I had to keep it on to cover the gun and holster, and the gun was bothering me, digging into my ribs.

"Frank? Come back to us, Frank."

Jane Hawthorne's soft, mocking voice drew me back into the company of the other people I was with right now. "Sorry," I said. "I guess I'm having trouble unwinding."

"If I had your job I'd never unwind," Arlene said. She and Jane were seated with me during lunch. Keith and Shannon were seated at the other little table with Charlie and Lori, about an arm's length away in the narrow aisle of the plane.

Keith said, "Have another glass of champagne, Frank. Or something stronger if that's what it takes to drive the boogeymen away."

"What boogeymen?" Shannon wanted to know.

"Frank's not just an ordinary FBI guy, he's on the Antiterrorist Squad," Keith told her with macabre delight. "He has to deal with some of the worst crazies you could ever imagine. Grisly and gruesome are part of his daily diet."

"Ugh! Murders?" Shannon recoiled, her eyes widening as she took another sip of champagne.

"Frank used to want to be a writer," Arlene told Jane. "Isn't that right, Frank?"

I nodded, not particularly wanting to get into that subject. My long-ago rejection slips still smarted.

"Lots of cops have turned out to be excellent writers," Jane said. "Joseph Wambaugh, for instance. I imagine you'd have some wild and interesting stories to tell, Frank, if you ever wanted to set them down on paper."

"Maybe someday," I said. "I don't know if I'm ready to relive any of it yet."

"It could be therapeutic," Jane persisted. "We should get together and talk. I'm not promising anything, but I'd love to pick your brain. There are a number of avenues a book could take, whether as fiction or nonfiction."

"Jane can help you a lot," Arlene interjected brightly.

"I don't doubt that," I said. "But I need some time to think about it. I'm not free to talk about a lot of my cases, especially the ones that are still in progress."

"Well, okay," Jane said. "I can certainly understand that. But when you're ready to talk, give me a call. Arlene has my number."

I wondered why I wasn't jumping at the opportunity that Jane was offering. A path I used to want to take seemed to be beckoning to me, and I was almost willfully turning my back on it. Maybe I was scared it would change my life too much at this point. Maybe I didn't want to be deflected from my obsession with Conrad Pryzor. Maybe I was just being stupid. Jane had been introduced to me as an editor for Kaiser Press, a prestigious publisher. I told myself that even if I didn't really want to write a book right now, I shouldn't pass up the opportunity for getting to know Jane better.

"I guess I'd like to bash some ideas around with you," I told her finally. "But I won't be in New York long after we fly back there. I have to be back in Pittsburgh by Tuesday."

"Let's have lunch Sunday afternoon, then."

"All right. Then I can still drive back on Monday."

"It's a deal. Cheers."

She clinked her glass against mine and we drank to it.

Arlene toasted along with us, her face beaming, and I wondered if all along she had been acting as a matchmaker. But that didn't make complete sense. After all, Jane Hawthorne and I were living four hundred miles apart.

CHAPTER 37

Missy and her fiancé, Dan Clanton, flew back with us the day after she got her diploma. Missy's big party was going to take place in New York several weeks hence. She and Dan had graduated together. They were both communications majors, both avid about becoming successful filmmakers, which in my mind conjured up remembrances of Carlisle and Brenda Dixon.

Keith's graduation present to his daughter was a gift of one hundred thousand dollars so she and Dan could start their own production company instead of going to work for someone else. Announcing the gift yesterday at a celebratory dinner, he said, "I don't want you to suffer like I did, honey. I was given a job by a woman named Margot Dane when I first started out, but she treated me like shit. I was never going to go anyplace with her. Luckily, I was smart enough to recognize a huge opportunity when the Leprechaun walked in one day and let me make both of us filthy rich."

He always referred to Ed Baumgardner as "the Leprechaun" when Ed wasn't around. And Ed wasn't around very much these days. He and his wife, Keith's mother, spent most of their time going on ocean cruises, while Keith ran their Natural Life Company and kept turning it into an ever more lucrative gold mine.

Missy had never flown in the new Gulfstream, and when she and Dan first boarded she laughed and said, "Oh, Daddy, this reminds me of the Liberace limo! Remember? With the purple rumble seat and that unbelievable hot tub? This airplane doesn't have a hot tub, does it?"

Keith pretended to be insulted. "Are you calling my airplane tacky?"

"No, I admit it's very tasteful -- probably excessive, but that's your style, of course." She turned to Dan. "My dad has to do everything in a huge way."

"I can see that," Dan said, with evident admiration. He was a rather bookish looking young man with wire-rimmed glasses and the obligatory long hair affected by almost all artists and filmmakers these days. His designer jeans, shirts and boots were obviously expensive, and his reddish hair was clean and neat, probably razor-cut in a salon, as opposed to the ubiquitously greasy, scraggly, ratty-haired look I had grown so tired of seeing on young males everywhere.

"Well, the company pays for my toys, so why shouldn't I enjoy them?" Keith was saying. "I get a kick out of them. To me, they're like comfort food."

By now we were all in our seats, buckled in, and the plane was taxiing, then lifting.

"How much?" Missy asked.

"None of your business, but ten million smackers," Keith answered impishly.

"Oh my God!" Missy exclaimed. "And children all over the world are starving -- but I expect Charlie already pointed that out to you."

"He did indeed," Keith admitted. "But he's not exactly giving all his money away either."

"Well, I donated heavily to Jimmy Carter," Charlie said from across the aisle. "And I'm fixing to get behind Mondale big-time. We've gotta kick the Great Communicator out on his ass before his trickle-down shit trickles the whole country right down the tubes."

"Well, I voted for Reagan, and I'm gonna vote for him again," Keith said. "All us rich guys vote Republican."

"Daddy, that's disgusting," Missy said.

"You should be a Republican, too," Keith remonstrated, "instead of a liberal like your mother. Ask yourself which party is buttering your bread."

"Reagan doesn't do enough for social causes," Guinard said. "He has a bully pulpit and he doesn't use it. He could help us put an end to Apartheid if he wanted to. "

"You sound like the Charlie Guinard of old," Keith jibed. "The campus radical reborn! Maybe the trip back to the Belmont campus did it to you. If so, I should have my ass kicked. You gonna start wearing flannel shirts and letting your beard grow wild again, Charlie?"

"We're selling Guinard Enterprises," Lori announced, surprising all of us. "We're going to devote ourselves to important social causes."

"But you have a new album coming out!" Missy said incredulously. "Your career is going to take off again. You can't give it all up again, Mom!"

"I'm not giving it up," Lori said. "I'm gonna keep on singing, and Charlie is still gonna represent me and a couple of other artists he loves to work with."

"Life is too short not to follow your heart," Charlie said.

"I heartily agree," said Arlene. "I've already put my life in a new direction, thanks largely to Jane."

I was actually quite proud of Arlene for the changes she had made. As a result of losing weight and exercising regularly, she looked better at age thirty-eight than when she was twenty. Her self-effacing, self-destructive impulses seemed to have vanished. Instead she was in the forefront of the women's movement as the business manager of NOW and a staunch supporter and confidante of Betty Friedan. The skills Arlene had developed when she was performing managerial functions for Lori had stood her in good stead. After she joined NOW her skills were readily recognized and she had risen swiftly to a prominent position in the organization.

I seemed to be the only one on the plane who wasn't making dramatic or imaginative life changes. Arlene was. Charlie and Lori were. Even Shannon Cristy, who didn't seem to be one of the brightest lightbulbs in the chandelier, was moving away from runway modeling into a fledgling acting career. Keith was helping her in this by co-financing a movie for her. Well, why not? Howard Hughes had done it -- why not Keith? -- so long as he didn't end up as a recluse in an old shack somewhere, unbathed and with dirty untrimmed fingernails grown as long as his penis.

As for Jane Hawthorne, she and I had gotten to know each other better during the time in Belmont, and she had told me she was thinking about forming her own literary agency. "A lot of top editors end up doing it," she said. "As a successful buyer of manuscripts, who should know better than I what will sell? Some of the richest agents in the business used to work for publishers -- that's where you learn not only about readers' tastes but how to tailor and promote a book and give it a shot at the bestseller list."

I listened, enthralled with her and finding her very easy to look at. I knew from Arlene that Jane was in her early forties, same as I was. She had some lines in her face, particularly around her eyes, yet she exuded a youthful vivaciousness. She wore her dark hair short, just above her shoulders, with bangs, and she didn't use much makeup. Her eyes were bright blue, alive with intelligence, one of her most attractive features.

I had noticed, to my surprise as I got older, how I could find women my own age beautiful and sexy now, whereas when I was a young man they had seemed merely "old" to me.

"Would you need a lot of start-up cash?" I asked her. "If you wanted to launch your own agency?"

"Not a whole lot. I could work out of my home. I already have a fully equipped office there. I have money saved up too, and I probably could get severance pay."

"You'd stay in New York, then?"

I wondered if I'd ever be able to get myself transferred back to New York. And I figured that, even though it would put me closer to Jane as well as closer to some of the things I missed, I wouldn't really be ready to take that step until I could put an end to Conrad Pryzor.

"Well," Jane said, "New York is where you have to be to take the right kind of meetings and do the necessary shmoozing. It's where almost all the big publishers *are*. And I love New York anyway. I'm not thinking about leaving."

"You sound like my ex-wife," I said, "Alice Kenton."

"Oh, *I* know her! The magazine writer."

"Yeah, we split up when I transferred to Pittsburgh. She wanted to stay where the action was, but unfortunately my kind of action was leading me elsewhere."

"Aren't there bad guys all over the place? Especially in a city like New York, I should think."

"Well," I told her, "I got into the FBI because of something that happened a long time ago. Something one particular bad guy had a lot to do with."

"Conrad Pryzor," Jane said knowingly. "He's never far from your mind, is he?"

Startled, I said, "How do you know about him?"

"Well, Arlene told me. She told me about your friends being murdered on a trip to Dealey Plaza." Reaching out and touching my hand, she said, "You really should write about it, Frank. It could be very therapeutic for you."

CHAPTER 38

By the time he was twelve, Delbert McCoy knew how to disassemble and reassemble M-16's, AK-47's and many different kinds of semi-automatic pistols, both American and foreign made. He knew how to handle and plant various explosives, and how to set them off from a distance, by wire or by battery. He also knew how to wield a razor-sharp knife flat side up so it would slide smoothly between the ribs of an enemy instead of being stopped by a rib or a breastbone.

He had learned the deadly effectiveness of firing a bullet into the base of the skull or beneath the ear, instead of aiming at other parts of the head where key areas of the brain might not be sufficiently destroyed. He had studied manuals on how to hijack airplanes and how to acquire, make and use a variety of deadly poisons. He had practiced crawling up to buildings and lobbing dummy grenades through windows. He knew how to dodge hostile patrols and how to hide in caves or crevices. He also knew which kinds of edible plants would yield water and nourishment in case he had to survive in the wild.

He liked practicing on the firing range with the AR-15, a civilian version of the Army's M-16. And several times he had gotten to fire one of the Aryan Confederacy's Breda 37mm heavy machine guns, so loud it hurt his ears and would have knocked him over if it hadn't been mounted on a truck. He was proud of how well and how quickly he had learned to load and handle the powerful gun, steeling himself not to flinch and succeeding in mowing down a group of dummy targets.

However, as proficient as he was in "adult" tactics and weaponry, what he still liked best was war games, which were played with toy guns that looked real. The boys would be divided up into two teams, and one team would be given some time to hide themselves in the woods, wearing camouflage gear and practicing concealment and ambush techniques, then the other team would go in after them. You had to be sneaky and silent, and Delbert was very good at it. If you spotted an enemy troop before he spotted you, you said, "Bang, you're dead!" and he would be out of the game. The first team to have all its soldiers killed would be the loser. Delbert's side almost always won. And he was the boy who usually had the most kills.

The Leader himself, Conrad Pryzor, had openly praised him for his accomplishments, including how tough and muscular he had gotten by devoting himself to calisthenics and other forms of strength and endurance training. Curb and Bash constantly encouraged him to do better and better, as did his stepfather, Harley Logan. Delbert desperately wanted to please them. He idolized these "Aryan Warriors" and felt the warmest of glows whenever he was allowed to be with them. His mother was proud of him, too, but after all she was "Mom" -- her affection for him was a given, and didn't necessarily need to be earned; the camaraderie of the big, tough men was much more satisfying.

He no longer cared what the boys at school thought of him. Besides, none of them picked on him like the boys in Cherry Hill had. They were scared to. Although still short and boyish looking, he was heavier and stronger than most of the other boys his age. Some of them had tried pushing him around when he was littler, but nowadays he could beat any of them up if they messed with him.

Many of the kids were a little in awe of him these days. This was because they had heard him on the radio, even if they weren't allowed to listen to ARYN and had to do it sneakily, out of earshot of their parents. The Leader, Conrad Pryzor, had started an Aryan Youth radio program, broadcasting every Saturday afternoon, and had designated Delbert as the host and program director. His on-air name was Del Logan. His last name had been changed a year ago, when his mother married Harley. He wasn't meek little Delbert McCoy anymore. He was a brand new person on the radio and everywhere else.

Some of the older girls, eighth and nine graders, had begun giving him the eye. But he wasn't greatly interested in girls yet, although certainly he felt stirrings. His activities and challenges in the Aryan Youth Brigade pretty much monopolized his time and energy.

As a treat when he turned thirteen and graduated from the Bear Platoon into the Lions, Harley, Curb, and Bash told Delbert they were going to take him on a motorcycle run. They passed around a bottle, taking swigs from it before heading out from the compound. They even gave Delbert a little swig, laughing and slapping him on his back when the whisky made him choke and splutter.

They were out behind the guardhouse and the sun was going down. Luckily none of the other boys in the Aryan Youth Brigade were around to see Delbert choke on the whisky. He wanted to be able to brag to them about how much he had drunk and how easily he had tossed it down.

He was surprised when the men told him they were headed to a nigger speakeasy in some woods outside of a little town called Hanksville, West Virginia, about two hundred miles away. Curb and Bash took up handfuls of mud and smeared it over the license plates on the motorcycles. Delbert knew when he saw this that something big was going to happen.

Slurring his words and staggering a little, Harley said, "Yer gonna be an important part of this mission, Delly, long as ya do what we tell ya and foller our cue." He laughed when he added, "We gonna help them niggers cook up some pork ribs."

"Gotta make sure they got a good hot fire for their barbecue pit!" Bash said with a drunken chortle.

Since the men were laughing, Delbert did too. He had learned not to ask too many questions, just hang in and keep his mouth shut. He had already noticed that the men weren't wearing any of their Aryan Confederacy gear, and their tattoos were all covered up too. He wanted to look just like them, no matter what, so he felt good when they made him take off his Aryan Youth sweatshirt and replace it with a plain denim jacket.

Watching him put the jacket on, Bash winked and said, "We don't wanna look like we're tryin' to come off like a bunch of badasses, Delly, elsewise them niggers might just turn on us and beat us up!"

"Might stick a switchblade in us or slice us up with a razor," Curb added with a sarcastic snicker.

Harley said, "Ya ain't never tasted nigger barbecue, Delly, yer in fer a treat!"

All the men laughed uproariously as they climbed onto their motorcycles. It was a hot, muggy August night. The sun was almost completely down now but there was an orangish glow on the horizon. Delbert clung to Harley's hips as he rode behind him, his short legs straddling the wide leather saddle.

He got a tingle of excitement over his sure knowledge that even if the men really were going to buy some barbecued ribs from the niggers, they sure as hell weren't going to leave the niggers be.

The three-hour high-speed motorcycle ride made Delbert tired and sore all over, but he sucked it up and didn't complain. He knew that good Aryan warriors were able to endure much worse torment than that.

Except for the bright bouncing beams of the roaring motorcycles, it was pitch dark by the time they got onto a narrow country road. They stayed on it for maybe thirty miles before they spotted glowing lights peeping through a tangle of trees and foliage out beyond an open field. With Curb and Bash in the lead, all three bikes cut straight across the field, headed for the lights. A path opened up through the woods and a short, bumpy ride took them into a clearing where naked light bulbs hanging from trees cast dim, shadowy light on three dilapidated, unpainted wooden shacks with tarpaper roofs.

A dozen or so black people were milling around the shacks, going in and out. They gawked and backed away when the three bikes roared toward them, but Harley, Bash and Curb innocently parked the bikes and turned the motors off. They dismounted, Delbert along with them, and looked all around.

There were other white people in amongst the niggers, and they all seemed to get along without any trouble. Seemed like they were all there to eat and drink and not bother much over the fact that they had different colored skin. In front of the shacks old men, white and black, sat together on wooden benches, talking and smoking and eating ribs and chicken, sopping up the red sauce with slices of white bread.

One of the old black men tossed a plateful of rib bones at a mangy-looking mongrel, and the dog bit into one and jumped back, yipping furiously. "Gonna burn yer tongue out, doggy!" one of the black men called out. "Big Rocky's hot sauce's is too damn much fer ya!" The dog tried tasting another of the rib bones and again leapt backwards, howling and yiping. Then he pounced on a bone and rolled it furiously in the dirt, his paws flailing.

The old men on the bench belched belly laughs, and so did Curb, Bash, Harley and Delbert. In between guffaws some of the old men spit gobs of tobacco juice into the dirt.

The dog got the rib bone pretty well coated with yellow dirt, then tried to bite into it again but it still burnt his mouth, sending him into another frenzy of yiping and pawing at it to roll it in some more dirt.

The old men kept on laughing.

Finally enough of the hotness must have worn off or got mixed with enough dirt that the dog was able to carry the rib bone in his drooling mouth. Delbert watched the animal disappear in the darkness behind one of the shacks. For him all this was a strange and exciting experience. It felt suspenseful too, like something big might be about to happen.

"C'mon, Delly," Harley said, and Delbert followed his stepfather and the other two men that he idolized into the nearest of the shacks. It probably measured about twelve by fourteen feet. The floor was hard-packed clay. There were no windows. For light there were two naked bulbs dangling from the rafters. The counter was a wooden plank held up on each end by stacks of battered and grimy Coca Cola cases. Behind the counter, tended by a gray-haired black man, there were a couple of tall upright coolers with dull red paint scraped up and chipped. The glass fronts of the coolers let Delbert see that one of them was packed with two different brands of beer and the other was filled with nothing but Coca Cola.

Curb, Bash and Harley bellied up to the counter and bought beers for themselves and a bottle of Coke for Delbert. Three black guys sitting at one of two dirty, banged-up, four-legged tables, averted their eyes as the white men and the boy walked by them. Delbert couldn't take his eyes off of the "wallpaper" -- dozens and dozens of calendar nudes thumbtacked to the raw planks, overlapping each other so as to keep wind and rain from howling through the cracks.

They took their drinks into the barbecue shack, which was lighted and "wallpapered" much like the other one. The place was hot and smoky enough to make everyone in there cough and sweat. The cook -- they heard some of the patrons call him "Big Rocky" -- dripped sweat over the huge barbecue pit, and there was no way some of it wasn't going to drop on the fat hot dogs, slabs of pork ribs, and half-chickens that he was tending with a long double-pronged fork. The sweatband on his dark brown forehead was stained yellow. His white T-shirt was soaking wet, clinging to his nipples and his large beer belly. As the meat turned golden brown, he turned it methodically, wearing an expression of pained indifference on his chubby, pock-marked face.

"Hey, Rocky! Give us two slabs and four plates!" Harley called out. "Mild sauce on one slab, extra hot on t 'other!"

"You been here before, Harley?" Delbert asked, lowering his voice.

"Naw, they don't know me from Adam," Harley answered in a hoarse whisper. "I wouldn't 've come here if'n they did. I learnt about this place from a guy in a bar in Wheeling. He gimme the lowdown, directions 'n' all."

Rocky split two slabs in two with a cleaver, then laid the halves out on paper plates, ladling mild sauce onto two of the plates and extra hot onto the two others. He laid two slices of white bread on top of each plate. "That'll be twenty dollars, ten bucks a slab," he said, mopping sweat from his face with a dirty, greasy towel.

Harley paid, and Rocky spun back toward the hot, smoky pit and started turning over a dozen or so half-chickens with his long fork.

There were no customer tables in this shack. Delbert, Harley, Curb and Bash stood at the makeshift counter and ate the wondrously delicious ribs with their sauce-coated fingers. Delbert was so hungry, and the stuff was so darn good, he kept on wolfing it down with scarcely a pause.

"Hey, Delly, ya ever gonna come up fer air?" Harley said, grinning broadly and patting Delbert on the shoulder.

"Dint we tell ya, ya was in fer a treat!" Bash said. "So whaddaya think, hey?"

"Yum, yum," Delbert said, rubbing his stomach in a comical, exaggerated way, making the men laugh and feeling darn good about that.

Beneath the counter was a row of cardboard boxes where they dropped each curved rib bone after sucking it white and clean.

They washed their meals down with the drinks they had brought from the other shack. They sponged up the remains of the rib sauce with their slices of store-bought bread, then licked their fingers and tossed their soggy plates and napkins into the cardboard boxes.

"C'mon," Harley said, and they left the hot, smoky barbecue shack, went back to the drink shack for another round of drinks to take with them, then entered the third shack, which they hadn't so far been in.

A card game was going on in there. There was an actual felt-topped table, almost new looking, and some pretty decent chairs for the players. A long, dusty green metal shade holding fluorescent light tubes hung low over the table, supported by chains, the gaming table as brightly lit as one of the tables in a billiard parlor. There were benches against the wall for men waiting to get into the game. The walls, like the walls of the other two shacks, were papered with garishly voluptuous nudes.

There were five players at the table, and the sixth seat was taken up by a hatchet-faced black man with long sideburns and a pencil-thin mustache. He was hunched over a gray steel strongbox with a revolver tightly clenched in his right hand.

When somebody won a hand, he counted the pot and took a percentage of it, shut the house share into the strongbox and held the lid down with the fist that held the gun.

Stacks of folding money were in front of most of the gamblers except the ones who apparently were losing, because they had smaller

211

stacks, some of them down to almost nothing. Delbert was amazed at the amount of money in play -- probably there was more than a thousand bucks on the table at any given time. And he figured there must be a lot more in the strongbox.

"They're playin' Skin, Delly," Harley said in a lowered voice. "See? Each player gits jes' one card every hand. They ain't allowed to look at their cards. The top card is skinned off the top of the deck after somebody shuffles and cuts, then they bet, raise or fold on whether they think their card'll beat the one turned up. Any player can bet, not jes' on his own card, but the other players' to boot."

They watched the skin game while they sucked on their drinks. Curb was standing a short distance away from the strongbox man, but facing the other direction from him, as if idly scoping on some of the wallpapered nudes.

"I gotta take a piss," Bash said, fixing his eyes on Harley when he said it, like some kind of signal was passing between them. He swilled down the rest of his beer and walked outside carrying the empty bottle.

Another hand of skin got played, a guy won a really big pot, and the man with the gun took out a big share of the cash and put it in the strongbox.

Bash came in carrying another bottle of beer that looked fresh, but he didn't drink from it, and he kept his thumb over the lip of the bottle. Delbert thought for a moment he had caught a whiff of gasoline; maybe it was on Bash's hands, from tinkering with his motorcycle.

Suddenly, Curb spun and smashed his beer bottle down onto the strongbox man's head. The man's grip on the gun slackened and Harley yanked it out of his hand. At the same time Harley drew his own gun, a big black semi-automatic, out from under his jacket.

Bash, still holding his beer bottle with his thumb over the lip, pulled out a long-barreled .22 Sportsman with a silencer, a favorite weapon of Mafia and CIA assassins, and shot the dazed strongbox man in his temple. The guy rolled sideways and sagged down onto the dirt floor and didn't stir anymore.

"Nobody move!" Harley yelled. "Delly! Grab all the money! Stuff it all in the strongbox!"

Even though his hands were shaking, Delbert managed to do as he was told. From his Aryan Youth training, he was familiar with the term "bag man" and he realized with a sharp thrill that all of a sudden that's what he was.

Bash held up his beer bottle. "There's gasoline in here!" he warned. "Don't follow us out the door or I'll light it and throw it, burn you all to hell!"

Delbert realized in a flash that Bash must've gotten the gasoline from his motorcycle gas tank when he pretended to go out and take a piss.

"Let's get outta here!" Harley shouted.

They backed out, the men pointing their guns and Delbert carrying the strongbox. Then they ran for the motorcycles, and Harley took the strongbox from Delbert and crammed it into an open saddlebag while they jumped on, cranked up and spun out.

Bash roared his bike right up to the barbecue shack and tossed his beer bottle in -- and it must've hit the hot grate and splashed onto the fiery coals -- because there was an instant explosion and the whole place went up in flames.

The motorcycles roared out of the woods, bounced across the open field, and humped back onto the blacktop road.

The three men let out rebel yells as they looked back over their shoulders at the huge fire they had started. Delbert was over-awed. He realized that not only had he been allowed to take part in a robbery, but he was also an accomplice in the burning up of some niggers.

Gradually he calmed down on the long saddle-sore ride back to the Aryan Confederacy compound, and it dawned on him why he had been allowed to come along. The men had used him as a shill. They wanted to make the speakeasy people let their guard down, and they figured that if they had a young boy with them, no one would suspect what they were really up to.

A few miles before they got to the compound, they stopped at a gas station and Harley took the money out of the strongbox and went into the men's room to count it. While he was gone, Curb and Bash used the squeegee out by the gas pumps to clean the mud off of the motorcycle license plates.

When Harley came out of the men's room he had the money divided up. He and the other two men got almost fourteen-hundred dollars apiece, and each of them gave Delbert a hundred dollars.

"I got a grand set aside for Mr. Pryzor," Harley said. "Gonna just hand it to him, prob 'ly tomorrow. He don't need to know where it come from. You know why, Delly?"

"Plausible denial," Delbert said, proud that he knew the answer and the correct terminology. He had learned it in one of his Aryan Youth classes.

The men laughed and clapped him on his shoulders.

He stuffed the three hundred dollars in his pocket. It was the most money he had ever touched in his whole life. Just thinking about it made his heart beat faster.

He figured that since the three men didn't seem to be suffering any pangs of conscience over what went down, and weren't at all worried that they'd ever be caught, he didn't need to worry either. His heart was still racing, his body pumped full of adrenaline, and he decided that, all in all, he felt- pretty damn proud of himself.

CHAPTER 39

In the seventies and eighties, death and destruction by explosion and conflagration became almost an American motif. Dozens of churches and synagogues were burned down, usually with no loss of life, but also with no arrests. Hate-crazed cowards hitting their targets in the middle of the night on dark country roads were notoriously hard to catch. They drove law enforcement half-crazy with futility. Pent-up emotions erupted in carnage.

When I heard about the ruthless extermination of the motley little band calling themselves the "Symbionese Liberation Army" I was appalled that fellow FBI agents had helped wreak such havoc, even though the outcome was probably not fully intended and could not be foreseen. It happened in 1974 when I had only been an agent for five years. I was three thousand miles away in New York at the time, while the SLA shootout took place in Los Angeles. Four hundred and ten L.A. police officers and one hundred and twenty-seven FBI men pumped thousands of rounds of ammunition and teargas into a little stucco house where six campus-bred, self-styled "leftist revolutionaries" were holed up, shooting back at the cops and stubbornly refusing a chance to surrender. They were shot full of holes and incinerated, their pitiful remains as black and shriveled as charred logs.

In June 1983, Gordon Kahl, age 63, leading a paramilitary rebellion against the government's right to collect taxes, killed two Arkansas police officers and wounded three more. Then he barricaded himself in a farmhouse surrounded by forty cops. A sheriff tried to go in and make an arrest, but Kahl shot him dead. The cops unleashed a barrage of automatic weapons and shotgun fire, and when Kahl's cache of ammunition was ignited, multiple explosions echoed in the hills and lit up the sky. Kahl's remains were identified by his dental records.

In December 1984, members of a neo-Nazi guerrilla group known as The Order hid in three little houses outside of Seattle, after gunning down a Jewish talk show host named Daniel Berg who had spoken out forcefully and adamantly against racism and bigotry. Dozens of heavily armed federal agents moved in, and the killers surrendered, except for the ring leader, Robert Mathews, who had founded The Order and wanted to go down in a blaze of glory. He got his wish. The feds fired flares to light up the house and blasted away with automatic weapons. Mathews' stash of ammunition blew up and he was burned to a crisp.

In August 1984, at a speakeasy in the woods near the small town of Hanksville, West Virginia, six black people and two whites were incinerated in a gasoline explosion in a barbecue hut. Four men who had been sitting on a bench outside the hut received second and third degree burns but managed to survive.

Several fire brigades showed up with sirens screaming, but due to an inadequate water supply they had to let the hut burn to the ground while they soaked grass and foliage in an attempt to prevent the blaze from spreading to some neighboring shacks and into the surrounding woods, where it would've started a forest fire.

By the time State Troopers and fire marshals could investigate the crime scene, eye-witnesses had scattered, except for the ones who couldn't drag themselves away because they were too badly burned -- they were taken away by ambulance.

A black man was found dead in one of the shacks, a .22 caliber hole in his head.

Because the speakeasy was illegal, nobody would admit to owning or operating it. Some of the surviving burn victims, too weak and in far too much pain to bother making up lies, admitted that illegal high-stakes card games had been going on day and night for months. This wasn't a well-kept secret, and the wrong people must have found out about it. All the money was stolen by three white men and a young boy who had seemed to be there to have fun till they made all hell break loose. In fleeing, one of the robbers had tossed a bottle of gasoline onto the barbecue grate, purposely causing the explosion and fire.

The FBI Anti-Terrorist Unit based in Charleston, West Virginia, was called in to augment the investigation, on the suspicion that what went down here had some of the earmarks of a racially motivated hate crime. But this remained in the realm of speculation; the only clear and obvious motive was robbery. The gasoline toss was perhaps only intended as a diversion, since whites as well as blacks were killed in the resulting inferno.

Nobody could identify the robbers. None of the burn survivors could recall ever seeing them before at the speakeasy. And nobody had been able to get any of the motorcycles' license plate numbers.

The case went cold, with no leads, no apparent avenues to pursue. Without an informant or a confession, probably nobody would ever be caught.

In May 1985, eleven members of a weird cult called MOVE were blasted and burned to death by a force of five hundred Philadelphia policemen. The MOVE people fortified a house in West Philly and refused to come out until nine members of their cult, who had been jailed for killing a policeman in a shootout in 1978, were pardoned and released.

MOVE members, mostly poor blacks and Puerto Ricans, espoused a return to primitivism and a life of total anarchy. They were so anarchistic that the name they had given themselves wasn't even an acronym; the individual capital letters stood for nothing. They wore dashikis and long dreadlocks and all took the same last name: "Africa." They occupied several houses in the city and bought weapons and explosives with money raised by selling drugs.

At first neighbors welcomed them and even fed their kids when they saw them eating out of garbage cans. But sentiment changed when MOVE members committed a string of robberies and burglaries in the community. They built a noisy, smelly shelter for stray animals, blocking off an alley that people had to use to get to their garages, and they kept up a habit of tossing their garbage into the streets, drawing rats. They began broadcasting long obscene rants over a public-address system blasting out of an upstairs window, and they used their roof as a lookout post, brandishing guns and wearing executioner hoods.

After numerous complaints, the cops tried to negotiate with MOVE, but the leader, Conrad Africa, refused to talk until his jailed followers were released. He jeered, "Send in the CIA! Send in the FBI! Send in your SWAT teams! Let it be the will of God!"

At first the cops didn't dare come into the open because the MOVE people had built a steel-reinforced bunker on the roof of their house, giving them a deadly vantage point for firing down into the street. After ten days of stalemate the mayor of Philadelphia approved the use of high-pressure water jets to dislodge the bunker. Once the bunker was out of commission, the police thought they would use tear gas to force the cultists out of their stronghold. But the water barrage was ineffective and led to a ninety-minute shoot out -- yet by some miracle, up to that point no one was killed. Family members of MOVE people were brought in by police. Using bullhorns, they pleaded from across the street: "Please

217

come out and save the children! We love you! Please save yourselves! Save the poor innocent children!"

All they got for their effort was a burst of gunfire that sent them scurrying.

This was the final straw for the mayor. He gave his approval for non-incendiary explosives to be dropped from a helicopter onto the bunker. But the blasts inadvertently set off some of MOVE's stock of ammunition, starting a fire. Officials hoped that the flames on the roof would finally force the cult members out without harming them. But the roof collapsed and the house was engulfed in flames. The fire raged out of control and spread through the neighborhood. Before it was all over, sixty-one homes were completely gutted and two hundred and fifty people were left homeless. Only two MOVE members survived. A woman named Ramona Africa and a thirteen-year-old boy, Birdi Africa, crawled out of the burning house and fled into the arms of police. The bodies of seven adults and four children, all charred beyond recognition, were pulled out of the smoldering ruins.

I followed all of these cases with a professional compulsion and a deep pervasive sadness over the ghastly, unnecessary toll of human suffering and death. But none of them happened on my own watch or in my own jurisdiction, so I didn't think I had a personal connection to any of them.

But I was wrong.

On a Monday in June 1985, I came home from a trip to New York, tossed a bundle of piled-up mail on my dining table, and started to unpack. I was seeing Jane Hawthorne every chance I got these days, irregardless of the expense, piling up plenty of frequent flier miles.

Jane had invited me to a party launching a novel that Kaiser Press felt was going to be a blockbuster. The author was one of the promising clients Jane had "discovered" after launching her own literary agency. I had read the book and didn't think it was so hot, but Jane -- and the critics -- thought it was wonderful. Advance sales were going through the roof.

The huge fringe benefit for me was that when Jane was flushed with success, her sexual appetite was wonderfully heightened. After the literary affair ran its course Thursday night, we lazed into a long, sensuous weekend and tried not to think too much about the fact that our incompatible careers would inevitably intrude once again, keeping us separated by four hundred miles.

On Sunday, the night before I left New York, I guess some of the bad stuff I was suppressing got to me while I was sleeping. I tossed and turned and woke Jane up. She said I was practically screaming in my sleep. She hugged me and caressed my clammy forehead, and I told her about my bad dream. I was back in the Army again, pinned down in a muddy trench, totally surrounded by the dead, torn-apart bodies of fellow soldiers.

I was the last survivor, and hordes of enemy troops were rushing at me, and there was no escape. I was paralyzed, rooted in fear, waiting for jack-hammering machine-gun bullets to slam into my chest.

This was a recurrent dream that I kept having at least once or twice a year ever since the sixties, even though I had never actually been under fire while I was in the Army. I had been shot at quite a few times as an FBI agent, but I never had nightmares about any of that, not even about the day when my friend and partner Cyrus Lumley was ripped to shreds by a pipe bomb. For some strange reason the fear of being sent to fight and die in a war in Cuba that had never happened was affecting my psyche more powerfully than the fears and horrors that I had faced afterwards. Perhaps the reason was that what I was doing now was a matter of choice. Jane and I talked about this but didn't come up with any definitive answers, and somehow I did not think the nightmares would ever go away.

On Sunday afternoon, a few hours before my flight back to Pittsburgh, Jane and I had lunch with Arlene Shoaf at the Grotto Azura, a fine Italian restaurant in Little Italy. Arlene smilingly handed us each a present, sans giftwrap -- copies of Lori's new album entitled *Lori McCoy ... Back Home Again*. I had already heard two of the cuts, one of which had made number three on the country music charts, and the other had made number seven. The album itself wasn't released yet, but it was expected to hit the national top twenty.

"Lori's happy as a clam," Arlene announced. "Right now she's touring down South. After that she's booked for two weeks in Vegas. And she's been invited to the Grand Ole Opry -- which is a lifelong dream come true for her."

Jane and I expressed how glad we were over the good news. Arlene brought us up to date about Charlie Guinard and his work against Apartheid in South Africa, and about an award that Missy and her husband David had won for a documentary about urban poverty that they had entered in the New York Film Festival.

Noting Arlene's vivacious good looks, I marveled at how completely she had remade herself. In her early forties now, her resemblance to her sister Lori was restored, even to the degree of poise and self-assuredness that she now displayed. I knew that Jane had aided and abetted Arlene's transformation, and I loved Jane all the more for it.

Arlene hadn't been able to come to the book-launching party Thursday night because she was immersed in a campaign for ratification of the Equal Rights Amendment. Over the past several years, she had worked tirelessly as a major fundraiser for the National Organization for Women, taking advantage of the many prominent show-business contacts she had cultivated when she was working for Lori. But she gave up her position with NOW and turned her energies toward the 1984 presidential elections, hoping to help make Geraldine Ferraro the first female vice-president of the United States. When Ronald Reagan and George H. W. Bush beat Mondale and Ferraro, Arlene was terribly discouraged and depressed for a while, but then she picked herself up and plunged into other causes, often working with Lori and Charlie.

"We've been trying to talk Geraldine into making a run for the Senate," Arlene said, "but she's afraid to do it. I was with her and her husband yesterday evening. They're hoping that if she doesn't run, the Reagan Justice Department will stop investigating their personal finances."

"That's one of their greatest coercion tools," Jane said indignantly.

"Well, let's get off of politics," Arlene said, "before I start getting indigestion."

We ordered pasta a la putana and roasted chicken, shared family style, along with side dishes of wedding soup, anti-pasto, and thick-crusted Italian bread dipped in olive oil and spices, all washed down with liberal quantities of homemade red wine.

Over tiramisu and espresso, the conversation inevitably succumbed to politics. Jane and Arlene began animatedly discussing what they considered to be the destructive policies of Eleanor Smeal, the former Pittsburgh housewife who had been president of NOW for the past six years.

"Eleanor doesn't have any tact," Jane said. "She fights with the politicos instead of shmoozing them. Her style is way too confrontational. She's such an extremist! She wants to throw all the men out of office and replace them with women. No wonder we get called feminazis!"

"She's already looking forward to the 1988 presidential elections," Arlene added. "She wants to try to push the Democrats into nominating Patricia Schroeder. All that would do is guarantee that our candidate would lose. It's suicidal. We have to be shrewd enough to campaign for somebody who's actually viable -- otherwise NOW will end up with no influence at all."

"We'll be totally marginalized," Jane said. "The movement will be set back by twenty years."

"If not forty," said Arlene.

They continued talking in that vein for the rest of our lunch, and I mostly listened and was enlightened. I didn't used to know much about the women's movement, even though I was always in sympathy with its major goals. Now that I was learning more of the inside scoop, I thought that the more moderate approach advocated by Jane and Arlene made a lot more sense than the angry militancy coming from other quarters.

While Jane was driving me to the airport, I asked her if Arlene was dating anyone.

"Why? Are you interested?" she said teasingly.

"I would be if I didn't have you," I responded, silently congratulating myself for displaying a bit of spontaneous charm and tact.

"I don't know if Arlene really has any wish to get married," Jane mused. "I think it was Flannery O'Connor who said that being a spinster is a lot like death by drowning, quite a pleasant sensation once you quit struggling. I think Arlene isn't struggling in that direction anymore. And she doesn't seem all that unhappy about it. Besides, at our age the statistics are against us. I read a study that showed that women who haven't married by age twenty-five have only a twenty-five percent chance of getting hitched. And ninety-five percent of single women over thirty-five will never marry at all."

"Well," I said, "I didn't ask you if Arlene wanted to get married. I just asked if she was dating anyone. "

"She spends time with guys, mostly the ones she works with. I don't think she's hit it off with anybody, romantically. Most of the good, decent guys are already taken, or else they've been recycled a couple of times. They only want to get married again because they can't get used to not having a woman around to pick up after them and do their laundry."

"I hope you don't think that's my motive," I said, and we both laughed. "Maybe we should get married now," I suggested, "even if we don't live in the same city."

"Why don't you apply for a transfer?"

"I will, I promise, soon as I get the albatross off my neck."

She sighed, knowing that I was referring to Conrad Pryzor. In the early stages of our relationship I had told her why I believed he was behind the long-ago murders that had led me to join the FBI Anti-Terrorist Unit. Although Jane understood where I was coming from, I knew it didn't mean she'd wait for me forever. I kept thinking about that after we kissed goodbye at LaGuardia and I got on the plane alone. I was forty-seven years old now. My hair was going gray and receding. Maybe it was time I should let someone else carry the ball, as far as Pryzor was concerned. There was certainly no shortage of bad guys I could chase, if I was operating out of New York instead of Pittsburgh.

When I let myself into my apartment the place felt empty. The four days Jane and I had spent together made it hurt even more when I suddenly didn't have her to talk to and to be with.

I didn't open the mail that I had plunked on the dining room table till I got into my pajamas and robe and made myself a pot of coffee. Most of it was junk mail, and I threw it away. But a business envelope of good-quality linen gave me a chill when I saw the artfully embossed return address: *Leonard Dixon, Certified Public Accountant.*

Leonard Dixon was Carlisle Dixon's father. The last time I had spoken to him I was still working out of the New York FBI office and had phoned to let him know that the four men who had killed his son and his daughter-in-law were dead. "What were their names?" he asked, and I told him.

He said, "They were the shooters? These four rednecks?"

"Yes. There was another man involved behind the scenes, a racist fanatic named Conrad Pryzor. I know he's guilty but so far I can't prove it."

"The big cheeses never get punished," Leonard said bitterly. "They let their flunkies take the rap. Been that way since the world began."

He hung up on me, and I never heard from him again until now. Scared that I might be in for bad news, I held the envelope in my hand for a long time before opening it and reading his letter:

Dear Mr. Williams,

> *I want you to know that my son Spencer died with the MOVE group in Philadelphia. He was 32 years old. When you came to see me at our house in Syracuse back in 1972, you didn't meet him because he was at Rutgers studying pre-*

222

med. But he dropped out after Carlisle was murdered. He lost all faith in organized (I don't want to say "civilized") society. He took the name Spencer Africa. He didn't want to be an American anymore. He said there shouldn't be any nation-states. He didn't even want to belong to our family. He said that there shouldn't be any banding together of anybody in any way. He believed in total anarchy. But yet he bonded with a bunch of angry, bitter folks who hated the world and just about everything in it. I'm trying not to allow myself to become that way, but I understand what made Spencer the way he was when he died. I consider him to be yet another victim of the crazy bigots who killed Brenda and Carlisle. I encourage you to keep up your pursuit of all these hate-filled people and bring them to justice the best way you can. You're a good and decent man. I have a lot of respect for you which I failed to express before, but I want to do it now.

Sincerely,
Leonard Dixon.

CHAPTER 40

In 1987, there were chapters of Women Against Rape in dozens of American towns and cities, including Pittsburgh. Jane Hawthorne and Arlene Shoaf were slated to attend a WAR symposium held that November at the University of Pittsburgh, where they both were to be featured speakers. They were invited because of their nationally known work on women's issues. I was looking forward to the occasion as a great chance for me and Jane to be together without my being the one who had to hop on a plane.

At this time, unbeknownst to me, Delbert McCoy was in the Lion Platoon of Conrad Pryzor's Aryan Youth Brigade, and was now known as Del Logan. His mother had married Harney (alias "Harley") Logan a few years back, and Harley had adopted her son and changed his last name. Lori and Arlene no longer had any idea of what had become of their nephew and their former sister-in-law, and it bothered them a lot, but I didn't think about it very much, other than to note how odd and unnecessary it was for Roseanne and Delbert McCoy to drop totally out of sight, shunning all their family members.

Although Lori was in much better emotional shape these days, she still had bouts of depression over Maylon's suicide and the unilateral estrangement from her nephew and sister-in-law. On the phone one day I told her, "You didn't do anything to cause them to turn away from you. Maylon was wrestling with his own demons, and you tried to help him, but he wouldn't let you. Underneath it all, I'm sure he knew that you loved him. Society let him down, you didn't. It's not your fault that he ended up turning his anger on himself. What he did was more because of what happened to him in Vietnam than because of anything else."

"But I feel responsible for his wife and son," she said. "Maybe I should reach out to them. I could hire a private detective to try and find them. That's why I called you. I thought you might know somebody good."

"If they don't want to be found, you're liable to piss them off all the more by putting a private eye on them. In time they might mellow and get back in touch with you."

"You think so?"

"Especially if they need something," I said pointedly, wishing she'd realize that her relatives had always put selfish demands on her and maybe she'd be better off letting them fend for themselves for a change.

She thanked me for my advice and said she'd think it over.

Even as this conversation was going on, none of us had any idea of what Roseanne and Delbert had gotten themselves into, and that they were both mixed up in the evil currents festering under the surface of our lives.

Down through the years, Conrad Pryzor had obsessively kept tabs on Lori McCoy and people close to her, and inevitably he read about the WAR symposium slated to take place in Pittsburgh. This was like dangling a mouse in front of a cat. Pryzor called young Del Logan into his office, complimented him on his recent promotion into the Lion Platoon, then showed him the article about his aunt Arlene and her participation in the anti-rape symposium.

He watched the boy's jaw tighten and his fingers clench as he stared at the newspaper. He gave him time to read. Then he said, "This other bitch, Jane Hawthorne, is your auntie's best friend, maybe even her lover. She's engaged to Frank Williams, that damned FBI agent -- the same one that could have gotten your father out of the bank safely instead of leaving him in there to die. And none of it would've ever happened if your two aunts would've done right by him."

Del Logan's face flushed with anger. "I hate them all!" he spat. "Especially my Aunt Lori and Aunt Arlene! I'd kill them both if I could."

"Would you now?" Pryzor said.

"Yes. sir!" Del responded immediately, clicking his heels and giving the Nazi salute.

"I want you to take that article with you," Pryzor said. "Learn as much as you can about this sickening event the dykes are putting on in Pittsburgh. Maybe you'll think of something. Maybe you'll make plans. But if you get any ideas, don't tell anyone about them, not even me. Do you understand?"

"Yes, sir. I do, sir," Del replied, feeling honored by the tone of this conversation and knowing he was being guided toward a mission that he had to flesh out for himself.

"I wish I had a hundred more like you," Pryzor said. "I've never told you this before, but you're almost like a son to me. Did you know that?"

225

A warm glow came over Del, and he didn't know what to say. He pivoted smartly and left the office before the tears welling up in his eyes could start to roll down his cheeks.

Afterwards, poring over the newspaper article as he sat on his bunk in the Youth Brigade barracks, he learned that the University of Pittsburgh had been chosen as the site of the WAR symposium because in September a seventeen-year-old student had been lured away from the campus and raped, and she had publicly accused her rapist and got him expelled, prosecuted and convicted. The article lauded her for her courage. Her name was Carol Henley and she was going to speak at the symposium.

In the article she said, "I was away from home for the first time, anxious to make friends and fit in, so I went on a blind date set up by one of my friends in the dorm. She said this nice boy named Howard in her sociology class had asked her out, but she told him she already had a boyfriend and didn't want to cheat on him. She offered to fix me up with Howard, so I checked him out on the phone, and he seemed really nice, sort of mild-mannered. Very polite. He told me he was a lot more religious than most boys, and he wanted a girl with old-fashioned tastes and proper morals.

"I figured I'd let him take me to dinner, where we'd be out in public and nothing bad could happen. But after I got in Howard's car, he said we should drive around for a while and just talk, so we could get to know each other, then he took out a flask and asked me if I wanted to try some whisky. I said no. I told him he could drink all he wanted, but not with me in his car. So he said, okay, he'd take me to his house and introduce me to his parents.

"When we got there he unlocked the door and we went in, but the house was dark. I asked where his parents were, and he said they must've gone out. Then he grabbed me and started kissing me and shoving his hands down my blouse and up my dress. I tried to fight him off, and he called me a bitch. He slapped me and choked me and slammed me down on the living room floor and raped me.

"Afterwards, I was in total shock. My clothes were torn and bloody. I had a cut on my face and bruises on my neck and thighs. He took me back to the dorm and told me to get out of his car or he'd push me out onto the sidewalk, like a piece of garbage. I ran up to my room and locked myself in. I cried and cried all night long. Even now, I'm still afraid of people. I don't like for anybody to touch me, even in the most innocent way."

Del Logan read and re-read the story of Carol's rape, getting more and more turned on by it. He scoffed at her sob story about all the "mental anguish and emotional damage" she claimed to be suffering. The bitch probably enjoyed having a big dick in her. Probably liked rough sex and didn't want to admit it. No doubt she'd sue the boy and his parents for a shitload of money. All because she got fucked, which is what she really wanted in the first place. She could act all sweet and pure when she wanted to, but she was nothing but a cock teaser, and she got what was coming to her.

Taking the article with him, Del Logan went into the latrine and masturbated.

Afterwards, he began thinking about me and my failure to get his father safely out of the hostage situation at the bank in Cherry Hill. He became consumed with the idea that since I had taken his father away from *him*, he ought to take someone away from me. I don't think this was exactly what Conrad Pryzor had been driving at. I think he wanted me dead, not someone close to me.

Or else maybe he wanted all three of us dead: me, Jane and Arlene.

On a Thursday, the day before the symposium was to begin, I was at my office at the Pittsburgh FBI Headquarters, and Jane and Arlene were settling in at my town house apartment in the Shadyside section of the city, not far from the Pitt campus.

The apartment was nestled in a warren of upscale, residential side streets that looked more suburban than urban. The neighborhood was quiet and peaceful under an overcast sky, with fresh snow lying on the dark, naked branches of the maple trees lining the sidewalks.

A blue camper van cruised slowly past my place. The narrow street was lined with parked cars, some of them still covered with snow. Harley Logan was driving the van. Curb Burton was in the passenger seat, and Bash Halsey and Del Logan were in back.

Scoping the place out, Bash said, "Lights're on. They're in there."

"Fer chrissake we know that," Curb said. "We seen 'em go in."

The stalkers had followed the two women from the Carnegie Library, which was hosting the symposium. By calling the number listed in the newspaper, they had learned that today was registration day, the day that all the speakers and guests would be signing in. They had watched and waited, eventually spotting Jane and Arlene coming out and getting into their rental car in the library parking area.

Now, cruising past my house, Harley said, "They coulda left when we drove around the block."

"Naw, their car's still there," Bash contradicted.

Squinting through the side window, Del said, "I can see movement behind the drapes."

"Attaway, son, yer usin' yer head," Harley said. "But don't let 'em see you. Yer auntie might recognize you."

"We know what our plan is so let's just do it," Curb said, snuffing out a cigarette on the floor of the van.

"Curb's like a dog sniffin' pussy," Harley snickered. "He can smell them bitches in there!"

"Well, don't cream yer jeans while I hunt fer a place to park," Bash grumped. "I never seen so fuckin' many cars linin' a fuckin' street."

"We coulda taken a taxi," Curb said. "Tell 'im to keep the meter runnin'."

They all laughed.

Del hoped they'd let him get laid, too. Not by his aunt, of course. He wasn't a pervert. He could do it with the other broad, Jane.

Harley had to take the van around the block again, and by the time he came back around the corner, the front door to the town house opened and Arlene stepped out, shutting the door behind her. She came down off the steps, carrying a leather briefcase.

Curb said, "What the fuck?"

Bash said, "She's goin' somewhere. Shit!"

Arlene was on the symposium steering committee, and Jane wasn't. The committee was having an afternoon meeting that Jane didn't have to attend.

Disgruntled, the four stalkers watched Arlene get into the rental car and drive off.

"Maybe she won't be gone long," Harley said.

"And maybe she'll be gone for seventeen hours," Bash said sarcastically.

"At least we got us a parkin' place now," Harley piped up, snickering.

"I tol' ya, we shoulda jumped 'em at the airport," Bash complained angrily. "Then we coulda taken 'em someplace nice and quiet."

"Fuckin' where at the airport?" Harley snapped. "A million fuckin' people around all over the place, and lots of 'em cops."

"Yeah, you're right," Bash admitted.

"Quiet down," Curb said sternly. "Let's go. C'mon, Delly. Gonna git yer first piece of ass."

Arlene and Jane had unpacked, each in a separate guest room, and Jane was relaxing and having herself a cup of tea when I phoned her around noon, just to touch base. She was in a holiday mood. Although the symposium was a serious matter, we expected to have fun this weekend, too. After Arlene got back from her meeting, she and Jane were going to have lunch and do some shopping, then they'd meet me at my house by the time I got home from work.

It was not to be.

Jane must have gotten attacked right after she talked to me on the phone. The medical examiner couldn't have pinned it down that close by means of his own expertise, of course; but a passerby came forward the next day and told the police that, at about twelve-fifteen, he had heard muffled screams coming from inside my house and assumed it was just kids yelling, playing some kind of game.

Jane was raped and sodomized in every way possible. Semen of multiple blood types was found in all of her orifices. She was strangled and stabbed to death. Her nude body was hung upside down from the shower rod in the bathroom adjoining my master bedroom. Her throat was slit. She bled out all over the tile floor, making a large puddle that seeped past the door and into the blue shag carpet. On the white tile of the bathroom walls somebody wrote in her blood:

DEATH TO FBI PIGS

WHITE POWER RULES

CHAPTER 41

Del Logan was proud of what he had done. He felt he had acted like a man, a true Aryan warrior. He savored each and every moment of the "guerrilla action."

Del had been the one to go to the door first. When he rang the bell he could feel that bitch Jane looking at him, sizing him up through the peephole.

He said, "Aunt Arlene, it's me, Delbert," pretending not to know his aunt wasn't there. He was dressed to appear totally innocent and harmless, in a blue wool coat, tan chinos and a dumb-looking red tassel cap. Normally he wished he didn't have such a babyish whiskerless face, but this time it came in handy since it helped make him look so unthreatening.

"Delbert?" the dumb bitch said through the door. "Delbert McCoy? Arlene's nephew?"

"Yeah, it's me. I came to see my aunt. May I come in? Who're you?"

The dumb bitch opened the door. Wide-eyed and smiling, she said, "Oh, your aunt has told me so much about you! I'm her friend Jane. How did you know she was here? She'll be so glad to see you!"

He stepped inside, and Harley, Curb and Bash pushed their way in right behind him. Her stupid smile was wiped right off her face as they knocked her flat on her ass in the hallway, then stomped on her solar plexus, knocking the wind out of her, to keep her from yelling.

By this time, they all had their knives out. Harley grabbed her by the throat and slammed her head on the floor, then Curb and Bash started slicing her clothes off. Del was surprised at how firm and youthful her body was, even though her face didn't look so young. He wanted to jump on her, but he knew he'd have to wait his turn.

They dragged her upstairs to the master bedroom, and Del got to put his dick in her mouth while Harley banged her. And finally he got to force himself between her legs. He wished he could've videotaped everything they did to her with the new VHS camera his mom had bought him for his birthday. But that would have been too dangerous, too incriminating. Where would he have hidden the tape? He couldn't have kept it at the compound -- in case the cops ever came there with a search warrant. He wasn't that dumb. He wouldn't put Curb, Bash and Harley in jeopardy. And he knew that his Leader, Conrad Pryzor, needed at all times to maintain plausible deniability.

Del knew that his Leader tacitly approved of the guerrilla action and would hold him in high esteem for carrying it out; Conrad Pryzor had been shrewd enough to realize that Del could take a hint and that he would enlist others to help him. But Pryzor couldn't be told that the mission had been accomplished.

The Leader was aware of which days were scheduled for the WAR symposium, and so he knew which days he needed to cover himself with an alibi. That's why he spoke at a Klan rally in Wheeling over that weekend. He would have plenty of proof that he was there, and not in Pittsburgh, because the Klan event in West Virginia was covered extensively by the news media and, furthermore, it was monitored by FBI agents.

The thing that was most delicious in Del's memory was the way he had plunged his knife into Jane's chest at the same time he was shooting his load into her. Her short dying scream and gradually weakening groans sounded like an orgasm going over the top, then winding down. This was so exciting that Del's dick didn't go soft immediately after he came. He kept on pumping and pumping and came again, just as powerfully as the first time. Later, he told this to the other three guys, and they laughed and clapped him on his shoulders and said, "Del Logan Big Chief. Heap Big Corpsefucker!"

They enjoyed talking about exactly what they had done to the bitch. On the way home in the van they told their stories over and over, embellishing them. Del kept reliving it all in masturbation fantasies for weeks and weeks afterwards, wishing an opportunity for another such exploit would come his way soon.

CHAPTER 42

I had to fly to New York once again to see Jane for the last time. It was a closed-casket funeral. Arlene was so torn up I thought she might have a nervous breakdown. Lori and Charlie tried their best to console us, but they were devastated too. Keith and his girlfriend Shannon weren't there; they were traveling in Italy. Hordes of show business people, political figures and literary notables showed up to pay their respects.

Jane's parents from Idaho, whom I had never met before, stayed as far away from me as they could. I was too shell-shocked to try to tell them how much I had loved their daughter. I don't think they would have cared. In fact they probably wished she had never met me. I couldn't say that I blamed them.

We had no leads so far, and few clues. The Pittsburgh police canvassed the neighborhood but found no one who had seen anybody strange entering or leaving my apartment.

The medical examiner got sperm samples that yielded the perpetrators' blood types, but this was in the days before DNA data banks, so the samples would be of limited value, and then only if we could come up with suspects.

It was clear that this was a hate crime because of what had been written in Jane's blood on my bathroom walls. It was also clear that some of the hatred, maybe even the brunt of it, had been directed at me through Jane. Lots of unsavory people had reason to hate the FBI. But the women's movement had plenty of vicious enemies, too, including members of the Ku Klux Klan, the Aryan Confederacy and other lunatic fringe organizations.

I couldn't directly connect Conrad Pryzor to Jane's rape and murder, but I had a gut feeling that he might have been involved. His dark, hovering presence loomed in the back of my mind. But we had nothing on him. As in the murders of my friends twenty-four years ago, he might be guilty as sin, but he was clever enough to stay behind the scenes, building a protective cocoon around himself, never getting his own hands dirty.

His headquarters was in Little Washington, a stone's throw from Pittsburgh, and this seemed too convenient to be passed off as a mere coincidence. Also, by the merest stroke of luck Arlene Shoaf had not been at my house right when the attack happened. She could have been the real target, not Jane, and Jane might have simply been in the wrong place at the wrong time.

I was torturing myself with endless speculations devoid of proof. And I was scared that, short of finding a snitch or coming up with a lucky break, there might be nothing I could do to prevent the case from going cold.

Haunted by the thought that Conrad Pryzor was still out there, free to make plans and lay traps, I asked the Agent in Charge of the Pittsburgh office for permission to place a "mole" inside the Aryan Confederacy. One of our guys went undercover for six dangerous months, but gleaned nothing to give us grounds for a warrant, much less an arrest and prosecution. Finally we had to pull the agent out. We were afraid he was taking too many risks and might end up in a ditch.

My need to find justice for Jane burned like a hot coal eating its way through my heart and brain. People said don't dwell on it, put it behind you and move on. But I couldn't do that. I didn't want to ever forget her. And I wanted to keep alive my memory of the awful things that had been done to her until I found her killers and gave them what they deserved.

CHAPTER 43

In the days and weeks following Jane Hawthorne's funeral, Arlene Shoaf sank into deep despair. She refused to go out. She seldom took food or drink, and the little she ate tasted like ashes in her mouth. She ignored phone calls from friends and family, including her sister Lori. They couldn't do anything to cheer her up, and she didn't want them trying to coax her into tasks or entertainments that she cared nothing about.

She cried so much that her eyes became painfully bloodshot, and one day when she blotted them, tiny red droplets were deposited on the clean white tissue. This at last was something she could not ignore. Her ophthalmologist prescribed a salve and an antibiotic to be taken by mouth. He made her wear dark glasses when she was awake, which was seldom, due to the sedative he gave her. She had to force herself not to cry anymore, or at least to cry less often, which meant that she must push her thoughts away from what had been done to Jane. But the disgusting, terrifying images insistently probed at the self-protective wall of numbness that her conscious mind was attempting to build with the help of the sedative.

As her eyes healed and her use of the prescriptions waned, so that she had more waking hours to deal with, she succumbed to her old, compulsive junk food habit. But in a fit of self-possession and self-loathing she flung bags of potato chips, corn curls, cookies, candies and cakes into the garbage. And this was her first major step up from her grief. Slowly and tentatively she began to think about how she might spend the remainder of her life. A life that she had almost wanted to give up on. But she knew that Jane would not have wanted her to think that way. Jane would have encouraged her to shed despair and go on to accomplish something worthwhile.

Five weeks after Jane's funeral, Arlene psyched herself up to attend a NOW meeting. She was welcomed warmly, with hugs and soft-spoken condolences. In the course of the proceedings, she announced her candidacy for the chairmanship of the committees that Jane had headed.

She was unopposed. The overriding sentiment among members was that Jane would have wanted it that way.

Arlene threw herself into the goals and strategies of the women's movement just as she once had obsessively immersed herself in the implementation of her sister's career. Nobody could deny Arlene's dedication and her capacity for hard work and long hours. But not only did she become thought of, once again, as something of a "hatchet lady," but many of those close to her started to notice a sternness, a stiffness, a so-called "lack of personality" that had manifested itself ever since Jane's death. Arlene seldom smiled, seldom laughed. Like a bitter crusading saint, she took on a fierce, unwavering zeal that was often implacable and quite hostile to compromise. But even so, her detractors had to admit that her single-mindedness often led to some rather striking and unpredictable successes.

One of the outcomes was that eventually, in a narrow vote, she was elected president of the New York chapter of NOW. The buzz was that in spite of those who now resented her, the new position she had taken would become her stepping stone to high office in the national organization.

Jane's murder still haunted Arlene's waking moments and her secret dreams, although she never spoke of it anymore. She was silently suffering from survivor's guilt, just as her sister Lori had suffered long after the murders of the Dealey Plaza trip.

On a rational level Arlene knew that she should not blame herself for what had happened to Jane and that she could not have saved her. The killers had purposely waited until Arlene had left Frank's house. Obviously they were out to take revenge on *him* by targeting Jane. But he wasn't to blame either. He was only doing his job. Hopefully he would continue to hunt down these vicious hate-filled killers till they were purged from the face of the earth.

PART SIX
BUSH

"Please, can't we all just get along?"
-- Rodney King

"I reserve judgment on whether God is a conservative or not.
-- John Kenneth Galbraith

"This monkey mythology of Darwin is the cause of permissiveness,
promiscuity, pills, prophylactics, perversions, pregnancies,
abortions, pornotherapy, pollution, poisoning, and
proliferation of crimes of all types."
-- Georgia Judge Braswell Deen

"The poor homosexuals -- they have declared war upon nature,
and now nature is exacting an awful retribution."
-- Patrick Buchanan

CHAPTER 44

Keith Santone thought that the Gulf War of 1990 and 1991 was President Bush's finest hour. The Democrats, including low-level personages such as Charlie Guinard, Lori McCoy and Arlene Shoaf, opposed it. But Bush showed them they were wrong. Saddam's "terrifying arsenal" of Scud missiles was shot out of the skies. His "formidable army" of five-hundred-thousand regular troops and a hundred-thousand "elite soldiers of the Republican Guard" were routed, killed or taken prisoner – they collapsed as if they were made of straw. American losses were negligible, except for a lucky hit by a Scud that landed in an Army barrack almost by accident, resulting in a couple of hundred casualties.

Keith lauded the outcome of the whole venture, except for the American casualties, of course. Luckily his daughter had come home unscathed. Michele and her husband Dan had been in Iraq filming a documentary about the trials, tribulations and bravery of our G.I.'s. Tonight Keith was throwing a welcome home party for the young couple at a fancy ocean-side resort in Keyport, New Jersey, where Dan and Michele had made their home.

Because of the victory in the mid-East, the mood of the entire country was in a zesty upbeat spiral that was very good for business. The American people were high on the proof they had gotten that all the tax money they had been shelling out for years and years in support of a strong military had actually borne fruit. The United States demonstrably had the most highly technological, overwhelmingly powerful armed forces the world had ever seen. The Russians were shaking in their boots. They had supplied Saddam with those supposedly awesome Scuds that bit the dust and burned up like paper airplanes. Many people thought that this Soviet humiliation might lead them to back out of the Cold War. The easy demolishment of Saddam's forces and their Soviet-supplied weaponry was a frightening "show-and-tell" for America's long-term enemies. They were forced to realize that they were so hopelessly behind us in the arms race that it would behoove them to start kissing our ass.

Some of the talking heads on TV were griping that Bush should've sent our troops all the way to Baghdad, but Keith disagreed. Bush was shrewd; he and General Colin Powell had done exactly the right thing. They didn't want to obliterate Iraq. They didn't want to have to occupy that country for years and years with American boys getting bumped off day in and day out in the streets and alleys. They just wanted to tamp Saddamn down and keep him on a tight leash without creating a power vacuum that could be filled by Iran.

In the euphoria that accompanied the winning of a war, the pulse of the stock market was racing like a nag hopped up on speed (pun intended). Keith's portfolio was bloated. He was in complete control of his Natural Life Company, with stock and stock options worth half a billion. Three years ago the Leprechaun had died of influenza complicated by pneumonia, and a year after that Keith's mother had to be placed in a nursing home, her once sharp mind eroded by Alzheimer's; she had been sporadically lucid during her slow lapse into dementia, and during a spell of lucidity she had given Keith her Power of Attorney. Freed from accountability to anyone but himself, he let his unrestrained ego and natural flamboyancy take him in bold new directions, and nowadays his handsome, smiling face constantly appeared on billboards and in advertisements everywhere, giving him the attention and visibility he always craved. He was a celebrity, a media star.

On his top-rated Sunday morning TV show, he preached as fervently and evangelically about health and wealth as the religious televangelists preached about God. His belief that he could pull off such a tour de force had its origin back in 1964 at the little church in Cherry Hill, West Virginia, where he had stood up in front of the entire congregation and snowed everybody, including the pastor and his own wife. Nowadays the "wonder of Keith's word" was issuing forth all across the United States, not just from the bully pulpit of his syndicated radio and TV shows but also from the podiums and stages of sumptuous five-star hotels and auditoriums. Spellbound millions were thoroughly convinced that his Natural Life products could help them lose weight, gain weight, ward off heart disease and cancer, prevent or cure baldness, provide them with overflowing reservoirs of energy, slow down or defeat the ravages of old age, and make them richer and more beautiful.

Of all these promises, the one about making them rich had at least some chance of coming true -- due to a quasi-legal marketing ploy that the Justice Department had tried unsuccessfully to prosecute on the grounds that it was nothing but a thinly-disguised "pyramid scheme."

The crux of the scheme was that it offered substantial incentives to those who agreed to pay a five-thousand-dollar franchise fee in order to become "Natural Life Spokespersons." The franchise entitled them to recruit sub-distributors, inside their own licensed territories, to sell Natural Life products door to door. The Spokespersons reaped a heavy commission on everything sold by their recruits. Those who got in at the top made out like bandits. But the latecomers at the bottom struggled and often went broke. And if they complained, they were told that they must not have worked hard enough to recruit sub-distributors.

So far, there was an uninterrupted flow of cash into Keith's hands, in spite of some erosion and some grumbling at the base of the pyramid, which didn't bother him in the least. With unabated exuberance he used everything from buttons to bumper stickers to promote himself and his "beneficial, life changing products."

He was fifty-one years old now, physically past his prime maybe, but his money and his notoriety were aphrodisiacs, for him and for the women that he dallied with. His marriage three years ago to the iconic fashion model, Shannon Cristy, had made them both darlings of the society pages. The tabloids touted them as two of the "beautiful people." The fact that Keith used to be married to the country music star, Lori McCoy, added to his cachet. He and his new trophy wife could fly anywhere, buy anything and do whatever it took to satisfy their every whim.

Why·was it, then, that not much of anything gave Keith a genuine thrill anymore? Why was it that somehow the excitement, the satisfaction, didn't last? If he was having a midlife crisis, he hoped it would soon pass. In the meantime he had to keep his juices flowing by constantly driving himself into new ventures and new conquests.

He wasn't incapable of joy. He could tell that because he felt it when he was with his granddaughter, Meredith, who was six years old. Keith doted on her, and so did Lori. He and his ex-wife had amicably taken turns grandparenting Merry while Dan and Michele were off foolishly risking their lives, filming in Iraq.

Thinking of his granddaughter, a smile came to Keith's face as he sat behind his desk, waiting for Frank Williams to show up. He had invited both Frank and Arlene Shoaf to the party this evening, even though a large part of him didn't really want to.

He thought of them as the doom-and-gloom duo. That old saying, life must go on, hadn't yet sunk into their craniums. They were still mired in a deep funk over what had happened to Jane Hawthorne, and true enough it was horrible, but wasn't three years long enough to wallow in it?

Frank wouldn't give up on his irrational hope of finding Jane's murderers, even though the case had gone as cold as a witch's tit. But he was the type who never knew when to give up, and his life was a bitter, futile mess because of his stubbornness. For God's sake, he was still obsessed with the murders that had happened almost three decades ago, even though the guilty parties had all been hunted down and killed. That wasn't good enough for Frank, though. He still had a burr up his ass about that moldy old fanatic, Conrad Pryzor, even though nobody had any actual proof that Pryzor ever did anything but shoot his mouth off.

Glancing at his Rolex, Keith noted that it was only a little past two, and Frank's plane wasn't scheduled to land at LaGuardia until four. What to do till then? Keith didn't feel like diving into any more work. He thought about his private secretary, Mary Ann Boyle (what an unfortunate last name for such a lovely young creature) who was in her office, probably not doing much of anything because he hadn't given her much to do. She was coming to the party tonight, too. He had told her to take off early to get ready because he had ordered a limousine that would pick her up at about six, right after it brought Frank in from the airport.

Mary Ann was a creature after his own heart, and not just because of her lovely blonde hair, ripe, full lips and luscious legs and ass. Two years ago she had married a thirty-something lawyer who was one of those avidly ambitious strivers that the media had dubbed Young Upwardly Mobile Professionals, or Yumpies. On her honeymoon in Las Vegas, Mary Ann took a side trip to Los Angeles for a job interview with a handsome showbiz lawyer who was wealthier and handsomer than her newlywed husband. She flew to Reno the next day, got divorced from lawyer number one, married lawyer number two and divorced him two years later, reaping a huge cash settlement. "I know it sounds shocking," she told Keith when she applied for her job with Natural Life, "but I firmly believe there are times in your life when you just have to go after what you want." Amused by her cold, self-serving flexibility, and thinking that he could put such ruthlessness to work for him, as long as he kept a close eye out for a knife in his back, Keith hired her at a hundred thousand a year.

Hoping she hadn't gone home yet, Keith buzzed Mary Ann on the intercom. When he heard her voice, he wondered if he really wanted her. Then he decided he might as well pass some time, so he called her into his plush executive suite and said, "Shut the door. I need something to relax me. "

He admired the shapeliness encased in her tight red mini-dress as she went to the bar and fixed him a Wild Turkey on the rocks. She fixed one for herself, too, so she could use the ice cubes on a certain part of his body as part of her relaxation and stimulation technique. Then she knelt and unzipped him.

His penis was flaccid, and he hoped it wouldn't stay that way for long. These days he didn't respond as quickly or as strongly as he used to, which made him wish that some of the wilder claims made for his products were actually valid.

She kissed his penis and took it into her mouth, and to his relief he began to respond. She cupped his balls and stroked his dick lightly and skillfully, and sure enough he became hard. He gave himself over to the welcome pleasure, and since he didn't intend to enter her vaginally this time, he considered it to be almost a monogamous act.

CHAPTER 45

I didn't enjoy being around people anymore, especially big crowds. The only reason I came to the welcome-home party for Dan and Missy was to see my old friends. I wanted to reassure myself as best I could that they were pretty much okay and not currently being stalked or threatened. For the past three years, ever since Jane's death, I had lived with the possibility that nobody close to me would ever be truly safe.

Other than at Jane's funeral, I had only seen Lori McCoy five or six times since our trip to Belmont in 1982, when Missy graduated from college and we all flew up there in Keith's private jet. It was hard to believe that nine years had gone by since then. I had met Jane on that trip, and now she was dead. And I still couldn't get her out of my mind.

The recurrent nightmares I used to have about being back in the Army and about to be killed in combat, had been replaced by recurrent nightmares of Jane being tortured and raped, and me trying to get to her and totally unable to, my mouth agape in a silent scream, my body frozen, my legs and feet rooted to the ground, heavier than a hundred tons of lead.

Somehow, over the years, my dreams of my father hanging in his jail cell had faded away as if I had finally burned out the circuits. Those bad dreams had been replaced by my dreams of getting killed in combat, and then the combat dreams had been upstaged by the terrible dreams about Jane. I told no one about any of this. I didn't want the Bureau to require me to see a psychiatrist and take a desk job while my mind was being wiped clean of all bad subconscious thoughts.

On the hour-long limousine ride from New York City to Keyport, New Jersey, I tried to be affable. I even had two stiff Wild Turkeys on the rocks to loosen myself up. With only three of us riding in the plush coach, there was plenty of room to spread out, but apparently Keith's private secretary, Mary Ann Boyle, preferred sitting very close to him, her thigh pressing against his. They were obviously quite used to this sort of chumminess. I did my best not to let it bother me. I realized that the task of getting me to the party had given Keith an excuse to have Mary Ann's company for the ride, while his wife got there by other means.

Conveniently for him, Shannon had a fashion shoot at one of the casinos in Atlantic City, and had the use of one of Keith's corporate jets to fly her to Keyport as soon as the filming was over.

It was bitterly cold for mid-April, and as we got out of the limo, a blast of wind from the Atlantic Ocean blew cold, wet snow into our faces.

Hustling toward the warmth of the restaurant, we ducked under an arbor of artificial poinsettias and a uniformed police officer stopped me from going in.

"Sorry, sir," he said, and started running a metal-detecting wand over my body. He was wearing a headset, so I guessed I must've set off a primary detector hidden in the arbor.

"He's okay," Keith said. "He's FBI. A close friend."

By this time, the cop had already located my holstered weapon, and before he could say anything, I showed him my Bureau card.

"Okay, sorry," he said. "I'm just following orders – right, Mr. Santone?"

"Right, Jerry, keep up the good work."

The rest of the people in our party made it past the artificial arbor without incident. While two bright and cheerful young ladies in hostess uniforms took our hats and coats, Keith told me, in a lowered voice, "I bought out the place for this shindig and invited two hundred people. You can relax tonight, Frank. There'll be two dozen security guys circulating among the guests at all times."

I have to admit this was somewhat reassuring, but I still was not about to let my guard down. I knew from the tabloids that paparazzi often crashed these kinds of celebrity-studded events, so why couldn't it be done by persons with more malevolent intentions?

The setting was gorgeous, elegantly Victorian, with marble pillars and red draperies and crystal chandeliers with dozens of bulbs glowing like candles.

The halls and alcoves were already crowded with beautifully dressed people holding drinks in their hands, smiling and chatting amiably. We made our way into the dining room, where there was an empty dance floor and an eight-piece orchestra playing Gershwin, and then gravitated toward one of the cocktail setups where one of the bartenders immediately recognized Keith and hustled to wait on us ahead of other people.

Glancing all around, surveying the crowd out of habit, I spotted my ex-wife, Alice Kenton, and my face must've showed my surprise.

245

Smirking at me, Keith said, "What's the matter, Frank? See a ghost?" During the limo ride he could have told me that Alice was going to be here, but I felt that he purposely hadn't; apparently he hadn't shed his perverse habit of toying with people's emotions just to see how they'd react.

"You should've told me," I said in a flat, even tone, so as not to give him the satisfaction of riling me. "Actually I don't mind seeing her again."

He just grinned at me, as if we both knew that my attempt at appearing blasé was at least partly an act. He said, "I'm going to go find Shannon. Come on, Mary Ann." And the two of them moved toward a group of newcomers and greeted them with kisses, hugs and handshakes.

By this time, Alice was coming toward me. We politely embraced, holding our drinks aside so they wouldn't drip on our clothes. Hers looked like a gin and tonic, which I remembered as one of her favorites. I had stuck with Wild Turkey, a double jigger on the rocks, which was starting to hit me.

Alice was wearing a dark blue evening gown, and I told her she looked good, which was the truth. She refrained from paying me any false compliments. I was well aware of how haggard and old I looked these days, with my bald spot larger and my hair grayer.

"I already found our placards," she said. "We're going to be sitting together at the same dinner table."

I said, "Keith must've had something to do with that. He likes to put people in uncomfortable situations."

She gave me a look.

I hastened to add, "I mean situations that he thinks *may* be uncomfortable. But I don't especially feel that way. Do you?"

"Not at all, surprisingly, other than I can tell you're still not taking very good care of yourself." Making a light joke, she said, "Do you think Keith's trying to patch us back together or something?"

"More likely torture us."

We both laughed.

"What brings you here?" I asked her.

"I'm writing an article about Shannon Cristy for *Cosmo*. That's how I got invited. My ulterior motive is that I want to do a brand-new story and photo spread with Lori, if she'll let me -- did you know she's been offered a part in a movie?"

"I didn't know she could act. Or even wanted to."

"Singing is acting," Alice said. "At least good singing is. Frank Sinatra proved that point when he got the Maggio role in *From Here to Eternity* and came out of it with an Oscar. But Lori's not going to have to do anything that heavy, I don't think. Her movie's called *Women's Work*. It's a campy comedy about liberated women taking revenge on their chauvinist pig bosses in a toy factory."

"What's she play, some kind of Gidget-like character?"

"I don't know. I hope it's not *that* silly."

Just then, Lori came walking over to us. She was holding hands with her granddaughter, Meredith, who was skipping along beside her. The little kid's nickname, Merry, suited her well; she was full of smiles and giggles, a basket of energy. She resembled both Missy and Lori, in a way, but she was kind of chubby at this stage, and she had Dan's reddish hair.

From about thirty feet away, Charlie Guinard waved at us to let us know he'd be coming our way shortly. He had gotten detained by an elderly couple, elegantly coiffed and dressed, with whom he was exchanging pleasantries. He was wearing a dark suit and a red tie, and I noticed that he had put on some weight, although he still wasn't as heavy as he used to be.

Lori was still a very attractive woman, and looked ten years younger than her true age. Her hair was still shoulder length and blonde, but maybe the coloring needed a little help by now. Her body was still quite shapely and youthful, in an obviously expensive and clinging low-cut dress. She hugged me tightly, then pulled back and said, "Oh, Frank, I'm so glad that you could be here."

"I wouldn't have missed it," I said. "I wanted to help welcome Missy back home. It must've been hard for you the whole time she was over there."

"Yes, all I did was worry. I was a nervous wreck. When that Scud missile killed all those soldiers, she and Dan were only two buildings away, interviewing some of General Schwartzkopf's officers."

"Yeah, Keith told me that. It's wonderful that they got home safe. Everybody expected the war to last a long time."

Charlie joined us in time to hear my last comment. He gave me a manly hug -- a showbiz-style greeting of the sort I didn't think I'd ever get used to -- and said in his big, booming voice, "Damned good to see you, Frank!" Then he launched into an indignant rap about Saddam Hussein's atrocities, including the gassing of thirty-thousand of his own

Kurdish citizens, and how we should have gone all the way to Baghdad to capture "the insane dictator" and put him on trial for his war crimes.

I wasn't in the mood for political discourse, and Merry saved me by saying "Pap-pap" and looking up at him with her arms raised. Beaming at her, Charlie scooped the child into his arms and nuzzled her with his beard, making her giggle.

Alice, who had been quiet all this time, said, "My gosh, look at the proud grandfather!"

"Darn tootin'," said Charlie. He rub-a-dub-dubbed Merry's face with his rough beard again, and she kept giggling even as she said, "Stop, Pap-pap, that hurts!"

"Oh, there's Arlene," Lori said, and waved her sister over to us.

Arlene looked terrible. And it hit me that her downtrodden, haggard appearance mirrored my own. We were the only two of our old group who hadn't maintained an appearance of youthfulness and verve. And I knew that was because we had been hit hardest by Jane's murder.

I hugged her and immediately realized that my cheek had gotten wet. She hadn't gained back the poundage she had once lost; instead she must have lost a great deal of weight. Her body felt hard, almost bony. She dried her tears with a tiny lace-edged hanky, then put it into her purse.

"Can I get you a drink?" I asked.

"Please ... maybe a glass of chablis."

I was glad to get away from her instead of wallowing in each other's grief. By the time I brought her her glass of wine, Charlie, Lori, Alice and Merry had moved off somewhere, and the lights were blinking to signal that we were to seat ourselves for the banquet.

"I'm sitting at your table, Frank," Arlene informed me, "I can show you where it is."

Following her, I hesitated, then detoured toward the head table, up near the dance floor, which the musicians had now vacated. It reminded me of a bridal table facing a hall full of wedding guests. It was adorned with flowers in crystal vases. Dan and Missy were sitting in the middle, at the place of honor, and Merry was next to her mother. Flanking them on Dan's side were Keith and Shannon, and on Missy's side, Lori and Charlie.

I wanted to go up to Dan and Missy and congratulate them right now, while I could get to them, when they weren't being pressed by a throng of other well-wishers. We couldn't hug from across the table, so we shook hands in turn. Missy managed to lean forward and buss my cheek. Both she and Dan had sunburnt faces, and their noses were peeling, each of them having skin that was unusually fair. Other than that, Dan looked about like I remembered him, except for a forehead that had started to recede. Missy wore her hair in blonde cornrows, a style recently popularized by Bo Derek in the movie, *10*.

I excused myself because Arlene was still waiting to lead me to our table. I hoped I would get to talk later with Dan and Missy because I was curious about their experiences in the Mid-East and wanted to learn more about how their husband-and-wife filmmaking partnership was progressing.

It turned out that Arlene Shoaf was sitting on my left, and Alice Kenton on my right while we were served dinner, which was lavish. From Keith I wouldn't have expected anything less. He had given us a table near the front, not far from the table of honor. The five other people sitting with us were strangers to us.

We introduced ourselves and chatted of insignificant things while we ate. I was glad that the presence of the strangers precluded talk of personal matters between me, Alice and Arlene, so that things couldn't get very sticky.

Since the restaurant looked out upon the ocean, its specialty was seafood. We started out with lobster stew, followed by a spinach salad, then platters of lobster tail, crab cakes, stuffed flounder, swordfish, clams and mussels. All this was washed down with liberal quantities of fine white wine. Then dessert of espresso laced with anisette, and tiramisu.

Afterwards, the speeches began. Keith stood up, thanked everyone for coming, and said how proud he was that his daughter had become a professional filmmaker, which was a career he had dreamed of following in his youth. This caused Charlie to raise his eyebrows and shake his head, but Keith didn't take notice because he had his eyes trained on his audience. "To continued good health and great success for Dan and Michele," he said, raising his wineglass, and everybody toasted and applauded.

Keith then asked Lori to say a few words. Surprised, she stood up rather reluctantly and said, "I 'm just glad to have my daughter and son-in-law back home with me. I thank God for it. I prayed day and night for them, and the Good Lord answered my prayers. I lost my brother Maylon in the Vietnam War, even though he didn't die over there, but that is what killed him nevertheless, and I will always believe that. This country has lost too many of its fine young people, and I just want all the wars to stop, and that's one of the things that Charlie and I will keep on working for."

She sat down, looking vaguely uncomfortable and embarrassed.

Charlie stood up without being asked, and I wondered if Keith even wanted him to. Keith shot a glance at him, and didn't look pleased.

"I'm not Missy's biological father," Charlie said, "but I love her as much as anybody could. I've known her ever since she was born. She's as beautiful as her mother, who has been my wife for the past sixteen years, and like her mother she has the soul of an artist. So does her husband, Dan. I just know that together they're going to do great things. In fact, they are already doing them. Our government doesn't always like to tell us the truth about everything, especially about the wars they keep on getting us into. But Dan and Missy are making documentary films that will tell us at least some of the truth, to the best of their ability, in spite of attempts made to obstruct them. I'm very proud of them for that reason. I passionately respect their courage. I'll support their efforts in any way I can, and I hope that all of you will do likewise."

Not everybody applauded when Charlie fell silent, but I'd say that maybe two-thirds of the guests did so. When the applause died down, Keith said, "And now I know everybody wants to hear from our guests of honor!"

Both Dan and Missy stood up.

Dan said, "My wife is a lot prettier to look at than I am. I don't think you'll mind if I let her do the talking for both of us." Then he sat back down.

Missy was quite poised and confident in talking to this crowd of wealthy, successful high-achievers. "Thank you very much for coming here to welcome us home," she said. "We feel we don't quite deserve to be so honored, but we can't help being flattered anyway. I want to thank my father for giving me my career. From when I was just a little girl I always knew it was what he really wanted to do with his life. He actually made what would have been the very first documentary exposé of the conspiracy behind the Kennedy Assassination, but four of his friends were murdered trying to bring the film footage back home from Dallas. After that, Daddy's career went in a different direction, and he's been highly successful, and I hope happy, but I think he still thirsts to be an artist. And I hope I can carry on where he left off. I hope my husband and I, together, can help my father realize through us some measure of his long-ago dreams."

She sat down to thunderous applause, and Keith was beaming.

Charlie and Lori were looking perplexed, if not slightly stunned. Alice was clapping her hands rather unenthusiastically; she knew what I

250

had told her about the Dealey Plaza fiasco and my interpretation of Keith's true motivations at the time.

Arlene wasn't clapping at all. She gulped down almost a full glass of wine and looked rather stricken, as if she had just been forced to digest an unpalatable sarcasm.

I was sure that Missy's comments were heart felt, but unwittingly misplaced. She still had her father up on a pedestal. Oh well, I told myself, what's wrong with a daughter idolizing her father? More power to him.

Suddenly I was wishing that I hadn't even come here. I felt like a third wheel, a failure, or worse, a Judas goat pursuing goals that could only wreak more destruction on the folks around me. Except for Arlene, who wasn't part of our original group at Belmont, all of my old friends were doing well and realizing their dreams on a grand scale. I was the exception. Lori had always wanted to be a singer, maybe even an actress, and that's exactly what she was doing. Charlie was a crusading attorney, just the way he had started out on campus, only a lot wealthier, and with a beautiful, talented wife. As for Keith, he had yearned to be rich and famous, and he had gotten there even though his methods were sometimes shabby or amoral. But I, who had wanted to be a writer, had abandoned that worthy goal and had landed in the FBI, chasing killers and drawing their wrath down upon my friends.

Who knew what might have happened if I had been able to push the Dealey Plaza murders behind me and stick to my original aspirations? Maybe more murders wouldn't have happened. Jane might still be alive, blissfully ignorant that I ever existed.

After I lost her, I moved out of my town house in the Oakland section of Pittsburgh because I couldn't bear to come home each and every day to the place where she had been killed. I took an apartment in the South Side, a charming ethnic neighborhood that was becoming rapidly gentrified. I hoped that its bustling youthful atmosphere might help me deal with my grief. But of course it did not. I carried angry bittersweet memories with me everywhere I went.

CHAPTER 46

Del Logan was eighteen when he graduated from the Lion Platoon in June 1991. He was the star of his class, the highest ranking cadet of his platoon. In front of the entire assemblage his outstanding qualities were extolled by Aryan Youth drill instructors Curb Burton and Bash Halsey. Conrad Pryzor beamed with pride, personally inspecting all the Youth Squads as they marched past his review stand, then lined up and performed a flawlessly precise, tightly coordinated rifle drill. The high point of the day's ceremonies was when Pryzor stiffly bestowed diplomas and handshakes upon each youth, making them full-fledged adult members of the Aryan Confederacy.

In the afternoon, everybody changed out of uniform and into clothes suitable for a picnic and beer blast. Heavy-metal music blared from an Aryan rock band called White Thunder, with lyrics that were anti-Jew and anti-nigger. Lots of people sang along, relishing the angry, openly bigoted musical profanity.

Roseanne Logan gave her son a warm hug, not holding him close to her bosom for too long, but letting him go off and enjoy himself with the other young men, like a good, stoical Aryan mother was taught to do. She hung around with her husband, Harley, feeling special just for being with him as his wife, because he was one of the most respected members of the Confederacy. They both got slobberingly drunk.

It was such a riotous good time, going on all day long and into the evening, that even the Leader, Conrad Pryzor, shed his crisp uniform and stiff demeanor and strolled around in a white T-shirt with the A.C. swastika logo on it, a pair of brown shorts, tan calf-high socks, red sneakers, a straw Budweiser hat and black, heavy-framed sunglasses. Showing good Aryan fellowship by having a mug or two of beer with each little group of picnickers, by sundown he was heavily inebriated and feeling lugubriously maudlin and mellow.

He went over to a picnic table where Del Logan was playing a chug-a-lug game with seven or eight other graduates, and gave Del a manly pat on the back.

"Listen up, everybody!" Del immediately cried out. "Heil to our Leader! Heil Conrad Pryzor!"

Everybody cried out "Heil!" and they all toasted and chugged a couple of times. Then they quickly refilled their mugs from a nearby keg and boisterously sang "For he's a jolly good fellow," slurring all the words.

Pryzor basked in the accolade, his arm around Del's shoulders. Over the past several years he had come to look upon Del Logan not only as one of his best and most reliable young followers but as an almost perfect embodiment of all the qualities that an ideal Aryan Youth was supposed to possess. Blonde, blue-eyed and zealously obedient, Del occupied a place in Pryzor's heart and mind that otherwise might have been filled by a favored son. Pryzor had never been married and had never sired children, but he felt that he was spiritually Del Logan's father even though genetically it was not so.

Suddenly he wanted to give Del a special gift for his graduation day. But what would be suitable? And available on the spur of the moment? At first Conrad Pryzor could think of nothing appropriate. He wished he had thought of perhaps buying a gold watch and having it engraved, but doing such a thing simply hadn't occurred to him beforehand.

Then he remembered the Mannlicher-Carcano rifle. He had kept it hidden away no matter where he happened to be living, whether down in Mississippi or here in Pennsylvania, ever since 1964. Nobody knew that he had the rifle. He himself had never fired it. The men who had committed murder with it were long dead. The weapon had never been used again. There weren't any recently spent slugs that could be compared and matched to the old ones, even if those potentially incriminating bullets were still being kept in an evidence locker somewhere.

Pryzor decided that Del Logan would love to own this particular rifle, and would covet it all the more once he was told that it had once been used to kill some of his Aunt Lori's old friends. Del hated both of his aunts now; he had narrowly missed killing one of them, and had vowed that he would gladly kill them both. Yes, young Del would get a perverse pleasure out of having the rifle in his possession, even if he couldn't tell anybody else where it had come from.

Furthermore, Pryzor thought, the rifle would be less dangerous and incriminating in Del's hands than in his own. Back in 1964 when those murders happened, the young man wasn't even born yet. He would know how important it was that he should safeguard the rifle, once he was

253

warned about it. And even if he somehow got caught with it, he could say that he had bought it unwittingly from an anonymous dealer at a gun show.

The next day, after bestowing the Mannlicher-Carcano upon Del, Conrad Pryzor further honored him by inviting him to attend a cadre meeting. In his dealings with the newly inducted young Aryan Warrior, Pryzor was being pragmatic as well as paternalistic. He was like an old Apache chieftain afraid that his leadership could eventually be threatened by a strong young buck chaffing to lead others onto the warpath. From time to time he had to show these rambunctious young troops that they weren't marching and drilling all the time for nothing. Their leader didn't intend to keep them marooned inside the compound without ever unleashing them to do bigger and better things.

Seated at the head of a conference table manned by Harley Logan, Bash Halsey and Curb Burton, Pryzor welcomed Del Logan to a seat next to his stepfather, then began to reveal plans that would be known at first only to this group of insiders.

Some of what was being disclosed was already known by all of the older men, but to Del the revelations were eye-opening and thrilling.

"Next Wednesday," Pryzor announced. "I will be signing a contract giving me sole ownership of the defunct store fixture factory in Shickton. Our plan is to put the factory back into full operation, totally refurbished and modernized with new, state-of-the-art machinery. The assembly lines will be manned by members of the Aryan Confederacy. In return for very good wages and benefits, they'll all be required to take up residence within the town limits -- that way they can vote in all the local elections. It's a small town, more properly a village right now, due to population loss when the factory went under. There are only about twenty-three hundred citizens and of those roughly five hundred are registered voters. Therefore if we organize ourselves and our supporters to vote as a bloc, we'll be able to take over the town council and the mayor's office. Our reopening of the factory will revitalize Shickton, and we'll get all the credit. That will give us unimaginable clout with the merchants, the chamber of commerce, the bank and any and all citizens that we choose to deal with. They'll know we have the power of the almighty dollar hanging over their heads. The whole town will be ours. Nobody will dare to challenge us. If they do, we'll freeze them out. They'll have to pull up roots and move somewhere else."

"You say we'll have to take up residence," Harley said. "I guess that means all of us, even us sitting here."

"That's correct," Pryzor answered. "We have to establish citizenship in Shickton in order to vote there. We'll be the new factory managers, but we'll also get ourselves elected to council, with me as mayor. It'll be an easy first position in a strategic sense. Our next move will be to take over as many elected positions as we can, on the county level. "

"What about in Little Washington?" Bash asked. "Are we giving up on that?"

"Not totally," said Pryzor. "But it's a little too tough to take on, for right now. Too many voters who don't like us. Shickton'll be a lot easier. We won't be biting off more than we can chew. But we'll be expanding our power base and enhancing our credibility as candidates for when we're ready to make a much bigger move. "

"I like it!" Curb declared.

He chuckled, and the others joined in.

Pryzor looked directly at young Del. "I suppose," he said to the boy, "that you're wondering what your role will be in all of this."

"Yes, sir," said Del. "But I'll do whatever you say, sir. I believe you already know that."

"I do, I certainly do," said Pryzor. "Do you recall what you were taught about dirty tricks and how they were used during Richard Nixon's presidency?"

"To help win elections."

"Yes, exactly. We're going to use some brand new dirty tricks on our opponents when we start to run for office in the town of Shickton. Some of the tricks will be best pulled off by youngsters, like you and your friends. I'm going to place you in charge of those tactics, Del. I know I can count on your total obedience and dedication to our cause. "

"You better believe it," said Harley. "This boy's a goddamn trouper, and nobody can deny it."

"Amen," said Bash Halsey. "Long live the Aryan Confederacy!"

PART SEVEN
CLINTON

"Death to America! Death to the Jews!
A curse on the Christians! America must pay!"
-- Shiek Omar Abdel-Rahman

"Bigotry of any kind ... it's just so unfair, and I've suffered
because of it in my own life. It makes me furious."
-- Neil Diamond

"The human race isn't far from going to the stars."
-- Astronaut John Young

"If the fetus is human life, as of course it is,
it ought to be accorded equal dignity with the
snail darter and the sperm whale."
-- Representative Henry Hyde

CHAPTER 47

The mid-nineties were marked by a wave of atrocities and law enforcement responses to those atrocities that brought intense scrutiny, wild accusations and widespread distrust down upon the FBI and the ATF. I was so disgusted and demoralized that I thought of giving up and getting out.

On February 26, 1993, Arab Islamist terrorists set off a powerful truck bomb in a parking garage beneath the World Trade Center. Six people were killed and more than a thousand were injured. It could have been far worse. The bomb was rigged to cause one of the twin towers to collapse upon the other, and to disperse cyanide gas through elevator and ventilation shafts, fatally poisoning any survivors of the explosion. Luckily the towers did not fall and the lethal gas was apparently burned up in the initial detonation, or the casualties would have been astronomical.

The ATF and the FBI deserved accolades for finding in the mountain of rubble a Ryder truck axle bearing the vehicle's VIN number, which enabled government agents to quickly track down and arrest the terrorists. But instead of appreciating such good detective work, crackpots promulgated a whacky theory that the solving of the case was somehow "too easy" and therefore the FBI must have had prior knowledge of the bomb plot but had done nothing to stop it. Various "government conspiracy" fantasies were whipped up to explain why the FBI would act so insidiously, and rabid talk-show hosts and Internet blatherers kept the spin alive and used it to pump up their ratings and land lucrative gigs as "talking heads" on TV.

Needless to say, this kind of crap infuriated all of us who worked in law enforcement, and the widespread distrust cast in our direction made our jobs much harder. I was proud of what I did for a living, but I found myself reluctant to mention it when I was among strangers, for fear of becoming a target of contempt and derision.

In the spring of 1993, ATF agents attempted to arrest David Koresh and members of his religious cult called the Branch Davidians, on charges of hoarding vast quantities of illegal weapons. Warned by a snitch that the arresting officers were coming, Koresh and his followers shot and killed two ATF agents and barricaded themselves inside their compound. During a fifty-nine-day standoff, the Davidians were given every opportunity to surrender without being harmed, but they steadfastly refused. When armored vehicles were brought forward to poke holes in the walls of the compound and inject tear gas, some of Koresh's fanatical henchmen doused the entire place with gasoline and set it on fire. Scores of men, women and children were incinerated.

The ATF, the FBI and President Clinton's newly appointed attorney general, Janet Reno, were reviled by persons who simply could not believe that "good godfearing folk" would have intentionally killed themselves and their own children in such a bizarre and horrible manner. Never mind that a similar "religious martydom" had taken place just a few years ago at the Peoples Temple commune in Jonestown, Guyana.

On April 19, 1995, the second anniversary of the "Waco Holocaust," Timothy McVeigh blew up the Alfred E. Murrah Federal Building in Oklahoma City, killing one hundred and sixty-eight people, including nineteen children. He had scouted the building beforehand to make sure that its day care facility was in full operation so he could kill lots of children as well as adults, in order to mimic the outcome at Waco.

McVeigh considered himself a hero and a true patriot. He believed that if he committed a "revolutionary act" by blowing up a government building with huge loss of life, Congress would respond by passing laws so draconian that the people would rebel, the government would be overthrown, all Jews and Negroes would be enslaved or exterminated, and White Power would reign supreme in America.

I had no close friends killed in the blast at the Murrah Building, although I did recognize on the victim list the name of a fellow I had known casually, years ago, in my class at the FBI Academy. Later I learned that he had left a wife, a son and three daughters.

People like me, in jobs like mine, were supposed to be a bastion against the criminals, the bad guys. But the horrors being unleashed these days made the task seem monumental, overpowering, even futile. Any nut so inclined could easily find out how to make a bomb out of fertilizer and fuel oil, and then terrorize and disrupt the entire country and send it into deep mourning. Desperadoes of the past, like Pretty Boy Floyd, John Dillinger and Machine Gun Kelly, who robbed and killed for mere money, seemed nostalgically preferable to the lunatics of today, all hopped up on religious and political ideologies and able to commit horrendous crimes against humanity with a complete lack of remorse and a fervent belief that God was on their side.

A recent study by FBI profilers had shown that hatred and bigotry in people had the effect of lowering their IQ scores by twenty to thirty points. The study postulated that since the bigots thought in "black and white," blotting out "shades of gray," they were victims of self-induced tunnel vision. When I read this it gave me pause. Maybe I had to guard against developing my own brand of tunnel vision because I was so fixated on certain kinds of criminals and criminal acts.

By 1995, I had been an FBI agent for twenty-six years. I was fifty-six years old now, and could retire any time I wanted to. But how would that bring to an end my misery, my despair? I'd still be watching the country go to hell in a hand basket, but I'd be doing it from the sidelines, helpless and ineffectual, a man without a mission, feeling even more frustrated than I felt now.

In a recent poll of the sixty-six million gun owners in the United States, twelve million said that they would be willing to take up arms against the government under the "right circumstances." When asked who they thought was in the right, the government or the armed militias, they sided with the militias. And, appallingly, right now there were over four hundred militia groups scattered all over the country. The FBI didn't have the money or the manpower to monitor them all, let alone infiltrate, prosecute, disband or destroy them.

If there was one thing that would give me at least some sense of closure to my own career, it would be to bring down Conrad Pryzor. But I was stumped, dead-ended. I had little hope of lucking onto somebody to rat him out for any of his past crimes, real or suspected. He always had flunkies and fall guys to take the rap for him, all the way back to Albert Crane, Cletis Barrett and the Stoddard brothers.

I didn't think Pryzor was a criminal mastermind of the first order, in other words an "evil genius" like Adolf Hitler. He probably believed he was Hitler incarnate, but to me he was just a pale and fuzzy carbon copy. Yet so far he had managed to stay beyond the reach of the law. And I couldn't abide that. It drove me crazy. I needed something new that I could nail him with. Something fresh. Some crime or conspiracy that he was fomenting right now.

Finally, in the fall of 1995, I caught a long overdue break when the FBI team working the Oklahoma City bombing case found out that Timothy McVeigh and his co-conspirator, Terry Nichols, had close ties to a network of militant neo-Nazi organizations. Based on that information, an effort to disarm and disband the most highly visible of such groups was given high priority.

At long last, I had the ammunition I needed to press the Special Agent in Charge of the Pittsburgh Field Office to reinvigorate our operations against the Aryan Confederacy.

CHAPTER 48

Lori's first movie, *Women's Work*, low-budget by studio standards at a cost of only seven million dollars, grossed over forty million domestically and another thirty-eight million or so overseas. That was in 1993. Since then she had co-starred in two more "politically correct" comedies of the sort calculated not to greatly offend anybody while dealing gingerly with themes that almost everybody could get on board with. This smattering of celluloid "social consciousness" was originally set in motion by *Tootsie*, a box office smash starring Dustin Hoffman in the role of an actor masquerading as a woman and in the process having his eyes opened to the realities of gender prejudice.

Lori liked writing and singing her own songs a lot better than she liked making these kinds of movies. To her they were just fluff. But they had the advantage of not forcing her to go on tour for months and months, as she was called upon to do every time she released a new record album. When one of her movies was about to premiere, her main obligation was to make some promotional appearances on TV, which did not put a big strain on her, since she and Charlie still lived in New York, where the major networks had their studios.

She was in her early fifties now; she and her husband were financially secure, and she was thankful that her career decisions no longer had to be motivated by a need for money. She still had the zeal to perform, whether on stage or on camera, but the one thing she could not live without was her music. Not just writing and playing her own stuff, but also listening to other people's work that she happened to admire. Music had been a major part of her life as far back as she could remember, and she knew it would be that way till the day she died. Matter of fact, her envisionment of heaven, ever since childhood, had included music. Otherwise it could not possibly be called "heaven."

In the summer of 1996, Charlie lined up a meeting with Aaron Spelling in Hollywood. Lori didn't really want to go but she did it to help Tammy Wynette. ABC, through Spelling, was interested in producing a pilot for a TV series spinoff of *Women's Work*, which would be set in New York City and would star Lori and Tammy.

The previous year, Tammy had suffered an abdominal infection that almost killed her. She was in a coma for six days, and Lori and Charlie had visited her in the hospital after she regained consciousness. They couldn't help thinking that Tammy's career might be over, but to their surprise she recovered enough to go on tour with her ex-husband, one of the biggest country music stars ever, George Jones.

Sometimes Lori didn't know how her friend Tammy managed not only to keep going, but to keep turning out hit records. Over the years she had endured twenty-six major surgeries, including operations to remove gall stones, kidney stones and nodules on her throat. On top of it, she was often harshly attacked in the media. One of the most hurtful comments was hurled at her back in 1992 when Hillary Clinton said on *Sixty Minutes* that she wasn't "some little woman standing by my man like Tammy Wynette." Tammy demanded and got an apology, and continued supporting Bill Clinton for president.

In spite of her desire to help Tammy land the TV series, if production would have been slated for the West Coast, Lori would have turned it down without even taking a meeting. She did not want to "go Hollywood." She wanted to stay close to her daughter, her granddaughter and her son-in-law, who were still living in New Jersey, and to her sister Arlene, who had never left New York.

When Missy heard about the Spelling meeting, she told Lori that she and her husband Dan had been thinking about a trip to Los Angeles, too. Their Desert Storm documentary had won top prize in several minor film festivals, and had even been shown at Sundance. This had brought them considerable notoriety as serious independent filmmakers and had whet their appetite to do more. But financing was always a problem, and Missy didn't enjoy having to go to her famous mother and father for help in raising money.

"Dan and I want to line up some meetings out there," she told Lori. "We've been putting together some concepts that we can pitch -- if we can get in to the right places."

Charlie said, "Aaron Spelling knows everybody, and when he talks they listen. I can press him for some entrées. Matter of fact, I can act as your agent, if you like. Let me see what I can set up for you."

"Do you think Aunt Arlene will let Merry stay with her? If she can't do it, maybe Daddy can."

"No, let's bring her with us," Lori said brightly. "We can take her to Disneyland. We can even go down to San Diego and show her the zoo."

"She's going to be more interested in seeing the movie studios and sound stages," Charlie said. "She's a little show biz wiz already."

"That's true," Lori agreed with a fond smile. She was delighted with her granddaughter's blossoming interest in music and entertainment. Six years ago, when she was only six, Merry picked up Missy's abandoned guitar, which for years had decorated the white granite hearth in Lori and Charlie's family room, and began to pluck at it, singing some of the words to a ballad from the *Coming Home* album. She couldn't strum the proper chords, but she had the rhythm right, and she surprised everyone with her precociously sweet and plaintive alto voice, a lot like Lori's voice at that age. She jumped at the chance to take guitar and singing lessons, and continued to develop quite amazingly. She loved going to Grandma's concerts and recording sessions. And now, at age twelve, she was starting to write some cute little songs of her own.

Even though the West Coast trip had turned into a family affair, part business and part pleasure, there would inevitably be times when the adults would have to take meetings in situations where it would be awkward or inappropriate to have a child along. So it was decided that Merry's nanny would watch over her during those times. Merry balked at this, saying that she was too grown up to have a nanny, but she stopped griping after she was told that she could invite her best friend from school, Alicia Carr, to come on the trip too, and that Alicia's parents would feel more comfortable and more apt to give their consent if they were told that an adult would always be around to look after their daughter.

Charlie called Aaron Spelling to firm up their plans, and when Spelling was told of the entourage Charlie was bringing, he insisted on booking rooms for everybody at the Beverly Hilton. "That's where our big party is being held on Thursday night," he said. "It'll be convenient for you. I'd love to have you come to the party. You can bring your granddaughter, too. I hate parties but I have to be there because we're launching a new season. You and I can sneak into a corner and talk business. That way the evening won't be a total bore."

Spelling was the most successful independent producer in television history, and everybody from the biggest stars to struggling wannabes coveted his attention. But Charlie Guinard was successful too, and for now he was being treated as an equal. He knew some of Spelling's history: how he grew up in a section of Dallas so shabby that railroad tracks ran right past his backyard, and how school kids picked on him because his father was a Russian Jew and a poor tailor who spoke broken

English. Tired of getting beat up by bullies every single day, at age eight Aaron escaped school by subconsciously willing himself into a psychosomatic illness: he became convinced that he couldn't walk. For over a year he stayed in bed and read stories by Hemingway, O. Henry and Mark Twain, till he was inspired to start writing stories of his own. To this day, he was still a bundle of neuroses going back to his childhood. His anxieties and insecurities were undiminished by all the hits under his belt, cash cows like *Dynasty, Mod Squad, Hotel, Love Boat, Charlie's Angels* and *Fantasy Island* that enabled him to live in a fantastic "dream house" of one-hundred-and-twenty-three rooms with an indoor skating rink, a bowling alley and a zoo.

He set Charlie and Lori up with three splendid suites at the Beverly Hilton Hotel, one for themselves, one for Dan and Missy, and one for the two kids and the nanny. "The kids'll have the suite that was on reserve for Tammy Wynette and her husband," Aaron Spelling said. "Tammy and George have been held over in Baton Rouge for another week. They'll be calling to tell you that, if they haven't already."

Sure enough, Charlie got a call that afternoon from George Richey, Tammy's current husband and manager. "We weren't held over," he confessed. "Tammy's sick, but don't tell Spelling. She's doubled over with pain. It's probably her kidneys again. She keeps passing stones. She can't get on a plane in that condition, but she'll probably be her old self in a couple of days. "

"Are you sure she's well enough to take on a series?" Charlie asked.

"She wants it so bad she can taste it. It'll be good for her, make her settle down in one place for a while. She can't take the strain any more on tour. But she's a trouper, you know that, Charlie. She'll be Johnny-on-the-spot for you, once she gets her health back."

Charlie had his doubts, but he didn't say so. Instead he asked if Tammy wanted to talk to Lori, but George said that she was sedated and finally getting some badly needed sleep. "You can speak for us with those television bigwigs, Charlie. We trust you to act in our best interests."

"It's not like we're gonna be signing any contracts right away anyhow," Charlie said.

"Yeah, this is just shmoozing time," George agreed. "We lay back and listen to their side of the story till we find out what's what. Thanks for everything, buddy. We realize Lori is getting on board for Tammy's sake."

"Just tell her we wish her well," Charlie said. "Lori's always thinking about her."

That evening over dinner, Charlie told Lori about all the arrangements he had made, and she covered his hand with hers and said, "I love you for taking such good care of us and being so easy-going about it. Any other husband might not have wanted to take so many extra people along."

In saying this, she could not help thinking back to the way Keith had acted, in contrast to Charlie. Her first husband had been more handsome, more charismatic. But Charlie was more solid, and far less selfish. For years now, they had had a very good marriage, not without its ups and downs, but always firmly grounded. Charlie was her anchor, her soul-mate, her island of dependability in a tempestuous world. Even in a career sense, she knew she might have floundered and gone nowhere if it hadn't been for his guidance and his unwavering dedication to her best interests. And he did it all without doting on her or being the least bit subservient. He wasn't Mr. Lori McCoy. He was himself, Charles Guinard, a fabulously successful agent and manager in his own right, and a champion of civil and political causes that he and Lori worked on together, gaining a sense of meaningfulness and commitment in their everyday lives. They weren't focused solely on succeeding in show business; they wanted to use their success to help people and to be good citizens. This might sound corny to some people, but it was something that Charlie and Lori truly believed in.

When the big day of travel to the West Coast arrived, the five adults and two children in Lori's party were taken to LaGuardia in a stretch limo and were picked up by yet another stretch limo when they deplaned at LAX.

The two kids, and even the nanny, Maxine Norello, who had never been to Los Angeles before, were utterly delighted when they got off the elevator at the Beverly Hilton and took a glimmer at their rooms. Each suite had two huge circular beds, a big-screen TV/VCR, a gaming station, and a living room/dining area with a big round oak table displaying fresh flowers, cheeses, candies, wine, bottled water and crystal glasses.

They settled in on Thursday afternoon, and went to the party that night. It was a "sweeps week" extravaganza, a first-class Hollywood gala, artfully designed to glean massive publicity and hopefully glittering reviews for Aaron Spelling's slate of attractions for the upcoming season.

The lavish spectacle resembled a scene from *Dynasty* or *The Love Boat* or any number of Spelling's equally stunning fictional confections. Charlie and Lori weren't overly impressed, since they had been to quite a few similar events. So had Dan and Missy. But Maxine Norello, a short, dumpy thirty-five-year-old woman of Puerto Rican ancestry, in an expensive bespangled dress that Lori had bought for her, was absolutely awestruck. And the two girls, Merry and Alicia, were thrilled over getting to wear fancy dresses and costume jewelry, and were trying their best to act sophisticated beyond their years. But the "sophistication" turned into giggles and blushes when they spotted cast members of *Beverly Hills 90210*, including Tori Spelling, Aaron's daughter, being fawned over by the gowned and tuxedoed crowd in the vast Empire Room of the hotel.

Champagne and hors de'ouvres were being served by waiters in white jackets and black bowties, and Charlie stopped one of them to ask for ginger ale for the kids and their nanny. Dan and Missy had moved off somewhere, anxious to mingle and perhaps make some important contacts. When Maxine and the two girls were served their ginger ale in tall champagne glasses, Merry and Alicia looked unabashedly pleased over the fact that their beverages looked just like everybody else's; they toasted each other, pretending to be drinking alcohol. Maxine got into this game too. Then the three hesitantly started circulating a little, stopping and staring at actors and actresses they recognized from their favorite television shows.

Lori noticed, with a touch of chagrin, that Alicia was prettier than Merry by conventional standards. Alicia was the blonde, blue-eyed, smoothly symmetrically-faced type often exemplified in TV spots or other syrupy portrayals of the "perfect American girl." In contrast, even though Merry had lost some of her baby fat, she was still a big robust girl whose unruly red hair and endomorphic physique were never going to put her in a beauty pageant. Yet Merry had already displayed loads of talent coupled with a captivatingly vivacious personality, and Lori hoped this would be enough to carry her through life and enable her to achieve a substantial level of success and happiness.

"Gosh, there's Jennifer Anniston," Lori suddenly said to Charlie. And look who's with her -- Lara Parker, I believe, from *Dark Shadows* -- wonder what she's doing here."

"Probably married to some network exec."

"I used to jump off the school bus and run home to see that show," Lori said. "I never saw so many stars in one place as are here tonight, did you?"

"Well, you forget that you're a star, too," said Charlie.

"Not a movie or TV star quite yet."

"But you've got how many platinum albums? A hit movie or two, plus a Grammy and three CMA Awards. And you're out here to have an audience with the so-called King of Prime Time -- and the people here all know it -- you've got lots of buzz. I can see them eyeing you up and trying hard not to be obvious about it. Some of them would give their left arm to have Aaron Spelling thinking about making a deal with them. Even the ones who're already in a hit series are scared to death it might be over for them as soon as the ratings drop. They don't want to give up the limelight. That's the power a guy like Spelling holds over them. They've got the gorgeous faces, the charisma and maybe the talent, but he's the one who makes it happen, he's the mover and shaker."

Right about then, the "mover and shaker" himself entered the ballroom, and the entire atmosphere changed. There was a heightened murmur, a heightened electricity in the air.

Aaron Spelling paused at the entrance to the ballroom, as if hanging back, reluctant to put his toe in the water, so to speak. "He looks so uncomfortable," Charlie said to Lori. "I guess it's true what people say: he's actually shy."

"Well, so am I," said Lori. "But I guess not too many folks realize it."

Spelling was slightly built and somewhat impish looking, his silvery gray hair neatly trimmed, cropped to the shape of his small head. His wife Candy was on his arm, a golden-haired beauty, much younger looking than her husband, wearing a shimmering black gown, with diamonds glittering on her fingers, throat and ears.

"That big ring she's wearing is forty carats," Charlie said. "It's called the Star of Malibu. I read somewhere, I believe in *Variety*, that it's been insured for over a million bucks. "

"Well, I'd be scared to wear it," said Lori. "If I went out like that on the streets of Manhattan, I'd never come back alive."

"I'm sure," said Charlie, "that the Spellings have an armed escort practically everywhere they go. There's probably an army of plainclothes security guards all over this place right now."

Charlie thought over other trivia concerning Aaron Spelling that he had digested in preparation for the trip out here. Although the man

269

wielded enormous power in the industry, most of his shows were reviled by the critics, who had labeled him a "schlock merchant." Even he had once admitted that his forte was in giving audiences big doses of "mind candy." But he also confessed that being disparaged for it hurt him deeply. Apparently he craved "respectability," and this led him to sometimes back programs that received lower audience ratings but a higher level of critical esteem, things like his Emmy-winning HBO movie, *And the Band Played On*, about the AIDS crisis in America.

Charlie's hope was that, if he could work out a contract for Lori and Tammy on the TV pilot that Spelling was interested in, that he could also land a side deal for Dan and Missy to produce a serious documentary for HBO or one of the other cable outlets. His thoughts were interrupted when Lori suddenly said, "Who's that, Charlie?"

She was referring to a distinguished-looking man who had kissed Candy Spelling on her cheek and was now throwing an arm around Aaron, hugging him as if they had been buddies in a foxhole together.

"He's the president of ABC," Charlie said. "I met him once, but I can't think of his name. Damn! I'll have to look it up."

Spelling drew a black briar pipe from an inner pocket of his dinner jacket and put it in his mouth without filling it. He and Candy spotted Lori and Charlie and started moving toward them, getting stopped on the way by various celebrities and executives who wanted to pay homage. When he finally got close enough, he somewhat shyly introduced himself and his wife to "Lori McCoy and her husband Charles Guinard," then he said, "I hate parties. What am I doing here?"

Candy said, "I'm afraid Aaron is never totally comfortable unless he's talking business. We had a tour of the White House about ten years ago, and Aaron scarcely took in anything Nancy Reagan was pointing out to us. She had fixed our son Randy some cinnamon toast, and when he dropped crumbs on the floor of the Lincoln Bedroom, Aaron squatted there and picked them up one by one, as if we had trashed the place. "

Aaron smiled sheepishly at this remembrance.

"I don't know who's the shyest, him or me," Candy said affectionately. "We both try to avoid this kind of fuss. Maybe you two men can find a corner to hide in and talk television, and I'll take Lori around and introduce her to people."

This suggestion was soon followed. Spelling didn't even pause to take proffered champagne or hors d'ouevres from any of the circulating waiters. He paid momentary attention to each of the fawning guests who came up to him, but at the same time did not deter from his purpose of leading Charlie into a little alcove, away from everybody. It seemed like he knew in advance that the alcove existed; beyond it was a swinging door that seemed to lead to one of the hotel's prep rooms, but the whole time they were there no one came in or out.

His social shyness gone, Spelling immediately took charge of the conversation. "People have a need to escape," he said. "Otherwise they'd have a nervous breakdown or blow their brains out, because they're so worried all the time about the cost of food, heavy mortgage payments, credit card debt, how in the world they're gonna afford to send their kids to college, and on and on. So my job isn't to pile on stress, my job is to help them escape for an hour or two."

Charlie took a sip of his champagne.

"I don't like to do violent shows," Spelling continued. "I don't think I have to. Some of the other shows are so totally violent and full of sex that I don't even want my wife to see them. And Candy isn't a prude. I love her. She does so much for me, she deserves all the stuff I give her."

Charlie knew that the Spellings had been lambasted for living so extravagantly, but he was surprised to hear Aaron promptly voicing his defensiveness about it. One of Charlie's favorite political columnists, Richard Reeves, once wrote that Aaron Spelling "should be held responsible for the respectability of Greed as the prime value on American Television."

But Charlie was willing to withhold judgment -- until he had a better idea of the artistic and aesthetic approach the man had in mind for Lori and Tammy's series.

"I know you've been a crusader all your life," Spelling said. "Some of my friends call you a liberal, a tree hugger. But I don't care about your politics. And I don't think you should care about mine. All we should care about is the good we can do with a series based on your wife's movie. We have to teach, not preach -- but we do it entertainingly -- and people hardly notice that their way of thinking is being changed. "

"They're learning things they never thought of before," Charlie interjected, speaking up for the first time. "Some of their prejudices against women in the workplace are slowly melting away, or at least their minds are more open than they were before."

"Exactly," said Spelling. "You can catch more flies with honey than you can with vinegar."

"That's something I had to learn over the years," Charlie admitted. "I used to try to win people over with the force and logic of my ideas. Eventually I realized I had to be a lot more tactful. People can be taught

271

and motivated in new directions, but they don't want to be hit over the head with a hammer."

Spelling smiled and clapped Charlie on the shoulder. "You got it," he said. "I believe you and I are actually on the same wave length."

The following day, while Lori, Missy, Dan and the kids and their nanny were taken on a tour of the sixteen sound stages and massive sets that Aaron Spelling and an army of two-thousand employees kept busy grinding out his many current productions, Charlie took a meeting with Aaron at his cavernous office where he was sequestered behind a cluster of secretaries and assistants.

When Charlie was ushered in, Spelling was on the phone assuring a lead actress that her hair color in an upcoming episode would be altered to her satisfaction. Hanging up, Aaron said, "I know an ABC exec who always puts his hand in the air after a meeting turns to a discussion of actor and actress complaints, in order to remind himself that that part of the meeting isn't serious."

Charlie chuckled obligingly.

Spelling picked up the phone again and instructed one of his secretaries to hold all his calls. Then he said, "Look, Charlie, let me tell you something. I'm not against serious drama, but let's agree up front that *Women's Work* isn't in that category. We'd be stupid to try to force it in that direction. We have to stick to the original tone and concept. If we mess with it, we blow it. "

"I have no problem with that," Charlie said.

"Good. Then, since you already understand that I'm thinking the same way you are, creatively, you shouldn't be afraid of giving me creative control. And that's what I need to have on all my projects. I didn't get where I am by not having a superior understanding and insight into what millions of people want to see."

"Nobody can quarrel with your track record," Charlie said.

"Let's not beat around the bush, then," said Spelling. "I have to re-edit a show that's going to flop if I don't get in there and fix it. So I'm going to be unexpectedly tied up for the rest of the day into tomorrow. I understand from George Richey that for the time being you're repping both Tammy and Lori, so I'm going to give you their deal memos to read over. It'll be a good start. Once we agree on the major points, we can call in the lawyers and finalize detailed contracts. "

"Sounds good to me," Charlie said. "But there's a side matter I want to bring up."

"What's that?"

"First of all, I'd like you to agree to let my son-in-law and stepdaughter try their hand at writing the script for the pilot. You don't have to accept it, all you have to do is read it and give them a decent chance. "

"I can go with that as long as you say it won't be binding," Spelling said. "What else?"

"I want a development deal on a documentary film that Dan and Missy want to make for HBO. It's about terrorist cells in America and the hidden danger right under our noses. Hardly anybody is talking about it or even aware of it, especially our politicians -- they all have their heads up their asses. It'll be such an important exposé that it might even go primetime. "

Spelling smiled his impish smile. "You must've read up on me. Must've done your homework. You probably know I've been looking for a project that'll make the snot-nosed critics dry up and blow away. I've done it before and I want to do it again. You talk about politicians with their heads up their asses -- I agree with you, but I think it applies to all the so-called critics who never put their own asses on the line but have the gall to give two thumbs up or two thumbs down to people like me who have the guts to enter the arena."

"Lori and I have quite a lot of experience with that syndrome," Charlie said drolly.

They both chuckled.

"What do you have in mind for the rest of your trip out here?" Spelling asked.

"Gonna take the kids around Hollywood tomorrow, we've got a car and driver. Might even stay two days. Then we're gonna head for the San Diego Zoo, maybe even take a detour into Mexico. I've never been there."

"Good place to stay away from," said Spelling. "Unless you enjoy dysentery. Better not go out into the countryside, gangs of peons will slit your throat for a quarter."

"I'll bear that in mind."

"Think I'll have myself a peaceful smoke before I head into that re-edit," said Spelling. "Candy is always telling me I don't know how to relax, so I've been trying to do it a bit more. You and I can shoot the bull while my secretary is holding my calls. Want another cup of coffee? Or something stronger, maybe?"

"Yeah, I'll take coffee," Charlie said.

Aaron Spelling rang the buzzer for coffee service, then sat back and started filling his pipe.

Charlie was under no illusion that what they had talked about was a done deal, but he congratulated himself that so far things were going about as well as could be expected. He had a motto that he always tried to live by when in the midst of negotiations: It's not a deal when they say it's a deal; it's not a deal when they shake your hand; it's not even a deal when you sign a contract. It's only a deal after you've spent the money.

CHAPTER 49

By the fall of 1997, the two undercover FBI agents that we had placed inside the Aryan Confederacy had fed us enough information to justify a take-down, and we were ready to pull them out before they got themselves killed. As a result of their efforts, we knew that Conrad Pryzor and his followers had accumulated a vast arsenal of illegal weapons that included machine guns, mortars, grenade launchers, land mines, armored personnel carriers, and crop-dusting planes that could be used to disperse anthrax and sarin. A huge cache of military materiel and munitions was being stored in the shafts of a depleted underground coal mine on Pryzor's land.

We were preparing to enter the armed compound with a search-and-seizure warrant, and we hoped our plans wouldn't leak to the media. To obtain the warrant, I went before a federal judge in Pittsburgh, accompanied by an assistant United States attorney, with an affidavit citing the facts and circumstances justifying not just the search and seizure, but any arrests that might follow.

We needed the element of surprise. If they found out we were coming, the contraband might be gone by the time we got there. And if only two or three agents showed up at Pryzor's gate, they might all too easily be turned away by the guards or gunned down by the sentries.

Mindful of the Waco disaster, we did not want to instigate a shootout, yet we needed overwhelming firepower in our favor in case worse came to worst. We hoped that a strong show of force right up front might actually discourage an outbreak of violence. Therefore it was decided that I would go in to serve the warrant at the helm of our Pittsburgh Anti-Terrorist Unit, backed up by a State Police SWAT team and a company of National Guard troops.

We knew of course that the two centers of operation for the Confederacy were the PDC factory and the compound. In our tactical meetings we had discussed the feasibility of arresting Pryzor and his closest henchmen at the factory, where they presumably would not have ready access to heavy armament and might not put up a strong resistance leading to a bloodbath. "On the other hand," I pointed out, "our objective is not merely to make arrests, but to confiscate their arsenal. We can only accomplish that at the compound. We should make our move when we can be pretty sure that the place is undermanned and Pryzor himself is on the premises. That's where he lives. He maintains a bungalow there, and he goes home each evening when the factory closes. So do most of the employees. Ever since the factory opened, they've been required to reside in Shickton, Pennsylvania, a town about ten miles south of Little Washington, because according to our undercover guys Pryzor wants to run for political office there. The Confederacy doesn't congregate en masse at the compound unless a rally or some other special event is going down."

We were on the verge of finalizing all of our plans when suddenly there was an outbreak of salmonella poisoning in Shickton. Dozens of people were taken violently ill with vomiting and diarrhea, and two little children died in the hospital.

The Centers for Disease Control and the DEA were under a lot of pressure to root out the source of the contamination and control the epidemic. The likely source seemed to be a buffet style restaurant in the heart of the town. Everybody who got sick apparently had eaten there. It was thought at first that a lazy employee, or perhaps one with a grudge, must have done something carelessly or purposely unsanitary. Health inspectors closed the restaurant, checked all the food and equipment for contamination, and discovered that the salad bar was infested with salmonella.

But where had the germs come from?

Who was responsible?

The scientists on the case couldn't figure it out.

Then the local sheriff got a shocking phone call. An anonymous female, her voice shaking with fear and desperation, claimed that members of the Aryan Confederacy had intentionally contaminated the salad bar in Shickton by spritzing the outlay of food with salmonella germs. It was supposed to be a test run to ascertain if enough people could be made so terribly ill that they'd stay away from the polling places in large numbers, come November of next year, when local elections were scheduled to take place. The Confederacy intended to run its own slate of candidates for mayor, sheriff and town council -- and to facilitate a win by spreading illness among their opponents' supporters, to keep them from coming out to vote. Now that the trial run had been successful, the strategy of poisoning the food supply would be carried out on a much larger scale come election time, when Conrad Pryzor and several of his cronies would be on the ballot.

"How do you know all this?" the sheriff asked the woman, scratching his head in consternation, almost positive that this phone call was a hoax.

"Because ... because my son and his buddies were in the Aryan Youth Brigade. They went to the restaurant lookin' all spiffed up and innocent. They're the ones that poisoned the food with their spritzer bottles."

"What're their names?" the sheriff demanded.

"I don't want to turn them in," the woman said. "I just don't want nobody else to die ... 'specially the little children."

"Who are you?" the sheriff barked.

But the woman hung up, and he shook his head in puzzlement. He wished he would have had some quick, easy way of tracing and recording the phone call. After mulling it over for a while, he punched in Star 69, and a robotic voice told him that his last incoming call had come from a number that he recognized as the one for the reception desk of PDC, the store fixture factory that had started back up again several years ago, bringing Shickton back from poverty. The initials "PDC" stood for the Pryzor Display Company. Most if not all of the factory's employees were members of the Aryan Confederacy, a fact that hitherto had been pretty easy for the sheriff to overlook, in light of the tremendous beneficial impact on the local economy. Conrad Pryzor was now one of the town's leading citizens and the most influential member of the Shickton Chamber of Commerce.

The sheriff didn't want to do anything that might bring down his town's largest employer. And he didn't want to risk losing the fat contributions that Pryzor had made up till now to his campaign committee, every time he had to run for reelection. If the store fixtures factory went out of business because of him, he'd be a pariah -- especially if this phone call turned out to be nothing but the blathering of a disgruntled employee or the hysterical ravings of a hopelessly neurotic woman in the throes of menopause.

On the other hand, if she was telling the truth, and if the crazy scheme she had babbled about was actually going to be put into play, the sheriff could easily lose the upcoming election. But not if he became a hero for solving an evil conspiracy that had led so far to the deaths of two children and had sickened dozens of citizens in its attempt to nullify the democratic process.

Motivated partly by a drive to uphold his sacred oath to protect and serve, and partly by a strong sense of political self-preservation, the sheriff finally put in a call to the FDA, figuring they could bring in the FBI if they saw a need to. Either way, the full responsibility of this mess wouldn't be solely on his own shoulders.

When Roseanne McCoy hung up, her hand shook so badly that she almost dropped the phone. She jumped when she jerked her head around and saw Harley coming toward her from down the hall. He wasn't smiling. Far from it. But for him to scowl at her for no reason at all wasn't unusual, and so for a brief moment she hoped that he hadn't heard anything that would draw his full wrath down upon her.

But those hopes were dashed when he hauled off and clouted her in the face, knocking her backwards into the heavy reception desk, then pulling her up by her neck. Her eyes smarted and tears rolled down her cheeks. Her lip was bleeding -- she touched the salty, coppery blood with her tongue, then wiped it with her hand so it wouldn't run down her chin and drip on her blouse.

"Who the fuck was you talkin' to, babe?" Harley demanded.

She didn't answer. Through her pain, she tried futilely to think of a lie that he might fall for.

Harley said, "You better tell me the fuckin' truth! Want me to smack you again, harder?"

His face was like a devil's face, beet red and all screwed up with anger. He started smacking her cheeks hard, first one side and then the other, pressing her body so tight against the wall that she couldn't budge. Each hard slap shot stabs of pain through her head and she thought her jaw would shatter and hang slack and unhinged.

"Talk, goddamn you!" Harley snarled, the blue veins popping out of his forehead.

She started blubbering, confessing just about everything she had told the sheriff. Hoping against hope that her husband would somehow take mercy on her, she pleaded that she just did not want any more little children to die.

"You ratted out your own son!" Harley sneered. "You betrayed him and his mission. He knows the penalty as well as you do. We can't let you live to testify against us if the police come. You're a traitor, worse than Judas. The punishment for an Aryan mother who sides with our enemies is death."

He spat in her face.

Then his big strong fingers tightened around her throat, and she felt her eyes bulging, her face swelling and turning purple.

In just a few short minutes all her pain went away for good.

CHAPTER 50

Del Logan was lying in bed masturbating while he tried to remember every detail of the rape and murder of Jane Hawthorne.

The phone rang, pissing him off. There was no telephone in his bedroom, so he'd have to go downstairs to take the call, unless he just let the damn thing ring till it stopped. But he was already losing his erection. He thought of keeping his hand on his penis as he went down the steps, not even bothering to pull his pants all the way up, but the phone was on a stand in the hallway between the kitchen and living room, and his mother might walk in on him. She was due home from work at any minute. So he pulled up his pants without zippering them or buckling his belt.

His mouth watered as he took in the delicious aroma of potatoes, carrots, celery, onions and chunks of beef slow-cooking in the crockpot that Roseanne had filled up before leaving the house this morning. His penis still tingled as he picked up the phone, ready to bitch out a telemarketer if that was who had interrupted his orgasm.

It was Harley. "You got to gitcher ass back out here, son. We got us a fuckin' emergency."

Del knew not to press his stepfather for details – the goddamn phone might be tapped. He had to do exactly what he was told, no time for bullshit.

"Patsy is comin' too," Harley said. "He's gonna stop for you. He'll be drivin' his pickup."

Harley was referring to Patsy Delmar, a tough, hard-nosed young guy who had graduated with Del from the Aryan Youth Brigade. They had been the best of buddies, all the way through. At one point they had tried to kick each other's asses and had fought to a draw. After that, as they rose through the ranks, they joined together to harass the younger, less experienced recruits.

Del decided to risk one little question. "Should I leave a note for my mother?"

"No," Harley said. "I'll explain when you get here."

He hung up the phone, and thought about turning off the crockpot. But he figured it would be okay on the "slow" setting.

And his mother was bound to come home and tend to it before it had a chance to overcook.

When Patsy and Del got to PDC, they hit the buzzer and Harley came to the door and let them in. Wordlessly, he led them to the employees' shower room, in a wing of the factory that also contained a well-equipped gym and a locker room.

Patsy was the same age as Del, but he looked much older and had a dark beard-stubble that Del envied. Both of the young men were in jeans and plaid flannel shirts, ready to do any kind of job, no matter how dirty. Their eyes darted all around as they wondered what kind of shit Harley was getting them into.

In addition to the various display racks, glass showcases, pegboards and merchandising accessories that the store fixtures factory manufactured and sold to retailers, it also sold custom uniforms for sales clerks, and the orders were packaged by the ten-count in big, opaque plastic bags which were then shipped out in cardboard boxes sized according to the total number of uniforms going to each particular customer.

Del worked in the shipping department, and so he was familiar with the normal usage of the heavy-duty plastic bags but now he had to wonder at why four of them were lying on the tile floor and why they looked all lumpy, pulled tight at the neck and sealed up with duct tape.

"Mebbe I shouldn't oughta tell ya what's in these here bags," Harley said. "But I'm goin' to, and ya gotta take it like a man, Del."

"I see a bloody knife over there on the bench," Patsy remarked. "Didja forgit to clean it up?"

"Gonna git to that," Harley said perfunctorily. Then he turned to Del, shaking his head, scowling, his hair and his scruffy beard wet from sweat or from the shower, it was impossible to tell.

"Spit it out," Del said.

"It's yer ma. She ratted us out. Lucky I caught her at it."

Harley's piercing eyes focused on Del, waiting to see if the boy was going to take it like a man. Del actually *was* a man now, twenty-three years old, but still baby-faced, barely needing to shave, and trying to sport sideburns that were made up mainly of head hair pulled down and trimmed straight across at the level of his ear lobes. Harley had to hand it to him, though, because he barely flinched when it dawned on him that his mother's cut-up body must be in those plastic bags.

"She called up the sheriff in Shickton," Harley explained. "I got it out of her, but I didn't really need her to confess, because I knew what I done heard. She told on you, Del. All about the spritzers and the salad bar. We ain't never gonna win no election -- and it's all 'cause of her. Fuzz'll be on us like stink on shit. "

"First of all," Del said, his high-pitched voice surprisingly under control, "I ain't gonna hold it against you, Harley. You done the right thing. I hate to admit it, but she was a traitor, and she knew what the penalty was, goin' in. But that fuckin' joke of a sheriff, he couldn't catch flies with flypaper. And now he don't got hisself a witness. He can say he got a phone call, but he can't prove it. "

"Right on," Patsy said. "All we gotta do is get rid of the body."

"And don't forget that bloody knife," said Del. "Just cleanin' it up ain't good enough. The cops got sophisticated lab equipment that can detect little wee traces of human blood, even sometimes get DNA where nothin' at all is visible to the naked eye."

"Yer a smart young fucker," Harley said, clapping his stepson on the shoulder. "One of these days you'll be runnin' the whole fuckin' Confederacy, you mark my words, boy."

They were down to the last plastic bag, ready to weight it down with heavy chains wired around it, like all the others, which had already been tossed into the river, when Harley heard his cell phone ringing and dragged it out of his pocket. He heard Bash's voice, all shook up, on the other end of the line.

"Harley, is that you?! Listen to me! Don't come back to the compound tonight -- we're surrounded by FBI!"

"Huh?!"

"They're here with SWAT guys and soldiers, armed to the teeth. We're gonna make a stand, we ain't lettin' 'em in -- we'll go down fightin'. But there's only twenty-six of us here."

"Why can't you get out? Get out or give up -- let 'em take you in. They can't hold you, we got good lawyers."

"Fuck 'em! Let 'em try to take us! If we let 'em in, they'll have us dead to rights, with evidence. They know we got illegal weapons -- that fuckin' FBI pig said so over the bullhorn. Claims they had two undercover agents in here for a long time. "

Harley started to say something, but then he heard loud gunfire over the phone.

"Gotta go!" Bash yelled. "The shootin's already started! Holy fuck! "

The line went dead.

Harley hastily told Del and Patsy what was happening, then they hurried up and finished dumping the weighted-down plastic bags full of body parts into the river. They jumped into the pickup truck and headed for Shickton as fast as they could go.

"We gotta get the fuck outta town," Harley said. "We can't help the ones at the compound, they're done for. It's every man for hisself in this kinda situation. We trained for it -- we know what we gotta do. Right, Del?"

"Damn straight."

Del flashed a thin-lipped, self-confident smile. He was quite pleased with himself because, even in this dire circumstance, he was cool and collected, almost devoid of fear. He knew what must be done, and he knew it with absolute certainty, without needing to be told. He and Harley and Patsy had to get to a safe house somewhere so they wouldn't be arrested. But first they had to bust into town to grab up their survivalist gear, their reserves of cash and their stash of guns and ammunition.

As they drove, Harley was on his cell phone calling up as many Aryan Brothers as he could, warning them to hide their weapons, lay low and act innocent, or else get out of town fast. Some of the ones he talked to wanted to head straight to the compound like the cavalry riding in in the nick of time, taking the FBI pigs and the SWAT pigs by surprise, outflanking them and mowing them down. But Harley said, "Forget that shit -- they got a fuckin' ton of National Guard troops -- we're fuckin' out-gunned and out-manned. We gotta be smart, run away and live to fight another day. Like George Washington at Valley Forge."

Del felt a tingle of excitement that overrode any vestige of regret over his mother's death. He and Patsy and Harley were going to become urban guerrillas now, like "Rambo" in the Sly Stallone flicks he had watched dozens of times, picturing himself as a Aryan superhero waging a one-man war against ZOG, whose soldiers would be puny and impotent in the face of his own bold, stealthy moves and superior military prowess.

A heavy burden had been thrust upon him because of his mother's betrayal. The blood of a traitor was in his veins, and he must wipe out that curse by demonstrating unparalleled loyalty to the Aryan Confederacy, even to the point of martyrdom. His mother's death sentence had been harsh but just. He would not allow himself to mourn her. She did not deserve his pity or his respect. He must banish her from his thoughts. From now on, his utmost allegiance, his skill, his bravery and his admiration, would be given solely to his Leader and mentor, Conrad Pryzor.

CHAPTER 51

Because the hotheads inside the compound refused to surrender peaceably, we had to use overwhelming force, and our hopes of coming out of it without any casualties went up in smoke. A half dozen of our troops were killed and twelve were wounded. On the other side, twenty-three were killed and three were taken prisoner.

Of course if we had hit at them at the wrong time, when they might've had several hundred fully armed fanatics against us instead of only a couple of dozen, things would have gone much worse.

After they opened fire from the guard house and the towers, we had no choice but to let the National Guard do its job. At this point there was no need for the guys in our Anti-Terrorist Unit or on the SWAT team to risk their lives. We kept ourselves back out of harm's way and let the battle unfold till it was time to go in and mop up.

Two Piper Cubs and two Cessnas parked on a little landing strip inside the compound never got off the ground. One of the pilots, running hard, tried to make it into one of the cockpits, but he was straffed from the air. Army assault choppers, circling above him, pounded the planes with machine-gun fire and rocket-propelled grenades, exploding their fuel tanks and blowing them to smithereens.

At the same time, cannons and mortars set back in the woods took out the sentries in the guard towers and blew gaping holes in the barrier of concentric chain-link fencing. It did not matter that the fences were topped with razor wire because now they would not need to be scaled.

The concrete guard house was taken out by a tactic reminiscent of World War Two. One of our Army squads laid down a barrage of small-arms and machine-gun fire directed so heavily against the firing slits that nobody in there could dare to pop his head up and shoot back. This gave four of our guys cover while they sneaked around to the sides of the bunker and lobbed in grenades. One guy staggered out, bleeding from his mouth, nose and ears, but still trying his damnedest to point a pistol at one of our grenade-tossers before he sagged to the ground and died without needing to be shot and without managing to pull his trigger.

Rottweillers were set loose and came snarling and slavering at some of our troops, and managed to inflict some serious bite wounds before they were shot. Luckily nobody got bitten in the face or neck. Their uniforms and flak jackets were so thick and heavy and laden with belts and straps for gear and ammunition that the dogs' fangs couldn't penetrate very well.

The toughest and most dangerous part of the assault was the need to neutralize four concrete redoubts that protected the main headquarters building, guarding it from approach on all four sides. As our troops poured in through the gaping holes in the chain-link fence and the demolished sentry towers, machine-gun fire opened up on them from the redoubts, mowing several of them down before they could hit the ground or take cover.

We lost five killed and three were wounded before heavy cannon and mortar fire could be brought to bear on the redoubts. In the end they were taken out in the same way as the guardhouse was -- a heavy fusillade against the firing slits, then grenades lobbed in till all was silent.

A cease-fire was called by the squad leaders.

The gunfire and explosions didn't stop all at once, but when they did, for a long moment the only sound was the whirring of the choppers, which were still circling above us.

Then we heard shattering glass, and all heads turned toward a window of the headquarters building where a white flag was being poked through, on the end of a broom handle. I saw it through my binoculars. I was still well back from the heavy action.

An Army captain barked an order for everybody inside the building to come out with their hands up.

After a long suspenseful silence, the front door slowly opened.

Two bearded, uniformed neo-Nazis stepped out, hands above their heads, their eyes nervously darting at the more than two dozen guns that were trained on them.

Then, at last, Conrad Pryzor came out, perspiring heavily, his brown uniform rumpled and limp with sweat, as he sucked in his gut and stepped forward to be flanked by his cohorts, all three with their hands in the air, looking as shabby, pathetic and vaingloriously evil as the Himmler, Hitler and Goering triumvirate that they had idolized and tried to imitate.

I lowered my binoculars and started toward them, shaking my head in disgust, and breathing a sigh of relief in spite of the carnage before me.

CHAPTER 52

Two days after the assault on the compound and the arrest of Conrad Pryzor, Del Logan was hiding out in an Aryan Confederacy safe house in Wheeling, West Virginia, with Harley Logan and Patsy Delmar. Patsy complained constantly that he was going stir crazy, and Harley kept bitching about having to leave his motorcycle behind when they split.

Del Logan was glad that he had hidden his Mannlicher-Carcano rifle in his secret place in the basement of the house in Shickton, because he was able to snatch it up along with his gear, guns and ammo before he got the hell out of there.

The Mannlicher-Carcano, which he knew was the same kind of gun used to kill President Kennedy, was one of his most treasured possessions. He also knew exactly where the rifle must have come from. As a little boy, he had overheard some of the adults in his family talking about Aunt Lori's trip to Dealey Plaza with her first husband and their friends. He got chills of excitement and wonder when he learned about the murders that had taken place back then and how his aunt and his cousin Missy, just a baby at the time, had barely escaped from the killers.

By digging up old newspaper articles in the dumpy little town library in Cherry Hill, and by talking to a few of the oldtimers loafing around town, he had fleshed out some of the details of the unique and astounding things that had happened to his family members all those years ago, before he was even born. He found out that a Mannlicher-Carcano rifle had been used to kill his Aunt Lori's nigger friends and two whitetrash friends, and then the rifle had disappeared. Quite a few years later, four Aryan Confederacy members had been ambushed by some FBI pigs in New York, led by fuckhead Frank Williams, and one of the Brothers named Albert Crane had died in a hospital after confessing to the killings of the niggers and nigger-lovers down in Mississippi, which happened to be where Conrad Pryzor had had his radio station and his Aryan headquarters at that time.

Del didn't need to be a rocket scientist to realize that the weapon that had killed his aunt's friends must be the very same Mannlicher-Carcano that now belonged to him. He was proud to own it. He felt that it had come full circle. God had ordained that it should end up in his hands.

Trying not to go crazy while he was holed up in the safe house, he avidly kept up with the media circus that erupted in the wake of the destruction of the Aryan Confederacy compound.

He ached to participate in some kind of counterattack against his enemies, but he knew that right now, at this inopportune moment, discretion was the better part of valor. He must force himself to lie low, reconnoiter, and strike wisely at the proper time.

Newspaper, television and radio accounts made clear that the compound had been razed and that the vast Aryan Confederacy arsenal had been confiscated by the federal government -- in other words, ZOG. The factory in Shickton had been shut down after the pigs figured out that salmonella had been cultured there in what they called a "secret scientific laboratory" making it sound like something worthy of Dr. Strangelove, when it was really only a little side room that used to be the plant foreman's private latrine.

Del thought it was stupid to shut PDC down -- what the hell was that dinky little town going to do for employment? Probably it'd soon become a ghost town. Which was what it deserved. At least that fat, stupid sheriff would be out of a job.

According to what was being said by the talking heads on TV, Curb, Bash and Conrad Pryzor would probably be put on trial sometime in 1999, a year or more from now. Meantime, the FBI would continue to hunt down members of the Aryan Confederacy and would press charges against them for possession of illegal weapons, criminal conspiracy, hate crimes, election rigging, salmonella poisonings and fatalities, and the "murders" at the compound -- which to Del were not crimes at all but acts of war and self-defense in a Constitutionally justifiable rebellion against an evil, corrupt, unlawful government.

ZOG was holding Curb, Bash and Conrad Pryzor in a jail in Pittsburgh pending trial, and Del dreamed of masterminding a break-out, a dramatic rescue that would make national headlines.

But so far he couldn't come up with a plan that seemed feasible. The odds against him were formidable. However, he took comfort from knowing that inside the jail there was a gang of Skinheads that ruthlessly kept all the other inmate gangs in line, including the nigger gangs. For sure the Skinheads would keep the Aryan Confederacy leaders safe and would treat them as respected comrades.

But, to Del's great shock, less than a week after they were checked into the jail, Curb and Bash ended up dead with numerous shank wounds, the shanks left sticking out of their torsos, and their throats slit for good measure. In the newspaper, one of the prison guards said, "It happened in the exercise yard, our eyes can't be everywhere at once, and the cons know it. Bunch of 'em formed a circle so tight we couldn't see what was goin' on -- it was all over in a few seconds. When they broke apart there was two dead bodies, and nobody was talkin'. Some of them Skinheads'll kill their own mothers, but they despise anybody comes in here for doin' somethin' bad to a child -- child rape, child murder and so on. No doubt in my mind that Burton and Halsey got themselves butchered up 'cause the cons knew they was behind the food poisonings that killed the two little kids in Shickton."

Reading the guard's statement shook Del up so badly that he sneaked into the john where nobody could see him, and wiped tears from his eyes. It seemed to him that his whole world was coming apart. He had never felt this kind of misery and anguish since back when he was a small boy trying to live down the disgrace brought down on him by his father's botched bank robbery and suicide.

He used to think that he'd always have a bunch of Confederates to protect him in case he ever ended up in prison, which after all was never going to happen, not only because he was so smart but also because he'd never allow himself to be taken alive. He didn't think it was fair that other Aryans might actually turn against him if they found out that he was one of the guys who had spritzed the salad bar with salmonella. He hoped it would never become known. But he didn't feel guilty about it. He had been following orders. The collateral damage could not be helped and surely was not his fault.

With great relief, Del learned from the news reports that Conrad Pryzor had not been killed by the Skinheads. But they had severely beaten him, which was a sacrilege, an outrage. He was in the prison infirmary, and the report said he was expected to make a full recovery. Why hadn't he been killed along with Curb and Bash? Maybe ZOG had designs on him and this was their initial move in an attempt to break him down, brainwash him and make him turn traitor. There was no doubt in Del's mind that some of the Skinheads must be ZOG agents disguised as inmates.

He brought this up with Patsy and Harley, and they decided to try to get someone they could trust to visit Conrad Pryzor in confinement. They had to make sure that their Leader was doing okay and find out what his

289

needs were and what orders he might have for them. They asked for help from the people at the safe house and were promised that prisoners and ex-prisoners would be questioned, and someone who had no criminal record would be sent to the jail as a visitor.

The news that came out of this was much worse than Del could ever have imagined. A young dude named Chris Terrell, who had been chosen for the jail mission because he looked so bland and innocent -- no tattoos and a fresh crewcut – arrived at the safe house in Wheeling after an hour and a half drive from Pittsburgh.

"Up till now I only seen pitchers of Mr. Pryzor from before he was arrested," Chris Terrell said. "I was like totally shocked, man. He shakes all over, and he ain't got no teeth. "

"Whatchou mean?" Harley said. "They stole his dentures?"

"Naw, he ain't never had no false teeth, but maybe he's gonna have 'em now. His real teeth all got knocked out, I mean bashed out, man. The Skinheads didn't do it – his cellmate did. They put him in with some big, mean, black dude that weighs about four hunnerd pounds, looks like the Incredible Hulk with black skin steada green. They done it on purpose, man. They knew this black dude wouldn't waste no time, and he sure didn't. Soon as the cell door slams shut, he grabs your man Pryzor by the neck and starts bashing his teeth against the steel sink -- right against the edge, you know? Knocks all the teeth out, down to the bloody stumps. Says he likes gum jobs from white dudes, 'specially White Power white dudes. Laughs like hell and says that with the teeth gone his big black dick gonna slide in nice and smooth."

"Who ... who told you this shit?" Del stammered, not wanting to believe it.

Chris said, "Pryzor hisself. He cried, lookin' for me to take pity on him. Says he didn't even testify against the black dude. Asts me if I blame him. He told the guards he knocked his own goddamn teeth out fallin' against the sink when him and the black dude got in a fight. He didn't even ask for another cellmate. Gonna stick with the black dude, be his kid. The Skinheads won't protect him, they wanna do him like they did Curb and Bash. He wasn't in the infirmary he'da been shanked, so I guess he's gonna do whatever he has to do now, so as not to get kilt."

"He's blowin' a fuckin' nigger!" Patsy spat.

"You got that right," Chris said.

"Jesus Fuckin' Christ!" Harley cursed.

"I'd rather be dead first," said Patsy.

"You got that right," Chris repeated. "I hate to say it but he looks like a baggy-eyed, toothless piece of shit, man, a little screamin' faggot just like he's turned into."

Del was devastated by all this, and he wanted to be alone.

But he and Harley and Patsy were all crammed into one little room. The only place he could ever be alone at the safe house was in the john. Or out on the back porch.

He got up from the kitchen table, where he and his fellow fugitives had been sipping from a jug of wine while getting all the bad news from Chris Terrell. He thought of strangling Terrell right then and there, to stop the young snot from badmouthing Conrad Pryzor to anybody else. But even though it would have made him feel good at this particular moment, in the long run it wouldn't help. The toothpaste couldn't be put back in the tube.

"Gonna go dryfire my rifle," Del said.

He got up from the table and left the kitchen. Went up to his room, pulled a leather case out from under his bunk bed, unzipped it and took out the Mannlicher-Carcano.

Taking the weapon out onto the back porch, he cradled it in his hands and squinted through the telescopic sight. It was a moonlit night, and as he aimed at a shimmering silvery tree trunk a powerful, hateful thirst for revenge came over him.

He pictured his Aunt Lori in the crosshairs as he sighted through the scope, held his breath, and squeezed the trigger ever so gently, making the hammer click in the empty chamber, picturing a loud explosion and an eruption of bright red blood as his aunt's head shattered like a pulverized pumpkin.

CHAPTER 53

On an icy, bitter-cold Saturday in March of 1998, Keith Santone flew into Pittsburgh to pay me a visit. He had phoned two days earlier, sounding distraught. "This is an urgent matter, Frank. I'll fill you in when I get there. I don't want to say too much over the phone."

Playing along with his cloak-and-dagger demeanor, I said, "I hope the hell you didn't rob a bank or something." But he didn't laugh, and that got me worried. I couldn't help recalling those "good old times" back in the sixties when he used to amuse himself by enticing me into disastrous misadventures and I was all too willing to allow him to do it.

He took a taxi into the city so I wouldn't have to pick him up at the airport, arriving at my apartment on the South Side at around two in the afternoon, shivering, plopping his leather briefcase down onto the carpet and tossing his leather jacket and leather gloves onto my recliner. I asked him if he wanted lunch and he said, "I snacked on the plane, crackers and caviar washed down with Scotch." He flashed his usual cocky grin, his wavy, sculpted hair chemically blonde now, his face unlined and unbaggy, the skin stretched taut over the bones, due to plastic surgery.

"You're looking young," I jibed, "especially from a distance. Wanna put me in touch with your surgeon?"

"Don't bust my chops," he said. "You need to lose twenty pounds and get yourself a hair transplant and a dye job. You'd be surprised how good it'd make you feel to look in the mirror and not see a bunch of bags and wrinkles. It does wonders for your ego, and fires up your libido, too."

"I don't think I could buy into the illusion."

"The chicks do, though. I still go after the young stuff. Can't help myself. Nothing like smooth young skin and tight pussy. "

"One of these days your dick will stop working," I said, "and you'll have to find some new goals in life."

He pulled out a chair and sat down at my dining table. "Let's talk here. Then we can go out to dinner, my treat. I smell coffee. Can I have some?"

I brought the coffee service in on a tray from the kitchen and we sat across from each other and helped ourselves to the fixings.

"This could be a helluva bachelor pad," Keith said, scrutinizing my digs. "But it's too goddamn mundane, like an old folks' home. It needs hip artwork, decorations, furniture and draperies, instead of those fucked-up Venetian blinds. "

"I don't spend much time here. The walls close in on me. "

"Well, no wonder -- there's nothing nice to look at. Hope you're getting laid once in a while, Frank. You're too glum all the time. You should've gotten married again."

"I almost did, and you know why I didn't. So let's just drop the subject."

"Touchy, touchy." He took a sip of coffee, then looked me in the eyes unwaveringly, which was the tactic he always used when he wanted to seem sincere and confiding. "Truth is, I might not be married for much longer myself. Shannon swears she'll stick with me, but I don't think she's the type to hang in when things turn ugly. The 'worse' part of 'for better or for worse' doesn't appeal to her."

"Why don't you just tell me what kind of trouble you're in, Keith? If I can help in any way, I'll be willing to do it. And nothing you say will ever leave this room."

He pushed himself up from his chair in a sudden fury, almost knocking the chair over. "I'm under attack from all sides! They're itching to wipe me out! Not just the state government but the feds, too! They glommed onto me and the fuckers won't let go. If I let them have their way they'll drive me broke. I might even wind up in jail."

He sat back down, shaking his head, grimacing at the implied injustice of it all. He rubbed his eyes, then abruptly stopped doing it. "Better not do that," he said. "My contacts will give me a corneal abrasion. That's all I need."

I didn't understand exactly what he was talking about yet, and I wasn't ready to gush sympathy. For years I had watched him walking a tightrope between legality and illegality in the operation of his business affairs. Sometimes he even bragged about how much he was getting away with, so I knew he would have no one but himself to blame if his house of cards started to crumble.

"Three years ago," he told me, "the FDA hit Natural Life with a Notice of Adverse Findings, and we've been fighting it ever since. It's been costing us a fortune in legal fees just to stave them off. I thought we'd eventually get them off of our backs, even if we had to go all the way to the Supreme Court. But now we're facing a civil suit and a possible criminal prosecution."

"What for?"

"Reckless endangerment, maybe even negligent homicide."

"How in the world could your products manage to kill anyone? I always thought they were little better than placebos -- probably not really beneficial, but not harmful either. To be frank, I never swallowed the farfetched claims you make on TV, it always amazed me that so many other people could be so gullible."

"Well, most of our claims are true whether you believe them or not," Keith insisted rather hotly. "Our diet pill has helped millions of people. Lots of celebrities swear by it. It's the most successful product we've ever put out. I can't stand the thought of having it driven off the market by a federal witch hunt and a bloodsucking class-action suit instigated by a bunch of money-grubbing trial lawyers! If that happens, my stock will nosedive right into the toilet. "

"Did somebody actually *die* from taking your pills?"

"Well, some old guy went to sleep and didn't wake up, and they're trying to blame it on our pills! But he was weak and malnourished, had a weak ticker and about seventeen other things wrong with him, and he was living all by himself in a cold, shabby apartment. The autopsy showed he only weighed about ninety-two pounds when he kicked the bucket. Apparently his heart gave out. Nobody can quite figure out what the hell he was doing taking a diet pill! Unless he grabbed the wrong thing, thinking it was a vitamin. He couldn't see too well, either. He was like Mr. McGoo. He had cataracts."

Keith snorted at the wry absurdity of this, and I had to admit to myself that there was some dark humor in it even as I managed to keep a straight face. "You mentioned a Notice of Adverse Findings from the FDA. What's that all about, Keith?"

"They say their tests show that our Natural Life diet pill contains mandrake, an herbal ingredient on their list of substances deemed unsafe for use in food -- but we're not selling it as food, we're using it in a fucking pill, for chrissakes! Damn near all the pills doctors prescribe can be harmful if you don't use them right! Ours are no different. But the FDA doesn't buy it! They've got depositions from scientists who say that mandrake was used by American Indians as a suicide drug. Sure! But *sleeping* pills are used to commit suicide, too, and you don't see *them* being taken off the market! And nobody gets put in jail for selling them!"

He got up, stomped over toward the recliner, picked up his briefcase, opened it up and handed me copies of the complaint filed against him by

New York's attorney general. While I took some time to read over the stuff, he paced around, muttering to himself.

One of the deposed scientists stated that mandrake would not only keep weight off indefinitely, as was claimed by its distributors, but had the capacity of keeping it off permanently. In other words, some unlucky people might die from it. He further stated that the 'wondrous weight-losing results' of the Natural Life Diet Plan were due mainly to the low caloric intake that the plan advocated, rather than to any beneficial effect of the diet pills. In addition to the pills, the dieters were to take twelve Natural Life Nutrient Supplements daily, washed down with glasses of skim milk, while restricting calories from "solid food" to one thousand per day or less. The hype was that this regimen would "cleanse the system" and make it more able to absorb nutrients, but the FDA branded this as a hoax, asserting that two of the main ingredients of the diet pills were cascara and senna, powerful laxatives that caused diarrhea and loss of normal bodily fluids, which the dieters misinterpreted as weight loss.

"We already removed mandrake from our diet pills," Keith griped, "but that's not good enough for the FDA. They're going after some of the celebrities in our ads, too."

"Why?"

"Well, of course we pay them well for their testimonials. We have noted scientists in our TV spots, as well as athletes and movie stars. They get twenty-thousand dollars a crack -- sometimes even fifty-thousand, depending on who's hot. The FDA accuses us of hucksterism. Never mind that we fund important research programs. A nationally published nutritionist called our diet plan the finest and most complete nutritional program he had ever seen."

"But of course he was being paid to say that."

"Not one red cent," Keith said, "before he expressed his opinion in a letter to us, totally unsolicited. Once we knew how enthusiastic he felt about our program, we compensated him for saying it on camera."

"And you probably funded one of his pet research programs as part of the bargain."

"For god's sake, quit trying to bust my chops, Frank! Are you on my side or not?"

"I'd like to be, but I'm not sure if I can become involved. I'm on some pretty tricky ground here. I need to know exactly why the federal government is coming after you because it's a potential conflict of interest for me."

"It's a fucking trumped-up case! The Justice Department is trying to penalize me for being successful! They're threatening to prosecute me for what they say is an illegal pyramid marketing scheme!"

"Well, I told you it was illegal the first time you laid it on me. But you said that by working the right loopholes you could stay out of trouble and get filthy rich."

"Hey, what's wrong with making money? The American way, right?"

"So long as you do it legally."

Keith said, "Listen, Frank, old buddy. I'm thinking of pulling a DeLorean. Only better and smarter. "

"I'll pretend I didn't hear that, and if you know what's good for you, you'll wipe those kinds of thoughts out of your mind. John DeLorean thought he was smart enough to beat the system, and look what happened to him. "

DeLorean was a suave, handsome, outwardly wealthy entrepreneur who got caught in an FBI sting operation back in the mid-eighties. He tried to destroy the careers and reputations of the agents who arrested him because it was his only hope of keeping himself out of jail. Up till then he had been wildly celebrated as a maverick genius in the automobile industry and had formed his own company to design and market the DELOREAN, an avant garde stainless steel luxury sportscar that debuted so promisingly that it was featured in the fabulously successful *Back to the Future* movies starring Michael J. Fox. But beneath his carefully cultivated aura of wealth and glamor, DeLorean was in a crushing financial bind, and he tried to pull off a multi-million-dollar cocaine smuggling caper to bail out his company. When he got caught with his pants down, he accused the undercover FBI agents, who had masqueraded as gangsters, of entrapping him by threatening to kill his daughter if he didn't agree to hide cocaine in the door panels of the cars he was shipping overseas. He and his defense attorneys snowed the jury and they acquitted him, but by that time he was flat broke and was divorced by his trophy wife, Cristina Ferrare, a beautiful fashion model. The obvious parallels must have been on Keith's mind earlier when he told me he might lose Shannon.

Eyeing me intently now, he tried another tack. "Listen, Frank, you know law enforcement people in high places – FBI, FDA, you guys're all tight with one another, right? You worked with FDA agents when you busted those Aryan Confederacy bastards for poisoning all those people and killing those two kids. You can put in a word for me, get them to call the dogs off. I can pay a fine, even a big fine, and I can go with a different marketing strategy, whatever will satisfy the Justice Department. I'm perfectly willing to modify my products and my advertising. But I have to get the FDA to back off or else they'll ruin me. I'll end up like DeLorean. He doesn't have a red cent. He's trying to start a new company to sell wrist watches!"

"Even if the FDA goes away, you're still in deep shit. What about the negligent homicide rap? That sounds way too serious to squirm out of."

"It's serious, but it's flimsy. Worse comes to worst, I can beat it. My pills didn't kill the old duffer -- there's plenty of reasonable doubt. He already had two feet in the grave. If the attorney general doesn't follow through with an indictment, the FDA depositions won't be a part of any court proceeding. The scumbag lawyers hired by the old man's fucked-up kids won't be able to use the mandrake testimony in a civil trial unless they find their own scientists, and even then we can dispute it or fight to have it excluded, and that will buy us some time. If I can delay things long enough, I can convert a lot of my stock to cash before it takes a tumble, and I can transfer the bulk of my assets off-shore."

"Keith," I said, "I hope you're not hoping I can influence somebody at the Justice Department to drop a case against you. I don't have that kind of clout."

"But maybe you know somebody who does."

"Not offhand, no. And if I start nosing around, asking fishy questions, it'll look like I'm trying to place a bribe. What about your expensive high-powered lawyers? Can't they pull the right strings? Don't they make campaign contributions so they can have influence in the right places? I'm just an ordinary FBI agent, not an ass-kisser or a wheeler-dealer. I try to stay away from Bureau politics. None of the higher-ups owe me any favors. They'd bust me and put me on trial if it looked like I was aiding and abetting any sort of corruption."

"Well, I don't want to take you down with me. I just want to save my company, that's my best-case scenario. My fallback scenario is to save my own ass in the event that I'm unable to rescue all the shareholders. "

"My advice to you is to start off by cutting a deal with the old man's survivors. Dangle enough money in front of their noses, they'll accept a settlement out of court, won't they? And wouldn't that influence the district attorney to back off?"

"Cart before the horse. If I make a settlement with the son and daughter, it's like cutting off my nose to spite my face. Plays right into the D.A.'s hands. Gives them more evidence to hang me with."

"Once you've paid them a bundle of money, why wouldn't they be motivated to go to the D.A. with an affidavit saying that they took the settlement because they came to a realization that your pills had nothing to do with their father's death; his ill health was to blame after all."

"I don't know, I don't know, Frank. So far they've turned down ten million dollars. "

"What! Are they crazy?"

"They're religious cranks. And they're vegans, both the son and the daughter. They refuse to eat animal products, even eggs. They don't take vitamins or medicines of any kind, and they won't accept treatment from hospitals or doctors. Neither of them's ever been married, and they're both in their forties. I doubt if they've ever been laid. Their thing against me is like their own little holy crusade -- they get off on it. When my lawyers tried to talk sense to them, they told them I should burn in hell for enticing people to put ungodly substances into their bodies. "

"Man, you could paint them as real nutcases if all this ever gets into court."

"Yeah," Keith said. "But that's where I don't want it to be."

CHAPTER 54

Well, Keith was right about one thing -- I still had a few friends in the New York FBI office, and I went out on a limb to pump them for information. I flew to New York to talk to them face to face, confidentially, without any threat of wire taps. Some of them absolutely refused to stick their necks out. I asked the more willing ones not to risk getting themselves in trouble, so I knew that their inquiries, if they deigned to make any, would have to appear offhanded. That being the case, I wasn't surprised when I got nothing out of them that was terribly helpful.

Keith got pissed off at me when I reported back to him at a restaurant near his office. He said I could have done more if I really wanted to. He accused me of being so uptight about protecting my own ass that I wasn't behaving like a true friend. But he had never done anything of comparable magnitude for me, and he had certainly never put himself in jeopardy on my account, because I would never have asked him for that kind of favor even if I needed it. I let him rant, hoping he'd blow off steam, and we parted with a great deal of animosity between us.

I had dinner that evening with Charlie and Lori, a welcome respite from Keith's antagonism. Lori was fifty-three now and still retained an ageless kind of beauty coupled with an aura of dignity and refinement that had accrued to her over the years. She reminded me of Linda Evans, the fiftyish actress who had starred on *Dynasty*, not so much because they looked like sisters but because they projected a similar allure.

Charlie, who had been growing rather plump at the time of Dan and Missy's coming home party, had gotten himself into fairly trim shape again. When I complimented him on it, he said, "Lori and I have been using the gym and swimming pool at our condo. What the hell, we're shelling out plenty for the so-called amenities. They have trainers there for us. And we don't have to go through the rigamarole of being cabbed or limmoed someplace just to exercise."

"Got a special motive for getting yourself in shape, other than good health?"

"Thinking about running for Congress, maybe next election or the one after that. But keep it under your hat. I don't want to start up a media fuss before I've made up my mind."

"My lips are sealed," I said, and made a show of zippering my mouth shut.

During our meal, I had it in my head to refrain from mentioning anything about Keith's problems, but I suspected that Charlie and Lori probably already knew at least some of the story if not all of it. Charlie seemed to be thinking the same thing about me. He beat around the bush for a while before confiding that Keith had asked him and Lori to help him "put the lid on a tricky situation."

"It's probably the same situation he came to me about," I conjectured, to see how he would follow it up.

"I figure you must know as much as Lori and I do," he parried.

"Yeah, Keith told me some serious shit," I admitted.

We felt each other out for a bit longer, till finally Lori broke the ice, saying, "He's in trouble and he needs help, but we're not sure what we can do for him."

"Obviously the three of us know exactly what the situation is," I said, "so there's no use being coy about it."

"He wanted us to use some of our political connections," Charlie said. "I was pretty blunt with him. I said that Lori and I only backed politicians who could convince us that they took their oath of office seriously, and so they'd be exactly the wrong ones to approach with anything that could considered shady. Well, Keith immediately took the heat. He told us to go fuck ourselves."

"Sounds like him," I said. "I guess all three of us are on his shit list now."

"That's sort of an Honor Roll, if you ask me," Charlie said with an unsuppressed chuckle. "Anyway, I didn't want to tell him right then that I'm thinking of running for office so I don't want to get involved with anything that might close off my options."

"I don't blame you for not wanting to get your hands dirty," I said. "He boxed me into the same kind of corner, and I tried to do some of what he wanted, but I could only go so far without getting my own head chopped off. Still, it bothers me that he thinks I didn't try."

"That's his way," Charlie said. "If he can't manipulate you, he lays a guilt trip on you. Either way, you lose. "

"Well, I'm not going to lose sleep over it," Lori said. "He can't twist my brain into little knots like he used to."

"Amen to that!" Charlie said, beaming at her proudly and affectionately and cupping his hand over hers.

"Let's not talk about Keith anymore," she said. "We've said quite enough about him. On a couple of other fronts, I have some good news and some bad news."

She launched into the bad news first, which concerned her friend Tammy Wynette. Tammy's severe health problems had persisted without letup. A botched stomach surgery had left her in such agony that she was in constant need of painkillers, and had become somewhat addicted to them. "To make things worse, she's developed an inflammation of her bile duct," Lori confided, "and it's put our TV pilot on hold. Aaron Spelling wants to cast somebody else in Tammy's role, but I don't want to do it at all if she has to drop out. We're praying that she gets better quickly. "

"I hope so too," I said. "I know how much it must mean to you. But did I hear you say that there's some good news?"

Lori broke into a bright smile. "My granddaughter Merry is going to appear with me on the Grand Ole Opry! It'll be a Christmas special, and we're taping it in October."

"That's great," I said. "I didn't know her career was taking off so quickly."

"Well, they wanted me, and I made them take Merry. The other singers are appearing with family members, too, so I really wasn't being a bitch about it. Actually, the producer loved the idea."

"I've been getting her gigs around Manhattan," Charlie said. "People like her a lot, she's following in Lori's footsteps. She's got her own material, and it's pretty decent, too."

"A lot better than just decent," Lori corrected.

"Sure is," Charlie said, "but I don't like to always seem to be bragging about her."

"Well, you can do it in front of Frank, he's like family," Lori said. "Keith's proud of her, too," she told me. "I hope he doesn't stay mad at us."

"Don't worry, the man has nine lives," Charlie scoffed, with a wave of his hand. "He always lands on his feet. It's the people around him who get crushed."

"At least he helps out Dan and Missy," Lori said. "And he dotes on Merry as much as we do."

"I'll give him that," Charlie said. "Somewhere deep inside of him there must be a soft spot."

"Well, I guess we can pray for him and Tammy both," Lori said. "The Bible says judge not lest ye be judged."

"Do you still go to church every Sunday?" I asked her.

"I go to St. Patrick's pretty often, because I can sneak in after the service has already started and sit in the back without anybody noticing. It doesn't bother me that the Mass is Catholic and I'm Protestant. If I don't feel like taking a chance on being recognized, I just stay home and watch the preachers on TV."

"I was wondering," I said, "where the heck in a city like New York you would find anything like the little church you belonged to in Cherry Hill."

"Well, I miss it," said Lori. "I think I might even go back there for a visit someday. I would for sure if Preacher Barlow was still alive."

"That's who Keith stole his act from," Charlie said. "That old-time country preacher -- Lori told me all about him. It's who Keith's playing when he hawks his phony products on television. He's got the spiel down pat, only he's using it to sell vitamins and diet pills instead of Christianity."

"I happened to be there when he first tried his act out on Preacher Barlow's congregation twenty-five years ago," I said, glancing uncomfortably in Lori's direction because we both knew that she was sucked in that day, too.

With a self-deprecating smile, she said, "Don't worry, Frank, I can admit he snowed me as much as he snowed everybody else back then. Thank God I'm not as dumb as I used to be."

"We've all come a long way," Charlie said. "But in one big important factor, Keith has stayed the same. Always working one kind of scam or another. He's one of the most seductive characters I've ever known."

The next morning, I flew back to Pittsburgh, and a few days after that I read in the *New York Times* that Keith had filed a countersuit against the FDA, charging them with making "false and defamatory statements" about him and his Natural Life Company. Apparently he was going to fight his battle on the basis that the best defense is a strong offense. I observed the legal wrangling at a distance by reading reports in the business pages of the newspapers. The parries and thrusts dragged on over the next several weeks, till the situation seemed to eventually become stalemated.

Meantime, the *Women's Work* pilot was cancelled before it even got out of development. Tammy Wynette was still unable to satisfy the terms of Spelling's contract, and Lori McCoy stuck to her guns and refused to go on with an alternate cast member. I found out about the cancellation when I got a phone call from Missy's husband, Dan Clanton. In spite of the demise of the pilot, Aaron Spelling was still living up to his commitment regarding the HBO Special that Dan and Missy were working on about terrorism in America. They wanted to interview me and maybe use me as a technical consultant. I agreed to meet with them in Pittsburgh to discuss terms and decide what kind of commitment I might be able to make.

Dan asked me if they could possibly interview Conrad Pryzor in jail, and I said I would find out about the legalities and the restrictions. I didn't want to take the slightest chance of jeopardizing the prosecutor's case against Pryzor.

Even though his two cohorts, Burton and Halsey, had been murdered in prison, we had videotaped statements from them in our files. Not long after they were hauled in, they had turned on Pryzor in an effort to save their own asses and get reduced sentences. But their sentences were reduced permanently when they got snuffed out, not for being ratfinks but for being child killers. We thought we might have a good shot at getting their taped depositions played in court when Pryzor went on trial, even though his lawyers would certainly fight to keep them from being admitted.

It turned out to be a moot point.

On March 8, 1998, Conrad Pryzor was found dead in his cell. He slashed his wrists with a jagged piece of sheet metal and bled to death in his upper bunk. His four-hundred-pound slob of a cellmate slept right through it all and woke up covered in blood that had soaked down through Pryzor's mattress. Guffawing about it, the big oaf bitched to guards and inmates that a blood drop plopping on his forehead had jolted him out of what had been building up to be a kick-ass wet dream.

CHAPTER 55

The death of Conrad Pryzor launched Harley Logan, Del Logan and Patsy Delmar on a spree of robbery, arson and murder.

Del suggested the Farmers and Merchants Bank in Cherry Hill for their first strike, and Harley and Patsy went along with it. It was the bank where Maylon McCoy had died, and the prospect of succeeding where his father had failed titillated Del's ego. He sized it up as an easy score, even though his father had blown it. He was thoroughly familiar with the layout of the town and the slow-paced day-to-day routines of the local yokels.

"They only got a four-man police force," he told Patsy and Harley. "More like a police *farce*. Buncha fat red-faced dudes waddlin' around writin' up parkin' tickets and chompin' on doughnuts. They think they done somethin' big if they toss the town drunk, but they'd shit themselves if they had to face three badasses with guns."

"We don't wanna git overconfident," Harley warned, eyeing Del coldly. "Jist when ya think ya got it made is when somethin's gonna jump up and bite ya in the ass."

"Yessir," Del said. "All I'm sayin' is, no bank is gonna be a piece of cake but this one's prob'ly the closest thing to it."

"You ain't lived there for a long time," said Harley. "A lotta things coulda changed. Cops might be better trained and better armed."

That was true, but Del doubted it. That penny-pinching town never would've sprung for enough money to upgrade its police force. There still wasn't much crime there. Del had never heard of anything big going down in Cherry Hill since that day back in 1978 when his father took hostages, got duped into letting them go, then gave up his own life for no good reason.

Harley, acting like big stuff because he had robbed a couple of banks early in his criminal career, told Del and Patsy that if they didn't stick to a carefully laid-out plan and make it come off like clockwork, they'd only succeed in fucking themselves up. "We gotta grab all the money in the tellers' drawers as fast as we can and git the hell out inside a couple minutes. That's the only way we don't git our asses in a sling. Our first heist together, we work the bugs out. Then, if ever'thin' goes smooth, next time we go fer a lot bigger haul."

During the planning stage, Del smugly believed that there was no way he'd be the one to fuck up while the job was actually going down. He clung to his image of himself as the perfect young Aryan warrior; he needed it to bolster him up after being badly shaken by the sudden and total destruction of the Aryan Confederacy compound, which was the best home he had ever known, and the murders in prison of Curb, Bash and Conrad Pryzor. He didn't buy that Pryzor's death was a suicide or that Pryzor had turned into a fag. He believed that the three top leaders of the Aryan Confederacy had been assassinated, martyred in a conspiracy masterminded by ZOG and carried out by secret agents masquerading as inmates or inmate turncoats paid off by the FBI.

During the weeks he spent in virtual confinement at the safe house in Wheeling, Del became as high-strung, fidgety and mean as a panther in a cage. He was quick to start arguments and fights, even with the people who were feeding and protecting him. He exercised a lot and masturbated a lot in an effort to take the edge off and calm himself down. He could barely suppress his urge to lash out at everyone and everything.

One bad thing about choosing Cherry Hill for the bank job was that Del grew up there and might be recognized. So he had to stay at the safe house while Harley and Patsy got out and did the on-site planning and mapping. Del looked so different from the way he had looked when he was a kid living with his mother in Cherry Hill that he didn't think anyone in town would recognize him these days, not even his own grandpap and grandma, who were probably half blind and half senile by now, even if they were still alive. But Harley didn't want to take any foolish chances, so he and Patsy did all the reconnoitering while Del lived in anticipation of the blow he was going to strike against the sanctimonious assholes who used to get their rocks off by making life miserable for him and his mother. He had little doubt that most of these stick-in-the-muds probably still lived in Cherry Hill and had checking and savings accounts in the town's only bank.

On the second day of casing the job, Patsy gave Del a list of the bank's employees and said, "There's three broads workin' the teller windows. You wouldn't wanna fuck any of 'em -- too old, fat and ugly. The guys are flabby baldheaded dudes -- two loan officers, a manager and assistant manager. I doubt all four of 'em could whup a sick pup."

"I'd *fuck* anything that walks," Del said. "Even a sick pup."

Patsy laughed.

305

Looking over the list, Del got a deja vu feeling when he spotted the name George Stanfield. "How old is this Stanfield guy?" he asked Patsy.

"Maybe twenty-nine, thirty."

"I know the fuckhead! I hate his guts. He used to pick on me when I was a little kid. You've got him listed here as a loan officer."

"Yeah. These days he ain't nothin' but a paper pusher. Got slumped shoulders and a pot belly, and I seen his pipe stem arms stickin' outta his short-sleeved shirt when his suit jacket was hangin' on the back of his chair."

"I'll be damned!" Del said, smirking. "Georgie's daddy was a fuckin' gung-ho Marine, wanted his son to be a jarhead just like him. Georgie got beat with a strap any time he didn't do what his daddy told him. I was scared of him back then, he was the big badass bully of the schoolyard. His daddy made him beat up on me all the time. He was a lot bigger'n me and three or four years older."

"Well, right now you c'd kick his ass from sundown to sunup 'thout workin' up a sweat. Dude ain't even got no calluses on his hands -- they's smooth as a baby's ass. I was you, I'd shoot him dead when we bust into the bank."

"The job'll turn to shit if we let personal shit interfere with the job."

"Job or no job, I'd be tempted to drill this Georgie dude if 'n I was you," Patsy said.

Del read the names of the tellers. All three had last names he didn't recognize, but they wouldn't be using their maiden names anymore if they had gotten married, so there was still a chance that he might have known one or two of them in grade school. He hoped so. If any of them turned out to be some of the prissy brats who used to razz him and stick their tongues out at him, making him feel almost as bad as he felt when he was getting beat up, he'd make damn sure to pistol-whip them before making his escape from the bank.

CHAPTER 56

Wearing black ski masks, black jumpsuits and bulky body armor, Del, Harley and Patsy burst through the front doors of the Farmers and Merchants Bank. They didn't give a shit who was in there -- anyone who resisted would be shot. Harley had a sawed-off shotgun. Del and Patsy had 9mm Glocks with fourteen-round clips.

"Tellers! Freeze!" Harley yelled. "Stay where you are! Everybody else, get down on the floor! Quick! Do what we say if you don't wanna die!"

The two customers in front of the tellers' windows didn't move fast enough, so Del and Patsy kicked their legs out from under them and pushed them to the floor. One was a guy in bib coveralls, and the other was a fat lady in a flower-print dress. The guy hit the floor hard and didn't make a move after that, but the woman thrashed and moaned and Harley silenced her by cracking her on the head with his gun butt.

A couple of people screamed, but Harley yelled, "Shut the fuck up!"

They clammed up and for a moment you could almost hear a pin drop.

Del and Patsy were carrying pipe bombs as well as automatic pistols. They placed one of the bombs on the ledge in front of the tellers' windows, and the other one on a desk in one of the glassed-in cubicles occupied by the bank's loan officers. Harley dragged the manager and assistant manager out from the rear of the bank and made them lie down on the plastic carpet-protector in the wide center aisle.

"These bombs can blow this whole place to hell!" Harley yelled, waving around a detonator that looked like a TV remote control. "Do what we say or nobody'll get outta here alive!"

While Harley stood guard over everybody with his shotgun, Del and Patsy made the three tellers scoop all the money from their drawers into canvas bags. Through the eye-slits in his ski mask, Del squinted into the faces of the tellers one by one and failed to recognize any of them from his childhood. This disappointed him. The sense of being all powerful, holding total sway over them, had given him an erection, and he wished he had time to rape one of the women or an excuse to shoot one of the men -- like if one of them would try to push an alarm button or make a move to get up from the floor. Turning toward Harley, he said, "Let's make 'em open up the vault."

"Naw, we'll have to force 'em and it'll slow us down. I told ya, remember? We'll make a decent score here, but mainly it's a run-through for bigger stuff to come. Don't get greedy and lose sight of that. "

"All right -- shit!" Del said. He felt his face reddening, his skin hot and sticky inside his ski mask. He was ashamed that his stepfather had to remind him how to behave as part of a well-coordinated assault team, and he was still pulling himself together when Harly barked at him again.

"Don't fuckin' freeze up on me! Get the fuckin' tellers out here! Don't make me hafta tell you every goddamn thing you're s'posed to do!"

Humiliated, Del jumped into action. He and Patsy yelled at the tellers, threatening them at gunpoint to make them come out from behind their windows, then punched and pummeled them to the floor and made them lie there face-down like the other bank employees and customers.

"Stay down! Don't move a fuckin' muscle!" Harley yelled. "We're gettin' the fuck outta here! If y'all don't remain perfectly still for twenty minutes while we make our getaway, the bombs'll be set off by motion sensors!"

Del was standing over George Stanfield, his old nemesis from his childhood, and it was too much for him to take. In spite of all the times he had told himself that he shouldn't let things get too personal, he shot Stanfield in the head and watched Stanfield's bald pate explode, then jerk and bounce, spurting blood.

One of the tellers shrieked and another started crying.

Del expected Harley to yell at him for acting like a loose cannon, but Harley just snickered. "Shut the fuck up!" he yelled at the sobbing tellers. "We'll kill every fuckin' one of ya!"

The women stifled their sobs down to whimpers and moans.

Underneath his ski mask, Del smiled at Harley's ability to get off on other people's acts of cruelty as well as his own. In spite of Harley's preaching about strict discipline, Del knew that his stepfather harbored a sadistic streak that was always on the verge of running amok.

Del looked at Georgie Stanfield's blood pooling on the plastic runner in the center aisle and grinned at the thought that Maylon McCoy's blood would no longer be the only blood that had been spilled inside this bank.

CHAPTER 57

The FBI office in Charleston, West Virginia, handled the investigation into the bank robbery in Cherry Hill, and so our Bank Squad in Pittsburgh didn't get involved, except to keep tabs on it and wait for the next one. That there would be a next one was a virtual certainty. Bank robbers didn't usually stop at just one, especially one with such a small take – less than seven thousand dollars. Like Jesse James, Bonnie and Clyde, and John Dillinger, they kept on chasing the big score that would let them retire and live in splendid debauchery, until not knowing when to quit took them down in a hail of bullets.

I made it my business to learn as much as I could about the bank heist in Cherry Hill. That it took place in Lori McCoy's hometown seemed ominously coincidental, especially when coupled with the fact that it was the same bank where I had failed miserably at getting Lori's brother Maylon out alive. I wondered if some of the Aryan Confederacy renegades that we had failed to capture when we raided their compound might be trying to reestablish and refinance themselves. Among them might be the cretins who had raped and killed my fiancé, still on the loose and hating me and Lori and everyone connected to us.

It seemed possible that the robber who had killed loan officer George Stanfield might have a Cherry Hill connection in his past, maybe something that caused him to harbor a personal grudge against Stanfield. According to the other people who'd been held at gunpoint, Stanfield hadn't put up a fight, hadn't given the robbers any lip, yet he was shot in the head execution style while lying face-down, completely helpless. Was it an act of revenge? Or just another killing without rhyme or reason?

Maybe the robbers figured that they needed to brutally kill one of their victims in order to keep the rest of them cowering in fear on the floor of the bank -- in case their bomb ruse didn't work. I say "ruse" because the two pipe bombs were fakes. An FBI bomb squad found this out. The devices didn't even contain any gunpowder. They were mere props, empty sections of galvanized pipe, electrical components and wires wound with tape, to scare people so badly that they'd keep still for a good long time while the robbers escaped.

The use of pipe bombs, fake or not, smacked of Aryan Confederacy. It sent my mind reeling back to that nightmarish day twenty-some years ago when my friend and partner Cyrus Lumley was ripped to shreds by a live pipe bomb rigged as a booby trap.

I didn't know what had become of Cyrus's wife and children. I had phoned them a couple of times in the early years following his death, but had gotten the sense that hearing my voice was more painful than comforting. They wanted to move on. They felt guilty for wondering why I had been spared while he had died.

If there was such a thing as closure, maybe I had gotten a measure of it when Conrad Pryzor slit his own wrists, taking the coward's way out. I told myself that Rorthal Cheatwood, Jimmy Green, Carlisle Dixon, Brenda Dixon, and Cyrus Lumley had finally been fully avenged. The four creeps who had committed the rapes and killings were long dead, and at last their sick leader had followed them to the grave.

But the bank robbery in Cherry Hill seemed like an omen, a warning that Pryzor's evil legacy hadn't yet run its course. Twisted minds were still out there, warped by the bigotry he had preached. And I couldn't shake an uneasy feeling that worse things might be yet to come.

CHAPTER 58

On April 7, 1998, a Tuesday, Tammy Wynette's husband George Richey telephoned Lori and Charlie to give them the sad news that Tammy had died Monday night of a blood clot in one of her lungs. Lori couldn't stop crying, even though she firmly believed that her dear friend had passed on to a much better place. She would never forget how Tammy had come to her rescue when she was totally depressed, encouraging her to go back to her musical roots, salvaging not just her career but her chance for a more rewarding life.

Lori and Tammy had remained close through the past two decades, even though the demands of movie studios, recording studios and concert venues kept them from seeing each other except for sporadic, all too brief interludes. Whenever they managed to be together in a relaxed and homey environment, at Tammy's place in Nashville or at Lori's apartment in New York, they gossiped and giggled like two teenaged girls.

Tammy was like another sister to Lori, and together they shared things that Lori couldn't quite share with anybody else, even her biological sister, Arlene. Lori sometimes felt guilty about placing Tammy above Arlene in this way, but even though Arlene understood the entertainment business as few other people did, she lacked the soul of a performer and could only vicariously relate to the stresses and joys, the highs and lows, that performers constantly went through.

Besides having pure girlish fun together, Lori and Tammy always talked about music, sometimes singing snatches of new material to each other, getting each other's opinions about lyrics or melodies. They encouraged one another and gave one another advice about which songs to put on which albums, and which ones should be featured in concerts or released as singles.

Tammy was in pain much of the time, but in spite of that she always had a vivacious sense of humor and an appreciation of the fact that life was meant to be enjoyed. Her husband said that she had passed away in her sleep, which was a comfort to Lori, knowing that Tammy wouldn't have to suffer any more from the cruel array of devastating illnesses that had plagued her all through her life, causing her to undergo more than two dozen major surgeries. Passing away peacefully while sleeping on her living room couch was better than a long, lingering death in a hospital bed with a conglomeration of needles and tubes delivering medicine that could only prolong agony. The pity of it was not just that she had had more than her share of pain but that she had died so young, only fifty-five years old.

George Richey asked Lori if she would like to sing one of Tammy's songs as a special tribute to her at a public memorial service that was going to be televised on Thursday evening from the Ryman Auditorium. Lori said she was honored to be asked, but was afraid she couldn't get through it without breaking down right in front of everybody.

"I understand," George Richey said. "I wish I didn't have to be there myself. But it's taken on a momentum all its own. They've already got Dolly Parton, Loretta Lynn, Lorrie Morgan and Randy Travis lined up for it. And I think the Oak Ridge Boys."

Lori and Charlie flew into Nashville for the more modest private funeral service that was held in advance of the televised one, at the Judson Baptist Church on Nashville's south side. George Jones, Garth Brooks, Naomi Judd and Crystal Gayle were there, and a host of other celebrities who had been close to Tammy in their own special way. Also in the church, right up front, were Tammy's five daughters, her son and her seven grandchildren.

To avoid the media clamor, Lori and Charlie flew back to New York as soon as the church service was over. It had been one of the saddest trips of Lori's life. But, thank goodness, Charlie was always steadfast, always there for her through thick and thin. Over the years, their love had deepened. Lori knew that she would feel empty without him. Sometimes, when she was in one of her most melancholy moods, she thought about one of them dying ahead of the other, and hoped she would not be the one left behind.

Every now and then she looked back in wonderment at how she had grown up, remembering the little patch of rough West Virginia farmland that she had come from, and was amazed that somehow most of her childhood dreams had been achieved. True, there had been some great tragedies in her life, but there had also been some wonderful triumphs.

At this stage, however, what mattered most to her was her family, small as it was: Charlie, Dan, Missy and Meredith. Merry had embarked on a singing career of her own already, with an album in release and another one in the works, at only sixteen years old. Lori saw herself in

Merry, and was beamingly proud when other people remarked that her granddaughter must have gotten her talent from her. She hoped that she and Charlie, with their wisdom and experience, could see to it that Merry didn't get ground up by the more cruel and heartless elements of the entertainment business, and that they could keep her from falling into some of the worst pitfalls that were always out there waiting.

CHAPTER 59

The unfairness of it all pissed Keith off. At this late stage of his life, after basking for so long at the summit of a fabulously successful career, everything he had worked for was coming unglued, and he was forced to come crawling to his first ex-wife.

His second ex-wife, Shannon Cristy, wouldn't give him the dust from the barely worn pairs of Guccis that she donated to the poor. She had divorced him in the midst of his battles with the FDA, kicking him when he was down, taking half of the money he still had left after getting hammered by the Justice Department for the past two years.

Even before Shannon had fled, Keith's executive secretary, Mary Ann Boyle, had left him for an older, balder but richer dude who was CEO of a Fortune Five Hundred company. But Keith didn't hold it against her. He had expected no less from a bitch so mercenary that she had had the balls to jump from one husband to the next in mid-honeymoon. Losing her was a blessing. He wouldn't have to try to keep up with her in bed anymore. He could stop taking Viagra. The Viagra was bad for his high blood pressure. Besides the hypertension, he was also suffering from constantly recurring, excruciatingly painful gout attacks. He did not want it to become public knowledge that he was not treating his ailments with his own products and instead was taking three different kinds of pills prescribed by a licensed physician. If the tabloids found out, they'd label him a hypocrite. And if the government lawyers arrayed against him found out, they'd say in court that the snake-oil salesman wasn't giving himself his own pills because nobody knew better than he that they were absolutely worthless. He could protest that Natural Life supplements were more preventive than curative, but that kind of argument would probably be pooh-poohed by a judge and jury.

He had to calm himself down, force himself to relax, redouble his efforts to put all of his troubles behind him. High blood pressure and gout attacks were caused by stress and anxiety. Viagra worked by pushing the blood pressure even higher, pumping blood into the penis but also into other major organs and blood vessels, inviting a heart attack or a stroke. Keith knew that he had been tempting fate by trying to keep up with a young nympho like Mary Ann Boyle. Lately he found himself toying with the idea of hooking up with a woman closer to his own age, but not too much closer, say maybe a judicious gap of only ten or fifteen years.

Sometimes he tried to imagine what his life would have been like if he had stuck with Lori. On the plus side, he'd have control of her money. On the minus side, although she was one of those women who managed not to look her age, he wasn't attracted to her anymore either sexually or romantically. To be turned on by a woman he had to feel superior, even dominant. But these days Lori was still riding high, comfortably rich and famous, and he was on the wane and trying not to show it. He had lost his edge over her, a turn of events that he found hard to stomach. But she owed him, and he hoped she still realized it. He had discovered her and jump-started her career back when she was a nobody, and now he desperately needed her to help him out of a jam.

He had to shield as many of his assets as possible before the courts allowed them to be frozen or confiscated. If his Natural Life Company went down, he did not want to go down with it. He felt no qualms about pulling his own marshmallows out of the fire while everybody else's went up in smoke. He was unable to envision himself as the noble captain of a sinking ship.

He needed a vehicle where he could dump ten million dollars that couldn't be seized by a federal court order or a civil lawsuit. It had to be a tax-sheltered investment that wouldn't pay off until several years down the road, after any monetary judgments against him had been settled or squelched, at which time he could reap the delayed profits.

He had seized upon the possibility of investing in a movie, a straw that he had grasped at after his daughter Michele and his son-in-law David Clanton had come to him with a screenplay they had written. They wanted him to help with financing and he had told them he would, without letting them glom onto the fact that he was no longer Daddy Warbucks.

Their screenplay, *American Murders*, was about a psychopath who kidnaps a young singing star and puts her through hell til she narrowly escapes from him. But she doesn't get away clean. He tracks her to a college campus where she's giving an outdoor concert, climbs up into a tower with a loaded rifle, and opens fire on her and her family. Although the plot was loosely based on actual sniper killings committed by Eagle Scout Charles Whitman on a Texas campus back in 1966, Dan and Missy had updated their fictionalized story to the nineties and loaded it with

315

suspenseful twists and turns that would make, in Keith's opinion, an exciting movie with tremendous box-office potential.

He hoped that Lori would come on board as a supporting actress and an investor. To seduce her into it he would push the fact that it'd be a huge career boost for Dan and Michele and also for Meredith, who could play the role of the kidnapped singer.

A few weeks ago, Tammy Wynette had died, a shame, Keith thought, but also good timing for his movie proposal. If the *Women's Work* pilot had gone into production as planned, Lori wouldn't have been open to another project. She would have felt no pressing need to help Dan and Michele since they would have been well taken care of by work thrown their way on the TV series.

Keith hoped that Lori wasn't completely bent out of shape by her friend Tammy's untimely demise. He had watched some of the televised wake, sipping Wild Turkey, expecting that Lori would at least sing a song or deliver a eulogy. But later Dan and Michele told him that she had been asked to, but had declined.

He thought it was smart of her to avoid associating herself with the tackiest part of the funeral. Maybe she didn't think this out for herself, maybe Charlie figured it out for her. Keith had to admit that his old pal was doing a pretty good job of guiding Lori's career, although he was sure that he would have done much better.

When he got out of his limo in front of Charlie and Lori's apartment, he congratulated himself for his decision to dress casually, in jeans and a blazer, instead of appearing in a suit and tie, like a supplicant. The tabloids were sticking a fork in him, but he had to show the world that he wasn't done yet. He reminded himself that Mike Nichols, who had once been married to Elizabeth Taylor, had gone broke a bunch of times and each time had bounced back and made millions.

He wished Charlie Guinard wasn't going to be present at today's meeting. His mind flashed back to the good old days when he was able to seduce Lori into doing just about anything he wanted. Even though she was a lot smarter now, he thought maybe he still had some of the old magic over her. But Charlie was a hard-nosed agent and negotiator nowadays and couldn't easily be snookered.

CHAPTER 60

Laughing and swigging whisky, Del, Harley and Patsy sped over the back roads outside of Shickton. In the back of their stolen van was a sack full of money from their second bank job. Also back there, hands and ankles bound with duct tape and mouths sealed with more duct tape wound around their heads, were two hostages. One was the Jew bank manager, Goldstein, and the other was a young nigger who had been standing in line to cash a check, probably one that would've bounced.

Del liked the strategy of taking hostages better than using fake pipe bombs. Nobody had come after them. Nobody in the bank had jumped up to call the cops. They were scared shitless that the Jew and the nigger would be dumped onto the road, dead. Which was what was going to happen anyways, sort of, but not exactly.

Del had argued beforehand that they ought to take female hostages. But Harley put his foot down, said this wasn't no goddamn time to think about gettin' their rocks off. A fucking shame. One of the tellers was such a cute young thing that Del had ached to rip her panties off and go to town on her right there on the floor of the bank, all the yokels watching with their tongues hanging out.

He and Patsy and Harley already had their ski masks off. Their faces weren't sweaty anymore, and the air conditioning was on high, cooling them down some more. No matter how calm and collected you tried to be when you were robbing a place, your sweat glands still went to work overtime from the thrills and excitement and the fear of getting caught.

Del took another swig of whisky from the bottle handed to him by Harley, who was driving, and said, "When we gonna start givin' 'em their sleigh ride?"

"Couple more minutes," Harley answered. "When we get to a mile or so from where we stashed my truck."

"We forgot to bring the fuckin' sleigh!" Patsy said, as if he had just thought of it, and they all brayed with laughter and swigged more whisky.

When they turned off onto a lonely dirt road, Harley hit the brakes and the van lurched to a sudden skidding stop. Del heard the hostages thumping around back there, and could hardly wait for what was coming next. In a jiffy he jumped down onto the road. So did Harley and Patsy, not bothering to shut the doors. They were primed to have a little bit of fun. Even though it would slow down their escape, they were well away from the bank job and the pleasure would be worth the risk.

They opened the back of the van and dragged out the Jew and the nigger by their bound-up ankles and wrists, not letting them down easy but dragging them past the rear bumper till they dropped about four feet down into the dirt, hitting the ground with a couple of hard thuds, then wiggling and kicking like as if they weren't helpless to save themselves. Del and Patsy got out a couple of ropes made into lassoes, tightened the lassoes around the hostages' chests, under their armpits, and tied the other ends of the ropes to the rear bumper of the van.

"Sleigh ride time!" Harley said. "Yer gonna enjoy this, fellers!"

"Fuckin Jew! Fuckin' nigger!" Patsy jeered.

Del worked up saliva and spat gobs of it on both of them, getting a thrill watching their teary eyes darting with fear and hearing their sobs, groans and pleadings, muffled by duct tape. He couldn't help snickering at them before he and Harley and Patsy climbed back into the van and slammed the doors.

Harley gunned it, picking up speed, and Del poked his head as far as he could out the passenger-side window to watch the ropes jerk taut and start bouncing the lassoed bodies over the ruts, kicking up clouds of dust as Harley pushed in a cassette of the Aryan rock group, White Lightning, and turned the volume up real loud.

"Yahoo!" Patsy yelled.

Harley cried out, "Ride 'em, cowboy!"

"Git along ya little dogies!" Del added, and they all laughed like hell and chugged whisky.

They stopped the stolen van behind Harley's truck, in a little clearing at the edge of a patch of woods, then got out and examined the two bloody bodies with their clothes and skin ripped to shreds. One wasn't moving at all, but the other was twitching a little. It was the nigger. Almost hard to tell the difference through the thick coatings of blood and dirt.

Del pulled his pistol.

"Go ahead," Harley said.

Del shot each of them in the head. They were so messed up it almost didn't feel like he was shooting anything human.

They weren't hardly human anyways. Just a nigger and a Jew.

CHAPTER 61

The bank job in Shickton confirmed my previous suspicions. Aryan Confederacy renegades were on the loose, mean and angry as hornets who had been trampled on but not killed.

We had videotape of the three robbers from surveillance cameras in both banks, and we could tell that the same three men had hit the bank in Cherry Hill as well as the one in Shickton. This time they got even less money: about five thousand dollars.

They also got me and my Anti-Terrorist Unit on their tails. The dragging deaths of the two hostages went down as racially and religiously motivated hate crimes.

My new partner and I, Harriet Stern, started our investigation at the Shickton Savings & Loan, and went from there to the murder scene. CSI photos had already been taken of the mutilated bodies, the stolen and abandoned van, and tire impressions of another vehicle, unknown, that the robbers must have transferred into in order to complete their getaway.

Harriet, who was usually called "Harry" by those of us who worked with her, was in her mid-thirties and had been an FBI field agent for ten years. She had reddish hair and dense freckles which did not detract from her attractiveness or her femininity. She didn't try to be as tough-looking as any male agent in the field, but instead generally wore stylish pants suits or dresses that neither disguised nor flaunted her lithe and shapely body.

She was also Jewish, a fact that probably added to the sick despair that came over both of us because of what we saw that day, and clung all over us like evil personified.

Chunks of skin and shreds of clothing were strewn for almost a mile along the dirt road, and clotty streaks of blood could still be seen in sodden patches of dust. One victim had his nose and lips missing, his gaping mouth filled with dirt and broken teeth. The other was missing both ears. Their eyelids were gone, the eye sockets caked shut with a muddy mixture of tears, mucous and blood.

The crime scene didn't provide much in the way of clues. It must've rained a little before the getaway vehicle had been pulled into the spot where it was left lying in wait for the robbers to get there in the stolen van, the moist earth then turning to dust, leaving us with a shallow, poorly defined tire impression, but still we might find something out from it, maybe the make and model of vehicles usually equipped with that brand of tire.

"The bastards we're after are stark-raving crazy," Harriet said. "They're going to make mistakes."

"Yeah, Harry," I agreed. "They can't control themselves. Too mean and reckless. But how many scenes like this one are we gonna have to look at before they self-destruct?"

She didn't answer my rhetorical question. She just shook her head sadly from side to side.

I didn't know how much more of this that I could take. I thought that maybe if we could catch or kill the three bastards who had started on this robbing and killing spree, I would finally retire from the FBI.

CHAPTER 62

Chris Terrell, the clean-cut neo-Nazi who had visited the jail in Pittsburgh to get the scoop on Conrad Pryzor prior to Pryzor's death, pleaded for a chance to take part in the next bank robbery. Harley finally said okay, thinking it'd be smart to have a getaway driver from now on. Terrell, with his blonde, innocent, All-American good looks, would make a perfect lookout and driver. Providing he didn't panic.

To test him out, they took him on a church burning at the tail end of September, 1998.

Riding in yet another stolen van, a maroon 1997 Plymouth Caravan with the backseat installed to accommodate four riders, they scouted out a Negro church in West Virginia, about a hundred miles south of the safe house in Wheeling. Patsy, who knew of the church beforehand, had told the others that it was an easy hit, out in the middle of nowhere. "Congregation, if you wanna call it that, is a buncha raggedy-ass niggers livin' in a patch of crappy rundown company houses useta remind me of roach motels -- I guess miners lived in 'em twenty thirty years ago after the coal mine down there petered out. That whole area is sick. Nobody got a pot to piss in, 'specially the goddamn niggers. "

On a Thursday afternoon, Patsy led his pals onto a lonely dirt road and they drove slowly back and forth a couple times, scoping out the church and the absence of anything but a few boarded-up houses, and not spotting anybody messing around in the woods or the fields. Nobody to get suspicious of them or try to upset their plans in some way.

The church was an old wood-frame structure with layers of grayish-white paint peeling off of it and no lawn at all, just gravel and weeds that started just a few feet from a couple of front steps made of unpainted stacked-up concrete blocks. The weathered front doors used to be red, probably, but now were a dirty nondescript brown with rotting plywood curling away in ragged strips.

Snorting contemptuously, Del Logan said, "Shit, we'll be doin' the niggers a fuckin' favor by burnin' it to the ground, puttin' it out of its misery."

"Like to put a bunch of *them* outta their misery," said Patsy.

"I'd like to sneak up on them niggers while they're clappin', shoutin' and singin'," Chris Terrell said. "Lock the fuckin' doors on 'em and charbroil 'em."

"I know yer anxious to do somethin' big, but hold yer goddamn horses," Harley said. "I'm like you, I'd like to burn up a bunch of churchgoin' niggers like Hitler's Storm Troopers burned up the fuckin' Jews inside their synagogues -- but we don't wanna risk that kinda thing just yet. We need to hit a couple more banks first -- big fuckin' banks with vaults full of money. Once we get ourselves bankrolled real good, then we can show the whole fuckin' world what we're made of."

"We make a big splash, it'll make it easy for us to recruit," Del explained. "We gotta build the Confederacy up again, more powerful and more militant. When the White Race gets into power, it'll be easy to get rid of all the goddamn niggers. We won't even have to make 'em wear yellow stars -- color of their skin is their yellow star. Goin' after the Jews'll be a little tougher. They'll run and hide like cockroaches when you turn the light on 'em. We might be able to use DNA samples to flush 'em out, get evidence against them."

"Fuck DNA, it's too complicated and too expensive," Harley said. "Kill the kikes we're sure of and make slaves outta the ones in doubt. That's the way to handle the whole fuckin' problem."

"Burnin' this crappy l'il church down looks like a piece of cake to me," Patsy said. "Won't take more'n a couple Molotov cocktails."

"Yeah," said Del. "Toss 'em through them cracked windows."

"I think we should catch us a couple of niggers walkin' around all high 'n' mighty shakin' their black asses," Chris Terrell suggested. "Beat the crap out of 'em, tie 'em up real good inside their church, tell 'em to say their prayers – then barbecue 'em."

"Sounds good to me," said Del. "Wouldn't be much more risky than if we just burned the church down. And we'd get a lot more satisfaction out of it. You remember, Harley, we done damn near the same kinda thing at that nigger rib joint back when I was just a kid, and nobody came after us, nobody ever even figgered out it was us that done it."

"Yeah, but maybe we was lucky. Keep on pushin' our luck too hard, we'll hit a brick wall."

"Aw, c'mon, Harley! Ain't nothin' to connect us with any church burnin' down here! None of us ever lived anywhere near these fuckin' niggers and we ain't about to come back and visit 'em."

"We ain't gonna show up at the wake?" Patsy said, feigning incredulity. "Shit. I wanna get me some fuckin' chitlins!"

They all laughed uproariously.

When the laughter died down Del said, "Listen, we could make better use of this here van, couldn't we? It don't seem right that we went through all the trouble stealin' it just to burn down one shitty little nigger church."

"Whatchou got in mind?" Harley asked.

"We ain't gonna come back here till tonight, right? We got all day to kill. Why don't we drive around, scout out some of these little hick towns with banks? We might see one that's easy pickin's. Chris ain't never done a bank job. This was s'posed to be a test for him. An initiation."

"I don't need no initiation," Chris said, somewhat offended. "I'm ready to rumble anytime you guys are. And I ain't no fuckin' pussy. I knocked over a liquor store and a convenience store after I got outta high school, done a little time in juvie for it. How much harder can it be to rip off a fuckin' bank? I'm only gonna be the getaway driver."

"You done time means you got caught," Harley squelched. "Yer in with us now and we don't do stuff half-assed."

"You think I don't realize that?" Chris countered. "At's why I wanted to throw in with y'all. You wanted to test me out and see if I'd crack. But I'm tellin' ya I damn sure ain't goin' to, Harley. Let's not fuck around, let's do some shit, I'm more than ready. "

"Well, okay," said Harley, "let's scout around like you said, Del. Bustin' a bank and burnin' a nigger church'd be a nice double whammy."

"A double whammy for your mammy," Patsy echoed. "Whaddyasay we crack open that bottle of bourbon you got under the seat, Harley?"

"Swig a jigger while you burn a nigger," Chris Terrell chipped in, proud of himself for following up Patsy's rhyme with another that he thought was much better.

He smiled as his pals rewarded him with laughter and Harley reached for the bourbon.

CHAPTER 63

Just as I had feared, the wild crime spree that these bastards were on got more and more sickening by September of 1998, when they robbed a small bank in Denton, West Virginia, took two hostages, a black man and a black woman, and killed them by binding and gagging them inside a church and then burning the church to the ground.

Harriet Stern and I interviewed people who had been inside the bank when the robbery went down, got a description of the getaway van from some folks who had seen the robbers bust out of the bank, and one of them even remembered the license plate number. We collected videotape from the bank's surveillance camera only to find out that the tape had been rewound and reused so many times that the images were worse than indiscernible. Later that week a West Virginia State Trooper found the van ditched in a field about twenty miles from the church.

We had thought at first that we might get a pretty good description of the getaway driver, but no such luck. He had kept the windows up, reflecting bright sunlight and curved, distorted images of his surroundings, and had kept his head down and turned toward the passenger side. One of the witnesses said it looked like he was wearing a Navy watchcap pulled way down over his forehead and ears.

Even with the dearth of hard evidence, the way the bank had been taken and the way the hostages had been abducted and killed convinced us that this was the work of the same gang responsible for the atrocities in Shickton and Cherry Hill. This time they had gotten only a couple thousand dollars, but money didn't seem to be their sole motive. No doubt they were getting their rocks off on the killing and burning, so we knew it was bound to continue. And continue it did. They kept on the move and found new places to lay low between wilding sprees, so we couldn't pin them down and move in on them. They were maddeningly adept at avoiding capture. And they were wise to exploding dye packs that could be hidden in packets of stolen money to go off and splatter them and their haul with tell-tale red dye; they never let that trick work on them.

Over the next two years, they fire-bombed two synagogues and three churches and robbed thirteen more banks scattered through West Virginia and Pennsylvania. Nobody died in the fire-bombings, but hostages were taken and brutally killed during each and every one of the bank robberies. Most of the murder victims were either Jewish or African-American. Autopsies showed that four out of the seven white female hostages were gang-raped before they were killed. We figured that the three other white women and two blacks were probably raped too, but they had been heavily doused with gasoline and set on fire, their corpses too charred and shrunken to yield evidence of sexual assault.

Some of these crimes might have been copycat jobs. We didn't know for sure. There was no exact pattern to where the gang had struck or where they might strike next, so we couldn't figure out where to do heavy surveillance or where we might be able to lay a trap. They seemed to be roughly moving from west to east, but with a lot of backtracking. Their most recent hit had been near Philadelphia, but that didn't mean they wouldn't double back again. If they crossed over into New York, my antenna would go up -- I'd have to start wondering if they might be heading toward Belmont, maybe to hit the same bank that had been robbed by Pryzor's flunkies back in 1975. So far, if there was any hint of a pattern to their madness, it was that they seemed to get a perverse satisfaction out of striking in places that had some connection to past escapades or past failures that they wanted to "make right."

Random crimes are the hardest type to solve, serial killings being one of the most frustrating examples. The perpetrator has no direct connection to his victims, so you try to find a pattern, a modus operandi based on his particular obsession or perversion. You hope he screws up. You hope you get lucky. Till any of that happens, you're running blind.

If the same gang had done all sixteen bank robberies, none of them being committed by copycats, by the summer of 2000, they had gotten away with more than five million dollars. We had to hope that the money itself might make them crack. Greed might set in and cause them to turn on each other. An increasing belief in their own invulnerability, a diminishing fear of getting caught, might make them careless. On the flip side, now that they were millionaires they might even abandon their fanatical ideology and run off to Argentina never to be heard of again. Fat chance of that, though. They were clearly too demented and too far gone to quit until they were stopped.

Knowing that these killers were probably Aryan Confederacy renegades that we had failed to capture at their compound or in the roundup afterwards, we tried to get a lead on them from the computers confiscated at the compound and the factory in Shickton. If we could separate the ones dead or in jail from the ones still on the loose, we might be able to focus on a smaller, more likely list of suspects. But if there was a comprehensive data bank of Brotherhoood members somewhere, it wasn't on the computer hard drives. At least not the computers in our possession.

We tried to pick up on a money trail that we could follow, but apparently they weren't spending their loot crazily. Neither had we tumbled onto any huge amounts being laundered or fenced. We had a network of informers, some of them with connections to neo-Nazi groups that were still operating, but so far the snitches had been useless to us.

Harriet came into my office one day and said, "The money is still the key. They haven't been splurging it around anywhere. So what are they holding back for?"

"Sit down," I suggested. "Let's brainstorm."

She took the seat in front of my desk, and her skirt hiked up. She was in her thirties, and quite attractive. Too young for me. And engaged to be married to a doctor. She had graduated near the top of her class at the FBI Academy, and had already shown me that her skills weren't purely academic. She was a whiz on the firing range. And she was street-wise enough to deal with scumbag hoodlums, as well as sophisticated enough to have insight into corporate-type criminals.

"The money," I said, trying to get my brain in gear. "What would they need millions of dollars for?"

"Well," Harriet said, "we've already speculated that they might want to reestablish themselves, bring the Aryan Confederacy back to what they think of as their glory days. What would they need in order to make that happen?"

"Another way of putting it," I said, "what have we taken from them that they would want back?"

"We took everything ... their land, their buildings, their money, their—"

"Weapons."

"That might be it, Frank. If they want to make any kind of splash, they're going to have to re-arm themselves in a big way. We've got to step up surveillance on known or suspected arms dealers. Wiretaps, satellite snooping. If we can make somebody rat out a big deal that's about to go down, we might be able to lay a trap. "

"Good thinking," I said. "Let's take it upstairs, see if we can put it in motion."

We ended up getting Harriet's suggestion approved, and I clung to it in hopeful desperation over the next few weeks because it seemed to be the strongest thing we had going for us. Sometimes I worried about how unhealthy my mental processes were. I was almost as obsessed with the killers as they were with killing. I thought about them day and night, dwelling on everything they had done and everything we knew about them, which wasn't much. My life hadn't been much of a life ever since Jane was killed. I had no close friends or regular companions outside of work, unless you want to count favorite bartenders and favorite waitresses in places that I frequented or "regulars" that I would bump into and chat with. I still read books and listened to music alone in my town house, but somehow my old passion for those things had flagged. Sadly, wistfully, I realized how much more they had meant to me back when I thought I would have a career in the arts. The townhouse that I lived in all by myself was in and of itself a sort of mockery, a lonely reminder of how I had bought it back when I still imagined I might someday have someone to share it with, even though I believed that no one could ever quite replace Jane.

One day while I was in my office wallowing in frustration and wondering where to turn next, Harriet Stern walked in and made a dramatic announcement. "Frank, I just got a phone call from the lab -- we have a couple of DNA matches."

"Great! What'd they do, rerun the tests?"

"Not exactly, no."

"Then how did they get any match-ups? How sure are they? Did they find something they overlooked?"

"Hold on a minute and I'll tell you. We actually got two DNA hits, and they came from one of the rape victims who was shot and partially burned outside of Philadelphia."

"There were matches in the CODIS system all along? Who screwed up?"

"Nobody. They weren't in the system. That's why they didn't pop out the first time we had them run."

CODIS was the FBI's Combined DNA Identification System. It didn't exist a few years ago, but by now it was getting to be a fairly comprehensive data bank and an extremely valuable tool for law enforcement. We had already submitted the DNA from the rape victim Harriet was talking about, and we hadn't gotten a match. Therefore what she was saying now didn't make sense to me. "This sounds like hocus-pocus," I said. "How in the world could we get two hits if the match-ups weren't even in our system?"

"We had the matching semen samples in evidence, but no DNA had never been extracted. Not till I thought of it," she said, allowing herself a trace of self-satisfaction. "They were very old samples, and I had to convince the lab to try to pull DNA from them so I could submit the charts to CODIS."

I could tell she was holding something back but I didn't know what. I rocked back in my desk chair and waited for her to say more, and all of a sudden she started apologizing.

"I didn't go behind your back on purpose, Frank, I swear. I just didn't want to shake you up if I didn't have to. I was taking a stab in the dark. It might not even pan out, and if so I didn't want to stir up bad memories for you."

"Harriet, please stop beating around the bush and level with me. I'm a big boy. I can take it."

She made eye-contact with me, took a deep breath and said, "Frank ... the semen samples I'm talking about are the ones that were taken from Jane Hawthorne's dead body, thirteen years ago. I hope you're not mad at me. If you are, I'm sorry."

I was stunned, not mad. The look on my face was due to the emotional impact of thinking about Jane's death anew, plus the necessity of wrestling with the forensic implications of what Harriet had discovered. It was a far-out angle that had never even occurred to me -- a break out of the blue, thanks to Harriet's good, imaginative detective work.

"I knew what had happened to Jane," she elucidated. "I knew her case had gone cold without any arrests, and I started wondering if something more could be done with the crime-scene items that had been collected back then. Maybe new avenues could be opened up with state-of-the-art laboratory methods."

It turned out that when she dug through the old evidence boxes, she discovered that some of the semen samples taken from Jane had been preserved on microscope slides. Not knowing whether DNA could be extracted after all this time, she decided it was worth a chance. She begged the scientists in our forensic lab to give it a try, and they ended up high-fiving each other. All of a sudden, by the magic of modern science, there was "new" DNA to be run through CODIS.

This time the system came up with two hits. They couldn't wait to call Harriet back with the results. They had two definite match-ups -- proof that two of the killers we were after right now had also taken part in the rape and murder of Jane Hawthorne back in 1987. We still didn't know who they were, but we knew that they had been raping and murdering for over a decade, and if we caught them we could convict them based on their DNA.

My head spinning with the ramifications of it all, I complimented Harriet on the great job she had done.

"So far, so good," she agreed modestly. "But DNA won't do us much good until we have suspects."

"Yeah, but at least we're further ahead than we were before. Thanks to you. I think I must've blotted out the details of Jane's death to the point where I would've been incapable of looking at it with any fresh insights."

"We'll get them, Frank," she said, putting her hand on my arm. "I know how you must feel."

I wondered if she really did. I wondered if she could know how badly I wanted to kill them.

CHAPTER 64

Del Logan and his buddies had enough cash to buy anything they wanted, and they wanted sophisticated stuff like machine guns and mortars. Harley knew of an arms dealer who specialized in heavy weaponry and operated out of an old stone farmhouse west of Gettysburg, Pennsylvania. Several times over the past eight or nine years Harley had made trips there with Curb and Bash to buy armaments and haul them back to the Aryan Confederacy compound.

In September 2000, after their rampage of bank robbery, rape and murder in the Philadelphia area, the gang backtracked toward Gettysburg. Harley and Del were in a rented Monte Carlo, and Patsy and Chris were following them in a U-Haul truck large enough for the anticipated load of weaponry and ammunition. In the trunk of the Monte Carlo was a suitcase full of one-hundred-dollar bills in thousand-dollar packets. The money was for show -- they didn't actually intend to pay any of it out. They had it with them in case they would have to demonstrate how well-heeled they were in order to gain access to the high-end goods.

The arms dealer, Gustav Streiter, did a little farming, cultivated a field of corn and a field of alfalfa, and kept a few cows, a few pigs and a flock of chickens. He also had a gun dealership in the town of Gettysburg. Both the farm and the gun shop were fronts for his illegal activities. The gun shop sales were licensed and above board as long as he filled out the proper paper work and abided by the law requiring a waiting period. But the money he got from legitimate sales was dwarfed by the huge profits he reaped by selling banned military ordnance to collectors, criminals and paramilitary outfits.

"He sees what's in that suitcase, his tongue'll be hangin' out," Harley said. "His greed's gonna get his guard down for us, you wait and see."

Del was looking forward to the weapons "purchase." More and more he found himself dreaming in earnest about revitalizing what was left of the Aryan Confederacy. He envisioned himself as Leader of a reborn movement with a new name, a new flag and a new logo. The Aryan Warriors it'd be called – a perfect name to conjure up images of jackbooted Storm Troopers. The White Race had won the Revolutionary War, then lost the Civil War, then slowly lost their grip on the America Dream. The Zionist Occupational Government had slyly usurped all their power. The White People had to take their country back. They had to rise up, overthrow ZOG, and kill all the Jews and niggers. Del Logan was ready and willing to lead the way. He had been preparing himself for this ever since he was eight years old.

Looking back on what he had learned under Conrad Pryzor, Del believed that Pryzor was a good organizer, a good recruiter, but too much a man of ideas instead of action. He didn't have the soul of a warrior. He was too weak. He failed to take the fight to his enemies. He got so comfortable in his barbed-wire bastion that he let the FBI swarm in and destroy him.

As for Harley, he was a man of action without wit or imagination. Basically he was a dimwitted but temporarily useful thug, like the blustery brown-shirted hoodlums manipulated by Hitler, Himmler and Goering in their initial rise to power. If push came to shove, Harley would need to step aside, or else Del would turn on him like Hitler turned on Ernst Roehm on the Night of the Long Knives. There was justification for this, and it had been festering inside of Del for two years. In the heat of the moment on the day the compound was attacked, he had helped dispose of his mother's body, but secretly he had never remained entirely convinced that Harley needed to kill her.

On their way back across Pennsylvania, the Monte Carlo cruised past the Civil War battlefield outside of Gettysburg, and Del wistfully told Harley how close Robert E. Lee had come to winning. "If he coulda whupped them Yankees' asses right here, he woulda marched straight to Washington, D.C., and had the place surrounded. Lincoln woulda been forced to sign a peace treaty. The Confederacy woulda survived and all the niggers would still be slaves like God sez they was meant to be, in the Bible."

"Shit!" Harley said. "You mean we come to within a cunt hair of doin' all that?"

"Yeah, we had all the best generals and the best soldiers, but the Yankees had all the arms factories and boatloads fulla dumb fuckin' immigrants to work in 'em. They didn't need slaves 'cause they had immigrants workin' for peanuts, and they wanted to make us free our slaves when it weren't none of their goddamn business. "

Harley griped and swore about the injustice of it all, then started bitching about Gustav Streiter when they got to within a few miles of the turn-off to Streiter's farm. "The motherfucker deserves what's comin' to him. He knows damn well I been here lotsa times and bought a shitload of his best firepower and paid top fuckin' dollar, but this time he has to give me a bunch of shit over the phone. Says he knows the FBI put us outta business. He don't wanna believe me when I tell him don't worry, me and my troops is still goin' strong. Wait till he sees the load of cash we're bringin' -- his eyes'll pop out."

"Fuck him," Del said.

"Well, don't fool yerself. He's not gonna be some kinda pushover. Like I told ya, he always has a couple mean-ass dudes carryin' sidearms and shotguns, but he trusts me and he sees we brung a suitcase fulla cash they'll relax a little, least they oughtta. But it still ain't gonna be no cakewalk to take 'em out. "

"You're the boss, Harley," Del said, playing the dutiful follower, ready and willing to take orders.

"Another thing I don't like about him," Harley said, "the fucker is German!"

"I'd of thought that'd make you like him," Del said.

"Yeah, but he got a chink wife, scrawny slanty-eyed bitch with a little pinched-up face and way too long scraggly black hair, makes her look like one them shrunken heads. They got a couple of slanty-eyed kids runnin' around, too. Streiter went on some kinda business trip to Korea about ten years ago and brung the chink over here when he come back. Don't know what the hell he was doin' over there -- maybe buyin' North Korean or Russian weapons on the Asian black market."

"Helluva thing for a German to have a chink wife and kids," Del said. "Führer's prob'ly rollin' over in his grave."

"We prob'ly won't have to kill the kids," Harley mused. "Prob'ly be in school. Not that I'd mind shootin' the slanty-eyed little fuckers."

He said this as he slowed down and turned off the main road. Patsy and Chris did likewise in the U-Haul. They followed the Monte Carlo along a sparsely graveled yellow clay road streaked black and shiny because it had been recently oiled, till they came to a fork and Harley pulled over. The U-Haul came up beside him and stopped, like it was supposed to, according to plan. Since Harley was familiar with the layout of the farm and its environs, he had described it and drawn a map for the others so they'd know beforehand exactly what they were expected to do. Here was where they were going to switch seats in the vehicles. Harley and Chris were going to get in the U-Haul and take the right fork over to Streiter's place, acting like they had come all by themselves in the truck.

Del and Patsy would get in the Monte Carlo and take the left fork all the way around, circling the valley, to approach the farmhouse and barn from the back, far enough to stash the car and go the rest of the way through some woods.

Harley got the suitcase full of money out of the car trunk and put it in the cab of the U-Haul. He and Chris both wore holstered Glocks under their denim jackets and knives in their boots. Streiter's bodyguards would probably frisk and disarm them, but they'd look stupid if they weren't armed to begin with, coming down here carrying such a large chunk of loot. If somehow they didn't get disarmed, so much the better. But even if they had to surrender their weapons, they still might be able to make a grab for them when all hell broke loose.

Del and Patsy were going to be hiding in the woods with binoculars and telescopic rifles. They were both good sharpshooters. Once they saw that the deal had gone down, a shitload of money paid out and a shitload of weapons loaded into the back of the U-Haul, they'd open fire and pick off Streiter and his goons, making sure to hit the goons first. At the same time, Harley and Chris would make a grab to get their weapons back or grab guns off of the downed bodyguards. They'd help finish off Streiter and his goons if need be, then they'd all go into the house on a search and destroy mission -- anybody in there, including the chink and her brats, would be shot dead on the spot. No use diddle-dallying around about it -- Harley had already assured the whole gang that the chink wasn't worth a good fuck. If they tumbled onto any of Streiter's cash or jewelry they'd boost any of the stuff that was easy pickings, but they couldn't take time to ransack, they had to get the hell out fast, making sure to leave no witnesses.

Del's whole body tingled with anticipation.

He wanted to be the one to make the most kills.

CHAPTER 65

We knew all about the arms deal. Gustav Streiter was cooperating with us, under pressure. When we confronted him with evidence gathered against him from wiretaps and satellite surveillance, he folded. Scared out of his wits that he'd be turned into a sex slave or outright killed if he went to prison, he begged us to put him in a witness protection program after we got what we wanted, which was to use him as a decoy. Two of his bodyguards were already in jail; we had replaced them with tough-looking FBI agents for today's take-down, both carrying shotguns and .357 Magnums.

We had two snipers in the house and a six-member SWAT team spread out, hiding in the corn field. Harriet Stern and I were in the barn, hiding in an empty horse stall, breathing in a residual aroma of hay and manure. Her nose was running and her eyes were watering, playing havoc with her contacts; she was apparently allergic to something in there and kept wiping her nose with balled-up Kleenex. Across the wide center aisle of the barn was a heavily padlocked room where Streiter's illegal arsenal was kept.

Our entire team had been airlifted in by helicopter early that morning so we could get in position before our quarry came on the scene. We didn't want to barge in with land vehicles because keeping the convoy out of sight after we got there would have been a big problem. Neither did we want the helicopter whirring around overhead, spooking the crooks and making them go on the lam. The chopper would hover about five miles out from the take-down site and keep in touch with our people on the ground by radio.

We knew from our wiretaps and from Streiter that the U-Haul was due to show up at around one o'clock in the afternoon, with two guys in it, ready to make the deal. Counting me and Harriet, there were eleven of us ready to go up against what we thought would be only two wannabe arms buyers. We thought we had the advantage of overwhelming force. We weren't wise to the fact that two more bad guys had gotten the drop on us by sneaking into the woods behind the place and taking up firing positions in the woods.

Maybe I'm being too easy on myself, but I don't think we could have anticipated the bloody scheme the gang had hatched. We knew they must have heisted around five million bucks from their string of bank robberies, so they could easily afford to pay Streiter a mere forty or fifty thousand. After all, they had dealt with him often in the past without harming him, so why would they go off on a tangent and screw up a long-term relationship they'd probably want to keep on the back burner for future buys?

We were going to let the deal go down before we pounced on them. We wanted to nail them after the cash changed hands and they had a load of illegal weapons in their truck. Our reasoning was that if they turned out to be accomplices of the bank robbers instead of the robbers themselves, we'd have evidence that would stand up in court, not only of intent but of actual commission of a criminal transaction, to pressure them into squealing on whoever sent them here.

At first, things started off the way we expected. The U-Haul turned onto Gustav Streiter's driveway right on schedule. Harriet and I were both wearing headsets so the agents in the house and the cornfield could clue us in as to what was happening out there. Also, the two agents pretending to be Streiter's bodyguards were wearing wires.

When the two guys got out of the truck, Harriet and I were able to catch the names "Harley" and "Chris" during the opening chit-chat. From then on we could recognize them by their voices.

Things heated up when the two "bodyguards" tried to frisk and disarm them.

"Fuck no!" Harley snapped. "You fuckers gonna shoot us dead, keep our cash and guns!"

"Oh, Harley, come on now," Streiter cajoled. "You know me too well. I'm not a violent man. Would I ever kill off a good repeat customer like you? It would be not only bad for business but real bad for my continuing health. I wouldn't want some mean-spirited plug-uglies coming after me if I failed to treat you right."

A chubby grandfatherly type fellow with wiry gray hair and wire-rimmed spectacles, he sounded like the gentle businessman farmer he had always pretended to be. Yet I had little doubt that the goods he trafficked in must have killed quite a few innocent people.

"We start loadin' the truck we'll be busier'n a one-legged man in an ass-kickin' contest," Harley said. "Your guys'll be able to catch us with our pants down. You don't let us keep our weapons, it's a deal breaker, Streiter. We'll jes' take our cash and mosey on. You ain't the onliest pebble on the beach. "

Streiter hemmed and hawed for a moment or two, then reluctantly gave in. "I guess I'll have to accommodate you, if you insist. But my guys aren't going to help you load. They're going to stand by and keep a close eye."

"Fine with us, just so they don't come up on us while our backs're turned. Right, Harley?"

It was Chris piping up, and Harley apparently didn't like it one bit. "No fuckin' way!" he barked. "Keep yer fuckin' trap shut till I ask fer yer opinion! We do this thing my way or we don't do it at all. One of yer guys can he'p us load, Streiter, and one of 'em can stand by. Me and Chris'll do the same. That way we'll have one guy busy workin' and one keepin' watch with his gun handy, and so will you. Things'll be even-steven, a Mexican standoff. "

"That's smart thinking," Streiter agreed. "I can live with that, Harley. But first let's have a look at what you're carrying." He chuckled amiably. "For all I know that suitcase could be full of cut-up newspapers."

"If it is I'll blow ya," Harley said.

Chris snickered.

"No need to be coarse," Streiter said. But he too allowed himself a chuckle. Over our headsets, Harriet and I heard the sounds of the suitcase being unlatched. Once more she wiped her nose and eyes with her Kleenex.

"Tell me that don't make you drool," Harley said.

"Satisfactory," said Streiter.

We heard the suitcase being closed and re-latched, then Streiter and our two agents led Harley and Chris into the barn.

Guns drawn, Harriet and I made sure our heads were down behind some bales of hay. She turned her head aside and tried really hard not to sneeze.

We heard the heavy oak door being unlocked, then squeaking open. After that, we had to stay put for an interminably long time while all the inspecting, hefting, choosing and dickering took place. Harriet was utterly miserable through all this because of her allergy.

Finally the sale was made and money changed hands. Then, doing it the way Harley wanted it, the alternating teams of two men each loaded crates of armaments onto a flat-bedded dolly and wheeled it out to the U-Haul.

Harriet and I crept out of the horse stall.

Suddenly shots rang out.

At first we jumped back.

More shots.

Then screams.

Harriet glanced at me, motioned with her Sig-Sauer for me to cover her. She broke for the front of the barn. A volley erupted, but I covered her -- unnecessarily, it turned out -- and she made it.

"Don't go out yet!" I yelled.

But I saw she was wisely hanging back. I darted toward the other side of the big wide-open double doors.

We both cautiously peeked around the corners with their huge iron hinges.

Streiter was face-down in the dirt and wasn't moving. One of our agents was flat on his back, shot in the neck, gouts of blood pumping from a severed artery, his shotgun lying across his thighs. His partner was sprawled against the side of the U-Haul, eyes wide open and unseeing, a bullet hole in the middle of his forehead. Harley was dead, too, blown half in two. Chris was bleeding from a shoulder wound, holding one hand up in the air in surrender while the other arm hung limp.

The SWAT guys were moving across the farmhouse's backyard, firing into the woods. There was a groan. They must've hit somebody.

Above a lull in the racket, I heard distant car doors slamming. Then, an engine starting up, tires squealing and peeling out.

The SWAT guys, advancing in squad formation into the edge of the woods, got off a few rounds before their leader yelled, "Cease fire!"

I couldn't see the getaway car, but I heard it faintly as it spewed dirt and gravel, accelerating on the dirt road.

CHAPTER 66

September 30, 2000, a Saturday, was officially my last day in the FBI. I put in my papers the week following the shootout at Streiter's farm. Two of the killers hiding in the woods had gotten away cleanly somehow. We didn't even know what they looked like or what kind of vehicle they were in, and by the time we could put up roadblocks they were long gone. Our so-called "dragnet" was superfluous, like shutting the barn door after the horse gallops away to God knows where.

I would've liked to keep after them, especially after forensics proved that one of the dead gang members, the one called Harley, had contributed some of the DNA from the Jane Hawthorne case. Either of the ones on the loose could have been the other donor that we still needed to find.

Harriet and I interrogated Chris Terrell in the hospital room where he was recovering from his shoulder wound. We got very little out of him. Though we pumped as hard as we could, he really didn't know much. He only knew his accomplices by their first names -- Harley, Del and Patsy – which after all might have been aliases.

However, fingerprints from Harley's corpse were entered into CODIS and matched up with a "Harney Logan" who had a long rap sheet and a prison record. FBI resources were hard at work trying to fill in his background and reveal as much as possible about him, in hopes of untangling clues to the identities of the two killers who had fled the scene of the shootout.

This part of the follow-up investigation was out of my hands. I still had a burning passion to see an end to it all, but at the same time I had had enough. If I waited for every single case I had ever worked on to resolve itself in a final conclusion, I'd be slogging and slogging till the end of time and beyond.

What tipped the scales of my decision to resign was the phone call I got from Lori McCoy. She and her husband Charlie, as well as her sister Arlene, her son-in-law, her daughter and her granddaughter were working hard to get Al Gore and Joe Lieberman elected, and this had led to harassment and even a few death threats from jerks of the extreme right-wing, anti-Semitic variety. Lori and Charlie wanted me to relocate to New York and hire whoever I might recommend and do whatever I could to make sure they had tight security. I'd be in charge of protecting them from now on, at a very enticing salary.

One of the reasons they felt that protecting them was now more complicated than usual was that their entire family, including even Lori's ex-husband Keith and her sister Arlene, were working on a movie production that Keith, Lori and Charlie had backed financially. Dan and Missy had written the script and Charlie had landed a distribution deal. Lori and Meredith were co-starring. Not only that, but the big wrap-up scene, a sniper incident at an outdoor college concert, was being filmed at our Alma Mater, Belmont University.

It all seemed to offer me far more fun and excitement, at a more relaxed, less dangerous pace, than what I could expect if I persisted in dragging out my time in the FBI. Lori and Charlie sweetened the deal for me by saying that Dan and Missy wanted me to be their technical director on the movie. I had already done this for them when they were making their documentary about terrorism in America, and I had found a great deal of satisfaction in it. I couldn't say it was the most creatively demanding job in the world of filmmaking, but at least it had put me in proximity to the kind of career I had dreamed of, early on.

By now, I had been an FBI agent for over thirty years. I was sixty-one years old, still wanting to believe I was tough and strong, yet knowing I wasn't, as they say, a spring chicken. I was more than twenty pounds overweight, and constantly wrestling with the realization that I'd have to pare myself down if I wanted to put less strain on joints and ligaments that were aching more and more from old football injuries.

I took Lori up on her offer, and sought to make Harriet Stern my first new hire. She was flattered and tempted, and said she would have to talk it over with her fiancé, Dr. Morgan Toth, who was about to extend his contract with a Pittsburgh hospital. To the surprise of everyone involved, all this ended up working out in a serendipitous way. Harriet would move to New York as soon as she could make all the arrangements, then come back to Pittsburgh long enough to be married. After the honeymoon, Morgan would batch it for a few months till he satisfied his contract, then he would join Harriet in New York and take a position on the staff of a hospital there, from whom he had previously declined an offer that he would now turn around and accept. Luckily the offer was still open when he changed his mind.

I told myself that maybe my own luck was changing too, and perhaps a few things were going to turn out right for a change.

Little did I know.

CHAPTER 67

Patsy was bleeding all over the interior of the Monte Carlo. One of those goddamned SWAT guys had gotten off a lucky shot, the bullet going through the trunk, through the back seat and through the back of the front seat into Patsy's back, blowing a ragged exit hole in his chest. He was groaning his ass off and trying to stanch the blood flow with a dirty white towel Harley had kept in the car to wipe off the windshield.

Del had no idea if the fuzz had gotten a look at the kind of car he was driving, but he figured he couldn't chance it. The Monte Carlo had to be ditched. It had more than one bullet hole in it besides the one from the slug that had penetrated Patsy. A shot-up car might be noticed even by a nosy fuckin' "upright citizen," let alone by a fuckin' cop.

Heading west, away from Gettysburg on a two-lane blacktop, Del took note of the fact that he was in an area of cultivated fields, green meadows, and prosperous looking farms nestled among heavily forested mountains.

Patsy kept on moaning and groaning, and Del wished the fucker would shut up.

"Goddamn it to hell!" he barked, and whipped the wheel on pure angry impulse, fishtailing the car onto a long stretch of fresh, clean gravel leading to a yellow-brick ranch-style home that looked too small for its large unkempt lawn. The place was kind of seedy and rundown, which together with the fact that the grass needed cutting and the bushes needed pruned, made Del think there must not be a man around to take care of the place.

There was a green pickup truck in the driveway, and an old woman on the porch, peeling potatoes. She stood up, looking wary, wiping her hands on her apron, as Del got out, slamming the car door. He didn't even bother hiding his pistol. "Hi," he said to the old woman, and shot her in the head. She was blown sideways against a brick pillar, bounced off it and fell almost without a sound, like a bag of old sticks.

Del waited.

Nobody came running out of the house.

Nobody charged at him from the backyard or from anyplace else.

He came up onto the porch, let himself into the house, did a quick eye-scan, and found the keys to the truck on top of a television set in the heavily draped living room.

When he came back outside, he dragged the old woman's body into the house, laid it out on the rust-colored carpet, and shut the front door so that it automatically locked.

He came down off the porch, walked over to the passenger side of the Monte Carlo, opened the door and shot Patsy in his right temple, putting him out of his misery.

Then he slammed the door shut. From the backseat of the car and from the trunk, he transferred all the guns, knives and ammunition into the pickup truck, a ten-year-old Ford in good condition. He got in and started it up, then backed it onto the lawn in order to clear the driveway.

He figured that the other key on the ring with the truck key was probably for the garage, and this turned out to be so.

He unlocked the door, lifted it up and slid it back, then got into the Monte Carlo, pulled it inside the garage, lowered the garage door and locked it.

Then he climbed into the truck, started it up again and drove back out onto the highway.

CHAPTER 68

On the Friday preceding the big Homecoming game, Harriet and I escorted Lori and Meredith on a walk around the campus. I kept my eyes peeled, but the throngs of students didn't show much interest in the two celebrities, who were dressed pretty much "incognito" anyway, in jeans, sneakers, and Belmont Bulldogs jackets and baseball caps. Harriet and I were dressed similarly except for the baseball caps, and of course we were armed and Lori and her granddaughter probably weren't, unless Lori still carried her old .32 revolver in her purse.

Today was October 15, 2000. Just two weeks after my final day in the FBI. I was still screening backup security people and hadn't yet hired any, but there would be plenty of police on the sidelines tomorrow. Harriet hadn't gotten married yet and hadn't yet moved to New York but had managed to be here this weekend. The two of us were monitoring this little excursion with Lori and Merry while Keith was in his hotel suite having a production meeting with Dan and Missy, and Charlie and Arlene were conferencing with some Young Democrats who were dedicated campaign workers for Gore/Lieberman against George W. Bush and Dick Cheney.

Merry had just turned sixteen and was a little too young to enroll at the University yet, but she intended to when the time came. I was already starting to wonder what the future security problems might be. Right now, because her singing career had taken off for her at such a young age, she was being home schooled. She often had a tutor with her while on extended engagements. So far, according to Lori, this was working out very well, thanks not just to the ability of the tutor but also to Merry's quick intellect.

I noticed her checking out some of the good-looking college boys and surreptitiously comparing herself to some of the well-built college girls. Merry was tall and full-figured, often dieting in an attempt to look as slim as she could for her photo shoots and personal appearances, which made her parents and grandparents worry that she might become anorexic.

When she was younger she used to say that she hated her green eyes and red hair, calling them "cat eyes" and "clown hair" but lately she had stopped saying that. Hopefully she was starting to realize that her physical attributes actually went quite well with the off-beat personality that came through in her music, and the entire package gave her her own special kind of beauty.

Lori was delighted, even sort of bubbly, about being able to show Merry all her old haunts on the Belmont campus – at least the ones that still existed. She and I were both interested to see how many of the hangouts we had been familiar with still remained and how many had been torn down or changed into something different.

Belmont University started out as a Land Grant college, founded in 1867, and the three original ivy-covered brick buildings, Ryan Hall, Farnsworth Hall and Belmont Hall, were still there in Belmont Circle, the central landmark of the campus, overlooking a grassy tree-shaded commons where students liked to lie in the grass, sit on benches and read, make out with each other, or toss Frisbees.

"I hope they never tear these beautiful old buildings down," Lori said, gazing up at their spires and towers.

"I don't think they're allowed to," I said. "They've been designated official historic landmarks."

"Thank God someone is saving them from the developers," Harriet commented.

She and Lori gave each other a look that said they were both already hitting it off. I had thought they would probably like each other and might even become fast friends, which appeared to be happening. That, along with Harriet's indomitable courage and ability, had been one of the reasons I wanted her on the job.

Neither of us had revealed much to Lori or her family about the shootout at Streiter's farm or the events that led up to it. I didn't think they needed to hear the grisly details. At this stage their lives would be much more pleasant if they didn't have to know about the connection to Jane's murder and Arlene's near escape.

"Coming down here, crossing Belmont Circle with the band playing, always used to make my fingertips tingle," Lori said. "It's gonna be the same for you, Merry. Right, Frank? Or was it totally different for you, being out on the field ready to do battle?"

"Well, I was all fired up and jittery as hell before every game, wondering if I was going to get my head torn off."

"You never acted scared, though."

344

"Men don't act scared," Merry said. "Right, Harriet?"

"I don't know about that," she said, casting a meaningful glance at me.

"Even us macho men get scared sometimes," I admitted.

I remembered the pregame band music whipping everybody up into a football frenzy as students and alumni filled the stadium, which I always thought must be one of the most beautiful stadiums in the country, especially on a crisp, sunshiny fall day. Above the bleachers you could see the tops of the original class buildings, and down below, the sparkling Belmont River wending through the valley with pleasure boats sailing by on it, and the surrounding hills lavishly decorated with autumn colors.

As if reading my mood, Merry said, "I think I'm going to love it here, Grandmother."

"I know I did," Lori said, as we left Belmont Circle and came out onto Campus Avenue.

The agenda for tomorrow was for Keith, Lori, Charlie and me to be introduced just before kickoff as "distinguished alumni." This recognition was being bestowed upon me not because of my FBI work but because I had been a star running back here in the late fifties, early sixties. Arlene wasn't an alum but she would be introduced as Lori's sister and a current vice-president of NOW, and would present Lori with flowers. Then Lori would sing the National Anthem.

There would also be halftime ceremonies, at which time Dan, Missy and Meredith would come out onto the field with us. The president of the university would announce that the movie *American Murders* was going to be shot here and that the producers were making a large donation to the scholarship fund.

He would introduce Keith and Charlie as executive producers, Michele Clanton as producer, Dan Clanton as director, and Meredith and Lori as co-stars. All of this had been ballyhooed in the newspapers and on TV already, so it would be a big surprise to absolutely nobody. But still the formalities had to be executed with suitable pageantry because Keith wanted the photo-op. He was going to present Belmont University with what Charlie facetiously called "a huge check" -- it was a biggy, measuring seven feet by three feet. The amount was one hundred thousand dollars.

Meredith would then sing *God Bless America.*

And after that the second-half kickoff would sail down the field.

As we approached the stretch of businesses along Campus Avenue, Lori cried out, "Oh, look! Jimmy's is still here! Let's go in!"

"Are you sure?" I asked with some trepidation. "It probably hasn't improved."

"Let's go in anyway," she said adventurously.

"Oh, no, you're acting like it's not so hot," Merry said, making a sour face.

"Well ... it's called Jimmy's Kampus Korner," Lori told her, "and we remember it as an old hangout. It's owned, or used to be owned, by a little old Greek guy named Jimmy Papajohn. I'll put it this way, the food wasn't bad enough to make you sick, and it was cheap, so it was always crowded with students who couldn't afford to fill their bellies with anything better."

"We used to call it Jimmy's Greasy Spoon," I said. "But let's go in anyway since Lori wants to. Maybe it's a lot better now," I added doubtfully.

We found that it hadn't changed one bit except for Jimmy Papajohn who was a lot more ancient now, even though we thought he was old back then. He was still behind the long gray Formica counter in a stained, wrinkled apron that was supposed to be white but was actually yellowish. The stool he was perched on looked like the same chrome-legged stool of forty years ago, and probably if he stood up I'd see that it still had the same badly cracked red plastic seat with the dirty-brown padding poking out.

Not wanting to call attention to Lori and Merry, we didn't stop to chit-chat with Jimmy Papajohn. But right behind him, along with cracked, fly-specked laminated "beauty shots" of burgers, fries, chicken and fish dinners (the photos obviously not of his own food) he had newspaper clippings of Lori and Merry thumbtacked to the grease-spattered wall, and he nodded at the two celebs as they came in, not making a big deal out of their appearance in his joint, and surprising me with his tact and his willingness to respect their privacy.

We took seats in a red Naugahyde booth just like the ones Lori and I remembered, except the upholstery must've been redone at some point because although it was lumpy and saggy like the upholstery of old it didn't have any cracks in it yet.

"Don't order coffee," Lori warned.

"Most awful coffee in the world," I agreed. "Tastes like battery acid. Or worse."

Merry grimaced and said, "Yuck!"

"What do you recommend?" Harriet asked with a show of intrepid courage.

"The only thing that was ever palatable in here was the grilled cheese," Lori told her. "And the tomato soup, because it comes out of a can, but it's a cheaper brand, not Campbell's. The soft drinks are okay if you order the ones in cans instead of from the fountain. "

"God, Grandmother, why did we come in here?" Merry griped.

"Just for the nostalgia, honey."

"Well, do we have to order?"

"I suggest we all have the grilled cheese with pickles," Lori said brightly.

After the college-age waitress took our identical orders, we started talking about the upcoming presidential election.

"Gore is going to lose Tennessee and West Virginia," Lori predicted dolefully. "Folks down there are afraid he's going to take their guns away."

"God, guns, gays and abortion," Harriet said. "That's all the Republicans ever run on. And it works for them every darn time. "

"West Virginia people like their guns, but they're also mostly Democrats," Lori said. "But Charlie thinks we're going to lose my home state and Gore's home state too, and the polls agree with him. He says the Democrats should be plowing more time and money into Florida. "

Merry eyed me and Harriet. "You two had to deal with the bad guys," she said. "So what's your real opinion on gun control? You know, those bumper stickers that say When Guns are Outlawed only Outlaws will have Guns?"

"I'm not worried about the outlaws as much as I'm worried about the law-abiding citizens who suddenly go postal," Harriet said.

"Me, too," I agreed.

As we ate what turned out to be the same kind of lunch Lori and I "fondly" remembered from forty years ago -- melted imitation American cheese pasted between two pieces of dry, hard, several-day-old toast, the unpalatible aftertaste washed down with Coca-Cola in cans -- Harriet and I explained to Lori and Merry why we didn't want American citizens to be able to buy military-style weapons, irregardless of the gun lobby's attempts to invoke the Second Amendment.

"I'm from Chicago," Harriet said, "and when I was in grade school a man went bonkers and started shooting at two hundred kids in a schoolyard at recess."

"At your school?" Merry said, aghast.

347

"No, it wasn't my school, it was across town, in a different suburb. But I read all about it and saw all the reports on TV, and I was absolutely horrified. I even had nightmares. I knew I could've been one of those kids. Eight of them were killed that day."

"How come only eight out of two hundred?" Merry asked. "I mean I'm glad there weren't more but—"

"That's the point," I said. "The shooter didn't have an automatic rifle -- or worse a machine gun. When the gunfire erupted and the very first kids were hit, the others were able to run like hell -- and the shooter had to reload."

"By the time he reloaded, the kids had run into the school building and the teachers locked the doors," Harriet said. "But suppose he had a machine gun with a full magazine, capable of firing six hundred rounds a minute? He would have mowed down a hundred or more kids before they even knew what was happening."

"He wouldn't have had to stop to reload," I emphasized. "The kids wouldn't have had time to react. By the time any of them realized what was going on, most of them would've been dead. "

"Too many crazy people in the world," Harriet said, "and you can't tell by looking at them what might be going on in their messed-up minds. Over and over again these rampage killers turn out to be the nice guy next door, or everybody's favorite Eagle Scout. You never know where the next one is coming from. Especially in this gun-crazy society."

"I've always thought random crime is the scariest kind," I said. "If you know you've made an enemy, or if you're facing a known criminal, you might be able to take steps to defend yourself. But what're you going to do if some stranger has picked you out for his next victim and you have no way of knowing?"

"Gives me the creeps!" Merry said.

"Worse than this grilled cheese sandwich does?" Harriet asked her, trying to lighten the moment.

We all laughed, maybe a bit nervously.

CHAPTER 69

Del Logan came back from the 7-Eleven with a large black coffee and a cream-filled doughnut. He let himself into the girl's apartment, jiggling her key a couple of times till he made it work.

She was slumped at the tiny kitchenette table, her head nodding onto her chest, her arms hanging straight down. Her complexion was pasty white, her eyeballs glazed. There were reddish splotches on the wall and on the checkered tablecloth. A trickle of dried blood ran from her left temple, down her face and arm, onto the floor.

He had met her last night in an off-campus bar. She told him she was a sophomore at Belmont and she had her own apartment. She hated the dorm, especially the dorm food. She wasn't very good-looking, but he needed a place to stay. She took him home with her, he screwed her, imagining she was someone a lot prettier, and then in the morning he shot her, using his long-barreled .22 Sportsman which didn't make much noise.

He sat down catty-corner from her at the kitchenette table and laid out a couple of napkins, one for his coffee and one for his doughnut. Then he picked up a stubby pencil lying on top of a folded-back Goldenrod tablet. He had filled up five pages before he took a break and went to the 7-Eleven, and he wondered why this girl who claimed to be a college sophomore didn't have a bunch of pens and sharp pencils on hand. He hadn't seen any textbooks around her place either. She was probably a goddamn campus prostitute. He would have bought more pencils at the 7-Eleven, but they didn't have any.

When he filled up the tablet, he intended to leave it here on the table in case he didn't come back. The girl could watch over it for him. He chuckled at that thought. Sipping his coffee and munching his cream-filled doughnut, he resumed writing, spewing out his inner rage, pressing hard with a duller and duller pencil, his scrawl becoming less and less legible but still decipherable, he thought, and even if he should be martyred, at least, as he put it, "the world will know why the Aryan Race needs to rise up and take back America from the craven parasites who have embedded themselves in her sick, rotting carcass and why some of

349

them are going to die today by my own hand -- Lefty Lori McCoy, Scar of the Silver Screen -- Charles Guinard, Zionist Shyster Scumbag -- Arlene McCoy, High Priestess of Lesbians and Fags -- Keith Santone, Purveyor Of the American Scheme -- Frank Williams, Secret Agent of Niggers and Jews ..."

When he signed his name, Delbert McCoy Logan, honoring his martyred father as well as his martyred stepfather, his fingers were terribly cramped and his head ached from the challenge of getting the words just right, but he had the satisfaction of knowing that the newspapers would print what he had written and the radio and TV would quote from it because of the brave revolutionary act he was going to perform. He had been inspired by a tabloid blurb about the movie *American Murders* but he did not mention this in what he thought of as his own little *Mein Kampf*. Let the world figure it out. Let the irony speak for itself.

He stood up and looked at the girl one last time. Then he went into her crappy living room and tried on her Belmont Bulldogs cap and sweatshirt. They were smelly and dirty but they fit him pretty well, making him look like any other student.

He picked up his heavy olive-green duffle bag, slung it by its strap over his shoulder, then stepped out onto the dinky little porch. He made sure the door was shut and locked tight behind him because he didn't want anybody to find the girl's body right away.

The sun was bright and hot, making him squint, and he was glad he had shooter's glasses in his shirt pocket. He walked toward the center of campus, the band music getting louder and louder as the pedestrian throng thickened. The weight of the duffle bag was starting to make the strap cut into his shoulder.

Nobody was sitting on the benches in Belmont Circle. The crowd was intent on filing into the stadium. It was almost game time and Del was later than he wanted to be, but he sat down to rest and rub his sore shoulder. He pulled a red bandana from his hip pocket and wiped his sweaty forehead. Then he headed into Belmont Hall.

He had scouted all three of the buildings in the Circle yesterday, and knew that Belmont Hall was the tallest and its lookout tower had the least obstructed view of the bleachers and the playing field down below. The girl back at the apartment had told him that Saturday classes were finished by noon, an hour before the start of the Homecoming game. Good. There shouldn't be any students hanging around.

Belmont Hall had seven stories and no elevators, and Del cursed the historic-preservation nuts for causing him to climb the long flights of banistered stairs carrying his heavy duffle bag. A guy with a beard, probably a professor, said a cheery hello to him on one of the landings, then kept on going down the stairs till there were echoing sounds of a door opening and closing and then no more sounds of his footsteps.

Del was sweating like mad by the time he climbed the last few steps to the look-out tower with its white wooden arches and pillars. He leaned his duffle bag against a banister, then wiped his sweaty face and rubbed pins and needles out of his cramped arm and sore shoulder.

He could hear the band music and the murmuring crowd fairly clearly from up here. It was a murmur of anticipation. Only twenty minutes till kickoff. He had to hurry now. He wanted to be in position by the time his aunt Lori started singing the National Anthem. He hated the thought that he was actually related to her. It was the way Adolf Hitler must have felt when a rumor circulated that he had a half-Jew ancestor.

He unhooked his duffle bag, took out three rifles in leather cases and leaned them against the banister. Then he pulled out an Army-surplus blanket, a cleaning kit with several different-sized cleaning rods, ten boxes of various-caliber ammunition, and eight spare clips already loaded.

He heard a sudden outburst of cheering from the bleachers below, and he crouched behind the railing to check out what was happening down on the field. He saw the home team running out and starting to warm up, doing calisthenics and tossing footballs around, while the Belmont cheerleaders got into their act, jumping around and waving pompons. Then the Darnell Tigers came out, to a chorus of boos.

He unfolded the Army blanket and spread it out so he could lay all his other gear on it, including the rifles as he took them out of their cases. One was the Mannlicher-Carcano, which he intended to use first. Then a sniper rifle. Then a shotgun in case anybody made it to the top of the tower and came charging at him; he could not lock the steel door that led up here from the main part of the building -- it only locked from the other side. He also was carrying a 8mm Glock in a holster under his Bulldog sweatshirt, for use if he had to ditch his other weapons.

He took his sweatshirt off because there was no longer any need to conceal the Glock and he didn't want to keep sweating so much in the hot sun. Salty perspiration could sting his eyes, making them water when he was trying to take careful aim. While he was thinking about this, he put

351

on his shooter's glasses with the special yellow UV lenses that drastically cut down on glare.

Suddenly he heard voices from the stairwell behind him. He wheeled around, grabbing for his pistol, sneaked toward the stairs and peeked around the corner. Two young people were coming up, a guy and a girl, holding hands. He said hi to them, holding his pistol behind his back, then when they passed by him he shot the guy in the head, splattering his brains. The guy dropped and the girl screamed. Del shot her twice in the chest. He grabbed the guy by the feet, thinking to drag him over and roll him down the steps so his body would come to rest against the steel door, making it harder for anybody else to push it open.

The loudspeaker started blaring and Del stopped to listen, for fear he was running out of time. Cripes! His intended victims were already being introduced! The people in the stands were cheering and applauding. Clunk! Del dropped the dead guy's legs back down onto the concrete. He really had to hurry up now. "Gotta go, go, go," he said out loud. "Gotta be ready when the fat lady sings." He meant his aunt, who wasn't really fat, but still the metaphor made him laugh.

He hurried back to the banister, took up the Mannlicher-Carcano and got into a firing crouch. He worked the bolt to chamber a round.

Bile rose in his throat as one by one he heard Aunt Lori and her ass-kissing entourage being introduced over the loudspeaker. Charles Guinard, Arlene Shoaf, Keith Santone, Frank Williams.

Del panned them with his telescopic sight, getting them one by one in the crosshairs.

The rifle came to rest on a red-haired bitch down there that he didn't recognize. He thought maybe she was Keith Santone's newest piece of pussy because she was standing on the end right next to him. Fuck her, she was going to die anyhow, no matter who she was.

He felt something brush lightly against his arm and he looked to see what it was. A wasp. Seven or eight of the little bastards were circling around, darting in close to his face. Shit! They must have a nest under the fucking banister! Well, he'd just have to ignore them and go about his business. No use stirring them up and making them swarm at him. When he was a little boy he was scared of wasps, but no longer. He knew they wouldn't sting as long as he didn't swat at them.

He peeped out over the banister. Aunt Arlene was handing Aunt Lori a bunch of flowers. The loudspeaker guy blathered about it and there was an enormous outbreak of applause, whistles and cheers that pissed Del off all the more because the two bitches didn't deserve it. Then Lori took hold of a microphone and started singing *The Star Spangled Banner*. The patriotic words were a fucking travesty coming from her commie-sucking lips! Damned if he was going to let her live to hit the final notes!

Squinting and sighting, he zeroed in on her, getting her in sharp focus in the crosshairs. She was wearing a white blouse, and he aimed for the middle of her breasts, held his breath, and started a slow delicate squeeze of the trigger, remembering what Curb and Bash used to tell him when he was a young kid in training on the firing range: seduce the weapon, don't rape it.

At that moment a wasp stung his cheek and the needle-jab of pain jerked his aim. BLAM! The gun went off when he didn't intend it to.

He got her anyway!

A red blotch appeared on her white blouse and she reeled backwards and would've fallen hard except Frank Williams caught her and eased her down.

Fuck him. Del shot Frank in the back and he sprawled on the grass face down, his arms twitching, like a stomped, half-crushed cockroach.

Charlie Guinard was kneeling beside his fallen wife. Del got him in the crosshairs. A squeeze of the trigger made him pitch onto his fat face.

Keith Santone was taken out with a belly shot. He sank to his knees for a moment as if praying, then fell slowly into a parody of a salaam, then flattened out and lay still.

Four targets down in probably less than fifteen seconds! Del was proud of himself. "Better than Lee Harvey Oswald," he muttered to himself. True enough, his victims had all been stupefied at first and slow to react, but still he could take credit for not letting anything distract him, not even wasp stings. The little bastards had stung him a couple more times while he was shooting. Fuck them. They couldn't rattle him. He was too pumped up, too full of adrenaline, too high on what he was accomplishing.

He spotted his aunt Arlene fleeing to the other side of the field, and he fired the Mannlicher-Carcano. She went down but somehow kept crawling, and he shot her again.

He didn't know where Dan, Meredith and Michele were -- in the press box, or in the stands? He wished they'd pop up somewhere so he could gun them down.

Suddenly the red-haired bitch darted out from behind an overturned bench on the sideline and came running in Del's direction, toward the wall at the foot of the bleachers where she'd be out of his line of sight.

He whipped the rifle onto her and squeezed off a round, hoping it hit home, but he wasn't sure. She got away and made it to the bleacher wall.

He laid down the Mannlicher-Carcano, took up his sniper's rifle and started picking off select targets in the wildly panicked stadium mob. He shot three football players and two hot-looking cheerleaders. And a fat guy in a coach's jacket. Then he concentrated on the fans.

It was like shooting fish in a barrel. Some of them he didn't even need to bother with -- they were being trampled under other people's feet. He wondered how many of them would die that way. How pathetic they were! And no matter how they died, he was the one responsible. They were all notches on his gun butt, so to speak.

He could take his time picking out choice targets now. There was no need to rush.

He heard sirens in the distance. Ambulance, police, whatever. He half expected to see helicopters. The fuzz would be closing in on him soon. He had a rented car stashed in a nearby parking garage and a shitload full of money in a rented storage unit outside of town. Maybe he'd get away clean and maybe he wouldn't. But what he had accomplished here today would be enshrined forever in the annals of Aryan Supremacy.

One last shot and then splitsville.

He picked out a blonde girl with tears streaming down her face. Instead of pushing against the frenzied mob cramming the exits, she had simply given up. She was sitting on a bleacher bench crying her eyes out. He zeroed in on her and started gently squeezing his trigger.

He heard a footfall. Somebody behind him again, near the top of the stairs.

He wheeled around, dropping the sniper rifle and going for the shotgun.

Too late.

The red-haired bitch stepped through the door and shot him.

The impact spun him around and jolted him backwards, his shoulder blades crunching against the railing.

He wondered if he was going to die.

He tried to lift the shotgun, but she shot him again.

She walked forward, pumping slugs into him, emptying her weapon.

He never felt the last seven rounds.

PART EIGHT
BUSH

"I am a person who recognizes the fallacy of humans."
-- George W. Bush

"I think everybody should get rich and famous and do everything
they ever dreamed of so they can see it' s not the answer."
-- Jim Carrey

"I want to fight in a war like World War Two. I want to fight
an enemy. And this (in Iraq) it's a faceless enemy."
-- Sgt. Christopher Dugger

"Men who believe in absurdities will commit atrocities."
-- Voltaire

CHAPTER 70

When two airplanes crashed into the World Trade Center. I was still in the hospital. It was the same one where Harriet's husband worked. He was a neurosurgeon, but he wasn't the one who worked on me.

Harriet was Mrs. Morgan Toth now. They had gotten married in December 2001, a few months later than they had originally planned. Their lives were in disarray after the massacre on the Belmont campus and the mass murders on 9/11, in which they had lost three close friends, including a young FBI agent whom Harriet had enlisted as a bridesmaid. Life (and death) is what happens while you are making other plans.

I know you're aching to know, so I'll tell you right now that Keith and Arlene didn't make it. They were both killed on the spot, down there on the football field.

Dan, Missy and Meredith were up in the press booth when the shooting rampage started and they tried to run out and do heaven knows what, probably get to Lori and Charlie, but the security guard made them stay in the booth and lie down on the floor. Even though they seem to be okay on the outside these days, they're still suffering inwardly from shock, grief and survivors' guilt.

Lori and Charlie both managed to hang on even though they lost a lot of blood by the time paramedics got to them. She sustained two bullet-shattered ribs and a bruised right lung. He lost his spleen and part of his small intestine. They both went through multiple operations and months of convalescence. They're still having a devil of a time coming to grips with the losses and the revelations -- especially finding out who the shooter was and how and why he came to use that particular rifle.

A year after I got shot I still didn't know if I was going to be able to walk again. I had gotten some feeling back in my toes, and Dr. Carlino said that was a good sign, but he was far too cautious to say more, for fear of stirring up false hopes. The bullet didn't sever my spinal column, but it came close enough to inflict paralyzing trauma. How long the trauma might last and to what extent the spinal cord might eventually recover wasn't medically fathomable.

I went through months of anger, denial and self-pity. I told myself I didn't want to live as a cripple. I toyed with the idea of asking Harriet to bring me a gun, but I knew that she wouldn't.

You might think that the destruction of the Twin Towers, the horrible loss of life there, and all the other ugly, terrible things that followed might make me grateful that I was still alive. But instead it only added to my gloom. Why did I want to be able to walk again? Why did I want to do anything? Why did I want to live? The world was too hideous, too shameful, too bent on its own destruction. Why did I ever think I could do something about it? Why should I believe people were worth the effort?

One night in a dream Jane Hawthorne appeared before me, standing at the foot of my bed, her face beatifically sad. I realized she was mourning for me. She wasn't going to give me glad tidings or even a kiss on the forehead. She stood over me like a saint in a vision, shaking her head in mournful despair over my loss of courage, fortitude and self-respect.

I woke up in a cold sweat. For days I didn't know what to do except the nothing on top of nothing that I had been doing ever since I landed in a wheelchair. Sure, I consulted with Dr. Carlino whenever he made his rounds, and I continued to put sufficient energy into my physical therapy sessions every time they were scheduled, but I was going through the motions merely to pass the endless empty hours, and not because I was looking forward to some kind of meaningful life.

Jane's appearance in my dream must have kept working on me subconsciously, because one morning, out of the blue, I woke up thinking about trying to do something that she would have wanted me to do. I wouldn't call it an epiphany; it wasn't that soul-wrenching, and I certainly didn't plunge right into it. It took me weeks to actually buy a ream of paper and ask for a typewriter. I didn't want to use a computer or a word processor. I wanted to write the same way I used to, forty years ago, like picking up where I left off. The staff psychologist I was talking to once a week thought it would be good therapy. I suppose he might have been right.

I was able to put a lot of the pieces together by reading the wild ramblings in Delbert McCoy's Goldenrod tablet. Also, when his former accomplice, young Chris Terrell, learned of the Belmont massacre, he discovered that he had enough of a heart, enough of a kinship with the rest of humanity to be appalled by what his old pal Del had done. He decided to open up to the FBI agents working the case. Of course his motive wasn't completely altruistic and he wasn't totally selfless. He and his defense attorney made the federal prosecutor take the death sentence off the table in return for his cooperation.

I've been working on this book for three years now, and this chapter will wrap it up. I've interviewed Terrell. I've interviewed Lori. I've interviewed Charlie, Dan, Michele, Meredith, anybody and everybody who could help me, even Carlisle Dixon's father and Brenda Dixon's family, in my effort to unravel threads winding through the past forty years of triumph and tragedy. I've had to use my imagination to fill in some of the gaps.

I'm not an in-patient anymore. I'm living in Manhattan, in a wheelchair-accessible apartment. A little more feeling has come back in my legs now, and I have a therapist coming once a week to my home.

Meanwhile, the beat goes on all around me. Misused and overburdened soldiers and innocent civilians are dying in Iraq, Afghanistan and damn near every other place on the globe. We have avenged three-thousand lives lost on American soil with several hundred thousand taken in the Middle East. Charlie Guinard sarcastically says, "The hawks who lied us into this war probably think we're winning because the Iraqui casualties are a hundred times greater than ours."

He's fighting off depression and ennui by reverting to his old bluster. He can't stand the fact that he wasn't able to stay on the campaign trail in 2000, because he flatters himself that his efforts might have made a difference. He's absolutely certain that the presidential election was stolen from Al Gore in Ohio and Florida. He says that the Supreme Court appointed George Bush, and that if Gore was President we would never have invaded Iraq.

Charlie came to visit me the other day, launched into a rant reminiscent of the ones he used to do back in our college days, and wound it up with a quote from H.L. Mencken:

"As democracy is perfected, the office of president represents, more and more closely, the inner soul of the people. On some great and glorious day the plain folks of the land will reach their heart's desire at last and the White House will be adorned by a downright moron. "

"That's good," I said.

"Damn right!"

"However," I said, "the inner soul of the people voted for Gore. He won the popular vote."

"But the people didn't rise up! They didn't *protest*! They let the election be stolen!"

"This is a conservative democracy," I said. "It takes a long time for the people to wake up and demand changes."

"Well, fuck that!"

"How's Lori?" I asked. "And the rest of your family?"

"As well as can be expected, I guess, at least physically. The funds are still in place to do that movie we were going to make, and I want Lori and Merry to start performing again and maybe do a nice entertaining family film instead. Dan and Missy are working on a script. I'm not going to go easy on them just to get something started, I want it to be really good. They all need to be immersing themselves in something creative and challenging right now."

"Makes sense. What about you?"

He flashed his old devilish, muckraking grin. "I'm thinking again of running for Congress. What do you think of that, Frank?"

I was surprised by what came out of my mouth. "Well, is there a place for me on your campaign staff?"

He laughed raucously and clapped me on my shoulder. I grinned and started thinking of how I could keep my gun velcroed to the inner arm of my wheelchair.

Charlie said, "What about your book? How's that coming along?"

"I think I'm just about ready to wrap it up."

ABOUT THE AUTHOR

With twenty books published internationally and nineteen feature movies in worldwide distribution, John Russo has been called a "living legend." He began by co-authoring the screenplay for NIGHT OF THE LIVING DEAD, which has become recognized as a "horror classic." His three books on the art and craft of movie making have become bibles of independent production, and one of them, SCARE TACTICS, won a national award for Superior Nonfiction. Quentin Tarantino and many other noted filmmakers have stated that Russo's books helped them launch their careers.

John Russo wants people to know he's "just a nice guy who likes to scare people" -- and he's done it with novels and films such as RETURN OF THE LIVING DEAD, MIDNIGHT, THE MAJORETTES, THE AWAKENING and HEARTSTOPPER. He has had a long, rewarding career, and he shows no signs of slowing down. Recently his screenplay for ESCAPE OF THE LIVING DEAD was made into a five-part comic book released by Avatar to great acclaim; it made the Top Ten of Horror Comics nationally and spawned two graphic novels and ten sequels.

Russo's recent novel is THE HUNGRY DEAD, was published by Kensington Books. He is also slated to direct two movies: a remake of his cult hit, MIDNIGHT, and a brand new take on the "zombie phenomenon" entitled SPAWN OF THE DEAD.

Russo's latest novel DEALEY PLAZA, was published by Burning Bulb Publishing. His short story CHANNEL 666 appears in THE BIG BOOK OF BIZARRO.

His popularity among genre fans remains at a high pitch. He appears at many movie conventions each year as a featured guest, and he considers his appearance at the Orion Festival, hosted by Kirk Hammett and METALLICA, one of the highlights of his career.

OTHER GREAT TITLES FROM

Burning Bulb
PUBLISHING

WWW.BURNINGBULBPUBLISHING.COM

ANTHOLOGIES
BIZARRO AND TRANSGRESSIVE FICTION

THE BIG BOOK OF BIZARRO

The Big Book of Bizarro brings together the peculiar prose of an international cast of the most grotesquely-gonzo, genre-grinding modern writers who ever put pen to paper (or mouse to pad), including:

NIGHT OF THE LIVING DEAD horror writers John Russo & George Kosana; HUSTLER MAGAZINE erotica contributors Eva Hore, Andrée Lachapelle, & J. Troy Seate and established Bizarro genre authors D. Harlan Wilson, William Pauley III, Wol-vriey, Laird Long, Richard Godwin and so many more!

From Alien abductions to Zombie sex, The Big Book of Bizarro contains OVER FIFTY STORIES of the most outrélandish transgressive fiction that you'll ever lay your capricious and curious hands upon!

WARNING: This book may be one of the most controversial and dangerous books you'll ever read.

WESTWARD HOES

Nine outlaw writers rode into town from obscurity to pen nine tantalizing tales of horror and fantasy, and leaving once they branded their own personal marks on the weird western genre and became living legends of the American Frontier experience.

Like drunken Indian scouts, the writers fervidly tracked down and captured the Western genre, tore off its fashionable veneer and ravished its exposed essence.

So belly up to the bar with your favorite soiled dove and enjoy perusing these thrilling tales of Old West debauchery, danger and desire; compiled by the publisher of The Big Book of Bizarro and featuring the bizarro novella *Big Trouble in Little Ass* by Wol-vriey.

Available at
amazon.com

Burning Bulb
PUBLISHING

ANTHOLOGIES
BIZARRO AND TRANSGRESSIVE FICTION

THE BIG BOOK OF BIZARRO SPECIAL KINDLE EDITIONS

VULGARITY FOR THE MASSES

A whole history of madness and struggle lie ahead for the disfigured children of Adam in this collection of nine tales from J.S. Lawhead.

Available at

amazon.com

Burning Bulb
PUBLISHING

GARY LEE VINCENT'S
DARKENED
THE WEST VIRGINIA VAMPIRE SERIES

DARKENED HILLS

When evil descends on a small West Virginia town, who will survive?

Jonathan did not start out his life to become a rambler, it just worked out that way. William was a troubled youth with something to hide. Both were from Melas, a small town tucked away in the West Virginia hills... a town where disappearances are happening more and more frequently.

After the suicide of a wanted serial killer, the townsfolk thought the nightmare was over. But when a centuries-old vampire is discovered they find out the hard way it's just getting started. Dark secrets can only stay hidden for so long and when the devil comes to collect, there will be hell to pay. Can Jonathan and William find a way to stop the vampire before it's too late? Find out in *Darkened Hills!*

DARKENED HOLLOWS

In the heart-stopping sequel to the award-winning *Darkened Hills*, Jonathan and William must return to West Virginia to face possible criminal charges stemming from their last visit to the damned town of Melas, where both had narrowly escaped the clutches of a vampire seethe.

And as livestock start mysteriously getting murdered with all of their blood drained, worried farmers are searching for answers - leaving the local Sheriff and his deputy racing against time to learn the cause before a more violent crime is committed.

Available at

amazon.com

Burning Bulb
PUBLISHING

WWW. DARKENEDHILLS.COM

GARY LEE VINCENT'S
DARKENED
THE WEST VIRGINIA VAMPIRE SERIES

DARKENED WATERS

When the world goes to hell, the chosen must arise!

As Talman Cane orchestrates a flood of epic proportions in this third installment of the *Darkened* series the towns of Melas and Tarklin are caught completely off guard by the deluge. Hell-bent on finishing what they started, the evil brothers return to the lunatic asylum to take care of the witnesses and add to the ever-growing army of the undead.

Aided by Lucifer himself and the insane vampire demon Legion, the stage is set to channel all of the forces of hell to come forth. In an all-out race to survive, Jonathan, William, and Amanda soon discover they are up against impossible odds as Lucifer opens the Gateway to Hell, ushering in the zombie apocalypse and the End Times.

DARKENED SOULS

Melas and the Madison House are about to be rebuilt.
True evil is about to be reborne!

Young ex-priest and vampire-killer William is drawn back to the West Virginian town that almost killed him, where his vampire arch-enemy Victor Rothenstein still stalks the earth.

The town of Melas lies destroyed after the battle of the End of Days. But why is wealthy Jackie Nixon so eager to rebuild it using the bone dust of murdered souls?

Terrible evil has visited before, but the Gateway to Hell is about to be reopened in a horrific climax. And this time – it's personal.

WWW.DARKENEDHILLS.COM

Available at
amazon.com

Burning Bulb
PUBLISHING

WEST VIRGINIA-THEMED HUMORROROTICA
BY RICH BOTTLES JR.

HELLHOLE WEST VIRGINIA

From the heights of Mothman's perch high atop the Silver Bridge in Point Pleasant to the depths of Hellhole Cavern in Pendleton County, evil lurks within the shadows as the sun sets upon the haunted hills and hollows of West Virginia.

Bizarro author Rich Bottles Jr. blows the coffin lid off horror genre clichés with this tour de force cast of Eco-friendly vampires, beach-yearning zombies and sex-starved she-devils.

LUMBERJACKED

If you are easily offended or do not possess a truly depraved sense of humor, this story may not be the light summer reading fare you desire. As for the four feisty female freshmen stranded on top of West Virginia's third highest mountain, they have no choice but to experience the sick, twisted debauchery and perverted mayhem described deep inside the tight unbroken bindings of this horrific missive.

Lumberjacked takes the reader to a nightmarish world where character development and aesthetic integrity are prematurely cut short by the swinging axes of maniacal lumberjacks, who are hell bent on death and destruction in the remote forests of Appalachia. And at the climax, when paranoia crosses over to the paranormal, Lumberjacked makes Deliverance look like a family raft trip down the Lower Gauley.

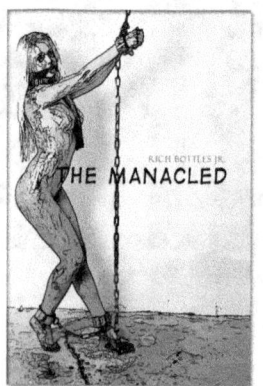

THE MANACLED

What happens when twin brothers lease out the former West Virginia State Penitentiary with the false purpose of filming a documentary on supernatural phenomena, but their true intention is to make a pornographic movie?

Chaos ensues as the disturbed spirits of murdered convicts, along with the reanimated dead from the neighboring Indian Burial Mound, take their vengeance on the unwary and undressed trespassers.

Zombies, ghosts, mobsters and porn collide in this bizarro tale from horror author Rich Bottles Jr.

Available at  amazon.com  Burning Bulb PUBLISHING

WOL-VRIEY
BIZARRO AND TRANSGRESSIVE FICTION

BOSTON POSH

Boston Posh: A Bud Malone Thriller! Why are the white robots trying to kill Malone?
In 2028 AD, the USA is a nation ravaged by hungry dragons and dinosaurs. In Boston, Massachusetts, private eye Bud Malone is hired to rescue a kidnapped heiress. But nothing is as it seems. Malone works to unravel a tangled web involving Boston Chinatown, a 200-year-old woman with a 9-year-old body, white humanoid robots, a human-liver-eating psychopath, a golem, a porcelain dragon, and a snake goddess with a crush on him. There's also a woman obsessed with chicken sex.

Then Malone meets Posh Lane, a gorgeous call girl who's desperate to quit her pimp. Romantic sparks ignite between Posh and Malone, but Posh's past suddenly catches up with her in a BIG way. To save Posh, Malone agrees to run a quest for Earth's new rulers, the Forks. The quest: recover ex US president Jefferson Lincoln's liver for them. Malone has no idea that agreeing to the Fork's odd request will send him on the weirdest trip he's ever been on in his life. *Boston Posh* - A total mind fuck! Reality like you've never dared imagine it!

VEGAN ZOMBIE APOCALYPSE

In the post-apocalypse worlderness, zombies rule the earth. They're allergic to meat, and brains literally make them explode. Zombies now eat blood potatoes, parasitic tubers grown in the flesh of humancows corralled in maximum security farms. The necros, barbaric human nomads travelling the worlderness in floating villages, worship the zombies. The necros both eat the zombies, and wear clothes made from them; they live in houses built of bricks of undead flesh. They also keep zombies as sex slaves. Two fugitives meet in the ancient ruins of Texas. The first is Soil 15-f, a womancow who's escaped her farm a week before she's due to be killed and her blood potato crop harvested. The second fugitive is Able Kane, former head necros food technician, now sentenced to death for heresy. But Soil is no ordinary humancow. Unknown to herself, she's the vegan zombie agricultural revolution, and the zombies desperately want her back. And the necros equally desperately want Able Kane dead. He's fled with a forbidden discovery which will reshape the world for the worse if used. And Able is just hardheaded/misguided enough to use it.

With android zombinators and the head necros assassin (Able's ex-girlfriend Morphia) after them, Soil and Able Kane have no choice but to climb the lemon tree to Haeven, residence of the zombie god Necro. And by anyone's reckoning, Soil and Able Kane are the two people in the worlderness who should never have been let into Heaven.

Available at
amazon.com

Burning Bulb
PUBLISHING

MINOR CONFESSIONS OF AN ANGEL FALLING UPWARD

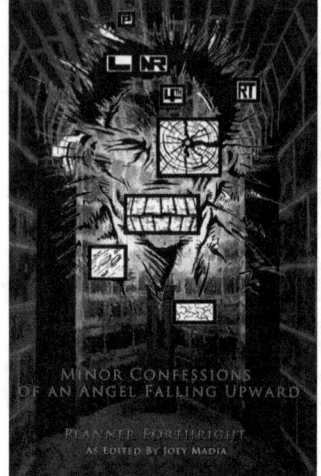

by Planner Forthright, as edited by Joey Madia

Confession. Revelation. Rant. *Minor Confessions of an Angel Falling Upward* is all of these... and more. Set in modern times and spiraling back to the swirl of Pre-Creation, this postmodern blend of genre-bending pop-prose and socio-political commentary is a classic tale of the (anti-)hero's quest for Reason and Redemption in a Universe gone mad.

Who is Planner Forthright? A fallen angel made Man. A once-winged evil with un-Divine purpose on this Plane. A cannibal prince chosen to inherit a castled landscape of destruction and despair. An Alchemist of sorts—a mental magician; a mortar-and-pestle wizard converting carbon lies to golden Truth, whose language is his own. A Vampire by nature and condition whose been walking the waters and thorny highways of our planet for over 40 years. And he's seeking a way out...

PASSAGEWAY

by Gary Lee Vincent with illustrations by Andy Hopp

When an archeological dig goes horribly wrong, the team is trapped in an alternate world where evil awaits them at every turn. Find out who will survive the *Passageway*!

From Gary Lee Vincent, the author of supernatural vampire thriller *Darkened Hills*, comes an unforgettable tale that spans four continents and takes the reader to the very realm of Hell itself.

Skeleton warriors, zombies, other undead beings and werewolves are allvery real inside the *Passageway*! In this Bizarrogenre tribute to H.P. Lovecraft and Indiana Jones, this deadly tale will keep you guessing and leave you breathless to the end!

THE TWELVE STEPS

by Zachary Crabtree

"A Man who Cannot Keep Awake Cannot Keep it Together." There is always something that pulls an alcoholic deeper into his unquenchable thirst – something degenerative to the human spirit. Indeed, there have been incidents in my life that carry tragic significance to me, yet I know they pale in comparison to the tragedies experienced by others.

When the jagged pieces of a disfigured past become a troubled, broken-up, glass-bottled mosaic in one's present life, all the innocent souls affected along the way become entangled in one's conscience; while the depression, pills, manic behavior and soul-searching coalesce in a series of twelve steps.

Alcohol affects the lives of hooligans, stubborn old fools, lovers, and families torn apart by drunk drivers – drunk drivers like me.

Available at
amazon.com   Burning Bulb
PUBLISHING

www.ingramcontent.com/pod-product-compliance
Lightning Source LLC
Chambersburg PA
CBHW072112250626
47159CB00007B/2416